MW01134613

THE CITY OF THIEVES

KYLE ALEXANDER ROMINES

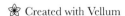

ALSO BY KYLE ALEXANDER ROMINES

To sign up to receive author updates—and receive a FREE electronic copy of Kyle's science fiction novella, The Chrononaut—go to http://eepurl.com/bsvhYP.

Five Kingdoms.
Five Kings and Queens.
One High Queen Sits Above All.
Her Wardens Keep the Peace.

Ard Ruide

Connacht, in the west, is the kingdom of learning and the seat of the greatest and wisest druids and magicians; the men of Connacht are famed for their eloquence, their intellect, and their ability to pronounce true judgment.

Ulster, in the north, is the seat of battle valor, haughtiness, strife, and boasting; the men of Ulster are the fiercest warriors of all Fál, and the queens and goddesses of Ulster are associated with battle and death.

Leinster, the eastern kingdom, is the seat of prosperity, hospitality, and the importing of rich foreign wares like silk or wine; the men of Leinster are noble in speech and their women are exceptionally beautiful.

Munster, in the south, is the kingdom of music and the arts, skilled ficheall players, and horsemen; the fairs of Munster are the greatest in all Fál.

The last kingdom, Meath, is the kingdom of Kingship, stewardship, and bounty in government; in Meath lies the Hill of Tara, the traditional seat of the High King or Queen of Fál.

—Adapted from Old Translation, Author Unknown

CHAPTER ONE

"WE'RE LOST." A crease formed on Morwen's brow as she pored over the map.

Berengar, sitting across from her at a table near the fire, said nothing. The pair had spent the last two days holed up at the Forgotten Stop, an out-of-the-way tavern deep in the heart of rural Leinster. Outside, the last vestiges of summer were fading, and soon the leaves would begin to turn.

Morwen held the map closer and studied it in the fire-light, as if there was something she had missed. "I don't understand. According to the map, we should have reached the Wrenwood by now." She jabbed a speck on the map with her finger. "We passed The Mount of Guarding not three days ago and turned north at the River Nore, just like we were supposed to."

Faolán, a wolfhound nearly Morwen's size, nudged her head over the young woman's shoulder and sniffed the weathered parchment. As a rule, Faolán disliked people almost as much as Berengar did, but in Morwen's case, she had made an exception. For her part, Morwen had taken to spoiling Faolán whenever she thought Berengar wasn't looking, and in her presence the fierce hound became as docile as a pup.

Exasperated, Morwen returned the map to the table and let out a protracted sigh. "Useless." She cast a glance at a stack of books beside her. "If only there was some enchantment to…" She stopped suddenly and narrowed her gaze in Berengar's direction. "You're awfully quiet. Even for you."

"You're the one who said you wanted a life of adventure. You can't adjust to a life on the road until you learn how to properly read a map."

"I'm a magician, not a cartographer." Morwen waved a hand in the air dismissively and patted Faolán's head. "And don't think I'm letting you off that easy—I can tell you're hiding something."

Berengar tried to keep the amusement out of his voice. Usually, she was the one to tease him. "Is that so?" He raised his tankard to his lips, gulped down a mouthful of ale, and wiped his unruly red beard with his forearm.

They drew a number of glances from the hall's other occupants, and with good reason. Berengar and Morwen made an unusual pair of traveling companions. Even seated, Berengar was easily recognizable as the tallest and largest man in the room. Unlike Morwen—who, at sixteen, was in the bloom of youth—he was well into his forties. Scars marred the right side of his face, and a patch covered his right eye. None would mistake him for anything other than a hardened warrior. In contrast, there was little to hint that Morwen—having discarded the blue robes she'd worn as Munster's court magician in favor of mundane traveling clothes—was about as far from an ordinary girl as one could get and still remain human. Anyone taking a look at the potions and spellbooks inside her satchel would quickly realize there was much more to her under the surface.

Morwen ran a hand through bushy brown hair and tucked a loose strand behind her ear. "You don't fool me. I know that look. You're waiting for something, aren't you?" She glanced around the room. "And you're not the only one. Everyone in here seems on edge."

The barmaid approached to refill Berengar's tankard. Preoccupied by the sight of his scars, she spilled a portion of ale, flushed a deep shade of red, and fled with a frightened yelp.

Berengar, accustomed to his appearance having such an effect, drank from the tankard without missing a beat. "I don't know what you mean." In truth, he had stayed at the Forgotten Stop some months back, and the proprietors were no less afraid of him now than they were then.

"In case you've forgotten, we're supposed to be looking for the Oakseers' Grotto so I can craft a new staff." Her previous magician's staff had been destroyed weeks earlier in a fight against a dark sorceress and a winged serpent.

Berengar shrugged. "So we are. I knew this tavern was in the area and thought it would be a good place to rest while we searched for your grotto. I spent some time here before receiving King Mór's summons."

Morwen was, in fact, Mór's illegitimate daughter—the product of a union between the king and a particularly nasty witch—though Berengar felt no need to call attention to that fact with prying ears about. When Mór was murdered, Berengar and Morwen had worked together to identify the king's killer—Morwen's half-sister, the princess Ravenna. Berengar, who owed Mór a debt, agreed afterward to allow Morwen to accompany him on his travels.

Intrigued, Morwen leaned closer. "The affair with the ogre?"

"Aye. I had some unfinished business when I left."

"I knew it." She flashed a triumphant grin. "I thought we agreed to stay out of trouble until I replaced my staff."

Berengar kicked his feet up on the table and gave a grunt. "Don't forget who's in charge. You may be clever, but you still have a lot to learn." He gestured to her stack of books. "Those aren't going to be much use to you in a fight."

Morwen folded her arms across her chest. "I might no longer have access to my library at Cashel, but I still need to learn and practice my arts—which would be a great deal easier if I had my staff." Their ages and appearances weren't the only things that set them apart. An avowed pacifist, Morwen had mostly resisted his efforts to train her in the ways of combat. "And I don't recall you complaining about my fighting abilities when we took on that coatl."

Before Berengar could form a response, the door to the tavern opened, and a gentle wind swirled fallen leaves inside. A nondescript man in simple clothes entered and made his way to a lonely table. A hood concealed most of his face. The hall's other occupants paid the newcomer little heed, but Berengar watched him closely.

Finally. Morwen's suspicions were well-founded, as he had indeed chosen the tavern for a very specific reason. "Don't stare."

Morwen lowered her voice to a whisper. "Who is he?"

Berengar remained perfectly still, doing nothing to attract the stranger's attention. "A member of the Brotherhood of Thieves, I'd wager."

"The Brotherhood of Thieves?" Her astonishment soon faded, and she chuckled softly. "And here I thought we were trying to keep *out* of trouble. What's a member of the Brotherhood doing in a place like this?"

"Before I rode south to Munster to answer King Mór's

summons, I spent the better part of the spring hunting a group of mercenaries called the Black Hand. Someone had hired them to retrieve a thunder rune."

Morwen's eyes widened with alarm. As a magician—and someone who carried a variety of runestones herself—she knew well the danger such a relic posed.

"I dealt with the Black Hand and recovered the rune, but it was stolen from me by hobgoblins before I could store it someplace safe. When I found them, the hobgoblins were starving and being hunted to the point of extinction. The money the rune would fetch would allow them to start a new life somewhere else. I chose to let them keep it." He hesitated, and there was a hard edge to the words that followed. "I came across their corpses on the road to Munster, just north of the border. They'd been slaughtered, and the rune was gone."

"I see. It seems likely whoever was after the rune hasn't given up on acquiring it."

Berengar gave an almost imperceptible nod. "I asked around. The Brotherhood uses this tavern to conduct business in the region at the end of each month. They trade in black market goods and dangerous wares. Whoever took the rune from the hobgoblins will come looking for a payoff, and when they do, I'll be ready."

Almost as if on cue, the tavern door opened again, and four men entered together. The companions were dressed in padded armor, and they wore bright red cloaks and swords sheathed at their sides.

Berengar recognized the sigil on their cloaks. "Lady Imogen's soldiers."

The soldiers laughed at some private joke and made a beeline for the bar. They were a long way from Castle Blackthorn, though not so far as to raise suspicion. Their presence in the tavern was far from unusual, especially if they were out on patrol.

Morwen shuddered, and her back straightened immediately. "They carry the rune. I can feel its power calling to me." Outside the tavern's walls, faint thunder murmured in agreement.

Armed with tankards and flagons brimming with ale and wine, the soldiers settled at the stranger's table. Berengar watched and listened.

"We've been waiting for you to show your face in here," the soldiers' leader said. "You Brotherhood lot are a secretive bunch, I'll give you that." He stared at the thief with a measure of suspicion. "You had better have our gold, Ryland."

Ryland laughed under his breath. "That depends on whether or not you really brought what you say you have."

The soldier's ruddy face broke out into a cruel grin. "Of course we did. Keenan, show Ryland what he came here to see." He nodded to one of his companions, who produced a closed pouch.

Ryland took a peek at what was inside. "My client will be pleased. Let's talk about your fee."

The ruddy-faced soldier raised his cup, and his companions clanked their tankards and cheered. "To new business ventures!" He slapped his thigh. "It was a stroke of luckfinding the thing. The lads and I stopped for a bit of fun with some hobgoblins near the border, and we found it among their things—not that we wouldn't have killed the little monsters just for the sport of it."

At the mention of the hobgoblins, Berengar's hands balled into fists. He pushed away from the table, and Faolán sprang to attention beside him.

Morwen winked at him with evident amusement. "Try

not to dismember anyone. Those are Lady Imogen's soldiers, after all."

"I know." There was a reason he preferred to keep his head down while in Leinster. He wasn't exactly welcome within its borders. Besides, he needed the men alive to tell him who wanted the runestone so badly.

Patrons cleared out of his path as he made his way across the room. The tavern went quiet as Berengar approached the table where the soldiers gathered, and onlookers exchanged worried glances.

"What the devil do you want?" the soldiers' leader demanded with the characteristic arrogance of authority. "Can't you see we're busy, you ugly brute?" The others at the table laughed—all except Ryland, who studied Berengar's cloak and weapons with growing recognition. "Now clear out of here, or we'll teach you not to intrude on matters that don't concern you."

Berengar hit him in the face, and the soldier's teeth broke against his knuckles. He grabbed the man's head and slammed it hard against the table, and the soldier fell from his chair to the floor. The man's companions were out of their seats in the next instant.

"I don't know who you are, stranger, but you'll regret that."

Berengar didn't flinch. "I want the stone—and the name of the person who paid you for it."

His knowledge of their affairs seemed to take them aback, if only for a moment. Berengar turned their surprise to his advantage. He snatched a tankard from the table and bashed it against the closest man's skull. When another went for his sword, Berengar seized his arm in a viselike grip. Before the third soldier could intervene, Faolán pounced on him and pinned him underneath her, her jaws inches from his throat.

7

Berengar and his foe struggled over possession of the weapon until he slammed the man against the bar and forced his arm behind his back. "Now talk. Who are you working for?"

"Go to hell," the soldier shot back.

With a twist, Berengar snapped the man's arm out of its socket, prompting a scream. "Try again."

The soldiers' leader rushed forward with an angry shout, wielding a dagger. Berengar took a step back and avoided the first jab. His leather armor bore the brunt of the next strike. Berengar grabbed the soldier's wrist, drove his forehead into the man's skull, and wrested away control of the dagger. With one thrust of the blade he anchored the man's wrist to the bar.

Faolán barked to warn him of danger, and Berengar caught a flash of movement out of the corner of his eye as a final assailant raised a sword behind him. Before Berengar could react, the sword toppled from the man's hand, and he slumped to the floor.

Morwen stood behind the fallen soldier, a wry smile on her face. In her hands was her satchel, stuffed to the brim with spell books. "I told you they'd be useful." She turned her attention to the soldiers, who were either unconscious or in considerable pain. "You left them all in one piece this time—more or less. Good work."

Berengar's gaze moved again to the table where the thief had been sitting moments ago. "Blast it. He's gone."

"He must have taken the stone with him." Morwen was already sprinting toward the door. "He can't have gone far. Come on!"

To the visible relief of the others within the tavern, Berengar followed her outside into the crisp fall air. Faolán sniffed out a set of fresh tracks left behind in the mud and bounded down the trail.

Morwen sprinted to her horse, Nessa, and unhitched her. She glanced at Berengar over her shoulder and aimed a wink at him. "Do try and keep up." With that, Morwen swung herself onto the saddle, seized the reins, and took off in pursuit of Ryland.

Berengar scowled and hurried to his horse. Despite her youth, Morwen was easily the better rider. Although the kingdom of Munster was most famous for its great wealth and vibrant culture, its people were also great horse masters. Morwen, whose father had spared no expense on all aspects of her education, was no exception. If anything, her sensitivity to magic gave her a greater connection to her mount.

Morwen had already disappeared down the path by the time Berengar put his foot in the stirrup. He kicked his horse in the sides and hurried after her.

"There you are," she called after him. "I thought I lost you. Come on, old man—he's getting away."

Berengar spurred his horse forward, but Morwen easily outpaced him. Faolán led them along a winding dirt road that ran northeast from the tavern, far removed from any vestiges of civilization. Trees grew on either side of the road, and the brush, weeds, and thorns intruding on the path were overgrown from the frequent rainfall common-place throughout Leinster. A signpost at a crossroads was the sole hint of human presence in the area.

Morwen veered right at the crossroads and galloped after Faolán across a shallow brook, leaving Berengar to do his best to keep up with both. The path straightened, and in the distance the thief—also on horseback—appeared, headed for a wooded area farther down the road.

"There it is," Morwen said. "The Wrenwood."

"I told you we were in the area."

According to Morwen, the Wrenwood was home to the

Oakseers' Grotto, a grove sacred to druids for centuries. The trees there possessed strong magical properties that made them ideal for fashioning a new staff. Berengar had strong misgivings about venturing anywhere touched by magic—and even more reasons to avoid druids—but Morwen assured him the area was safe.

Ahead, Ryland drew nearer to the wood's entrance.

"We're losing him." Berengar ground his teeth together. "We can't let him slip away."

"Leave it to me." Morwen made a clicking noise with her tongue, and her horse picked up speed. The mare galloped past Faolán and quickly closed the distance with Ryland. "Give us the stone! You don't know how dangerous it is."

When Ryland ignored her request, Morwen pulled alongside him and leaned sideways in the saddle, grasping for the pouch containing the thunder rune. Ryland jerked the reins to the right, and Morwen came up empty. She caught up to him again, said something to her horse Berengar couldn't hear, and let go of the reins.

Berengar frowned. *What's she doing?*

Before he could stop her, Morwen jumped from the saddle and landed on the back of Ryland's horse. Ryland produced a hidden blade and stabbed at Morwen, who deftly avoided the knife while the thief's horse followed the road into the Wrenwood. Berengar spurred his horse forward, but he was too far behind to be of help. Before Ryland could thrust the knife at her again, Morwen reached over and touched the horse's coat with the flat of her palm. The stallion reared up, throwing Ryland to the ground, though Morwen maintained her hold. He scrambled forward in the mud only to find himself face-to-face with Faolán. He looked to his fallen knife, which lay just out of his reach, and the wolfhound bared her fangs.

Morwen dismounted and stood victoriously over the thief. "I wouldn't do that if I were you." She turned her gaze to Berengar. "Took you long enough."

Berengar suppressed a smile. "Show-off." He snapped his fingers, and Faolán backed away from Ryland. "Unless you want to be my hound's next meal, I'd suggest you start giving me some answers."

Ryland stared back at him with open defiance. "I'd sooner lose my tongue than reveal the details of a contract."

Berengar growled impatiently, kicked Ryland flat on his back, and planted his boot on the man's chest. "That can be arranged. The last time I came across a Brotherhood member who wouldn't talk, I took his hand."

Ryland's eyes flickered over to Morwen, who simply nodded.

"It's true. I was there. Calum, I think, was his name. Perhaps he was a friend of yours?"

At the mention of Calum, all the color drained from Ryland's face.

Berengar reached for his axe. "Let's see how well you thieve without fingers."

"He means it," Morwen said. "This one isn't a man you want to cross."

"Wait!" Ryland held up his hands in a show of surrender. "Take it!" He reached for the pouch containing the thunder rune and tossed it to Morwen.

She stiffened suddenly, and her eyes widened with dread. Berengar knew that look. She sensed danger.

"We're not alone."

Berengar searched the swaying trees for the source of Morwen's discomfort. Suddenly, an arrow streaked by and missed him by inches. A second arrow struck Ryland's horse, killing it almost instantly. *Black arrows.* "Goblins!"

Faolán barked loudly, and Berengar, Morwen, and Ryland took cover under a fallen tree.

"They must've followed us from the tavern." Morwen fixed her attention on Ryland. "I'm guessing whoever hired you doesn't like loose ends. What'll it be, Berengar? We've got the rune. Maybe we should leave him to the goblins."

Three goblins approached on foot while others rode horses or scurried through the trees above. Goblins came in a variety of shapes and sizes, but the three moving toward them were all slender and just a bit shorter than the average human man. Their skin had a dark green hue, and their ears were sharply pointed.

"Have mercy." Ryland clutched at Morwen's cloak. "Get me away from those monsters and I'll tell you anything you want to know."

"Remember that. Morwen, meet me back at the crossroads. You know what to do." Berengar stepped out to meet the goblins with his axe in hand. The goblins continued, undeterred by the sight of him. Although many goblins were capable of conversing in the human tongue—their native language was full of harsh, discordant sounds —the goblins did not extend the courtesy of surrender, and neither did he.

Berengar charged, his axe held high, and the goblins rushed to meet him. They pressed him on all sides, wielding clubs and rusted iron blades. They were fast and agile, but Berengar had been killing goblins for a long time, and he had become very good at it. He used his size to his advantage and overwhelmed them through sheer strength. A single swing of his axe cleaved through a goblin's armor and opened the creature's chest wall. Berengar wrenched the axe free and beheaded the next goblin in his path with one swipe. The third goblin hissed and launched himself at Berengar, who tossed the creature aside as if he were weightless and stomped on his head until the goblin stopped kicking.

Another arrow sailed by his head. Faolán sprinted by him into the trees, and moments later the goblin archer shrieked and went silent. Berengar heard a whistle, and soon Morwen and Ryland were riding away on the back of Morwen's horse. His distraction had worked.

At the sight of Morwen escaping with their target, the remaining goblins ignored Berengar and went after her on horseback. Berengar called to Faolán and sprinted to his mount to give chase.

Though Morwen was clearly the superior rider, the goblins outnumbered her, forcing her to go deeper into the Wrenwood rather than heading for the crossroads. She led her horse off the path and jumped over a fallen log to keep out of range of the archers' arrows. Berengar followed behind, picking off goblins one by one.

He looked up from raking his axe along a horse's flank in time to witness an archer take aim at Morwen, who was too busy evading the others to notice. The goblin was beyond the reach of his axe, which left him with few options. Berengar swore and drove his mount directly at the other rider, resulting in a violent collision. The two horses crashed together, and Berengar was thrown from the saddle. He hit the ground hard, and the impact knocked the air out of his lungs.

Berengar pushed himself up and crawled away from the thrashing horses.

He looked around, searching for the archer. His axe lay just out of reach. The goblin was on him in an instant. The creature's claws dug into his armor, and the goblin's jagged teeth strained toward his face.

As he pushed the goblin away, Berengar glimpsed another with its face hidden behind a helmet scurry up a tree ahead of Morwen. Before he could shout out a warning, the goblin tackled her off the horse, and Morwen, the creature, and Ryland were scattered across the dry leaves. Berengar heaved his attacker off him with an angry growl and bashed the creature's face until he felt bones cracking under his bloodstained fists. He released his hold on the goblin's mangled corpse, snatched his axe from the ground, and hurried toward Morwen and Ryland.

Morwen's characteristic confidence faded as the helmeted goblin bore down on her and clawed at the pouch bearing the thunder rune. Ryland attempted to flee only to find himself surrounded by three mounted goblins. Berengar looked from one to the other. There wasn't time to save both.

He lowered his shoulder and charged the goblin atop Morwen. The creature rolled away unharmed, holding the pouch.

Berengar tightened his grip on the axe and stared down the goblin. "Let's finish this, vermin."

A hiss sounded nearby, and the goblin leapt onto a companion's horse. The remaining creatures followed suit, and soon the Wrenwood was quiet once more.

Berengar's gaze fell on Ryland, who lay in a pool of his own blood. Even as they hurried to the thief's side, he could tell it was too late. Multiple stab wounds covered Ryland's abdomen, and his face was white from blood loss.

"The pain…" Ryland trembled. "It hurts."

"A name," Berengar said. "Give me a name, and I'll ease your passing."

Morwen glared at him, reached into her satchel, and retrieved a bottle containing a murky scarlet liquid. She pried off the lid and held the bottle to Ryland's lips. "Drink this. It will help with the pain."

Ryland did as she said, and his trembling slowly

subsided. "Thank you." With that, he breathed his last and fell still.

"Blast it." Berengar kicked a goblin's corpse to vent his anger. "They got away with the stone."

Morwen wore an impish grin. "No—they didn't." She opened her satchel to reveal the thunder rune gleaming inside. "Goblins are tricky, but so are magicians. I switched out the stone."

"Aye, but they don't know that. If the goblins think they have the stone, we can track them to whoever they're working for." He frowned. "Of course, we wouldn't have to if you hadn't gotten Ryland killed, and yourself nearly with him. Magician or not, if you ride with me, you'll need to learn how to defend yourself properly."

Morwen offered no retort, a sign she took his criticism to heart.

Berengar started toward his horse, which seemed to have recovered enough for travel. "Can you track them with a spell?"

Morwen shrugged apologetically. "Without my staff…"

Berengar sighed. "All right. We'll stop by the Oakseers' Grotto before picking up the goblins' trail. Where I grew up, the country was filled with goblins. I don't need magic to track them, as long as the trail's still warm."

Morwen brightened immediately. "It won't take long to gather the wood. I can do most of the enchanting on the road." She led her horse by the reins and accompanied him along the trail with a renewed spring in her step. "The Oakseers' Grotto shouldn't be far."

Wind rustled through the trees, scattering multicolored leaves. "So, what *can* you do without your staff?"

The question was innocent, born out of ignorance and curiosity, but Morwen took it as an insult. "Plenty! I can still sense magic and human emotions. For example, right now you're feeling angry and hungry."

Berengar snorted. "I'm always angry. And hungry."

Morwen quickened her pace, and her annoyance with him seemed to fade, replaced by a palpable wave of excitement. "We're close. There is old magic in this place." She came to an abrupt halt, and her brow furrowed. "It can't be."

The Oakseers' Grotto was a ruin. The trees had been cleared away.

CHAPTER TWO

"I HEARD stories about this place as a girl." Morwen wandered the area with Faolán while Berengar looked on. "The Oakseers' Grotto was one of the most sacred sites in all Leinster. It was said the trees were alive with magic. Magicians, mages, and witches would come from far away to submit themselves to the trees' judgment, sometimes undergoing great quests to be deemed worthy to fashion wands or staffs from the trees' branches."

Faolán whined, as if she too sensed a great loss. Not a single tree remained where the grove once stood. Only their stumps lingered, a final insult.

Morwen approached the grotto itself, where a statue with three faces hung above the entrance to a shallow cave. "Brigit—goddess of life and nature." Each face reflected one of the goddess' aspects. Scorch marks marred the faces on either side, leaving only the face of the mother. Brigit's shrine had been destroyed, and stones filled in a pool of water. Morwen turned back to look at him, her usual cheerfulness overcome by sorrow. "How could this have happened?"

Excluding the trees in the Wrenwood, Berengar doubted there was enough wood left in the whole area to serve as kindling, much less a new staff for Morwen. Even the portion of the Wrenwood surrounding the grotto had been cleared away, beyond which empty fields went on for miles.

He noticed smoke rising over a distant hill. "I'd wager there's a settlement there. The settlers probably cleared the grove and the neighboring trees to build their homes."

Morwen looked horrified at the idea. "This forest is under the druids' protection."

"The druids are gone. Most died out during the purges." There was a time when few would have dared risk the druids' ire. In centuries past, druids served as a bridge between humanity and the elder gods. They were priests, soothsayers, healers, and conjurers. Their political power declined with the arrival of Padraig and the worship of the Lord of Hosts in Fál.

Morwen stared at him in disbelief. "I heard stories, but I never imagined…"

"Those were dark days. The High Queen's reign was still young, and riots and purges broke out across the five kingdoms." Attitudes toward magic changed greatly in the aftermath of the Shadow Wars, when the dark sorcerer Azeroth had attempted to conquer Fál with an army of monsters. "The riots in Dún Aulin were the worst. I was there. Queen Nora sent me to quell the violence. Blood flowed in the streets. An alchemist was crucified outside the city gates."

"But alchemists can't even use *magic*—"

"Do you think that mattered to the mob? Fear makes people capable of terrible things. They can't be reasoned with. Violence is the only language they understand."

"What did you do?"

Berengar looked away. "What I had to." He left it at that. There was more to the story, but it wasn't something he felt like sharing. "There's a reason we need to keep a low profile while in Leinster. It's not safe for you here."

Morwen folded her arms across her chest. "The people of Munster weren't exactly fond of magic either."

"You don't understand. Magic is hated here more than in any other kingdom. The people here are pious, and the church teaches that sorcery is of the devil. Fairies were few in number even in the time of Áed, and monster hunters have driven them to extinction. It won't be long before goblins follow. As long as we're here, you need to be careful about who you use magic around. Got it?"

Morwen nodded.

"Good."

While by no means helpless, Morwen was vulnerable without her staff, which meant he'd have to keep a closer eye on her in the near future. Berengar, who largely avoided the company of others when he could help it, was unaccustomed to looking out for anyone but himself. Unlike most of the High Queen's wardens, he had always walked alone until Morwen came into his life. Although they had journeyed together for some time, it was still a strange feeling having someone at his side. At times it was a bother—he might have saved Ryland had he not been forced to come to Morwen's defense—but it was useful having a magician around. To his surprise, he had grown to enjoy her company, when she wasn't busy teasing or pestering him with questions.

Morwen let out a disappointed sigh. "I suppose I'll have to look elsewhere for materials to craft a new staff. There are other places I know of, but most are far from here."

"That will have to wait until we've dealt with the

goblins." With the matter settled, Berengar started toward his horse. "We should get back to the trail."

Morwen noticed an acorn lying on the ground, picked it up, and added it to her satchel before mounting her horse. Berengar whistled to Faolán, who began following the goblins' scent.

A cool breeze greeted their return to the road. After a particularly hot summer spent in Munster, Berengar welcomed the change in seasons. He had come of age in the kingdom of Ulster, Fál's northernmost realm, and preferred cooler climates. Dark clouds on the horizon hinted at the potential for rain, which came as no great surprise. The last time Berengar was in Leinster, it had stormed almost the entire time.

Aside from his axe, Berengar carried a short sword sheathed at his side and a silver dagger hidden in his boot. He kept a quiver full of arrows and a bow strapped to his saddle in case the need arose, and although he had only one good eye, he was a very good shot. He wore a bearskin cloak, which, coupled with his facial scars—the product of his fight with the bear whose skin he now wore—gave him a very distinct appearance. His hair and beard, both the color of an open fire, had grown long and unruly. He usually shaved whenever he returned to the Wardens' Keep, but between hunting down the Black Hand and avenging King Mór's murder, over half a year had passed since he last laid eyes on Tara.

They passed a settlement in short order, and it was clear the settlers had put the trees from the Wrenwood to use in the construction of their huts. The world was changing. The peace and prosperity ushered in by the High Queen's reign allowed trade and commerce to flourish across the five kingdoms. New towns and villages popped up at an ever-increasing pace, and the wilds continued to shrink, leaving many nonhuman creatures without homes.

"How do you think the Brotherhood of Thieves is mixed up in this?" Morwen asked.

"Most likely they're just intermediaries—like Calum." The incident in the tavern wasn't the first time they had crossed paths with the Brotherhood of Thieves, Leinster's thieves' guild. In Munster, Berengar and Morwen had prevented the sale of a coatl egg orchestrated by the Brotherhood. "I doubt they'd have any real interest in the stone other than its worth. Whoever wants it is risking a lot if they were willing to double-cross the Brotherhood."

"Maybe we should start there. We might be better off questioning the Brotherhood directly."

"Out of the question." Although Morwen understood magic and monsters far better than he could ever hope to, she had spent much of her life sheltered in her father's castle at Cashel. Berengar knew how the world worked outside of books, and a life of adventure was a great deal more dangerous than stories made it out to be. "The Brotherhood is one of the most dangerous organizations in Fál. Its reach extends into all five kingdoms, but Dún Aulin is the seat of its power. We should do our best to stay out of their affairs."

"What about the goblins? I can't think of many people who would employ goblin mercenaries to do their dirty work—not when there are plenty of disreputable humans willing to do the job. It suggests whoever hired them is eager to cover their tracks, or perhaps isn't entirely human themselves. I'd be willing to bet they want the rune in order to use it, and that makes them very dangerous indeed."

Berengar nodded grimly. "Then it's a good thing we have it." The purges that followed Azeroth's defeat had drastically reduced Fál's population of magic-capable humans. In times past, it was magicians or sorcerers who dealt with magical threats. Now, the duty usually fell to monster hunters or the High Queen's wardens. He caught Morwen glaring at him. "What?"

"I might have talked the goblins down if you hadn't gone charging in with your axe. You shouldn't have called them vermin."

"Morwen, they tried to kill us!"

"Even so. Maybe relations between the races would be better if we weren't so quick to reach for a weapon every time something green jumped out from behind a bush. In Munster, goblins live side by side with humans."

Berengar scoffed at her. "As second-class citizens, maybe." Munster prided itself on being tolerant of magic and nonhumans, and while it was true there weren't bounties for goblins plastered across Cashel's city square like there were in Dún Aulin, tensions between races had risen considerably in the wake of King Mór's assassination.

For his part, Berengar had spent too many years at war with goblins to ever count them as friends, but neither did he believe they were all evil, as some in the church taught. Goblins—and most nonhumans, for that matter—were just like people: capable of both good and evil. As an outcast himself, he could understand why Morwen, who would never quite fit in on account of her magic, was sensitive to the treatment of nonhumans.

Although illegitimate, with Mór dead and Princess Ravenna banished, by right Morwen had a claim to her father's crown. The people of Munster would rather the throne go empty than accept a magician as their queen. The people of Leinster liked magicians even less, which made the danger to her all the more real.

Morwen wasn't the only one who faced danger in Leinster. Berengar hadn't told her the whole truth about what happened at Dún Aulin all those years ago. He had more than his share of enemies there who would gladly see him dead. He kept his thoughts to himself and focused on the task at hand. Once they tracked the goblins to their lair and dealt with whoever hired them, they could move on.

The sooner we're gone, the better.

T hey hunted the goblins for three days. The trail led through pastures and open fields, and there were fewer trees and forests than he remembered encountering the last time he was in the area. With fewer potential hideaways, the goblins proved easy to follow—almost *too* easy. It was as if they weren't even trying to cover their tracks. Goblins were sly and crafty by nature, so why would they risk traveling out in the open? Berengar didn't like it.

Gradually, the path turned southeast. Berengar said less and less as time went on. After they passed the Hill of Allen, the terrain became more familiar to him, and he had an unpleasant suspicion about the destination that awaited them. Morwen, who undoubtedly sensed a change in his mood for the worse, wisely chose for once not to press him on the matter. On the third day, they reached the trail's end at a four-arch stone bridge that ran across the River Liffey, and Berengar's suspicions were confirmed.

"Blast it. It's as I feared."

Ahead stretched the Slighe Chualann, one of five *Slighe* roads spanning Fál's kingdoms. All the highways met at the capital at Tara, where the High Queen ruled. At the moment, the road was busy with travelers of all stripes moving in either direction. There were nobles in fine carriages, merchants and farmers with wagons overflowing with wares, soldiers marching in formation, and countless others. Faolán looked back at Berengar with an irritated expression, and it was clear that with so many travelers on the road, the goblins' trail had gone cold.

Although many travelers stopped at the thriving town of Kilcullen, Berengar looked past it to a great city rising farther in the distance. "Dún Aulin."

"The City of Thieves." Morwen stared at the city in wonder.

The one place in Leinster he most wanted to avoid. Worse still, the goblins would be far more difficult to track in a city of thousands. He sighed and prodded his horse over the bridge. "Come on."

Morwen followed slowly, and her gaze remained set on the looming city. Although Cashel, Munster's capital, was more beautiful and prosperous, Dún Aulin was unquestionably the larger of the two cities. Its sheer size was staggering, even at a distance. Morwen's excitement grew evident as they approached. Their search for the Oakseers' Grotto had marked her first time beyond Munster's borders.

There were five kingdoms in the land of Fál. Munster was its southernmost realm while Ulster was its northernmost. Leinster, Connacht, and Meath fell in between. For much of recent history, the five kingdoms had quarreled and warred among themselves, until Nora of Connacht assumed the High Throne after her defeat of Azeroth. At the moment, Fál was enjoying a time of tranquility not seen since the days of the high kings of old, but always there were threats seeking to unravel the peace.

Berengar and Morwen made their way onto the road, which was unusually crowded, even by Dún Aulin's standards. He wondered if there was some occasion of interest drawing spectators to the city. The heavy traffic turned what might have been a short ride into an hour-long slog.

Leftover mud from recent rains caused a number of carriages and wagons to become stuck just off the road.

So much for slipping into the city unnoticed. The lines ran all the way to the city, where guards carefully screened newcomers at each gate to determine whether to grant entrance. It seemed the city watch had learned its lesson from the riots, when an out-of-control populace completely overwhelmed the guards. "Let's stop at Kilcullen first. We might get lucky and pick up the goblins' trail."

It was a few hours past noon, but already the sky darkened with ominous clouds. He doubted they would have reached the city before the storm. Besides, Kilcullen was the best place to find information on current happenings in the city, and Berengar had no intention of heading into the dragon's den unprepared.

They continued along the main road until they reached Kilcullen. Though by no means small, the specter of Dún Aulin dwarfed the town. Kilcullen was also known as Kingstown, for in centuries past it was where kings and queens from neighboring kingdoms stayed as guests for Leinster's royal coronations. The name was a bit of a misnomer, as nobles and lords largely eschewed the town, whose population consisted mostly of commoners.

"We should resupply here. The merchants in the city gouge their prices." As a warden, he rarely wanted for coin, but that had not always been the case. In any event, spending too freely invited unwanted attention.

Berengar and Morwen dismounted and led their horses through town. Numerous travelers bolstered an already booming population, and the narrow streets were cramped and congested. Berengar's size made it difficult to maneuver, and he quickly grew annoyed at the number of times strangers bumped into him.

Morwen paid a stableman to put their horses up for the

night, and the pair ventured into the market in hopes of making their purchases before the storm hit. Despite the impending weather, the market was lively, and it appeared many fellow travelers had similar ideas. Fish fresh from the waters of the Liffey were on abundant display, and farmers from surrounding lands traded in produce and livestock.

"Do my eyes deceive me? The Bloody Red Bear, right here in Kilcullen." Three men barred their path forward. The men were dressed like soldiers, but their armor bore the insignia of a sword drenched in blood in place of the sigil of a noble house.

Monster hunters. The insignia belonged to the Acolytes of the True Faith, a group of fanatics so brutal the church had officially disavowed them.

The man in the middle took a step forward. "What's the High Queen's Monster doing off his leash?" His companions laughed with malicious intent.

Berengar's jaw tightened in anger. "Get out of my way. Now."

The monster hunter's smile, and those of his companions, faded. "You should watch your tongue, dog." He turned to his friends. "What do you say, lads? Shall we teach him some manners?" His hand inched toward his sword.

"Do it, and you won't live to regret it." It wasn't Berengar's first run-in with the Acolytes, who had played a key role in the purges. Bad blood ran deep on both sides, and the people of Leinster had long memories.

"You killed the grand marshal's son during the riots. We'll not let that pass." The man unsheathed his blade, and his companions did the same. "You're a fool to show your face here. Last I heard, you were excommunicated after what happened at St. Brigid's. You have no protection here."

Berengar reached for his axe. "This is all the protection I need." Ready for a fight, Faolán let out a menacing growl and bared her teeth beside him.

"You lot are making a serious mistake. I've seen what happens when he loses his temper." Morwen shot Berengar a look, as if to remind him to keep his head. "He's a Warden of Fál. He can kill with impunity."

It was true, at least in theory. When Nora of Connacht became High Queen of Fál, she appointed five wardens to keep the peace between realms. As a warden, Berengar answered to Nora alone. In practice, there were limits to even the High Queen's influence, and Berengar was often required to back up his authority with force.

The monster hunter ignored Morwen's warning. "Save your fancy words, wench." He glanced at his friends. "Warden or not, we'll be celebrated as heroes for killing the Bloody Red Bear."

Thunder sounded above, and a light rain began. Berengar's hand tightened around the axe's handle in anticipation of violence. Unlike the soldiers he had brawled with at the Forgotten Stop, the Acolytes were lethal warriors trained to hunt and kill dangerous creatures.

"Stop this at once!" The voice belonged to a stout man in brown robes. A crucifix hung from his neck. He carried a walking stick in one hand and jabbed the other, made of wood, at the monster hunters. "What is the meaning of this?"

The monster hunters' leader kept a wary eye on Berengar. "Friar, it is our sacred duty to kill this man where he stands. He has been excommunicated for violating the right of sanctuary and committing murder in the house of the Lord. He's—"

"I know who the Bear Warden is. I expect mindless

violence from a man like him, but the three of you should know better than to draw blades on today of all days."

The man hesitated and lowered his sword.

"It's the first day of the Festival of Atonement," the friar went on. "Surely devout men such as yourselves should know it is a grievous sin to spill blood on this day."

"Of course. The Festival of Atonement." The monster hunters' leader returned his blade to its sheath, and his companions reluctantly followed suit. "Forgive us, friar." He bowed and shot Berengar a withering look. "This isn't over."

"Many blessings, brothers." The moment the monster hunters were gone, the friar's face broke into a wide grin. "It's good to see you again, Warden Berengar, though I'll admit you're the last person I expected to meet today."

Morwen looked from one man to the other, confused. "Wait—you two know each other?"

Berengar nodded. "It's a long story. Morwen, this is Friar Godfrey. Our paths crossed in Alúine when I was last in Leinster. Godfrey, meet the Lady Morwen of Cashel. We owe you one."

Morwen raised an eyebrow. "I'm no expert on church lore, but I've never heard of the Festival of Atonement."

Godfrey winked at them. "I'd imagine not. I just made it up." Thunder crackled loudly overhead, and the rain intensified. "Have you found lodging for the night?"

Berengar shook his head. "We've only just arrived."

Godfrey lifted his hood and beckoned them to follow him. "Then come! Have a drink with an old friend and tell me what the devil has brought you back to Leinster, of all places."

"Lead the way."

Morwen leaned over and lowered her voice. "So you *can* make friends. I thought I was your only one."

"Who says you and I are friends?"

She punched him playfully on the shoulder.

They followed Godfrey past a round tower and the churchyard to a secluded monastery at the edge of town. According to local legend, Padraig himself started the monastery, and judging by its apparent age, Berengar almost believed it. Moss crept up the sides, and there were signs of neglect everywhere he looked. He suspected the church preferred to spend funds on the extravagant cathedrals and churches in the city instead of a lonely abode of solitary monks and dusty scrolls.

Although the worship of the Lord of Hosts extended throughout Fál, nowhere was the church's influence greater than pious Leinster, and Dún Aulin served as its political center.

Centuries ago, most of Fál worshiped the elder gods, which included the benevolent Tuatha dé Danann and the monstrous Fomorians. That changed with the arrival of Padraig, who brought the word of the Lord of Hosts to Fál. The old ways persisted in many parts of Fál—especially in the north—but were almost nonexistent in Leinster, which had made the worship of the Lord of Hosts the official state religion and prohibited shrines to the elder gods.

"It's quiet," Morwen said once they were out of the rain.

"Most of the monks have traveled to the city." Godfrey lowered his hood. "Old Bishop McLoughlin has finally died, and all the holy men in Leinster have come to Dún Aulin. Officially, they're here to attend the funeral, though I suspect a great deal are really there to ingratiate themselves to McLoughlin's eventual successor in hopes of advancing their position. You'll be safe here, at least for the night."

Berengar appreciated the irony. "I doubt many would think to look for me at a monastery, at any rate."

Godfrey chuckled. "It would be quite a shock, arriving for prayers to find the Bloody Red Bear. Now if you don't mind waiting here for a moment, I'll see about food and rooms for the two of you." He set his walking stick aside and disappeared down a forlorn corridor.

Berengar and Morwen lowered their hoods, and Faolán shook excess water from her coat and curiously sniffed the monastery's interior. The falling rain produced a sweet, earthy fragrance detectable underneath the musty odor that hung in the air. The entrance hall was sparsely decorated, in keeping with the monks' austere lifestyle. Rain dripped from cracks in the ceiling.

Strictly speaking, Berengar was barred from setting foot on holy ground and had no right of sanctuary on account of his excommunication. Still, it was better to risk spending the night in the seclusion of the monastery than in a busy inn or tavern where he might be recognized.

"I bet you feel right at home," he said to Morwen. They first met when King Mór sent Berengar to Cill Airne to retrieve his court magician. When he found her, Morwen was under siege from a group of superstitious farmers who believed she was responsible for the pestilence affecting their crops. The monks at Innisfallen had given Morwen refuge within their monastery. When Berengar threatened to kill the farmers to lift the siege, Morwen had managed to convince both sides to stand down and achieved a peaceful resolution.

"I've spent enough time trapped inside monasteries to last a lifetime, thank you very much—though I do miss the smell of parchment." She smiled wistfully. "Who were those men?"

"Part of a group of fanatics who call themselves the

Acolytes of the True Faith. Their leader is a butcher named Winslow. Calls himself the grand marshal."

"Did you really kill his son?"

"Aye. Made him suffer, too. Bastard deserved far worse. I would happily have killed Winslow too if I could have managed it, but my hands were occupied at the time." Berengar knew people thought he was a monster—and deservedly so—but at least he only killed those who deserved it. The Acolytes slaughtered innocents without hesitation, all in the name of their blind devotion to a perverted interpretation of the scriptures. They truly thought they were carrying out the Lord's will. There were few foes as dangerous as those who truly believed in their cause. "I've a feeling we haven't seen the last of them."

Godfrey reappeared moments later. "It's all taken care of. I found a place in our dormitories where you won't be disturbed. Come, and we'll see about getting the two of you something to eat."

Berengar and Morwen followed him deeper into the monastery. Faolán trailed behind and kept to the shadows, her amber eyes gleaming in the dim light. They passed a library full of shelves stacked with books and scrolls, which Morwen regarded with a longing expression, before starting down a set of stairs leading to the undercroft. Candles and torches illuminated the refectory, a wide, somberly lit chamber that served as the monks' dining hall. Like the rest of the monastery, the chamber was relatively bare, which made it seem all the more spacious.

Godfrey, Berengar, and Morwen washed their hands in a basin of water and settled at a long bench where simple wooden plates and goblets waited. At the moment, the other benches sat empty. Footsteps echoed across the chamber, and an aged man in brown robes placed a tray of food before them and limped off without a word.

"Don't mind Father Ulrich," Godfrey said to Berengar, who watched the old man with caution. "He's quite blind, but he's a decent enough cook by monastery standards. I'll put it this way—I'm glad I'm a friar and not a monk."

Berengar grabbed a flatbread wafer and helped himself to a piece of *tánach*, an exceptionally hard cheese, while spooning *menedach*—a porridge made from kneading grain and butter together—onto his plate. Monks were known for their moderation, and the food in front of him was no exception. The fare was largely flavorless, but Berengar wasn't particularly choosy, so long as he could eat his fill.

Morwen raised an eyebrow. "How exactly did the two of you meet?"

"After I tracked down the Black Hand, their leader fled and took refuge inside a church," Berengar replied between mouthfuls. "I killed him at the altar. I didn't know at the time it was St. Brigid's Church. Laird Margolin promised to keep it quiet if I would help find his niece, Lady Imogen. He told me she'd been abducted by an ogre, but the mad fool really wanted to sacrifice her to Balor, King of the Fomorians. Godfrey gave Imogen sanctuary and helped put her on her uncle's throne."

The whole affair ended disastrously. Imogen proved as bloodthirsty as her uncle in her own right. Word of Berengar's deeds at St. Brigid's resulted in his excommunication from the church, and only the timely arrival of King Mór's summons had saved him from having to return to Tara to face the High Queen's wrath.

"In the end we prevailed, though the cost was dear." Godfrey bowed his head.

"Aye." Berengar stared off into space, and for a moment the only sound in the refectory was the pitter-patter of rain outside the monastery.

Godfrey raised his goblet. "To Rose and Evander."

"To Rose." The pair clinked goblets, and Berengar took a swig of ale. "Any news of Saroise?"

"I believe she was headed north."

"And Lady Imogen?"

"The last I heard, Imogen had cleared the trees around Móin Alúin and drained the swamp. The land is changing, Berengar. New roads and settlements sprout up all the time. Now I believe you owe me a story. What brings the Bear Warden back to Leinster?"

Berengar downed another mouthful. "Not much of a story. Some of Imogen's soldiers massacred the hobgoblins near Alúine and stole the thunder rune I gave them. Morwen and I are looking for the person who hired them."

"And you tracked them here?" Godfrey scratched his beard. "They'd be fools to come within ten miles of Dún Aulin. There are monster hunters everywhere, and most folk would gladly string up anyone with even the slightest whiff of magic."

Morwen watched Godfrey with interest. "What about you?"

The friar laughed. "My dear child, I believe everyone has magic of a sort. It simply takes different forms."

"Very wise." Morwen leaned closer to Berengar. "I like him."

"Still, if it's goblins you're looking for, you might ask Tavish, the head of the city watch. Perhaps his scouts have seen something. The Brotherhood is also said to be a good source of information—provided it's not about one of their contracts and you're willing to pay."

Berengar exchanged a glance with Morwen. "We've run afoul of the Brotherhood before. I prefer to avoid them if possible."

"Understood. You could always try a bard. That lot seem to know everything that happens around here—puts most innkeepers to shame, I'd say. The Revels have drawn a fair number to the city."

Morwen's brow arched. "The Revels?"

"An annual celebration of the arts. Men and women come from across Fál to see the greatest poets, musicians, and bards compete for the golden quill. The contest lasts the whole month. Don't know why they bothered holding it this year, though. Jareth has won the competition three years straight."

Morwen looked to Berengar, intrigued.

"Don't get too excited. We don't have time to waste listening to a bunch of storytellers. We have a job to do." Berengar had a particular dislike of bards, who wove truth and lies together to suit their stories. More often than not, the truth was bad enough as it was.

He resumed eating and spent the remainder of the meal in silence while Morwen peppered Godfrey with questions about himself and the monastery. It amused Berengar to see someone else subjected to the weight of her curiosity for a change, but the priest took each question in stride.

"We can resupply when the rains pass," Berengar told Morwen when he finished his meal. "We'll spend the night here and set out in the morning." It was early, but he wanted to be sharp and well-rested when they entered the city. In the meantime, they could ask around Kilcullen and see if anyone had heard of the goblins.

Godfrey refilled Berengar's goblet and returned to his seat. "You would do well to leave early. The guards are inspecting everyone entering the city, and it can take hours to get through the lines."

"Why so much traffic?" Berengar accepted the goblet. "Is it on account of the Revels or the bishop's death?"

Godfrey's brow furrowed, and he looked from

Berengar to Morwen with increasing incredulity. "You mean you don't know?"

Berengar frowned. "Know what?"

"The people are coming for the Ceremony of the Cursed Blade. It's been thirteen years. In four days' time, the most dangerous relic in Fál will be on display."

CHAPTER THREE

"THE CURSED BLADE," Morwen muttered. "What strange turn of fate has led us here?"

Torchlight flickered across the refectory's stone walls. Thunder reverberated outside the monastery, causing Faolán to stir at Berengar's feet.

The sword used by Azeroth in his conquest of Fál. It was a famous weapon, even to Berengar, whose knowledge of most things magical in nature was limited at best. "What's so important about a broken blade?"

Morwen appeared taken aback by the idea he would even entertain such a question. "Even broken, it's no ordinary blade. The sword is one of four treasures forged by the Tuatha dé Danann."

Godfrey shifted uncomfortably in his chair. "The four lost treasures—magical objects of great power scattered across Fál. I thought they were a myth."

"The sword is no myth." A chill settled over the chamber, and Morwen shivered and held her hands out to the hearth for warmth. "The fairies called it the *Cliamh Solais*— the Bright Sword. According to legend, no man could stand before it. Much blood was spilled over the blade, and wars were waged for possession of it.

"Centuries ago, the sword passed to King Lorc of Leinster, who saw the endless cycle of destruction that followed the blade and attempted to bring peace by other means. Lorc signed a treaty with the fairies that ushered in a time of peace between races unheard of before or since. Every thirteen years, the blade changed hands between Lorc and the fairy queen. It was said the two had fallen in love, and neither would use the sword against the other.

"The practice continued long after the king's death, and for centuries the blade went unused—even in times of great need. As the old ways died out and relations between humans and fairies deteriorated, the ceremony continued with the church taking the fairies' place. Still the blade went unused."

Berengar stared into the flames. "Until Azeroth."

"Aye. The Lord of Shadows took the blade for himself and corrupted it with dark sorcery. Even without the blade, he was already the most feared sorcerer in Fál. With it in hand…" She shuddered.

"I know. I was there." Berengar had first encountered Nora of Connacht during the Shadow Wars, when the queen raised him up and gave him purpose. Nora was made High Queen after the war, and much to everyone's surprise—including his—she named him as one of her wardens.

"Queen Nora defeated Azeroth, and the blade was broken in the final battle," Morwen finished. "Nora returned one of the two shards to Leinster, and the kingdom resumed the ceremony."

"And the other shard?"

Morwen shrugged. "No one knows what happened to it. I suspect Nora hid it to prevent the two shards from being reunited, though only powerful magic could accomplish such a task."

Godfrey drained his goblet and set it aside. "For the last thirteen years, the cursed blade has been under the church's care for safekeeping. It is one of the most closely guarded objects in Fál on account of its power. Even the Brotherhood of Thieves wouldn't dare lay a hand on it. In four days, the blade will change hands again and be presented to young King Lucien."

Berengar wasn't sure how much of the story he believed. It was often difficult to disentangle truth from exaggeration where legends were concerned. Based on Godfrey's expression, the friar shared his skepticism. Still, he could see why the ceremony would interest the masses. With the old ways in decline, such a powerful relic was a link to a long-forgotten past.

"An interesting story, but we have more important matters to deal with at the moment." Thanking Godfrey for his hospitality, Berengar pushed away from the table and gestured for Morwen to follow. While the crowds drawn by the ceremony and the Revels would no doubt complicate efforts to locate the goblins and their mysterious employer, the cursed blade was no concern of theirs.

F riar Godfrey remained behind when they set out early the following morning. Although the storm had passed, the sky remained bleak and overcast. Despite the early hour, heavy traffic again blocked their path to the city. Berengar doubted most would-be spectators would ever get close enough to see the cursed blade for themselves. Many probably came to take part in other events and attractions surrounding the ceremony, or to take advantage of the influx of trade and commerce.

Berengar found himself growing more restless the closer they got to the city. Many years had passed since he last laid eyes on Dún Aulin, but the things he'd witnessed during the riots were forever seared into his mind. He still remembered the scene that greeted his approach. Fattened crows circled overhead. Bodies hung everywhere—from gallows, trees, and the walls themselves—as a warning to any who dared draw near. The waters of the Liffey were red with blood and teemed with bloated corpses. The memories stirred a familiar surge of anger, which earned him a reproachful look from Morwen.

"We're close now. You don't want to lose your temper in front of the guards."

"I've told you not to go poking around in my head."

"I'm not. You give off anger like a fire gives off heat. Anyone with a hint of magic could sense it."

"Next!" bellowed one of the guards, and Berengar and Morwen inched closer to the city's North Gate.

"How dare you?" A few spots ahead in line, a noble in his early thirties berated another traveler as others looked on. "You've gotten mud all over my new clothes." The noble was tall and well-groomed, and his fine clothes were spotted with mud.

The other man, a portly farmer in shabby clothes, bowed low and stammered a string of apologies. "Pardon, good sir. Please forgive me." From the look of things, the farmer's wagon had splashed over a puddle and sprayed the noble's carriage with mud. His face reddening by the moment, the farmer hastily reached for his coin pouch. "I don't have much, but I'd gladly pay what I can to have them cleaned."

The noble's lips curled into a thin sneer. "These clothes were tailored specifically for the Revels. They're ruined now, and on the final night of the event."

"Please, sir, I meant no offense."

"Your very presence offends me." The noble turned to his companions and retainers, as if to belabor some previously discussed point. "I find it offensive that I am made to wait in line with peasants. I am Baron McCullagh, son of Uriens. I think perhaps we should teach this man a lesson about careless manners." One of McCullagh's retainers gave the farmer a shove, causing the man to land in the puddle on his backside. McCullagh's companions laughed heartily.

The farmer scrambled to find his footing. "Mercy, please! I'm only here to beg the church to bless my little Sophie, sick with St. Anthony's Fire. She's just a girl."

"I don't think he's learned his lesson yet." McCullagh nodded at his retainers, who advanced toward the farmer.

"Is there a problem?" Berengar all but growled. The retainers stopped in their tracks.

McCullagh glared at him. "Stay out of this affair. This isn't your business."

"I'm making it my business."

"Do you have any idea who I am?" McCullagh demanded. "I'm—"

"I heard you the first time. I just don't care." He'd killed princes and lords. He certainly wasn't afraid of some lesser noble. Berengar punched McCullagh in the face. He smirked at the sight of blood gushing from McCullagh's broken nose. "Looks like you have something new to wear to the Revels."

"Don't just stand there!" McCullagh shouted at his retainers. "Do something."

The retainers exchanged nervous glances and chose to keep their distance.

"Guards!" someone exclaimed, and Berengar saw men in green cloaks approaching through the crowd.

"Now you've done it." Morwen shot him a dark look before helping the farmer to his feet. "I told you so."

Berengar shrugged. "I don't like bullies."

Morwen delved into her satchel and handed the farmer a sealed vial containing a turquoise liquid. "Give this to your daughter when the fits take her. It should help with the convulsions. The disease is caused by a fungus that grows on grains. You should deep plow your fields. Take your yield and submerge it in a brine solution—the healthy grains will sink. In the meantime, keep your daughter away from rye."

The farmer bowed low in a show of gratitude. "Many thanks, friends. May the Lord of Hosts bless you and keep you."

"You there!" said one of a trio of guards. "What's the meaning of this?"

Berengar grunted noncommittally. "He slipped."

The guard looked from Berengar to McCullagh. "Do you take me for a fool?" He waved a hand dismissively. "Get out of here, the lot of you."

"Wait." Another noticed the potion in the farmer's hand, and his gaze fell on Morwen's satchel. "Turn out your things. That's an order."

"That won't be necessary." Berengar saw Morwen tense as he reached into his cloak, but to her visible relief he produced a coin pouch rather than a weapon. "My friend and I have come a long way to pay our respects to the bishop. We'd be very appreciative if you let us inside the gates." He offered a handful of silver coins to the guard. "That enough to cover it?"

The guard eyed the silver with a greedy expression. "For one of us, maybe."

Berengar handed each of the guard's companions the

same measure of silver, and the guards motioned them through the lines.

Once they were through the gate, Berengar held up three gold coins. "This is so you never saw us. Understand?"

The guard took the coins and handed two to his companions. "Look, friends, at all these coins that have fallen into our pockets by accident. The Lord smiles upon us." He waved Berengar along. "Many blessings, stranger."

"You handled that surprisingly well," Morwen remarked as they entered the city.

"Don't sound so surprised. I don't solve *all* my problems with violence."

Morwen grinned. "Just most of them."

Berengar led his horse down a cobblestone road toward the dense web of packed buildings. The last time he passed through the gates of Dún Aulin, the streets were abandoned. Mobs had reduced whole neighborhoods to ruin and ash, and the smell of smoke and death hung in the air. In contrast, the city he saw before him was vibrant and full of life. Homes and businesses had been rebuilt, and aside from a visibly increased presence of the city guards, there was little evidence of the riots.

Dún Aulin consisted of a large number of districts, each with its own distinct character. The city streets were paved and well-maintained, except in poorer neighborhoods. There was a new sight to see everywhere he looked. Vendors and merchants of every stripe imaginable peddled their wares in businesses or vending stalls. Musicians and entertainers performed on street corners.

"Hear me!" a man in sackcloth proclaimed to a crowd of onlookers. "King Mór of Munster is dead at the hand of assassins!"

Although some appeared to have heard the news already, others greeted it with alarm.

"King Mór welcomed monsters and cavorted with witches. He even kept a magician as a member of his court. Is it any wonder he invited divine judgment upon himself?"

Morwen stared with clenched teeth at the street preacher, and her hands balled into fists at the insult to her father. "If I hadn't vowed to use my magic only for good, I'd show *him* some divine judgment…"

The preacher continued. "Give thanks for the wisdom of good King Lucien, young though he may be. Let us pray our prince regent repents of his sins and follows his cousin's example."

Although the five kings and queens of Fál—the *Rí Ruirech*—were sworn to Nora, each was largely left to rule his or her own realm as they saw fit. Beneath these overkings were the *Rí Tuaithe*, underkings who wore iron crowns. Lucien, like the monarchs of Ulster, Meath, Connacht, and Munster, wore a silver crown. Only the High Queen wore a crown of gold.

Leinster's current monarch was Lucien, a boy-king of twelve who had not yet come of age. He was said to be a devout follower of the Lord of Hosts, though Berengar had no idea if the stories were true or wishful thinking on the part of Leinster's populace. In contrast, Prince Tristan, who ruled as regent, was anything but pious. Tristan was an open drinker, gambler, and womanizer who preferred merriment to governance. Despite his many vices, the people loved him, much to the consternation of the church —which also had a hand in governing the realm.

"Let's go, Morwen. We have better things to do."

Her mood improved as the street preacher's voice receded behind them. "Why is it called the City of

Thieves? There's so much more here than the Brotherhood."

"Thieves take many forms. Dún Aulin is the most corrupt city in the five kingdoms. Much of the city watch is in the Brotherhood's pocket. The Church of Fál levies heavy fines and taxes on the populace in addition to those imposed by the crown."

"So much for piety."

"Aye. There are plenty of true believers, but there are also those who pay homage to faith with their lips while their actions say otherwise." On the surface, Dún Aulin was a shining example of holiness to the rest of Fál, but there was a shady underground operating behind closed doors.

The multitudes grew the farther they advanced into the city, and while the roads were a good deal wider than those in Kilcullen, the influx of travelers resulted in congested lanes. Berengar blended into the crowd and kept his head down to avoid drawing unwanted attention. Fortunately, despite his size and scars, most passersby appeared too preoccupied to take note of him.

"Stay close to me. We need to stick together while we're here. I don't want you wandering off."

Morwen, apparently still cross over the remarks about her father, sounded vaguely irritated by the warning. "I'm perfectly capable of looking after myself. In case you've forgotten, I was Munster's court magician long before you came along. In fact, I could probably handle this whole affair without your help."

Before she could continue, Morwen's mare tore free of her grip. The horse reared without warning and knocked down a woman in a hooded cloak.

Horrified, Morwen calmed the horse with her touch and ran over to help the traveler up. "Are you all right?"

The young woman stumbled and put her arms around Morwen for support. Her lower face was concealed by a scarf. "I think so." Her eyes were the deepest shade of blue Berengar had ever seen.

There was something pure about her voice, and Berengar felt a sense of warmth when she spoke. Faolán, usually wary of strangers, sat on her haunches and stared at the woman with a vacant expression, as if under a spell. Her behavior reminded him of how she had acted when she first met Morwen.

"Are you sure?" Morwen held out a hand to steady her.

"No harm done." The stranger dusted herself off and started on her way.

Morwen turned back to her horse and stroked the mare's muzzle. "Nessa, what's gotten into you?" She shook her head and glanced at Berengar. "She's normally more even-tempered than this." She started to speak but stopped suddenly and reached into her satchel. "The thunder rune —it's gone."

Berengar peered into the crowd, where the hooded woman had almost disappeared from sight. "I think your new friend is a member of the Brotherhood of Thieves."

When the woman glanced over her shoulder and saw them staring, she broke into a sprint.

"What was that you were saying about handling yourself?"

Morwen glared at him and took off running. "Shut up. We can't let her escape."

The dense crowd was too difficult to navigate on horse-back, so Berengar let go of his horse's reins and followed on foot.

"After her!" Morwen shouted to Faolán.

Faolán bolted forward and outpaced them both. Fellow travelers cleared out of the way at the sight of the wolfhound racing toward them. The young woman attempted to lose them in the crowd, but Faolán barked loudly to alert them to the thief's presence.

"There she is!" Morwen yelled. "Don't let her get away!"

Berengar shoved two men out of his way. Ahead, the thief weaved and dodged through the crowd, avoiding collisions with others while maintaining her speed. *Whoever she is, she's fast.*

With Faolán at her heels, the thief leapt over the side of a footbridge. Berengar reached the bridge just in time to see her hit the ground below and execute a perfectly timed roll that put her back on her feet. It was at least a twelve-foot drop.

"She's headed to the market!" Morwen called over her shoulder. "Come on."

Berenger swore and hurried down a nearby staircase. The city's expansive market made that of Kilcullen seem insignificant in comparison. Banners of various colors and shapes, announcing all manner of goods and services, rippled in the wind. People were everywhere. It would be easy for the thief to lose them in such a crowded place.

He quickened his pace and kept the thief within his line of sight. She deftly spun away from a woman with a wash bucket and gave it enough of a nudge with her fingers to spill its contents over the road. Morwen slipped and lost her balance, and Berengar pushed past her, inadvertently knocking over an apple cart in his effort to keep up. The thief jumped over a passing herd of sheep that blocked his path, and as Berengar tried to get around them, he spotted a group of bored-looking guards on patrol nearby.

"Stop, thief!"

The guards instantly took note of the young woman,

who deftly evaded them, leapt onto the back of a moving carriage, and jumped off in front of an alleyway.

Berengar pulled Morwen to her feet. "You go after her. I'll go around to the other end and we'll trap her in the middle." The long alley had only one outlet, and unlike the vast network of alleyways in other parts of the city, it was easy to see where it ended.

"With pleasure." Morwen rushed into the alley with Faolán close behind.

Berengar reached for the dagger in his boot, hurried around the building, and slipped into the shadows at the alley's far end. He heard footsteps coming his way and readied the blade, only to stay his hand at the last moment when Morwen appeared around the corner.

"You let her get past you?"

"Of course not. There's no way she could have reached the end before I got there."

"If you didn't see her and I didn't see her, the only way she could have escaped…" Morwen trailed off, and Berengar followed her gaze up the side of the building. "But that's impossible." It was as if the thief had vanished into thin air.

"It doesn't matter. She's gone." Berengar put the dagger away and stormed off. "We've lost the rune."

Their horses were gone too, as it turned out—most likely stolen. They had been in Dún Aulin all of half an hour and already they'd lost the rune, both their mounts, and the supplies in their saddlebags. He wasn't in a pleasant mood.

Morwen checked her satchel to make sure nothing else was missing. "How did they find us so quickly?"

"The Brotherhood of Thieves knows everything that happens in this city. They probably knew we were here from the moment we set foot inside the gates." *At least they didn't take her satchel.* If the wrong people discovered Morwen in possession of spell books, runes, and potions, they might attempt to have her tried as a witch. Berengar would kill every man in the city before he let that happen.

Despite his intent not to get involved with the Brotherhood, it seemed trouble had found them anyway. If the Brotherhood didn't already know about their involvement with Ryland and the thwarted sale of the thunder rune, they would soon. After the business with Calum and the coatl egg, it was unlikely they would look favorably upon a second slight.

"Nessa was a gift from my father. I'm not leaving without her."

Berengar didn't bother arguing. There was little anyone could do to sway Morwen once she made up her mind. It was one of the few traits they had in common. "We'll find her. Come on."

They followed the main road farther into the city. Like Cashel, Dún Aulin had been built at high elevation for defensive purposes. The city had expanded outward over the centuries as its population grew, but most of the older, central parts of the city were still made of stone. The differences between the districts were more pronounced than when Berengar had been sent to quell the riots, and clear class distinctions were evident between neighborhoods.

The nobility, priesthood, and wealthiest citizens occupied the highest position in the city's social structure. Beneath them were an extensive middle class of merchants, soldiers and guards, craftsmen, and many more. The trades had guilds of their own, and the strict laws and regulations imposed by the church had simply driven many businesses underground. At the bottom rung were a great number of the dispossessed, who lived in cramped slums in less affluent city districts. Starvation and disease were common among the poor, who mostly depended upon the benevolence of the church to meet their earthly needs. For all the corruption in the church, there were many true believers like Friar Godfrey who gave generously to help those in need.

Morwen glanced around. "Where are we going?"

"To the grand square. I want to have a little talk with the city watch."

"I thought you said the guards were in the Brotherhood's pocket."

"Even the Brotherhood's influence has its limits. Besides, there are more than a few in the watch who owe me their lives. The mobs killed guards by the dozens during the riots."

It was a long walk without their horses, but Berengar was accustomed to traveling great distances on foot. Dún Aulin buzzed with excitement over the Revels and the Ceremony of the Cursed Blade. The teeming masses impeded their progress through the city. After almost an hour, they reached the looming walls of Padraig's Gate and passed under a tall triangular arch to enter the grand square, arguably the city's most influential district.

The royal palace and the great cathedral—symbols of the twin pillars of Leinster's government—were both visible from the square. Inner walls and a plethora of guards were meant to keep unsavory elements at bay, though the square appeared nearly as busy as the rest of the city. The buildings were taller and more imposing than their counterparts elsewhere, and scores of statues depicted storied characters from history and myth. The trees, grass, and flowers that grew in centrally located road verges represented the final remnants of the old forest long ago cleared away to allow for the city's expansion.

Berengar ignored the crowd of nobles, religious leaders, and government officials and followed the sound of an elaborately dressed bellman to a place where notices were posted along a section of wall. There were also a number of bounties naming rewards for the death or capture of human criminals and monsters. Most bounties for monsters were for goblins, though one in particular stood out among the others.

"Azura," Morwen read. "The last fairy." The bounty depicted an artist's rendering of a blue-skinned woman with dark hair, pointy teeth and ears, and solid violet eyes. Unlike the rewards of silver listed for the goblins, the bounty promised considerable gold for information leading to Azura's capture. "Do you think she's really here in Dún Aulin?"

Berengar shook his head. "She's probably just a myth. There are no more fairies left in Leinster." He grabbed another bounty and tore it free of the nail where it was posted. "Does this goblin look familiar to you?"

Morwen's gaze ran over the goblin's image. "It looks like the goblin that attacked me in the Wrenwood." The rendering depicted the same helmet worn by the goblin that had attempted to steal the stone from Morwen.

"I thought the same. According to this, it's the mercenaries' leader." It almost seemed fitting that they had lost the thunder rune now that they finally had a lead on the goblins. Berengar turned his attention to the bellman. "I'm looking for a man named Tavish. I'm told he commands the city watch."

The bellman tipped his tricorne hat at Morwen, who stifled a giggle. "Look no further. Here he comes now." As the bellman spoke, a middle-aged man in uniform flanked by guards began nailing another bounty to the wall. "It seems you are in luck, good sir."

Given how his day had gone so far, Berengar was skeptical, though he was at least grateful he didn't have to waste even more time in search of Tavish. "You there—I'd like a word."

Tavish took one look at Berengar and swore before noticing Morwen. "Forgive me. Something else to confess on the holy day."

"I've heard worse." Morwen stifled a giggle.

Tavish glanced from Morwen to Berengar. "If you're traveling in *his* company, I bet you have." He let out the exasperated sigh of a man weary beyond his years. "You're not supposed to be here, you know. The last thing I need right now is the Bear Warden stirring up trouble. I've got my hands full enough as it is with the Revels, security for the ceremony, and the fairy dust epidemic."

Morwen raised an eyebrow. "Fairy dust?"

"Aye. Stuff's worth its weight in gold. Some people will do almost anything for a taste of real magic, but they don't have any control over it."

"Of course they don't." Her alarm was evident. "Even a fully trained magician can have difficulty using fairy dust. It's far too dangerous to sell to ordinary people."

"We've had deaths all across the city. One poor sod thought he could fly and threw himself off Labraid's Tower. Took hours to clean him off the street. Another fellow went invisible and broke into the vaults of Gemstones only to reappear in front of the guards. Until we find whoever's supplying the dust, the problem is only going to get worse. And now I have to deal with the Bloody Red Bear."

Berengar smirked. "The sooner you help us, the sooner I'll be gone."

"Somehow I doubt that."

One of the men under Tavish's command stared at

Berengar with clear disdain. "I saw the bodies you left in your wake the last time you were here. You're every bit the monster they say you are. Your kind has no place in this city." Some of his companions murmured in agreement.

Berengar took a step forward. "I saved this city while you and your friends were still in swaddling clothes."

"You butchered men like cattle."

"I did what I had to, and I'd do it again."

For a moment, it looked as if the man might reach for the sword at his side until Tavish held up a hand.

"Stand down—all of you. That's an order." He took Berengar and Morwen aside. "I haven't forgotten. I was in the guard when the riots broke out. I saw the corpses stacked at the gate. What do you need?"

"The Brotherhood of Thieves took something that belongs to us. We want it back."

Tavish chuckled but broke off abruptly when he noticed the look on Berengar's face. "Good luck. I've been trying to run the Brotherhood out of the city for years, and they've only grown stronger. Half the guards are in their pocket, and the rest would rather look the other way than get involved. Tell me what it is they've taken and I'll put the word out, for all the good it will do."

Berengar quickly relayed the details, along with a description of the thief, to Tavish. "There's something else. We tracked a group of goblin mercenaries who were after the rune." He removed the folded-up bounty from inside his cloak and held it out. "I think this was their leader."

Tavish pointed at the goblin illustration. "Teelah the Strong-Willed. A bold one. This one single-handedly killed an entire band of monster hunters. Some of my scouts have encountered that lot and barely made it out with their lives. Nasty bunch, just like the rest of their kind."

Berengar elbowed Morwen to keep her from speaking

out in protest. "Do you know who the goblins are working for or where we might find them?"

Tavish stroked his beard. "I believe they've been spotted near the Elderwood on more than one occasion, though I'm afraid I can't tell you anything more specific than that. A fair number of nonhumans have taken refuge within the forest, and there have been a lot of strange happenings in the area lately."

"What sort of happenings?"

"Soldiers have disappeared at the border, and monster sightings have increased. The villagers nearby believe magic is involved. They say a man in a mask spreads pestilence and disease and calls forth dark powers. Rumors, most likely, but one of my scouts claims to have seen him too. Poor lad returned half-crazed. If you ask me, the sooner we raze that cursed forest to the ground, the better."

Anger flashed in Morwen's eyes, and she put her hands on her hips. "Is that so?"

Berengar gave her a warning look. "Thank you. You've been very helpful."

"Wait," Tavish called when he turned to go. "A word of advice—do what you need to and be on your way. This city is dangerous for you and any who walk with you. I'll help you as I'm able, but you have powerful enemies here. Watch your step."

Berengar offered a grim nod and returned to the road.

They didn't get far. A messenger waited for them under the arch. "I have a letter for you, Warden Berengar."

Berengar groaned. Word of his presence in the city had spread even faster than he anticipated. "Who sent you?"

The messenger extended a sealed envelope by way of reply. Berengar opened the letter and quickly scanned its contents.

Morwen handed the man a coin, and he promptly disappeared into the crowd. "What does it say?"

"It's from an old friend," Berengar muttered. "He wants to talk."

"Who?"

He showed her the message.

Berengar,

Meet me tonight at the Coin and Crown. The matter is urgent.

Tell no one.

Niall, Warden of Fál

CHAPTER FOUR

"What's he like? Warden Niall, I mean."

Foreboding clouds drowned out the sky's pale light. Berengar didn't need Morwen's magician's senses to know another storm was brewing. *Blasted weather.* He hated Leinster. The sooner they were finished, the better. Unfortunately, the theft of the thunder rune and Niall's mysterious request only complicated matters further. *As if we didn't have enough to worry about already.* Still, Niall wouldn't have asked to see him on such short notice unless it was about something serious.

"He's clever, I'll give him that. A little too sure of himself. You two should get along just fine."

Morwen flashed a wide smile. "I like him already. You know, for all your talk about walking alone, you have more friends than you let on."

"If it were up to me, I'd be left alone. It's not my fault people keep dragging me into their problems." He cast a glance in her direction. "What's your point?"

She shrugged. "Honestly, I don't know why everyone is so afraid of you. Sure, you have a bit of a temper and you're too quick to reach for your axe, but you're not so bad."

Berengar laughed quietly. "For the daughter of a poet king, you have quite a way with words." His expression turned serious. "Make no mistake, I've hurt as many people as I've helped—probably more. I've done things that would make your blood run cold."

Morwen rolled her eyes. "You also rescued me from the mob at Innisfallen and saved Cashel from destruction. You know what your problem is? You're too hard on yourself. Have you ever stopped to consider that maybe you're not the monster everyone seems to think you are? Maybe you're the hero."

Berengar didn't reply. He knew exactly what he was, and he was no hero. Morwen always wanted to find the good in everyone, even when there was none to be found. She hadn't seen the horrors he left behind at the Fortress of Suffering or the men he butchered at Laird McAuliffe's table. Dún Aulin itself was a living reminder of the kind of man he was. There was a reason why men called him the High Queen's Monster, even if most were careful to do it behind his back.

After Morwen casually covered her head with her hood, a light rain began almost on cue. Berengar raised his cloak's bear-headed hood and quickened his pace. Mercifully, they didn't have far to walk. The Coin and Crown, the most infamous alehouse in the city, was part of the Rookery, a popular off-color area at the intersection between the more affluent Hightower neighborhood and the tawdry Riverside District. The alehouse was one of the few places where those of all classes intermingled in pursuit of vice and other less-than-savory endeavors frowned upon by the church. It was said Prince Tristan spent more time at the Coin and Crown than in the palace.

Even the bishop, with all his influence, had failed to shut it down under threat of a full-scale revolt.

The rain intensified as they cut through the Lord's Crossing on their way to the Rookery. A number of fellow travelers were seeking refuge from the storm, though the streets remained relatively full despite the downpour. The sky grew darker with night's approach, and torches glowed brightly in the distance, revealing the frame of a three-story building built over a waterway.

"There it is," Berengar said. "The Coin and Crown."

Morwen regarded the alehouse's lofty heights with growing awe. "That's the largest pub I've ever seen."

Lights emanated from no fewer than four dozen windows. Loud music and lively cheers carried through the walls. A sizable group surrounded the alehouse, and Berengar remembered it was the last night of the Revels. Given that people had come from far and wide to see the best performers in Fál and beyond gathered in one place, why had Niall chosen it for their meeting?

Faolán slipped away to seek shelter from the storm, though Berengar knew she wouldn't go far. He pushed through the crowd and made his way up the steps to the entrance. A feast for the senses greeted them inside. The hall was brightly lit and full of warmth. The aroma of hearty stews and freshly made breads blended with the scent of free-flowing ale and wine, stirring hunger and thirst simultaneously. Most notable were the varied sounds coming from every direction.

Berengar ground his teeth and stepped around a group of men and women dancing to a lively tune. There was barely enough room to maneuver. He hated large gatherings. A passing barmaid nearly spilled wine on his boots and shot him a brief look of apology before scurrying off to a table of disorderly patrons. Cheers sounded nearby, where a smaller crowd flocked around a pair playing ficheall, a strategy game played with pieces on a board with one player as the aggressor and the other as the defender. Morwen had taught him the game during their search for the Oakseers' Grotto, and despite his initial inclinations, he found he enjoyed it, though she almost always won.

Morwen lingered near the match before hurrying to catch up. "We're staying here."

Berengar would sooner fight the bear that took his eye all over again. "You couldn't pick a more auspicious place?"

Morwen's enthusiasm remained undaunted by his sarcasm. "There are bathhouses here, Berengar! Bathhouses! I don't think I've had a decent bath since we left Cashel, and that was months ago."

"We're here to track down those goblins and recover the rune. Don't forget that."

She smiled innocently. "There's no reason why we can't do those things and be clean at the same time."

Berengar groaned. "Let's see what's so blasted important that Niall asked us here. Then we'll decide where to stay."

At least the thief hadn't stolen his gold, though the rune was far more valuable. He was surprised she had managed to locate and extract the rune from Morwen's satchel with such ease. The last time he witnessed someone attempt to wield the rune, the idiot almost brought down a tower on top of his head. Even Imogen's soldiers had displayed enough sense to keep the stone in a pouch.

"Keep your eyes peeled. Niall could be anywhere." He brushed past more strangers on his way to the bar, where he finally succeeded in getting one of the bartenders occupied with the never-ending line of patrons to take note. "I'll have a pint."

The bartender placed a flagon brimming with mead before another patron and turned to Berengar. "That'll be twelve coppers."

"Twelve?" Berengar raised an eyebrow and gave an irritated grunt.

The bartender only shrugged. "Blame it on the new vice tax levied by the church. They can't run us out of business, but they can still help themselves to our earnings."

Berengar swore under his breath and put down the coins. *Twelve coppers for a pint.* Where he came from, that amount could feed a family for weeks.

As if sensing his hesitation, the bartender quickly made the money disappear. "They've tried to impose the tax before, but the prince regent has always vetoed the measure." He filled the pint and handed it to Berengar. "For what it's worth, this is the best in Leinster."

"It had better be." Berengar leaned forward and lowered his voice. "I'm looking for someone. Maybe you've seen him?" He gave a brief description of Niall.

"In a crowd like this? In case you haven't noticed, I haven't had much time to pay attention to faces." The bartender turned his attention to the next man in line before Berengar could ask any more questions.

Morwen winked at him. "Looks like we'll have to find him ourselves."

Scowling, Berengar took his tankard from the bar, wishing he was somewhere—anywhere—else. He'd rather fend off a hundred goblins than take part in the festivities. In contrast, Morwen appeared to thoroughly enjoy observing the many spectacles before her. There were cards and dice, feats of strength and brawling, and jesters and jugglers, to name only a few sources of amusement.

The sounds died away farther inside the alehouse, where a troubadour was performing on a stage. The audience watched with rapt attention from a vast auditorium that surrounded the stage on three sides. Every seat was full, and countless others observed from the hall. Unlike the rest of the alehouse, the auditorium and the balcony above were somberly lit, presumably to keep the focus on the performers. Morwen watched, transfixed by the troubadour's viuola, a long, figure-eight shaped instrument with tuning pegs and five gut strings.

As far as Berengar could tell, Niall wasn't among the audience. His scowl deepened. Niall's absence might mean trouble.

Morwen seemed to sense his thoughts. "Relax. We probably just arrived first."

"It's not like Niall to be late." He took a drink from the pint and gulped it down. It wasn't worth twelve coppers, but it *was* good. *Nothing to do but wait.* "It looks like you'll get to see the Revels after all."

Morwen's face filled with utter delight, and she rubbed her hands together in excitement. The troubadour finished his song to a generous helping of applause and offered a gracious bow before stepping off the stage. Some in the audience left for ale or conversation while others stomped and clapped their hands in anticipation of the next performance. Berengar lingered in the shadows at the back of the room and nursed his pint while listening to those nearby. A number were discussing the death of King Mór and what Munster's vacant throne might mean for the peace between the realms. The details were obscured by a new round of applause as the next performer took the stage.

"That's Roland of Gallive," a woman in the crowd whispered to Morwen. "He's one of Leinster's greatest storytellers—and the only one who has a chance to beat Jareth for the quill, if you ask me."

Roland was a grizzled old man with a long white beard who used a walking stick for support. In his nondescript gray robes, he almost looked like a clergyman.

Morwen leaned close so Berengar could hear her amid the noise. "I've heard of him. He was famous long before the Shadow Wars. It's said he even met Thane Ramsay himself in the days of Áed. Can you imagine?"

Roland held up his hands in a show of humility and waited for the audience to quiet before he opened his mouth. He spoke softly, with the ease of a practiced story-teller, and many had to strain to hear. The man reminded Berengar of a kindly old grandfather imparting secret knowledge from a bygone age.

"In the time when the elder gods were still worshiped throughout Fál, there once lived a great lord who possessed unimaginable wealth. Despite his abundant riches, the generous lord was beloved by all in the realm—all save the jealous king, enraged by any more prosperous than he. The king invited the lord, his family, and all his retainers to an extravagant feast, where his soldiers murdered them in cold blood.

"Only the lord's son—a boy of thirteen—escaped alive. Forced into hiding, he learned to steal to survive a life on the streets. He found he had a talent for it, and as he grew, his skills grew with him. He realized a network of conspirators could accomplish far more than one man alone and began employing the knowledge he'd gained from his boyhood tutors to forge the Brotherhood of Thieves. He was the first thief king.

"The Brotherhood grew in strength and influence over

the centuries, and its reach spread across all five kingdoms. At the height of their power, nothing could be sold or traded without the Brotherhood first receiving a cut. But the thief kings and queens of old grew arrogant. They wanted to rule. They began contracting assassins and employing mercenaries. This overreach provoked a backlash that nearly destroyed the entire Brotherhood. Those who remained returned to the shadows, where they thrived on growing corruption and indifference and waited for their time to come again."

Morwen listened, entranced, as Roland continued the story of the Brotherhood of Thieves. Bored, Berengar scanned the audience for any sign of Niall. *What's keeping him, blast it?* Cheers filled the auditorium at the conclusion of Roland's tale, and the old man bowed and basked in the crowd's praise. A sudden hush came over the crowd until all that could be heard was a single man clapping.

"What a tale! Perhaps not the most *original* story, but certainly well-told nonetheless." The newcomer took the stage and aimed a wink at Roland, who glowered at him with the clear disdain of a rival. "Of course, if you ask me, the *true* thieves in this city are those pompous hypocrites in the church." This statement was greeted by a chorus of cheers from the audience.

"Jareth," Morwen said. "It must be."

In sharp contrast to Roland, the newcomer appeared somewhere in his twenties or early thirties. He wore elegant, stylish clothes and a bright green cloak that seemed to shimmer in the dim lights. "How, then, am I to outshine such performances?" Although not exceptionally tall, he seemed to cast an outsized presence on the crowd. His hair was shaggy and unruly, and he spoke with vigor and ambition. "I could give you a song, but the church has ears everywhere, and young maidens have been known to lose their virtue at the sound of my voice. I could give you poetry, but good Lyra has already left you in tears with the *Madness of the Fair Folk*. What, then, shall it be?"

Jareth stopped suddenly, and Berengar realized the bard was looking right at him with unmistakable recognition.

Jareth's eyes lit up, as if a new thought had occurred to him, and his mouth twisted into a grin. "A story, then. It's one you should all know—at least in part. I give you a tale of blood, rage, and the birth of monsters—I give you the story of the purges."

At the mention of the purges, every soul in the room fell deathly still.

"The years that followed Queen Nora's ascension to the High Throne were uneasy. The Lord of Shadows had been defeated, yes, but had left his mark on the land. Petty jealousies and old rivalries remained between the realms, and nonhumans were hated and feared.

"Five years into the High Queen's reign, the druid leader Cathán came to Dún Aulin and asked King Percival to prohibit the persecution of nonhumans within the kingdom. The king refused, hoping to avoid stirring the unrest spreading through the realms.

"In his youth, Cathán was a healer and philosopher, but shifting attitudes toward magic in the wake of the war radicalized him. Druids worship nature. Their magic is entwined with the land. Cathán saw an assault on magic as an affront to life itself—one that must be stopped at any cost. He wanted a return to the days of old, when kings and lords feared and respected the druids' power.

"Cathán gathered all the druids in Leinster under him and returned to Dún Aulin. In the midst of summer, he and his followers used their mastery over the elements to shut the heavens so no rains would come. He hoped the demonstration of power would force the king to reconsider his demands. Instead, the drought and famine turned the men and women of Dún Aulin against each other.

"Fanatics stoked long-simmering resentments by blaming the trouble on magicians and nonhumans. Riots broke out in the streets and quickly escalated beyond the ability of the guards to control. The king recalled his army to the capital, but his forces were at war with the goblins and too far away to intervene in time. It wasn't long before the purges spread to include anyone who followed the old ways. Eventually, the mob killed for no reason at all.

"Chaos reigned. Nobles, peasants, saints, sinners— none were safe. Hundreds were slaughtered. Businesses were looted and destroyed. Smoke from fires raging across the city could be seen from miles away. Corpses filled the streets."

Jareth paused for a moment to let his words sink in. The silence from the audience continued, and it was clear to Berengar many in the crowd remembered the horrors of the riots all too well. Some had tears in their eyes, and others still were ashen-faced.

"The uprising threatened the tenuous peace between realms that had existed since the war. Only five years into the High Queen's reign, Leinster's fall would signal to Fál's enemies—both within and without—that her rule was vulnerable. In this dark hour, Nora sent a warden to quell the violence." Again his eyes found Berengar. "Knowing full well what such a task might require, and to avoid sullying the reputation of the others, the queen entrusted the undertaking to Esben Berengar."

A few boos came from the audience at the mention of Berengar. Surprise registered on Morwen's face, and her brow furrowed as Jareth went on.

"Even in those days, the Bear Warden was known

throughout Fál. Tales of his actions at Dún de Fulaingt and the Ford of Blood had spread across the land. Unlike the other wardens—beloved heroes all—Berengar was hated and feared. But Queen Nora knew that when heroes fail, sometimes it takes a monster.

"It is said that Warden Berengar is a killer without conscience, but when he beheld the horrors at Dún Aulin, whatever shred remained of his humanity recoiled at what he saw. Even monsters can understand suffering, sometimes better than most. As he entered the city and encountered the legions of dead, he was overcome with rage.

"Those of you familiar with the tale may doubt that one man could have suppressed riots in the city of thousands. It is not uncommon for those in my trade to embellish the truth for dramatic effect. That is not the case here. In truth, even I, with all my skill, cannot do the story justice.

"Berengar tracked the druids to their lair, where Cathán mocked the Bear Warden to his face. How could one man stand against those who wielded the forces of nature itself? He scoffed at Warden Berengar's scars and laughed at his ugliness, for Cathán was known for his striking appearance.

"Alone, armed with only his axe, Warden Berengar slaughtered the druids one by one. Some even tried to surrender, but he struck them down until only Cathán was left. In the final battle, Warden Berengar crushed and mangled Cathán's hands to prevent him from using his magic. Then he dragged Cathán to the fire and held the druid's face to the flames. Cathán begged for death, but Warden Berengar refused. Cathán had wanted a return to the old ways, but instead he had brought about the violent deaths of the very magicians and nonhumans he had hoped to protect. So great was Warden Berengar's wrath that he spared Cathán to force him to live with that knowledge and left him to the mercy of the mob.

"With the druids dealt with, Warden Berengar turned his attention to the rioters. After taking command of the city guard, he met violence with violence and repaid blood for blood. He cut down any who stood in his way—including the fanatics who stirred up the trouble in the first place—and displayed the bodies for all to see. By the time the king's soldiers finally entered the city, all was quiet. Order had been restored.

"When Queen Nora learned what Warden Berengar had done in her name, she was furious. Some claim she even considered ordering his death, but stayed her hand because it was better to have such a danger as a friend than an enemy. Whatever the case, that was the day when Warden Berengar became known as the High Queen's Monster."

Unlike the boisterous applause that greeted previous performances, silence filled the auditorium when Jareth finished speaking. For a moment, no one said a word. The audience just sat there, stunned by what they had heard. Then one man leapt to his feet and cheered. Soon every man and woman in the auditorium was on their feet. Flowers flooded the stage as the thunderous standing ovation built to a roar, leaving little doubt at who had won the Golden Quill.

Morwen, however, was no longer smiling. She stared at Berengar, horrified, and quickly stormed away. He sighed, cast a murderous glance at Jareth, and went after her.

He followed her through the crowd and caught up to her near a lonely storeroom. "Morwen, wait."

She turned around, trembling. "It was you. You killed the druids."

Berengar's voice was quiet. "Aye." He was the reason

why there were no druids guarding the Oakseers' Grotto. There were none left.

Morwen jabbed a finger at his chest. "I *knew* you were hiding something when you told me about the riots." She shook her head. "Tell me it isn't true."

"I can't do that, Morwen." He met her gaze and held it. "You weren't there. You didn't see the bodies. Cathán and the others had to answer for what they did."

"So you butchered them? Even the ones who tried to surrender?"

He felt his temper rising. "And I'd do it again if I had to. They were too dangerous to be left alive."

"Is that how you see us—how you see me?" Morwen looked away. "I thought you were different, but maybe you're just like all the others."

Her words took him by surprise. *That's what this is about?* Morwen had faced resentment and ostracism her whole life on account of her magic. It was easy to see why she might identify with the druids. His expression softened, and he nodded slowly. "You're right. I've always been suspicious of magic. I helped the High Queen fight a war to drive the Lord of Shadows from the land. I saw the terror that one dark sorcerer could unleash." He paused, searching for the right words. "But then I met you, and I saw your great heart, and I know now that magic can be used for good or ill."

Morwen's anger faded instantly, and she beamed from ear to ear.

He raised an eyebrow. "What?"

"Nothing. You know, sometimes, despite your temper and gruff manners, you manage to be rather sweet."

Berengar laughed. "I've been called a lot of things, but never that."

"Pardon, sir and madam," a barmaid said. When she

saw Berengar's scars, she averted her eyes. "There's a man asking to see you. You'll find him in a private room on the balcony." She promptly withdrew.

"It must be Niall. It's about time."

Morwen continued grinning.

"What?"

"Great heart, eh?"

"Shut up." He started up the stairs, leaving her to trail behind.

The balcony was only slightly less crowded than the auditorium, though the area seemed mostly reserved for wealthier patrons. Berengar and Morwen escaped notice as they passed others by, their faces masked by shadows. The spectators watched quietly while the performances continued below, even if there was little doubt who would win the night.

"There," Morwen whispered.

Berengar followed her gaze to one of several private rooms, where a lone figure sat at a candlelit table partially hidden by a curtain. The man waiting for them inside was younger than Berengar by several years. His hair, which was brown and wavy, framed a thoughtful face and a pair of intelligent blue eyes. Like Berengar, he wore a brooch with the image of a silver fox—the sigil of the line of Áed —pinned to his cloak.

"Niall," Berengar said.

"Berengar. It's been a long time."

"It has. I've been busy."

"So I hear." Niall inclined his head at the empty seats across him and waited for them to sit. "Word is the High Queen wasn't pleased by what happened at St. Brigid's."

Berengar shrugged. "Darragh's her favorite. I'm just her monster."

The two men clasped arms. "It's good to see you again,

my friend." Niall's eyes settled on Morwen. "And who is this, if I may ask?"

"My companion, Lady Morwen of Cashel."

"Indeed?" Niall chuckled to himself. "Times have changed more than I thought. I never imagined I would see you of all people with a companion, let alone Munster's court magician."

"You're well-informed." Morwen sounded impressed.

Niall flashed a brief smile. "It's my job to be." He pointed to his head. "My mind is my weapon, and I must keep it sharp. I'm sure a scholar such as yourself can relate. I was sorry to learn of King Mór's passing. What happened? I've heard only rumors."

"The king was assassinated by his daughter, Princess Ravenna."

"So it is true."

"Ravenna was a sorceress," Berengar explained. "She wielded shadow magic and unleashed a coatl that nearly destroyed Cashel."

"Shadow magic?" Niall's face grew somber. "Most interesting. Do you suspect the Lord of Shadows' involvement with Mór's death?"

"I don't know. Ravenna had cause to want her father dead."

"I suppose we'll never know now. Munster is fortunate you were there to stop her, though I wish I could have questioned her before you finished her. Impressive work defeating a sorceress, by the way. Even with a magician at your side, I'm sure it was a difficult feat."

Berengar looked away. "I let her live, Niall."

For the first time, Niall looked truly surprised. He studied Berengar with curiosity. "You've changed more than I thought."

When he leaned forward, Berengar noticed blood on his clothes in the candlelight. "Are you hurt?"

"The blood's not mine."

Berengar smirked and folded his arms across his chest. "Finally getting your hands dirty for a change?"

"I'm the warden of the most corrupt and dangerous city in Fál. My dealings with scheming nobles and treacherous officials are just as dangerous as your local disputes and monster hunts, I assure you."

"Don't mind him," Morwen said. "If he teases you, it just means he likes you. Besides, it *was* a big coatl."

Niall laughed. "I like her, Berengar. Don't push this one away."

"He's tried. I'm not that easy to get rid of."

"I believe it."

Berengar cleared his throat. "We do have other business in the city. Your message was light on details. Why ask to meet, and why here?"

"There are eyes watching me all over the city. I thought it best to hide in plain sight. With everyone here preoccupied with the Revels, we can converse safely without fear of being overheard. I need your help, Berengar."

"Go on."

"All is not well in the City of Thieves. The mood is tenser than any time since the purges. The ceremony has the whole city on edge. The bishop's passing, the murder of King Mór, and Munster's empty throne have created a sense of unease—not to mention whispers of trouble in the north."

Berengar scoffed. "There's always trouble in the north."

Niall's face grew grim. "Things here are worse than you understand. King Lucien is not himself. He has shut himself up in the palace and hidden away from the world.

There are those who say he has gone mad. Now the prince regent has gone missing."

"Missing?" Morwen repeated.

"Vanished—without a trace. I think he's in grave danger." Niall's voice grew firm. "I sense a sinister plot afoot in Dún Aulin. I've heard stories of an evil that has taken root to the west, and the Brotherhood of Thieves grows bolder by the day. There are those who say a member of the Brotherhood has taken on a black contract. I must find Prince Tristan before it's too late, but I cannot be everywhere at once."

Berengar studied him carefully. "What would you have us do?"

"I am leaving tonight, under cover of darkness. In my absence, you must take over my duties and supervise the Ceremony of the Cursed Blade."

CHAPTER FIVE

IN THE END, Berengar was left with no choice but to agree to Niall's request. Even if he hadn't owed Niall more than a few favors, the cursed blade was far too dangerous to allow it to fall into the wrong hands. Morwen got her way —much to Berengar's considerable annoyance—and he paid an exorbitant amount for a room at the Coin and Crown. It seemed their departure from Dún Aulin had been indefinitely delayed.

Anticipating pushback from the higher-ups in the palace and cathedral, Niall had already secured an agreement to allow Berengar to take his place in preparation for the ceremony. As long as Berengar remained excommunicated, he was unwelcome, though as a Warden of Fál, he could ignore the laws as he saw fit. They could banish him from Leinster, but they could not enforce it without drawing the High Queen's ire. It was an arrangement to no one's liking—least of all Berengar's. Neither the government nor the church wanted him in the city, and Berengar would rather be anywhere else. Unfortunately, until the ceremony was over, both sides were stuck with no alternative.

Berengar retired for the evening not long after Niall took his leave. As he suspected, Jareth wasn't the only one to recognize him. He drew a number of curious glances and outright stares when he paid for his room. Unlike in Munster, where he had stayed as a guest at King Mór's castle, he most certainly would not be welcome in the royal palace. With the bard's tale still fresh in the minds of the alehouse's patrons, it was better to lie low while he still could. His presence in Dún Aulin would be widely known soon enough as it was.

Morwen, on the other hand, was not finished taking part in the night's festivities. After weeks spent bored on the road, she relished the chance to indulge her inexhaustible curiosity and implored him to allow her to remain in his absence. Berengar, unwilling to argue with her further over the matter, agreed on the condition she not set foot outside the Coin and Crown. He was her companion, not her nursemaid. He'd warned her. If she wanted to play with fire, that was on her—just as long as she didn't come running to him when she got burned.

It was quiet when he returned to the main hall the following morning. Patrons sat hunched over their breakfasts, nursing hangovers. Some were still unconscious, having slumped over the bar or fallen asleep at tables. Their intermittent snores were a welcome reprieve from the music that had filled the alehouse the night before. Even with the staff hard at work sweeping floors and wiping tables, it was clear the task of cleaning the mess left behind would take quite some time.

Berengar looked around for Morwen. Although the crowd had thinned a great deal overnight, there was no shortage of guests within the hall. A few hurried about making preparations to depart Dún Aulin. To his surprise, Berengar spotted Morwen sitting wide-awake at one of the tables. He headed to join her after obtaining a heaping portion of breakfast.

Morwen wrinkled her nose at the bounty of food on his plate. "For your sake, I hope we don't run into another thief today. I don't think you could keep up with all that weighing you down."

Berengar stifled a yawn. "You're looking chipper this morning."

"What a night! You should've heard them, Berengar. Jareth won the Quill, of course, but the others were outstanding. And the songs and ballads! I haven't heard such talent in ages. It reminded me of my time in the king's court." She stretched her arms toward the ceiling as if to emphasize her point.

Berengar noticed a sizable stack of coins before her. "Where'd those come from?"

Morwen sat back in her chair and gave a self-satisfied smile. "My ficheall winnings. I *may* have joined one of the tournaments last night, and I *may* have won said tournament to great fanfare from the crowd."

"Morwen…"

"It was glorious! Do you know how long it's been since I've had a proper challenge—no offense, of course." She shoved the stack of coins toward him. "This should be more than enough to cover the cost of our stay here for a good long while."

"Morwen, that's not the point. I told you to keep a low profile, not join in a high-stakes ficheall tournament."

She held up her hands. "Relax. I'm sure no one recognized me."

"There she is!" bellowed a man sitting with his friends at a nearby table. "Three cheers for Morwen, the best ficheall player to ever grace these halls!" The friends clanked their tankards and cheered to the visible irritation of those hungover.

Morwen flushed a deep shade of red and turned back to Berengar. "Sorry."

Berengar sniffed the air. "What's that smell?"

Morwen ran a hand through her hair. "Do you like it? It's lavender."

"You had time to visit the bathhouses *and* win a ficheall tournament?"

"I also brewed a few potions and worked on a number of enchantments that were easy enough to manage even without a staff. The next person who tries to steal something from my satchel is in for a nasty surprise. And don't worry—I made sure to do both away from prying eyes."

Berengar stared at her, at a loss for words. "Did you sleep at all last night?"

Morwen shook her head.

"And you aren't tired?"

"I'm a magician, remember? I can draw off my magic stores for energy. Don't look at me like that. I wasn't wasting my time. I managed to pick up some valuable information during my ficheall matches. You'd be amazed at how the prospect of easy coin loosens lips." She lowered her voice. "It seems a number of gamblers have quite a few friends in common with the Brotherhood of Thieves."

"Go on."

She grinned. "I thought that might get your attention. I asked after the go-betweens the Brotherhood uses to fence their ill-gotten gains. As it turns out, there's a fence named Edrick who recently acquired a pair of valuable horses from Munster. According to my source, he's putting them up for sale at noon near the East End District. Not bad, right?"

"It's a start." With any luck, the information might prove useful beyond leading to the return of their horses and belongings. Berengar finished his breakfast and wiped his beard with his sleeve. "Let's go. Noon is still hours away, and we have a lot to do before then."

They emerged from the alehouse and started down the stairs. The storm had ceased overnight, and the sun shone brightly for the first time in recent memory. The air was unseasonably warm, though nothing approaching the summer heat that had marked their time in Munster. People swarmed the streets even in the early hours, and despite the Revels' conclusion, Leinster's capital hummed with life.

Faolán waited for them outside.

At the sight of her approaching, Morwen reached into her satchel and tossed the wolfhound a treat. "I take it we're not abandoning the hunt for the rune then."

"I don't like leaving things unfinished." The thunder rune wasn't as powerful as Azeroth's sword—broken or otherwise—but it was still dangerous, as was whoever had hired the goblins to retrieve it. "Niall set up a meeting with the king and his advisers at the palace later today. Until then, we can focus on other business."

Morwen produced an apple seemingly out of thin air and polished it before taking a bite. "So, where to now?"

"First we'll see about finding you a new staff. If we're going to be here a while, you should at least be able to defend yourself." He smiled briefly at having caught her off guard for once.

"Not that I don't appreciate the sentiment, but I shouldn't have to remind you that you can't just buy a magician's staff at the corner market. Even if you could, Dún Aulin is the last place in Fál I would look for anything associated with magic."

"Just follow me. There's a place where we might be able to find some of the materials you require. More likely than not we won't find anything at all, but it's worth a shot."

The Coin and Crown fell behind them as they left the Rookery. Instead of returning to the grand square by way of Padraig's Gate, Berengar led Morwen north to another of the city's older districts. While the area's stone buildings were impressive in size, most were in various states of disrepair and neglect, and the spot was notably less crowded than other parts of the city.

"Where are we?" Morwen asked.

"The Scholars' District. Or what's left of it. It was the center of knowledge before the trade guilds took over." There was a time when craftsmen, artists, and others came to Dún Aulin to study their chosen professions, though the city's status as a hub of learning declined in the years before the Shadow Wars.

Berengar fell silent, and Morwen followed his gaze to a tower looming above the others. "What's that?"

"The Institute."

Her eyes widened in amazement. "Truly? I thought it was destroyed in the purges."

"It might as well have been." Scorch marks and piles of rubble were visible even at a distance as evidence that not all signs of the purges had been erased.

Morwen bowed her head in reverence. "So this is what's left of it."

In times past, magicians and mages were trained at the Institute. Only the various academies at Cill Airne rivaled the Institute's prominence as a center of higher learning for the mystic arts. Healers, alchemists, and herbalists, though they could not use magic, also studied within its walls. By the time of the riots, their numbers were greatly

77

reduced. Like the Oakseers' Grotto, the Institute was evidence of a world intent on leaving the old ways behind.

"What makes you think there's anything left to find? Rioters would've picked the place clean. Even if they hadn't, the entrance is caved in."

"There's another way inside. Come on."

Morwen started after him. "Wait. How do you know so much about this place? You didn't…"

"No. Jareth didn't have the whole story. Typical bard. Not long after I arrived in the city, the druids poisoned me with a substance called the Bewilderer's Bite."

"The Bewilderer's Bite? That would have knocked you on your backside."

"It did. One of the students at the Institute found me before the rioters. He brought me back to the Institute, where a herbalist administered the antidote." He hesitated, one foot in the past. "The whole place was under siege. The mob's torches lit up the night."

Morwen's face was full of concern. "That's horrible."

"Aye. The Institute's leaders struck a deal with the Brotherhood of Thieves to smuggle them out of Dún Aulin in return for valuable magical wares. They asked me to help get them across the city to the Brotherhood. I knew I should leave them…that I had more important things to take care of…but I couldn't."

"What happened?"

"I tried my best, but I couldn't save them all." He looked at her for a long moment. "That's why I showed Cathán and his followers no mercy. All the killings—all the death—it was their fault. I made them pay." His hands began to tremble with anger. Even after all these years, his rage burned just as hot.

Morwen must have sensed his anger, for she reached out her hand to him. "Peace, my friend."

Berengar pulled back and shook his head to warn her away. In addition to sensing emotions, he'd seen Morwen influence them with her touch, and he wanted no part of it. "I've told you before to keep out of my head. I won't tell you again."

Her brow arched in anger. "You don't have to live with all that rage all the time."

"You're wrong. Someone has to remember when others have forgotten. Someone has to avenge."

"What about making the world a better place?"

Berengar stared at her. "Sometimes you sound just like Nora. I'll leave that kind of talk to the two of you. Now come on." He led her away from the tower.

"So you saved them," Morwen mused. "Was Jareth wrong about anything else?"

"It's true I was told to end the purges by any means necessary, but that didn't come from Nora. He got that wrong too. Nora would never have given such an order. She's too good—like you. When she learned what I did…I don't think she's ever forgiven me."

"I'm sorry."

He shrugged to show her he didn't care. In truth, the High Queen's opinion was one of the only ones that mattered to him. His actions during the riots had strained their relationship to the breaking point, and it had never really recovered. Berengar had simply accepted that it was his job to do the dirty work so that she could keep her hands clean.

The pair kept to back roads and shadowed corners until they reached a secluded alleyway that ended in a wall.

Morwen glanced around suspiciously. "There's magic in this place."

"Aye. The Institute's inhabitants used a secret passage

underground to come and go. The entrance should be here somewhere. It was hidden by a spell of some sort."

"Do you remember the spell?"

"Do I look like a magician to you?" He gestured to the wall. "Your domain, I believe."

Morwen cracked her knuckles and stepped up to the wall. "Stand back and watch." She ran her hand along the wall and muttered a phrase under her breath. When nothing happened after a few moments, she frowned and tried again.

"What's the matter?" he asked after a few failed attempts. "Having trouble?"

Morwen gritted her teeth and wiped a loose strand of hair away from her eyes. "They used a spell of greater concealment to hide the door. Illusion magic. It's not as easy as it looks without the password."

She reached into her satchel and removed a purple rune similar to the one stolen by the thief. It was a rune of illusion, and Berengar had seen her use it to cast spells when it occupied a slot at the head of her staff. Morwen held the stone close to her lips and whispered to it, causing it to glow with purple light.

"Should you do that without your staff?"

"I won't tell if you don't." She looked around to make sure they were alone and held the stone toward the wall. Suddenly, the faint outline of a door materialized along the stone surface. Morwen turned back to him with a look of satisfaction, only to wince and drop the stone, which slightly burned her hand. She hastily returned the stone to her satchel and massaged her hand. "Not to worry. Nothing a little healing ointment won't fix."

A keyhole stared back at them from the door.

"What's your plan to deal with that?"

Morwen glared at him. "You could have told me that

was there." She tried for almost half an hour to unlock the door before finally throwing her hands up in exasperation. "It's no use. Whoever enchanted this lock had attained a level of mastery far beyond my capabilities. I'm a magician, not a thief." She paused. "You don't suppose…"

He nodded. "It's not long until noon. I think it's time we had a chat with that fence you discovered."

Morwen cast a parting glance at the door. "Do you really think there's a staff inside?"

Berengar shrugged. "Honestly, I don't know what we'll find inside. I wasn't there long—just long enough to know the inhabitants were crafty enough to conceal what they wished. There might be something the rioters didn't find."

Morwen wore a wistful expression. "Either way, I'd like to see what's inside. To roam the halls where the great mages and magicians of old once walked."

Their path took them away from the older and more affluent parts of Dún Aulin to its poorer areas, where the discrepancy between the haves and the have-nots was readily apparent. Beggars pleaded for coins from passersby while unsavory-looking characters lurked about in the absence of the guards relocated elsewhere to provide added security for the impending ceremony. Priests and monks provided care to the sick and administered last rites to the dying in the plague-infested neighborhoods of the Warrens. Other men and women of the cloth distributed food to starving children in rags.

Without warning, Faolán's ears perked up in alarm, and she sprinted after a figure trailing behind them. Faolán tackled the man to the ground before he could flee.

Berengar grabbed the man. "Who sent you? How long have you been following us?" When the man kept his mouth shut, Berengar shoved him into the wall. "Talk!"

"Look." Morwen pointed to the insignia of a bloodstained sword hidden under his cloak. "He's with the Acolytes."

"Get your hands off me, you filthy bastard," the man told Morwen. "We know who you are, witch, and you will burn alongside the Bloody Red Bear."

"What did you say?" Berengar twisted the man's hand to the breaking point and forced him to his knees. "Apologize. Now."

"They're just words," Morwen said.

The man sneered at them. "Do what you will, monster. My body is a temple. Others will follow. The grand marshal put a bounty on your heads. Your lives aren't worth spit."

Berengar reached for his axe. "Funny you should say that. Neither is yours."

Morwen attempted to restrain him. "Berengar, stop. He can't hurt us. There's no need to kill him."

"Fine." Berengar put his axe away. "Have it your way." He tightened his grip on the man's hand, drawing tears. "On second thought…" He pulled the man's index and middle fingers apart until they broke. "Now you have something to remind you this 'witch' showed you mercy when you deserved none. Tell Winslow I'll be waiting." He left the man to cradle his mangled hand and returned to the path.

"Was that necessary?" Morwen asked.

"I should've killed him. If he was following us long enough, he might know we were poking around the Institute."

Morwen looked back over her shoulder. "Killing isn't always the answer to every problem, you know. Besides, it's too late to do anything about it now. He's gone."

It took them another half hour to cross the Warrens. The neighborhoods in the bordering Muckbottom and

East End Districts contained fewer slums but were no less disreputable. After stopping to ask for directions, Berengar and Morwen finally arrived at a relatively small market-place in the shadows of an overhead bridge. The vendors, along with the proprietors of nearby stores, traded in unusual goods and services compared to the standard wares found elsewhere in the city.

"Nessa's close." Morwen looked at him with certainty. "I can feel her."

Berengar ignored entreaties from ambitious merchants and scanned the area for any sign of their horses. "Find them, Faolán."

The wolfhound sniffed the area a moment before picking up a trail. With her nose held low to the ground, she followed the scent through the busy market while avoiding the shoppers and obstacles in her way. It wasn't long until she came to a stop at a stand where a boy of no more than twelve addressed spectators from the top of a stack of crates.

"You there," he called to Morwen. "Come see my jewelry. A special discount for a beauty such as you." With pale blond curls and freckled skin, he had the look of a Dane.

Morwen approached. "Where's your master? We're looking for Edrick."

The boy bowed low and flashed a mischievous smile. "At your service, my lady. How may I be of help? Name whatever you like, and you shall have it." He casually scratched the back of his neck. "Of course, it may take some time to procure what you need, and my services aren't cheap, but there are none who will serve you better than I."

"We're looking for a pair of horses. I understand they came into your possession recently."

Edrick's gaze wandered to the coin pouch hanging from Berengar's belt, and he lowered his voice. "A pair of majestic beasts from Munster. Finer mounts you'll not find."

"Is that so?" Morwen suppressed a laugh in a transparent effort to conceal her amusement.

"Aye. Brian Boru himself did not have steeds of such quality. I imagine they are of fairy stock, though I suppose we will never know." Edrick jumped down from the crates and motioned them over to a pen where their horses were tied.

Morwen opened the door to the pen and ran a hand along Nessa's neck. "There, there. I knew I'd find you."

"She likes you." Edrick turned his focus to Berengar. "Thirty silver pieces each, I think—but only because you're first-time customers."

Berengar put his hand on his sword. "How about we pay you in steel instead, you little whelp?"

Morwen glared at him. "Berengar, he's just a boy!"

When Edrick heard Berengar's name, his face whitened, and he inched backward. "Berengar, you say?" His eyes settled on Faolán with growing apprehension.

"Warden Berengar to you." Berengar took a step forward, leaving Edrick with no route of retreat. "These horses are ours. They were stolen from us."

Edrick held up his hands in a show of surrender. "This is all a misunderstanding. I'm merely a humble purveyor of…"

Berengar took out his axe and smashed through one of the stacked crates, causing apples to spill out. "Save it. We know you're a fence. Now fetch the rest of our belongings before I lose my temper. Try to run, and my hound will rip out your throat."

Edrick scrambled behind his booth to remove the

possessions previously held in the horses' saddlebags. "I assure you, I had no idea these horses belonged to the Bear Warden." He flinched as Berengar took the bow from his hands and looked it over.

"We're not done here. The Brotherhood stole something far more valuable than these horses, and I want to know where it is."

"I've given you what you've asked for. There's no need to cause a scene." Edrick peered past Berengar's shoulders at the other vendors, who had taken note of the disruption.

Berengar didn't bat an eye. "No one's coming to help you. We both know the guards don't come around here. They're too busy looking the other way. Now, where's the rune?"

Edrick looked from Berengar to Morwen, confused. "I don't know what you're talking—"

Berengar smashed another crate with his axe. "Don't make me ask again."

"Please! I don't know where it is!"

When Berengar raised the axe, Morwen put herself between them. "He's telling the truth." She stared hard at Edrick with an unflinching gaze. "We're looking for a magical relic called a thunder rune. It's a white, translucent stone filled with energy. It's very dangerous. Surely you must have heard something about an object so valuable."

Edrick hesitated. "The most valuable thefts rarely go to ordinary fences like me—especially if they're magic. Those at the upper levels of the Brotherhood handle them themselves."

"True—and yet that's not what I asked. I sense you're hiding something from me, Edrick. The thief who stole our horses—where can we find them?"

Edrick looked past her to Berengar, who loomed behind her, axe in hand. "Do what you want. I won't tell.

She's my friend." For a moment, he looked less like a worldly youth and more like a vulnerable young boy.

Morwen smiled and put a hand on Edrick's shoulder to reassure him. "We won't hurt her. We just want to ask her a few questions, that's all. I am Morwen of Cashel, and you have my word as a magician."

Edrick pulled away, and his expression hardened once more. "Are you mad? The Brotherhood has unfinished business with you both. You'll never make it out of there alive."

Berengar pointed his axe at Edrick. "I'm not that easy to kill, boy. You'd do well to remember that." He returned the weapon to its harness. "It might prove useful having you around. Tell us where to find your friend and we'll let you be—for now."

Edrick looked to Morwen. "Are you sure about this? I don't really care what happens to him, but you seem nice enough." His brow furrowed. "Are you really a magician?"

"I am. It's very important we find the rune. A lot of people could get hurt."

The boy sighed. "Fine. Just don't say I didn't warn you. Go to the Thieves' Quarter and look for the Court of Sorrows near the statue of the Crooked Lord. Ask for Azzy."

Berengar stared down at him. "Good lad. I trust you'll keep this conversation between us. If I find out you've tipped off the Brotherhood, you won't be so lucky next time. Got it?"

Edrick nodded to show that he understood.

"Let's go, Morwen." Berengar whistled to Faolán and turned to leave.

"Don't hurt her," Edrick called after them before kneeling down to pick up the apples from the smashed crate.

"It seems we're headed for a confrontation with the Brotherhood after all," Morwen said as they made their way to the Thieves' Quarter. "Better let me do the talking."

"You're the one who tried to steal the coatl egg right from under Calum's nose, in case you've forgotten."

"Aye, but it was you who took his hand."

Berengar grunted without argument. *She has a point there.*

The Thieves' Quarter was a bit of a misnomer, as the Brotherhood had no official headquarters—at least not one that was public knowledge. Instead, there were multiple factions spread across the city. Brotherhood affairs were notoriously secret, but Berengar knew the organization operated under a diffuse hierarchical structure. Each faction had its own leader, all of whom answered to whichever thief king or queen was in power at the moment.

The Thieves' Quarter was, in fact, a gateway of sorts between the older and newer portions of Dún Aulin. Its location allowed for easy and fast travel to most districts in the city, and its proximity to the river and a vast network of back alleys made it easy to evade guards giving chase. Not that any guards ever came near the area. Over the years, the Thieves' Quarter had become a favorite haunt of Brotherhood members of all ranks and factions in leisurely pursuits during the daylight hours.

"Interesting place. You seem to know your way around."

"I've been here before." The last time Berengar set foot in the Thieves' Quarter had been under very different circumstances. Although their more recent actions in Cashel had made him a fair number of enemies, he was not without allies in the Brotherhood. Still, the riots were years ago. Much had changed since he led the desperate group fleeing the Institute to the Thieves' Quarter to be smuggled out of Dún Aulin.

Like most of the city's districts, the Thieves' Quarter boasted its own unique flavor. Even the boldest guards knew to stay well away. While residences were fewer than in other places, there were an abundance of taverns and alehouses and no shortage of amusement to be found. A single, worn-down church was mostly abandoned, save for the number of lost souls found buried in its sizable grave-yard—a solemn reminder of the danger inherent in thievery.

It was easy to spot the nervous-looking nobles there to discuss business or potential contracts with the Brother-hood. They hid their faces under cloaks and awkwardly shuffled along, keeping their heads down while roving bands of young pickpockets sized them up from the side-walk. Berengar growled to frighten the pickpockets away. Almost all were orphans. The lucky ones—those who showed promise—might be initiated into the Brotherhood. The others would likely starve or meet their deaths at the end of a hangman's noose. Justice was harsh in the City of Thieves, especially for those without means or connections.

Berengar and Morwen came to the statue of the Crooked Lord and passed through an open, unguarded gate to enter a secluded courtyard with no outlet. Men and women sat scattered at tables grouped around a fountain. A few threw darts at wanted posters nailed to the wall. Some conversed in hushed tones or played cards or dice while others kept to themselves at solitary tables. A wooden staircase led up the side of a tavern from which occasionally appeared to bring tankards and flagons to those outside.

At the sight of Berengar and Morwen, much of the

laughter ceased. Berengar ignored the stares and searched the area for Edrick's contact.

"I gather you two didn't find your way here by accident." A lone woman at a table with a ficheall board regarded them with a curious expression. "Looking for someone?"

Berengar guessed she was somewhere shy of her twentieth birthday—probably only a few years older than Morwen. She wore nondescript clothes under a light cloak, which he suspected concealed a number of tools for thieving. In contrast to the other thieves, who often wore their hair short or bound, her luminous black hair fell freely to her waist. Thief or not, she was without a doubt one of the most beautiful women Berengar had ever seen. Still, there was something otherworldly about her appearance he couldn't quite place.

"Aye." Morwen approached. "Do you know where we can find Azzy?"

The young woman's blue eyes seemed to glimmer with inner amusement. "That depends on who's asking."

"We don't have time for this." Berengar struggled to keep his temper in check. "We didn't come here to play games."

"A pity, for I'm quite fond of games. It's been far too long since I've had a decent game of ficheall." She gestured to those in the vicinity. "The others are much too boring to play." Her face lit up with excitement, and she snapped her fingers. "I know! How about a match? Beat me, and I'll tell you whatever you wish to know."

Morwen interrupted before Berengar could protest. "And if you win?"

The young woman stroked her chin and seem to consider her reply. "Let's say you'll owe me a favor. Why don't we make it interesting? Just one game, rather than the usual set." She held out her hand. "Do we have a deal?"

Morwen grinned with self-assurance and shook the woman's hand. "Deal." She pulled Berengar aside. "Let me handle this. It'll be easy. I almost feel sorry for her. She has no idea who she's playing."

"Have it your way." Berengar had seen Morwen play enough times to know her confidence was justified.

Morwen plopped down across from the young woman and gathered her pieces. "Shall you toss the coin, or shall I?"

The thief held out a coin that had clearly been pick-pocketed from Morwen's coin pouch. "Allow me."

Maybe you should have enchanted the pouch as well, Berengar thought, amused at Morwen's consternation.

"Heads," Morwen declared.

The young woman threw the coin up in the air, and it landed on tails. "Luck is on my side today, it seems. Fear not—'tis only a coin toss. I'll be aggressor, if it's all the same to you."

Morwen shrugged. "You won the toss." She arranged her pieces around the center of the board. Ficheall was played on a grid of seven by seven squares. It was the defender's job to clear a path for their king to reach one of the grid's edges, and the aggressor won by capturing the king beforehand. "We haven't been properly introduced. I am Morwen of Cashel."

Her opponent flashed a mischievous smile. "Azzy, at your service." Morwen blinked in surprise, and the thief uttered a friendly laugh. "How did you find me?" She nodded at the board before Morwen could reply. "Your move."

Morwen hesitated and put a hand on one of her pieces. "Edrick sent us."

Azzy took a turn. "I imagined as much when I saw your horses. It's not often a mark seeks me out to talk." She inclined her head toward Berengar. "I'm guessing this one prefers to talk with his axe."

Morwen moved another piece. "More than you know."

"Is he all right? Edrick, I mean." Azzy's face was suddenly serious. "You didn't hurt him, did you?"

Berengar noticed two knives holstered at her side—hinting she was much more dangerous than her cheerful disposition suggested.

Morwen shook her head vigorously and looked her opponent in the eye. "No."

"Good. Ed is a cheeky little git sometimes, but he's loyal." Azzy sat back, any temporary animosity forgotten. "So, why seek me out? Would you like me to recover a family heirloom, or perhaps rob a quarrelsome neighbor?"

Morwen appeared to be off to a good start, and she began to visibly relax. "There is something you could help us with. There's someplace we need to break into. It could be dangerous, but we'll pay you for your trouble."

"The job—is it soon? I have something else coming up that will require all my focus."

"It is. We have other matters to attend to as well."

"Before I agree, I'll need to know the name of your companion."

Morwen bit her lip. "Esben Berengar."

"Truly?" Azzy looked entertained rather than intimidated. "Not that it wouldn't be interesting, but I'm afraid I'll have to decline. I work hard to keep my head down, and I can't afford that kind of attention at the moment."

"That's not the only reason we're here. We want information. Something of great value was stolen from us, and we want to know where to find it."

Azzy wagged a playful finger at them. "I can't discuss that sort of thing with anyone outside the Brotherhood."

Morwen advanced her king toward the grid's outer edge and folded her arms across her chest in triumph. "Too bad. A deal's a deal."

Azzy rubbed her hands together with glee. "I agree." With her next move, she captured Morwen's king. "It appears I win."

Morwen's smile faltered. "I…I lost?"

Azzy kicked her boots onto the table. "You played exceptionally well. I haven't had that much of a challenge in years."

Morwen remained motionless, staring at the board in complete bafflement. "But how?"

Berengar was equally stunned. Morwen was a master ficheall player, but Azzy had strung her along with ease. He laid a hand on Morwen's shoulder. "Let's go. We'll find someone else to help us with the Institute."

Azzy's eyes widened at the mention of the Institute. "What did you say?"

"Well, well. Look who it is." The words came from a woman in a black cloak with severe scarring along her jawline. "The Bloody Red Bear and Munster's court magician, all alone." At the sound of her voice, the courtyard's other occupants fell silent, and all merrymaking came to an abrupt end.

Faolán growled as a number of thieves rose from their seats to join the woman and her lieutenants, who moved to surround Berengar and Morwen. Many wore hoods or masks to conceal their faces.

"I always heard you were clever, Warden Berengar. Never thought you'd be fool enough to show your face here."

"Someone in the Brotherhood stole a thunder rune

from us. I want it back. I'll pay double whatever you're asking, if that's what it takes."

The woman appeared confused. "If there was such a theft, I would know of it. None in our ranks would dare take something so valuable for themselves without handing it over to leadership. But don't worry, we'll help ourselves to your gold soon enough."

Her surprise seemed genuine. Berengar frowned. Whoever had stolen the rune was playing a dangerous game by keeping it for herself. "And you are?"

"Reyna, ringleader of the Whisperer Faction."

"Listen—whatever you've heard, I'm not here for trouble. I've done business with the Brotherhood in the past. Velena can vouch for me. She helped me get the survivors of the Institute to safety, and in return I took care of a little problem rotting in the cells at Tara."

"Her rival Diego, you mean. You murdered him before he could talk—right under the High Queen's nose."

"Aye. Velena owes me. She must be high in the Brotherhood's leadership by now."

"She was. She's dead. There's a new thief king in charge, and he does things differently." The circle of thieves tightened around them. Berengar reached for his axe, and the thieves drew knives in unison. "We know about Cashel and what you did to Calum. Did you think we would let that pass?"

"What, was he a friend of yours or something?" Morwen asked.

The remark only served to anger Reyna further. "No. We were much closer than that."

Morwen swore.

"You took his hand and his eyes."

Morwen bit her lip. "Technically, we only took his hand. A sorceress took his eyes."

Reyna advanced on them. "We're thieves, not assassins, but in your case, I think we'll make an exception."

Tension mounted as Berengar and Morwen stared down a sea of sharpened knives. He raised his axe, ready to defend himself, but there were far too many thieves to fight at once.

"You can't kill them." The words came from Azzy, who had slipped out of her chair unnoticed and now stood between Berengar and Morwen and Reyna.

Reyna sneered. "Mind your own business. This doesn't concern a low-level journeywoman like you."

Azzy didn't flinch. Despite her short stature and wiry figure, she seemed totally unfazed by the threat. "I have to disagree. These two just hired me for a job."

Reyna pointed her knife at Berengar. "You accepted a contract from *him*? Do you know who this man is? What he's done?"

"It's done. Coins have changed hands. Whatever quarrel you have with them, it will have to wait until the job's done. Same goes for the other factions. If you disagree, you can take it up with the thief king."

"I don't need the hassle." Reyna thrust her knives into their sheaths. "This isn't over, Warden Berengar. Once the contract is complete, you're fair game." She regarded Azzy with disdain. "As for you, your ringleader will be hearing about this." With that, she marched off, leaving her subordinates to follow.

When they were alone, Azzy held out her hand expectantly. "The contract's not official until you pay me."

"I don't understand," Morwen said.

"I've been trying to find my way inside the Institute for *years*. Just one of the magical relics inside would be worth its weight in gold."

Berengar shook his head. "We'll find another way. I don't trust her."

Azzy followed them from the courtyard. "I'm a thief. Of course you shouldn't trust me. You need me, or else you wouldn't be here. Tell me you know where to find the secret entrance. I've been searching for it for ages."

Morwen stopped dead in her tracks. "How do you know about that?"

"I told you—I've been trying to get inside for years. Even if you know where to find the door, you won't be able to get inside without one of the keys used to unlock it."

"Do you have a key?" Berengar asked.

Azzy's grin widened. "No—but I know where we can find one."

CHAPTER SIX

BRINGING a thief into the king's court wasn't one of his better ideas. Then again, given the disdain Leinster's nobility and the church hierarchy held for him, Berengar felt a perverse sense of satisfaction watching Azzy accompany them to the Sovereign's Gate.

According to her, the key they were after was inside the palace. With all the added security for the Ceremony of the Cursed Blade, gaining access to such a place was a near-impossible task for even the most accomplished thief. Fortunately for Azzy, Berengar had an invitation.

A series of outer and inner walls and gates shielded the palace from the outside world. The imposing walls cast shadows across the land below. Sentries and guards patrolled the gates or observed from walls or towers. It was a highly effective defense system—and probably the only reason why the royal family managed to survive the purges.

For someone faced with the task of thieving in one of the most closely guarded places in the city, Azzy was in considerably good spirits. She seemed to greet the prospect of danger with enthusiasm and excitement, humming and whistling as they walked.

Morwen listened with interest. "What's that song? I don't recognize it." Despite Berengar's reservations, she was becoming fast friends with their new acquaintance. Not that it was particularly surprising. The two were close in age, and like Morwen, Azzy possessed a cheerful disposition and a fondness for humor.

For a moment, Azzy's blue eyes appeared to shimmer in the sunlight. "I doubt you would. 'Tis an old tune, long forgotten, of the founding of Dún Aulin. Aulin—or Ailinne, as it was once called—comes from the word *ail*, which means rock or stone. The sight of the palace walls brought it to mind."

"How does it go?"

Azzy flashed a radiant smile and began to sing as they approached the gate.

> *"Three mighty men made essays of trenchings,*
> *Burech, Fiach, and Aururas:*
> *it is they who without flagging (clear fact!)*
> *dug the rampart of Alend.*
>
> *Burech cast from him straightway*
> *across the rampart (no weakling he!)*
> *a stone he cast from his spear-arm;*
> *and that is the ail in Alend."*

Morwen applauded. "Bravo! You're every bit as good as any of the performers at the Revels."

Azzy gave a mock bow. "You are too kind, Lady Morwen."

She *was* good. Even Faolán seemed under her spell. In another life, Azzy might have made a name for herself as a bard, and Berengar wondered what turn of fate had brought her to the Brotherhood of Thieves. "You sure this is the only place we can find a key? There are less dangerous places to steal from."

Azzy's smile widened. "That there are. The Institute's inhabitants used multiple keys to enter the secret passageways, but most were lost after the purges. I spent a long time trying to track one down. Without knowing the location of the hidden door, attempting to retrieve the key from the palace wasn't worth the risk until now."

"I hope you know what you're doing. This isn't a joke. No funny business, either, or I'll leave you to the guards." Causing trouble in the king's court was the last thing he wanted.

Azzy gave him a three-fingered salute. "Thief's honor." She didn't seem fazed by his coarse manners. Nor did she shy away from his scars. Most women averted their eyes rather than look at his ruined face for any length of time. There were exceptions—Queen Nora, Ravenna, and Morwen—but they were few.

"Halt!" ordered a guard stationed outside the gate. "State your business here." The man's hand inched toward his sword at their approach.

"Put that away, you fool—unless you mean to bring the High Queen's fury down on our heads." The voice belonged to Tavish, the commander of the city watch. He had just arrived on horseback with a few of his lieutenants. "That's a Warden of Fál you're threatening, and the Bear Warden at that. He's here at the king's invitation."

The guard removed his hand from the blade's hilt. "Apologies, sir."

Each of the guards remained stone-faced. The veterans among them would have remembered Berengar from the purges either as monster or savior. The others would have heard the stories. If any were alarmed or uneasy at his presence, they gave no hint of it, a sign they were well trained.

"Your caution is appreciated. That goes for the rest of you as well." Tavish waited for the gate to open and nodded to Berengar and the others. "You three —with me."

Berengar and his companions followed him through the entrance, and the gate closed behind them once more.

Tavish eyed Azzy from his mount. "I see you've picked up another companion, Warden Berengar. I thought you said you weren't long for the city."

"Trust me, I wish it were otherwise. Things changed."

Tavish appeared unsurprised. "I heard of Warden Niall's sudden departure. Nothing serious, I hope."

"Nothing you need concern yourself with."

"Don't worry, I don't mean to pry into wardens' affairs. I've got enough on my plate as it is. Curiosity comes with the job, I suppose. Still, with the ceremony at hand, we need all the help we can get right now. Just between us, I'm glad you're here—not that your presence hasn't caused a fair amount of trouble already."

I'm sure it has. Berengar didn't even want to think about the arms Niall would have had to twist to arrange an invitation to the palace.

The green banners that waved from the ramparts depicted a crown at the foot of a cross—the sigil of Leinster's king. Morwen regarded their surroundings with eagerness as they made their way from the outer courtyard. She'd been raised in the halls of one of Fál's royal houses, and to Berengar's knowledge, this was her first time setting foot in another. While the royal palace at Dún Aulin shared many similarities with the castle on the Rock of Cashel, the differences were readily apparent. The palace was far more overbearing and austere than the castle at Cashel. Munster was a kingdom of beauty and culture, and the halls of its royals were full of splendor. In contrast, the monarchs of Leinster prided themselves on their prudence and devotion to the Lord of Hosts.

"You're lucky to gain an audience with the king," Tavish remarked. "It's a sign of the ceremony's importance. He's been acting rather odd lately, from what I hear."

Niall said something similar. "What do you mean?"

Tavish shrugged. "Good King Lucien is quiet and reserved by nature, but lately he has shut himself away and refused to see anyone other than his chief adviser. I expect he's simply at prayer, but there are rumors he suffers from a malady of some kind. Of all the times for the prince regent to take his leave of court…"

They passed through another fortified gate to a busy inner courtyard, where servants tended to the company's horses, before starting up a steep stair that led to the palace. Tavish, Berengar, and the others surrendered their weapons outside the entrance—Azzy had left her knives behind to avoid drawing the wrong kind of attention—and were ushered past the threshold.

A formally-dressed chamberlain met them at the head of an escort. "Welcome, honored guests. King Lucien and his advisers are already in discussions on the subject of the ceremony." His nose wrinkled with thinly-veiled contempt when he spotted Berengar. "Do not come within twenty paces of the throne. Do not speak to the king unless spoken to. You are to address the king as 'Your Highness' or 'Majesty.'"

Berengar fought back a sigh. He hated the tediousness of court. He had little use for the vanity of the noble classes or the games they played. At least when he faced an enemy on the battlefield, the conflict was honest. Perhaps it was his humble background, but he saw no reason why it should matter whether the royals of Leinster styled themselves "Majesty" or those of Munster used "Your Grace." The ranks of the nobility varied among kingdoms. In Ulster, where Berengar was born, power was hereditary or seized at the point of a blade. Leinster, heavily influenced by the foreign kingdoms of Albion and Caledonia across the sea, boasted a variety of ranks and titles unused elsewhere in Fál.

Music emanated from the throne room, where three dogs yapped at a colorful court jester while a boy clapped loudly from the throne. One of the hounds successfully bit the jester's backside, and a guard restrained the animals long enough for the jester to catch his breath.

The figure on the throne doubled over with high-pitched laughter and slapped the seat's armrest. "More wine." The jester stared at the snapping hounds with wide-eyed fear before scrambling to his feet and refilling the king's goblet. Lucien lifted the goblet to his lips and drank deeply with satisfaction. "Again! Do it again!"

The guard released his hold on the hound, the jester took flight, and the king howled with glee as the dance began anew.

Berengar frowned. Everything he'd heard so far suggested King Lucien was pious, sober minded, and shy —anything but the impish creature occupying the throne. Lucien had an almost feral look about him. His skin was waxy and discolored, his hair mussed and unruly, and his clothes were ill-fitting. Even his eyes didn't set quite right. One was reddened and larger than the other, with a significantly dilated pupil.

"Around he goes! Watch him run, watch him run!" There was a dissonant melody to the king's slurred speech.

Like their comrades at the gates, the guards within the chamber remained expressionless. The room's other occupants, however, looked on in revulsion. The jester tripped and landed on the stone floor, and the hounds were on him in an instant.

"Enough." A figure approached the king from behind. He motioned to the guards, who forcibly removed the hounds from the room, and laid a hand on the throne. "The king has business to attend to. His guests are waiting."

Tavish spoke in a hushed tone. "That's Father Valmont. He's been King Lucien's closest adviser since the bishop first took ill."

Apart from Berengar, Valmont was the tallest man in the room. He wore black robes in the fashion of a priest, and his long white hair was neatly clasped behind his head.

King Lucien's brow furrowed at the mention of guests. "What guests?"

The chamberlain nodded to a herald, who bowed low. "Tavish, of the city watch, and Esben Berengar, Warden of Fál."

A devilish gleam crossed the king's face, and he sat straight up in his seat. "Shall we make them dance?" He glanced at the members of his elite guard beside the throne. A steel helm concealed each guard's face, and heavy armor protected their bodies. Each wielded a crossbow.

Valmont flashed an irritated expression at the king. "We shall not."

The king sank back into his seat and folded his arms across his chest with a rueful look, but remained silent.

Morwen observed with rapt attention. "Interesting."

Wonder what she means by that. Berengar glanced around

the room but failed to see any sign of the key Azzy mentioned. The thief remained quiet at his side.

The king's thane beckoned to them. "Welcome. We've been expecting you." In many kingdoms, the thane served as the monarch's right hand. In Munster, for instance, the thane was second-in-command of the entire kingdom. In Leinster, the position was less significant due to the influence of the church. The thane gestured to a group of government officials and representatives of the church. "This is Vicar Flaherty, who served under Bishop McLoughlin. Vicar, I'm sure you know..."

Flaherty's lips formed a thin line. "I assure you, Warden Berengar needs no introduction."

"Ha!" The young king's attention settled on Berengar, and there was something unbalanced about his manner. "Beware the bear, the witches' words. Too true, in two, spells doom for you." He threw back his head and roared with disquieting laughter.

The chamber fell silent at the mysterious pronouncement, and members of the king's court exchanged puzzled glances. Azzy's smile vanished, and she stared hard at Lucien and his adviser with an unflinching gaze. Any similarity to Morwen ended there; Berengar had never seen a look of such unrelenting hatred grace his companion's face.

Valmont's shadow fell over the throne. "The king has had too much wine. He will now be excused."

Lucien started to protest, but Valmont's eyes narrowed in his direction, and the king hopped off the throne and scampered away, trailed by the elite guard.

"The witches' words?" Morwen whispered to Berengar. "What did that mean?"

"Nothing. It was nonsense." Even if that wasn't strictly true, he had no intention of concerning Morwen with the details. He looked intently at the empty throne. *How did he know about the witches' words?*

Despite Berengar's general disregard for magic, he'd been forced to battle its practitioners on more than one occasion. The last time he was in Leinster, he slew the Hag of Móin Alúin, a cruel witch who had tormented the villagers of Alúine for years. With her last breath, the hag had cursed him to regain all that he had lost only to lose it again. And at Cashel, the witch Agatha—Morwen's mother—predicted he would soon face betrayal and death. Of course, it was possible the words referenced Princess Ravenna's attempt to seize the crown of Munster by murdering her father, but what if Agatha's prediction had yet to come to pass? Berengar, who didn't trust the witches or their words, had never shared what they told him with anyone. There was no way Lucien should have knowledge of it.

Valmont glanced their way and saw Azzy staring at him. He regarded her with interest from the throne. "You. You have a familiar look about you. Have we met before?"

Azzy's lips formed a forced smile. "I don't believe we've had the pleasure." Berengar noticed her hand inch toward her side, as if to grab one of the knives she'd discarded.

"Ahem." The king's thane cleared his throat to get the others' attention. "Back to the matter at hand. We were discussing preparations for the ceremony."

"Where's the blade now?" Berengar asked.

"Hidden somewhere within the cathedral," answered Flaherty. "Its exact location shall remain a closely guarded secret."

"We also hide the blade when it is in our possession to ensure its safety," the thane said. "It is only on public display during the ceremony, once every thirteen years."

"And this time it's the church handing it over to the

crown." Berengar glanced back at the throne, where Valmont lingered, observing at a distance.

The thane nodded. "Aye. In two days' time, King Lucien will leave the palace and journey to the cathedral to receive the cursed blade from the new bishop. The exchange will take place at midnight. There will be hundreds of onlookers within and thousands crowded outside in hopes of catching a glimpse of the blade. As always, security is at an all-time high, but with a relic of such power, one can never be too careful. Before his departure, Warden Niall had several ideas to address gaps in our preparedness."

"Good. We'll start there. I want all the details. And I'll want to see the cathedral for myself in advance of the ceremony."

"There is the small matter of your excommunication," Flaherty said. "I am sure I can persuade the others to permit such a visit, provided you are willing to arrive in secret."

Berengar grunted by way of response. With the king's departure, they adjourned to a neighboring chamber to continue discussions in private. The rest of the conversation followed the same course. All parties quibbled over their various interests, and Berengar's involvement only complicated matters further. Getting everyone to agree on anything was nigh impossible. When it was over, Berengar, Morwen, and Azzy were promptly dismissed from the palace. For his part, he was as glad to go as they were to see him leave.

He turned his attention to Azzy once they were safely outside the gate. "You've got some explaining to do. I don't know what game you're playing, but I didn't see any key."

Azzy held up a long black key tucked between her

fingers. Berengar recognized its likeness. He'd seen it years earlier, the last time he was at the Institute.

Morwen's brow furrowed in consternation. "You were with us the whole time. Where—how did you get that?"

Azzy grinned. "A good thief never reveals her secrets. Now I believe I've held up my end of the bargain. The sooner you show me to the secret door, the sooner we can both get what we want."

Berengar clenched his teeth. There was still something about her that he didn't trust. "Maybe I'll just take it from you."

Azzy laughed. "You'll find I'm not so easy to catch."

"She did help us with the Brotherhood," Morwen reminded him.

Berengar shook his head. "Fine."

"That's the spirit." Azzy tossed the key into the air, caught it, and returned it to her pocket. "Lead the way."

The three set off north, headed for the Scholars' District.

Morwen tugged on Berengar's sleeve and lowered her voice. "Niall was right. All is not well with King Lucien. I fear it involves magic."

"Go on." Even if Morwen was correct, Lucien's advisers would never allow a magician to examine the king.

"Did you notice the king's red eyes and his dilated pupil? Taken with his strange behavior and the magic I sensed coming from the throne, I suspect he's become addicted to fairy dust. It would certainly explain the change in him. That's not the only thing that concerns me."

"What?"

"Something's not right about his adviser, Father

Valmont. I sensed great darkness in him—darkness and malice."

"That's obvious enough."

Morwen raised an eyebrow. "Oh?"

"He doesn't wear a crucifix. Odd for a priest. Besides, chief advisers are rarely good people. Something about power attracts the rotten among us like flies." Still, given his apparent sway over the king, Valmont bore watching. Berengar's gaze moved to Azzy, who walked ahead, just out of earshot. "What can you sense about her?"

Morwen bit her lip. "Almost nothing beneath the surface. I haven't encountered anyone so difficult to read since Ravenna."

"Don't sound so surprised. Thieves are practiced at concealing their true intentions. They wouldn't be very good at the job otherwise."

"Perhaps." Morwen appeared unconvinced.

"I thought you liked her."

"I like nearly everyone. That doesn't mean I trust them."

Berengar fought back a grin. "There's hope for you yet."

When they returned to the secluded alleyway they visited earlier that day, they again found themselves facing a dead-end.

"Time to see if that key of yours does the job." Berengar wasn't entirely sure if the key would work for Azzy, who wasn't a magician.

Azzy looked around, searching for the door. "Where's the entrance?"

Morwen hesitated, her hand on the clasp of her satchel. "Not a word of this to anyone. Got it?"

Azzy dragged a finger across her lips. "My lips are sealed."

Morwen again used the rune of illusion to reveal the secret entrance. She claimed that she was not an exceptionally powerful magician—even with her staff—and her magic usually was of an ordinary variety. Berengar, having spent much of his life hearing of magic only in stories, was still amazed every time he saw such a feat. Morwen grimaced with discomfort when the rune burned her hand again, and she looked paler than she had before.

As the rune's purple glow subsided, Berengar watched Azzy to ensure she didn't make an attempt on the stone. One missing rune was enough. To his surprise, the thief seemed entirely unconcerned by Morwen's use of magic. Instead, Azzy clapped her hands together with glee.

"Well done!" She produced the key with a flick of her wrist and raised it to the keyhole. "Let's see what secrets lie within." The door vanished, leaving a gaping hole in its place, along with a set of stairs leading down into darkness.

Berengar started down the stairs and motioned for the others to follow while Faolán remained above to keep watch.

When they reached the bottom, Morwen stumbled on the last step and leaned against the wall for support.

Berengar held out a hand to steady her. "You all right?"

"I'll be fine." An unlit torch waited below. Morwen wiped blood from her nose and again delved into her satchel to retrieve a quartz stone. "Solas." The stone glowed with white light, sending a wave of illumination down a long underground corridor. Just as suddenly as it began, the light flickered and went out. Morwen scowled and returned the stone to her satchel. "I must have used more magic than I thought."

"Don't worry. I think I can bring this flame to life." Azzy lifted the torch from the wall and scraped one of her knives along a flint from her cloak to create a spark. She moved the torch to her lips and breathed on it, causing flames to burst into life.

Morwen's eyes widened in astonishment. "How did you do that?"

Azzy winked at her. "Any thief worth her salt has to be ready to find her way in the dark." She held the torch out to light their path through the corridor.

Morwen quickened her step and followed Azzy with renewed interest. "Reyna called you a journeywoman. What did she mean by that?"

"There are many different ranks within the Brotherhood. New recruits begin as novices or apprentices. They do as they're told and get the scut work. Almost all their earnings go to the Brotherhood's coffers. Adepts, or journeymen, have more independence. We can take on our own contracts—though the Brotherhood still takes a cut. Master thieves can largely do as they please, and those who wish can become ringleaders. And, of course, the thief king sits at the top."

"Any idea where we can find him?" Berengar asked. If anyone knew the location of the thunder rune, it would be the Brotherhood's leader—unless Reyna was telling the truth, and the theft was committed by someone with no intention of handing over the stone.

"No one knows who he is, and I wouldn't tell you even if I did—as much for your safety as my own. The new thief king is exceptionally clever and cautious. He's a dangerous man."

"So am I."

The thief's appearance seemed to shift in the corridor's shadows. Her angular features grew sharper and more pronounced, and her porcelain skin appeared darker under the flickering torchlight.

"What's a black contract?" Morwen's voice sounded stronger.

Azzy looked back at her over her shoulder. "Why do you ask?" Her tone was casual, but Berengar noticed she was no longer smiling.

Morwen shrugged. "It's just a word I overheard. I was curious about what it meant."

Berengar knew exactly where she'd heard it. Niall had mentioned that someone in the Brotherhood of Thieves had taken on such a contract.

"A black contract is a contract for a job so dangerous, so risky, that it requires approval by the thief king himself. Anyone who agrees to a black contract without approval faces death—whether or not the contract is completed."

Berengar wondered what kind of contract could pose such a threat that even the Brotherhood would refuse it.

The trio came to the end of the corridor. A wooden trapdoor loomed at the top of a ladder. When Morwen started toward the ladder, Azzy held a hand out to stop her.

"Wait." Azzy removed one of her knives, bent low, and cut a tripwire that ran along the ground.

Morwen regarded the thief with awe. "How did you see that in the dark?"

"I have *very* good eyes." The amusement in her voice was evident.

"That wasn't there the last time I was here." Maybe the Institute wasn't as abandoned as he believed. Berengar climbed the ladder and put a hand on the trapdoor. "You two stay close."

He emerged into darkness on the other side. Azzy passed him the torch, which revealed a spacious chamber in its fiery light. The candles and lanterns that once illuminated the room lay scattered or turned over, having long ago fallen dark. The last time Berengar came through the trapdoor, delirious from the Bewilderer's Bite, he found himself face-to-face with two dozen frightened souls, all waiting for their end. Now the chamber lay quiet and forgotten.

Azzy helped Morwen through the trapdoor. "Be careful. There could be more traps."

"So this is the Institute." Even in the dim light, it was clear Morwen was disappointed.

"It was different once." The room still smelled vaguely of sulfur, but everything else had changed. The strange instruments and unfamiliar relics he remembered had been smashed to pieces. The scrolls and tomes that once stacked the shelves lining the walls were gone. A few burnt fragments of parchment were all that remained. "Come on."

He raised the torch and crossed into a long passage lined with pillars. Morwen and Azzy followed close behind, and together they wandered the Institute's long-forgotten halls, searching for anything of value. They passed empty rooms that once contained alchemy laboratories and empty herbalists' stores once full of every ingredient imaginable. There was little left behind. The mobs had done their work well.

Morwen's disappointment quickly turned into a mix of wonder and sorrow as they reached the atrium and came to a series of staircases where the full enormity of what had been done to the Institute became apparent. "How could they have done this? Why would anyone destroy something so beautiful?"

Azzy seemed to share Morwen's regret. "'Tis human nature to hate and fear what's not easily understood. There may come a day when all that is magical and special about this world is lost and forgotten." She stopped suddenly and held a finger to her lips. "We're not alone."

"I didn't hear anything," Morwen began, but Azzy had already slipped into the shadows.

Berengar groaned. "I knew we shouldn't trust her."

"Don't move another muscle." The voice came from a man holding a lantern that had been dark only moments ago. In his free hand, he wielded a crossbow, which he trained on Berengar. "Do you like it? I made it myself. Make another move toward your sword, and I'll pull the trigger."

"That'll be the last mistake you ever make." All the same, Berengar eased his hand off the blade's hilt. "Who are you?"

"I'll ask the questions, if you don't mind. You're the intruders here." The stranger was somewhere in his late forties. He wore a set of gray alchemist's robes.

Suddenly, there was a knife to his throat, and Azzy's face was illuminated in the lantern's light. "I'd put that down if I were you."

The man dropped the crossbow, which clattered to the floor.

"Now would be a good time to start talking." Berengar nodded to Morwen, who retrieved the crossbow and aimed it at the stranger before Azzy lowered the dagger.

The man held up his hands in a show of surrender. "Elias is my name. I was an alchemist by trade before the purges. Now I'm the guardian of these halls. There are few who know of the secret entrance, and they have no keys. I made sure of it."

"You live here?" Morwen looked astonished. "Why?"

"It was my home once. I had friends and a life here. You people took that from me."

Morwen lowered the crossbow. "You're wrong. My companion helped your friends escape the Institute. He risked his life to get them out of the city."

Elias stared at them with new interest. "Who are you?"

"My friend is Esben Berengar, Warden of Fál. And I am Morwen the magician."

"Magician, you say? What on earth are you doing here? They'll kill you if they catch you."

"I lost my staff in battle. I need another, and with the Oakseers' Grotto felled, my companion thought I might find one here."

"I see. Thought you'd do a bit of thieving, did you? Well, you can bugger off." He stopped short and stroked his beard, as if pondering some hidden matter. "Wait. As it happens, there are several magical items the rioters failed to find that I managed to salvage. I can help you attain what you seek."

Morwen's face lit up with excitement.

Elias held up a hand. "Not so fast. I would be willing to part with such a valuable possession only for a price. And it's no use threatening me, either. I know these halls in a way you can't even fathom, and you'll never find what you're looking for without me."

"Out with it," Berengar said. "What do you want?"

"You might've heard of the fairy dust epidemic sweeping the city."

Azzy perked up at the mention of fairy dust. "What of it?"

"I want you to put the distributor out of business and bring him to me. If you really are the Esben Berengar the tales speak of, you'll have no problem with such a task."

Morwen regarded Elias with suspicion. "Why? What's in it for you?"

"That's my business. Do the job, and we can both get what we want. Otherwise, good luck finding another staff in this city."

.   .   .

T hey returned from the Institute the way they came. Morwen scratched Faolán behind the ears when they emerged from the secret door. Evening had fallen across the face of Dún Aulin in their absence, and the sun hung low. "Don't look so glum, Berengar. We found what we were looking for! I thought it would take ages to acquire a new staff."

"Assuming he even has a staff. Maybe he was lying to get us to do his dirty work."

"I'm a magician, remember? If he was lying, I'd know. Besides, you remember what Tavish told us. The fairy dust is causing a real problem in the city. This is a chance for us to do some good. And with a staff in hand, it'll be easier to cast a spell to help us locate the rune."

"This is exactly what I meant by getting dragged into other people's problems. Have it your way." He turned to Azzy. "You're good. I'll give you that much. I don't suppose you'd be willing to help us with the job?"

Her face remained unreadable. "I'll help—on one condition. When we return, I get to keep anything I find in the Institute."

"Deal."

"Good. Then meet me tomorrow night, just before dark. Send word to the Thieves' Quarter." She gave a self-satisfied smile, raised her hood, and disappeared into the impending night.

Berengar and Morwen returned to their mounts and began the journey to the alehouse. Even on horseback, there was a considerable distance from the Scholars' District to the Coin and Crown.

Morwen stifled a yawn. "How much farther?"

"Not far now." Berengar glanced over at her. "Tired?"

"Not at all." She yawned again. "Well, maybe a little."

Berengar laughed. "I thought you didn't get tired. What was all that talk about drawing on your magic to keep awake?"

Morwen offered a weary smile. "I think I might have pushed myself a little too hard today. Do you mind if I ride with you for a while?"

Berengar pulled back on the reins and slowed his pace. Morwen dismounted, and after fixing Nessa's lead rope to his saddle, climbed onto the saddle and put her arms around him. Berengar resumed the journey to the alehouse as Faolán followed alongside, keeping watch.

The horses' hooves reverberated against the paved road. The streets of Dún Aulin were relatively quiet, which Berengar found a welcome change. A curfew was in effect in advance of the Ceremony of the Cursed Blade, and although some unsavory elements lingered, most of the city's occupants had returned to their homes and lodgings. The city watch was out in full force, and guards told loiterers to move on in no uncertain terms.

Morwen rested her head against his shoulder, and within moments she was asleep. Berengar chuckled softly and readjusted his position to make sure she was comfortable. Sometimes he forgot just how young she was. For all her vast knowledge of magic, she was really just a girl.

He thought on the day's events. After a series of false starts, at least they were headed in the right direction. The Ceremony of the Cursed Blade would be over soon enough, and if Elias proved good on his word, Morwen would have a new staff. Then they could return to the task of locating the stolen thunder rune. With any luck, Tavish and the watch might come through on that end as well. Still, with various Brotherhood factions and the Acolytes after blood, he couldn't rest easy so long as they remained within the city's walls.

Streetlamps lit their path as night descended over the City of Thieves. By the time the glow of the torches and lanterns in the windows of the Coin and Crown appeared, Berengar realized—much to his surprise—he was humming the tune Azzy sang earlier that day. Unlike Morwen, Berengar wasn't musically inclined, and yet he couldn't get the thief's voice out of his head. There was something about her he couldn't quite put his finger on.

He gently shook Morwen awake when they neared the Coin and Crown.

"Is it morning already?" she asked, half-asleep.

Berengar helped her from his horse and led their mounts to the boarding stables. He tossed a coin to the stableboy. "Make sure they're fed and well looked after." Then he gathered their recovered belongings and started on the path to the Coin and Crown on foot. Although the numbers inside had diminished in the aftermath of the Revels, there was no shortage of patrons inside, and lively music again filled its halls.

Morwen leaned against him for support, oblivious to the sights and sounds that had so captivated her the night before.

"Come on. Let's get you to bed." Berengar helped her up the stairs to her room and eased open the door.

Morwen stirred. "Wait. Something's not right."

A cold chill permeated the room. Moonlight filtered in through an open window. Bedsheets were scattered and drawers and cabinet doors were ajar. Someone had turned the room upside down. Fortunately, thanks to the prior theft of their belongings, there was nothing for the would-be thief to find.

Morwen looked around the room. "Who could have done this?"

"Whoever it was, they were looking for something. I'll

give you three guesses what." The blasted thunder rune was still causing them trouble, and they didn't even have it anymore.

"Do you think it was the Brotherhood?"

Berengar gestured to the mess. "It's too obvious. If it was the Brotherhood, we would never know they were here."

Morwen started toward the nightstand to light the candle but stopped short, instantly alert. "We're not alone."

A floorboard creaked somewhere in the darkness. Berengar inched forward and reached for his sword. He caught a glimpse of movement to his right, and a goblin scaled the wall and dropped down behind him. Berengar pulled his blade too slowly. The goblin tackled him, and they crashed to the floor. When the goblin's eyes fell on Morwen, he launched himself at her, but at the last moment Berengar seized the creature's ankle to restrain him. The goblin kicked him in the face and broke free in time to pounce on Morwen, who lost her hold on her satchel.

When the creature went for her satchel, a strange expression came over his face, and he toppled over and hit the floor.

It looks like her enchantment worked.

Morwen stooped down to retrieve her satchel. "The goblins must have followed us to Dún Aulin."

"I'm guessing they led us here. We thought we were chasing them, but the slippery bastards tricked us. Who knows how long they've been following us? With any luck, this is the only one who knows where we're staying. I say we kill him and be done with it." Berengar started forward with his sword, but Morwen held up a hand to stop him.

"Wait! Don't kill him."

"Morwen…"

She knelt over the goblin. "It's all right. I won't hurt you. You're feeling the effects of a spell, but it won't last long."

The creature studied her with interest. "You're a magician?"

Morwen nodded. "Enough blood has been spilled over the stone already. Tell us what we want to know, and we'll let you go. You have my word. Now, who sent you? Why do they want the stone?"

The goblin regarded her with an unblinking gaze. For a moment, it seemed he might speak, but then Berengar stepped forward. When the goblin's eyes settled on him, he let out an angry hiss.

"He hasn't forgotten you, Berengar Goblin-Bane." The goblin jumped up from the floor, crossed the room, and crawled out the window before Berengar could catch him.

"Blast it!" Berengar hurled his sword to the ground and turned back to Morwen. "This is on you. If we'd done things my way…"

"You would have done what, exactly? Cut off his fingers until he talked?" She put her hands on her hips, her exhaustion temporarily forgotten in her anger. "There's a reason the goblins hate us."

"So you just let him run back to the others? What happens when they come for us in the night?" He closed the distance between them and felt his temper rising. "You believe he's going to care that you spared him? You think that man from the Acolytes you let go won't still burn you for a witch?"

"And you think killing is always the answer and compassion is a weakness!"

"Because it is." Berengar shook his head with disdain. "In the real world, monsters don't change just because you show them mercy. Do you want to know what happened the last time I was in Leinster? A woman named Rose rescued me from the bog—saved my life. She was good and kind. She was also a werewolf." He stared hard at her. "She ate her fiancé. I put her down. Put a blade between her ribs. *That* was mercy."

"What about Ravenna?" Morwen shot back. "Should you have killed her too?" There was silence between them for a moment. "I'm sorry, Berengar. I'm just tired, I guess. I didn't mean that."

He said the next words before he could take them back. "Maybe if you had found out what she was earlier and done the job yourself, your father would still be alive."

Morwen's mouth opened in shock. "You don't care at all what I think, do you? I thought you wanted me as a companion, but you just want me as your pet magician."

"I don't need you. I don't need anyone."

Anger flashed across her brow. "You're impossible! Get out and let me sleep."

"Fine by me." He marched from the room.

"And Berengar? If you're going to lie to me, you should at least try to be good at it!" She slammed the door shut behind him.

Berengar let out a frustrated sigh. *She's too stubborn for her own good.* Then again, so was he. She was who she was, and he was who he was. There was no point to either trying to change the other.

It was the mention of Ravenna that had stirred his anger. Although he hardly spoke of Ravenna, he still thought of her more than he would like. His feelings for her were complicated, to say the least. With Ravenna, Berengar felt something he hadn't felt for anyone since the death of his wife. Like him, Ravenna was deeply broken. She had suffered greatly at the hands of her father and others, resulting in scars—visible and otherwise—Berengar understood only too well. Maybe it was on account of what happened with Rose, but when the moment came, he'd found he couldn't kill her. Stripped of her crown and kingdom, Ravenna fled Munster on the back of a winged serpent. He often wondered what became of her after that. Berengar suspected Morwen sensed his feelings but chose not to pry.

He knocked on the door to Morwen's room to apologize, but she was already fast asleep. Berengar hesitated, pulled a blanket over her, and sank into a chair in a corner of the room. He kept his sword across his lap and took turns with Faolán standing guard in case the goblin returned.

Before long, his eyes grew heavy.

"He hasn't forgotten about you, Berengar Goblin-Bane," the goblin had said.

Who the devil was he talking about?

CHAPTER SEVEN

THAT NIGHT, Berengar dreamed of the purges for the first time in years. The rioters' screams for blood built to a deafening roar. The air reeked of smoke and death. He remembered crushing Cathán's hands and listening to the shrieking cries as he forced the druid's face into the flames. He watched himself cut down everyone in his path until the streets ran red with blood and all who looked upon him trembled in fear.

He woke covered in a cold sweat. Faolán, perched at the foot of Morwen's bed, regarded him curiously. Berengar leaned back in his chair and rubbed the sleep from his eyes. It was early, and weak sunlight streamed in through the window. Morwen remained fast asleep. He considered waking her but thought better of it. He wasn't sure if it was because she needed rest to recover her strength or because of the harsh words that had passed between them.

Sorry, old friend. I'm sure you would have picked a better guardian for your daughter, given the chance. Mór wasn't exactly a saint himself—there were his numerous affairs, not to mention an illicit agreement with the Witches of the Golden Vale—but Berengar knew he was the very last person who should be entrusted with looking after a sixteen-year-old girl.

As if sensing his mood, Faolán approached and pushed her muzzle against his knee.

Berengar patted her head and scratched her behind the ears before rising. "Keep an eye on her for me, will you?" He cast one look back at Morwen, eased the door open, and shut it behind him without making a sound.

Despite the early hour, the alehouse was crowded again. Berengar coughed up payment for another night's stay, along with a little something extra to repair the damage the goblin left in his wake. The managers didn't ask for the specifics; he expected the Revels had resulted in a fair amount of property damage, though not enough to offset the influx of coin. He helped himself to another generous portion of breakfast—the only perk of staying at the Coin and Crown, as far as he was concerned—and took a seat by himself.

A barmaid handed him a message from Vicar Flaherty, summoning him to the cathedral to oversee final preparations for the ceremony. The visit was timed to coincide with the bishop's funeral to keep the knowledge of Berengar's presence on sacred ground to as few as possible.

He had just begun eating when he noticed Friar Godfrey making his way toward him.

"Ah! Just the man I was looking for. I heard I might find you here."

Berengar gritted his teeth. *Does* everyone *in this blasted city know we're here?* He kicked a seat out and motioned for Godfrey to join him. "Finally abandoned that monastery of yours, I see."

Godfrey propped his walking stick against the table,

leaned closer, and lowered his voice. "Just between us, I'm glad to take my leave. Father Ulrich's cooking is starting to take its toll." He glanced around the hall. "Where is your charming companion?"

"Still asleep."

Godfrey rapped his wooden hand on the table. "Youth is wasted on the young. I've come to the city to tie up some business before the funeral. The bishop's successor will be chosen shortly—just in time for the Ceremony of the Cursed Blade. Word is you're caught up in that, by the way."

"Don't remind me. You're not in the running for bishop, are you? Maybe you could see about lifting my excommunication."

"I'm afraid I've broken a few too many rules for that." Godfrey smiled and paid a passing barmaid for a drink. "I expect you know a thing or two about that." He stopped to take a swig from the cup. "I suppose you're wondering why I sought you out—other than the pleasure of your company, of course."

"Get on with it, friar. I haven't had a particularly enjoyable last few days, and it doesn't appear that will change anytime soon."

Godfrey laughed, undaunted. "Same old Berengar. Very well, I'll get to the point. There's been some strange talk around the monastery of late."

"What sort of talk?" The friar wouldn't have bothered him if it weren't important.

Godfrey's manner was no longer jovial. "Talk of things better left buried and forgotten. There are whispers of someone in the west who seeks to resurrect the old ways. I've heard of accounts of human sacrifice remarkably similar to what we encountered at Alúine."

Berengar raised an eyebrow. Godfrey's implication was

clear. "Laird Margolin is dead, and the cult of Balor died with him. You were there. We stopped the ritual."

Godfrey appeared unconvinced. "We prevented Margolin from sacrificing Lady Imogen, but not before he began the invocation. What about the entity you saw?"

Berengar clenched his teeth. He hadn't forgotten. "I don't know what I saw." It wasn't entirely true. After they thwarted the ritual, a nightmarish being of shadow and flame attempted to possess him.

"If someone is endeavoring to revive the Fomorians…"

Berengar cut him off. "Look around you. The Fomorians are gone. The old ways are done."

"All the same, there is a man in the city who has witnessed these things firsthand. A scout by the name of Horst who barely survived a goblin ambush. His companions were not so fortunate, I hear."

That must be the scout Tavish spoke of, Berengar thought. So that was the business Godfrey referenced earlier. "And?"

"I would like you to come with me to meet him."

"Godfrey, in case you haven't noticed, I have enough to worry about at the moment."

"I would consider it a personal favor if you would accompany me."

Berengar groaned. "Fine—but you owe me one." He finished his breakfast and pushed away from the table.

Godfrey slapped him across the back. "That's the spirit!"

The friar took hold of his walking stick, and together they left the Coin and Crown and made their way through the city. The pale sun was barely visible, and while the previous day's warmth was all but forgotten, at least it wasn't raining. A somber mood, perhaps on account of the bishop's funeral, seemed to have taken hold of Dún Aulin.

"This had better not take long." On top of his existing

obligations, he still had to track down whoever was supplying the fairy dust.

Godfrey whistled cheerfully by way of response.

Eventually they came to a busy neighborhood on the outskirts of the city, where the delineations between classes were blurred. Travelers came and went by way of the neighboring Beggars' Gate, which offered easy access to and from Dún Aulin. Godfrey led him to an almshouse in a secluded area, where priests and monks tended to the infirm.

It was quiet inside. Many beds were empty, and most of the patients appeared to be guards or soldiers suffering from some injury or other malady. "Are you sure this is the right place?"

Voices carried from below, and Godfrey lifted a candle from a bracket on the wall and started down a flight of stairs. They came to a dark room in the cellar where two rows of additional beds lined the walls on either side. Only one bed, at the end of the room, was occupied. A visitor with a candle sat at the patient's bedside. The man's features were cloaked in shadow, but as Berengar drew near, he recognized Jareth, the bard from the Coin and Crown.

His brow furrowed in anger. "You. What are you doing here?"

Jareth set his candle aside and studied him in the faint light. "Same as you, I suspect—to hear this man's story."

Before Jareth could move, Berengar grabbed him and shoved him against the wall. "That's what you do, isn't it? Take others' suffering and use your lies to turn it into gold? Not so brave without your adoring crowds, are you?" When Jareth tried to speak, Berengar tightened his grip around the bard's throat. "Next time, you should take more care choosing whose stories you tell." He eased his hold, and Jareth slumped against the wall, clutching his throat.

"And what lies am I supposed to have told?" To Berengar's surprise, Jareth appeared neither frightened nor resentful. "I believe you misunderstood the point of my tale. You weren't the monster of the story. You were only a mirror. I don't believe in heroes and villains—only interesting people." He nodded at the bed's occupant. "And this man certainly has an interesting tale. I'll leave you to it." He started from the room.

"Wait."

Jareth stopped short.

"I still have half a mind to give you a good thrashing, but as you're so fond of talk, I'll let you convince me otherwise if you can give me some straight answers. Since you seem to know everything that happens around this city, maybe you can tell me where the fairy dust is coming from."

Jareth's lips formed a thin smile. "I would ask about your interest in this matter, but I have a feeling you wouldn't tell me." He held up two fingers. "Very well. There are two sources of fairy dust in the city from competing dealers. The first lives in a secure villa, protected by private guards. Elazar is his name. From what I understand, he has powerful friends. As for the second…little is known about him. Whoever he is, he understands the value of secrecy. Does that answer your question?" He turned to go.

"One more thing. King Lucien's chief adviser—what do you know about him?"

"Curious. Your questions surprise me, Warden Berengar. It's not often that happens." Jareth studied him for a moment. "Valmont's past remains a mystery, even to those in the church. He arrived in Dún Aulin ten years ago.

Bishop McLoughlin had served as the king's adviser since the boy-king's infancy, but it did not take Valmont long to gain influence at court. When McLoughlin's health deteriorated, Valmont took his place at Lucien's side. Some suspect Valmont himself had a hand in the bishop's death. Any of McLoughlin's potential successors, however, would have a motive to poison the old man."

"You're saying the bishop was murdered?"

Jareth laughed. "Don't look so surprised. The church is full of separate factions vying for power. They just do a better job of hiding it than others. Not all monsters have scars. You would do well to remember that. Farewell, Warden Berengar. I suspect we will meet again." With that, Jareth took his leave.

"That man is more than he appears. I would know." Godfrey, the only surviving heir to Margolin's former rival, Laird Cairrigan, had rejected his worldly title in favor of a life of service to others.

A low moan came from the bed. Its occupant, who had lapsed into unconsciousness during Berengar's conversation with Jareth, bolted upright with a start. "Are you here to kill me?" Even in the darkness, it was clear he was young —hardly old enough to be a scout. Then again, Berengar had been drafted to fight goblins in the north at an even younger age.

Godfrey's voice was kind. "No, son. We're friends."

Horst's eyes darted about the room, as if seeking invisible threats. He held his sweat-drenched bedsheets in a tremulous grasp and shivered violently.

Godfrey picked up a washcloth at the bedside and applied it to the scout's forehead. "There, there. You're safe now."

Horst's voice was weak. "Nowhere is safe."

Godfrey glanced at Berengar. "He's delirious with fever."

Horst moaned again and briefly convulsed before slumping back in bed, semiconscious. Berengar noticed numerous cuts and scratches on his skin, including some that appeared self-inflicted.

"The voices…make them stop…"

Tavish said he returned half-crazed. Berengar regretted leaving Morwen behind. She was a gifted healer. Perhaps she could have helped the frightened wretch before him. "What happened to you?"

When Horst ignored him and began murmuring unintelligible babble, Berengar looked to Godfrey for answers.

"He and his friends were stationed at Cobthach's Hold near the border with Connacht, where the last of the wilds remain. They left the fort to track a band of goblins and never returned."

Teelah. Berengar thought of the helmeted goblin he and Morwen had encountered in the Wrenwood. If the attacks were linked, there was a chance Horst could point him toward whoever paid the goblins to retrieve the thunder rune. "Did goblins kill your friends?"

"*Monsters.* Terrible monsters. They were everywhere." Horst went quiet for a moment. "There were too many. I couldn't save the others. The spiders got them. When I went back, I saw…I saw…"

"What did you see?"

At that, Horst became more himself. "*Him.* The man with the face of a monster. I watched as he tied my friend Arland to an altar and drove a dagger through his heart. Then he turned and looked right at me. I ran and didn't stop running."

"Who is this man? Were the goblins working for him?"

Horst's eyes widened, and his hands shot out to clasp at

Berengar's cloak. "I know where they're keeping him…the king…"

"What about the king?"

"Valmont…said to keep it secret…" He convulsed and again lost consciousness before he could elaborate.

Berengar stared at him, pondering those last cryptic words. *What did he mean by that?*

Godfrey was first to break the silence. "There you have it. Human sacrifice. Monsters, pestilence, disease—you can see why I thought of Alúine."

"Aye." Church bells tolled outside the almshouse. It was almost noon. The bishop's funeral would begin soon. "I will think on what you've said." Berengar left the almshouse behind and parted ways with Godfrey. He followed the main road farther into the city, where he scrawled a message for Azzy detailing what he'd learned about Elazar and paid a messenger to deliver it to the Thieves' Quarter.

Crowds of onlookers arriving early in hopes of catching the funeral procession slowed his progress through the city, and Berengar briefly regretted leaving his horse stabled. He returned to the grand square by way of Padraig's Gate and headed in the opposite direction from the palace. The cathedral was impossible to miss even at a distance. It was easily the most impressive structure in the city. Even the splendor of the Rock of Cashel fell short of the cathedral's grandeur. Unlike the palace's austere court-yards, striking statues and beautiful fountains adorned the area around the cathedral.

Berengar pushed his way through the teeming masses gathered to watch McLoughlin laid to rest. Men, women, and children from all walks of life were tightly packed in such numbers they filled the square. *I bet the Brotherhood's pickpockets are here in full force.* The multitudes rivaled those who came to watch King Mór's funeral, signaling the church's importance in daily life.

Berengar wrapped himself in a nondescript gray cloak, as Flaherty's message instructed, and raised his hood to avoid attention. He slipped from the crowd and made his way around back.

"Identify yourself," said a member of the holy guard.

Berengar lowered his hood. "I'm here to see Vicar Flaherty."

The guard glowered at him, a reminder of the low regard in which he was held in religious circles. "This way."

An armed escort led him inside. Berengar, not easily impressed, couldn't help feeling awestruck at the sight of the cathedral's interior. Ornate stained-glass windows depicted various stories from Fál's history, including many centered around Padraig and his deeds. Frescoes covered the walls and ceilings, and the floors were made of marble and mosaic tiles. Breathtaking arches and pillars were everywhere, and the level of architectural skill on display was staggering.

Bells continued tolling outside as the funeral unfolded, and the cathedral's quiet halls only added to the sense of grandeur. Berengar followed the guards to the sanctuary, where the ceremony would be held the following day. An immense chandelier that hung from the ceiling cast a dazzling array of light across the vast chamber. Rows of uncomfortable-looking wooden pews spanned the length of the room and ended at the altar. The guards promptly withdrew and shut the doors, leaving him alone.

Footsteps echoed over the marble floor, and Vicar Flaherty approached.

Berengar looked over his shoulder. "Is all the secrecy really necessary?"

"It might have been avoided, but for your deeds at St. Brigid's."

Berengar bared his teeth. "Skinner Kane and his men tortured and killed dozens of innocents. He deserved worse."

"There it is. That infamous temper." Flaherty held up a hand before Berengar could speak. "I went through a great deal of trouble to arrange for your visit here today, and I would prefer to avoid an argument. Although I voted for it for appearances' sake, I was against your excommunication. Not because of any fondness for you, mind you, but because of the political headache it has caused with Tara. Unfortunately, your actions forced Bishop McLoughlin's hand."

"What's your point?" In retrospect, ignoring the right of sanctuary to cut down a defenseless man at a sacred altar wasn't one of his best decisions, even if Kane did have it coming.

Flaherty stared hard at him. "You have a rather direct manner, Warden Berengar. Bishop McLoughlin—may the Lord rest his soul—is dead. His successor may see your actions differently."

Berengar studied Flaherty carefully. "And you aim to be that successor."

"At the moment, there are two candidates—Father Valmont and myself. Valmont cannot be made bishop. Since his arrival, he has quickly amassed power by manipulating those around him with his words. If he did not murder Bishop McLoughlin himself, one of his pawns did. Look at what he has done to King Lucien. You saw what the boy has become. I fear for the realm if it is allowed to continue."

"I fail to see what part I will play in all this."

"I want your word you will stay out of Leinster when

the ceremony is finished. Do this, and as bishop, I would see your excommunication lifted." Flaherty's stone face grew impassioned. "These are dark times. Much has changed, and there is more change yet to come. The peace is more fragile than you know. The people need a shepherd to guard against their worst instincts."

Berengar scoffed. "Like you did in the purges? You lot stood by while the crowds slaughtered countless innocents. I haven't forgotten."

Flaherty's voice quieted, and his expression betrayed remorse. "You're right. It is our secret shame, one that can never be put right. I could tell you the fanatics among the Acolytes of the True Faith were responsible, but there are those among us who support their aims." He turned away, approached the altar, and stared up at the cross. "The girl you travel with is a magician, is she not?"

Was that a threat? Berengar felt anger rise within him. "What of it?"

Flaherty turned back to him without a hint of malice. "I do not hate magicians and nonhumans, Warden Berengar. Nor do I believe all magic is evil. I grew up hearing the tales of Thane Ramsay. I know magicians are capable of good, but magic is simply too dangerous to be allowed to flourish. It is the church's job to bring light into a dark world. Science and progress must replace the old ways, so the day will come when magic is no longer needed and forgotten altogether."

The sentiment echoed Azzy's words inside the ruins of the Institute, and Berengar remembered what became of the Oakseers' Grotto. The world was changing. Azeroth's war had broken something that could never be mended. Were it not for Morwen, he might have agreed with Flaherty about magic, but something about the priest's words nonetheless left him with a melancholy feeling.

"I've no desire to remain here any longer than necessary. I've no love for Leinster, and it certainly has none for
me. Now, if you don't mind, I didn't come here to discuss
your ambitions."

Flaherty appeared satisfied they had reached an
accord. "We are in agreement. Let us discuss security
measures for the ceremony."

Outside, the bells fell silent. Berengar spent the
following hours going over security details with the cathedral's guards. Despite his protests, both the crown and the
church insisted on permitting an audience inside the sanctuary in accordance with tradition. However, admittance
to the cathedral would be strictly monitored and limited to
those of title and rank. As previously agreed, the city watch
would bolster security for the ceremony, and King Lucien's
elite guard would be on hand to protect the king.

Berengar left nothing to chance. He combed every inch
of the cathedral looking for gaps in security and drilled the
guards repeatedly to assure their preparedness. Evening
approached by the time he was satisfied all the necessary
precautions were in place. Flaherty excused himself to
attend the conclave where the new bishop would be
chosen, and Berengar departed as quietly as he arrived. It
was almost time to meet Azzy. With the information he
had gleaned from Jareth, they could do the job for Elias
and Morwen would get her staff.

Morwen was waiting for him at the Coin and Crown.

"Hope you're done sleeping. We've got work to do." He
whistled to Faolán and began the walk to the rendezvous
point.

Morwen stifled a yawn and flushed, clearly embarrassed at having slept so late. Berengar filled her in on the
day's events, including his conversation with Jareth.
Morwen listened with interest but remained unusually

quiet. Berengar wondered if she was still sore over the cross words they'd exchanged the night before.

They reached their destination just before dark and waited for their companion to show.

"Ready to get started?" Azzy emerged from the shadows without making a sound.

Startled by her sudden appearance, Morwen jumped. "How did you do that?"

"Do what?" Azzy asked after she finished laughing.

Morwen's gaze narrowed in her direction. "Sneak up on me." As a magician, Morwen was uniquely aware of her surroundings. More often than not, she was the one who could move about unseen.

Azzy flashed a mischievous grin. "I'm a thief, remember? I wouldn't be very good at my job if I couldn't come and go without being seen."

Morwen remained skeptical.

Azzy turned to Berengar. "I received your message. According to my contacts, the fairy dust is stored in a warehouse by the docks."

"And Elazar?" Raiding the warehouse was only the first step. It would only interrupt the distribution channel of fairy dust temporarily. To put the supplier out of business, they needed to put a stop to the production of the dust, which meant dealing with the source.

"He spends his days in a highly secure villa watched by private guards. I could manage breaking in easily enough, but getting him back out again…I have a much simpler plan in mind."

"Go on."

"Every week, Elazar and his guards leave the villa to drop off another load of fairy dust at the docks." Azzy grinned. "We're in luck. The delivery is tonight."

"Good work. I hope you're both well rested. We've a long night ahead."

They settled on a plan and made their way to the docks under cover of darkness. The area was mostly quiet, save for creaking shipping vessels on the water. Azzy held a finger to her lips, and they took cover behind a stack of crates. From the outside, the warehouse Azzy had discovered appeared abandoned. No light came from within, and the building's exterior was splintered and faded.

"Look." Azzy pointed to the entrance, where two guards stood watch. Their attire suggested they were private guards or soldiers hiring themselves out for supplemental income.

Azzy raised her hood, emerged from cover, and silently stole around to the other side to pick the back door's lock. When she finished, she returned to Berengar and Morwen with the guards none the wiser.

Then they waited. After a few hours, Berengar heard the sound of wheels. Lanterns glowed in the distance, and a wagon approached the warehouse. The guards unlocked and opened the front entrance, and the wagon rolled inside, but not before Berengar caught a glimpse of a bearded man flanked by guards on either side.

"Remember the plan," Azzy said once the guards stationed outside the entrance shut the doors. She stepped out from behind the crates and started toward the warehouse, humming a cheerful tune.

"Stop right there. No trespassers allowed." The guard raised his torch for a better look.

Azzy waved at the guards and continued undaunted. "Evening. 'Tis a fine night for a stroll, don't you think?"

"Stop. I mean it." The guard made a show of touching the hilt of his blade.

Azzy did as he said. She faced the guards, standing an

arm's length away, and Berengar was struck by the contrast between her petite stature and the guards' stocky frames.

With the guards distracted, Berengar and Morwen slowly edged toward the rear entrance. Voices came from inside the warehouse.

Azzy's gaze moved to the coin pouch at the guard's side. "So many coins. That must be an awful weight to carry. Allow me to relieve you of it."

The guards looked at each other, stunned by her beauty or confused by her choice of words. Berengar blinked, and a knife appeared in Azzy's hand. She moved before either could react. The knife flashed in the moonlight, and coins spilled from the cut pouch and into the thief's purse without one landing on the dock.

"You little…" When the guard reached for her, Azzy easily evaded his grasp and kicked his backside, knocking him over. When she severed the other guard's belt to obtain his coin pouch, his pants fell to his boots, and he tripped and landed beside his companion.

Azzy doubled over laughing. "A profitable night. Thank you, gentlemen, for your patronage." With that, she bowed gracefully and sped into the night.

"What are you waiting for?" asked the guard clutching his pants. "After her!" They took off in pursuit, leaving the entrance unattended.

"It worked," Morwen said. "I hope she knows what she's doing."

"It would've been easier to kill them. Now come on."

Morwen shot him a dark look, and they rounded the warehouse before the guards inside emerged through the front entrance to investigate the commotion. Berengar eased the door open and reached for his axe. A floorboard creaked under his weight.

"Who's there?" demanded a bearded man with a

lantern.

Berengar bashed the man's skull with the flat of his axe, and his victim sank to the ground, unconscious. He quietly advanced on the guards lingering outside and subdued one from behind. Faolán brought another low, and a kick from Berengar put him out like a light.

Morwen pried open a lid and tossed the contents of a vial containing a dark powder at the remaining guard, who instantly crumpled to the ground. "Sleeping powder. My way's easier."

"Help me with the bodies." They dragged the guards inside and closed the front entrance behind them. They would be gone long before the men regained consciousness. Berengar put a bag over the bearded man's head and bound his hands before lifting him onto the wagon.

Several sacks were stacked against the wall. Morwen inspected one, which was full of a powder that shimmered in the faint moonlight. "This is it."

"Help me move these sacks before the others return." Together they loaded the fairy dust onto the back of the wagon. Berengar hauled two at a time while Morwen struggled to lift even one.

"Don't forget Azzy." She grunted and heaved a sack onto the wagon. "We'll have to go back for her."

Azzy stepped out of the darkness. "That's not necessary."

Morwen lost her footing and landed on her backside with a sack in her lap. "Stop doing that!"

Azzy raised a hand to her mouth and suppressed a chuckle. "I gave the guards the slip and came back to see how the two of you were faring. It looks like you handled this lot easily enough."

After loading the last sack, Berengar climbed onto the wagon and—after Morwen calmed the horse—took the reins.

"Let's go before they return." When the wagon rolled out of the warehouse, Faolán jumped onto the back and curled up at Morwen's feet. It wasn't long before they were away from the docks, again headed toward the Scholars' District.

Morwen's eyes lingered on the sacks of fairy dust. "I expected we might find enough dust inside to fill one of these sacks, but this? Fairy dust has been incredibly rare since the fairies abandoned these lands." She gestured to the stacks. "Where did this come from?"

Berengar shrugged. "We'll have to ask the dealer."

Morwen was quiet for a moment. "Perhaps a fairy gave it to him."

Berengar shook his head. "I told you—all the fairies are gone. Those who weren't killed by monster hunters fled these lands years ago." Morwen was probably thinking of the wanted poster they saw in the grand square, but he doubted the creature depicted even existed. Many of the monsters on the posters were simply figments of frightened villagers' imaginations.

Morwen sat back and folded her arms across her chest. "It's a shame. I would've liked to see one once. It's said their voices were so lovely they could ensnare men's minds or even influence nature itself."

"Aye." Azzy peered into the night with a wistful look. "None were more graceful or beautiful to behold. The splendor of the fairy halls surpassed anything human minds can fathom." She stopped, as if suddenly aware of Morwen's gaze. "According to the stories, at least."

"They were also dangerous, short-tempered, and cruel," Berengar muttered. "They played nasty tricks for sport and replaced human children with changelings—and those were the decent ones."

Azzy's expression soured. "Harmless amusement. I

expect if you lived for hundreds of years, you'd bore easily too."

When they reached the Scholars' District, Berengar parked the wagon in the alley with the secret entrance and grabbed the unconscious prisoner while Morwen and Azzy opened the hidden door. A lit torch waited for them at the bottom of the stairs. Together they made their way down the underground corridor.

Elias waited for them on the other side of the trapdoor. "Well? How did it go?"

"See for yourself." Berengar dropped the prisoner's body at his feet.

Unlike before, lanterns and candles illuminated the Institute's halls. The light revealed the full extent of the wreckage within. Dust clung to every surface, and cobwebs hung about the chamber.

"What of the fairy dust?"

"Outside in the back of a wagon."

Elias knelt beside the bearded man and removed the bag from his head. "It's him. Just as I thought. You've done well."

"Why did you want him?" Morwen asked. "What's he to you?"

"It's obvious." Berengar's eye remained fixed on Elias. "Jareth said there were two sources of fairy dust in the city. You're the other, aren't you? That's why you wanted his business shut down. He's your competition."

"Aye, but that's only half the truth." Elias delved into his robes to retrieve smelling salts, which he held to the bearded man's nose. "Wake up."

At the sound of Elias' voice, Elazar's eyes flashed open, and he sat up with a start. "I should've known." He tugged to no avail at the ropes binding his arms. "It's come to this, has it? You've sent mercenaries after me—your own brother?"

Morwen's brow arched in surprise. "Brother?"

It made sense. Berengar gathered both were alchemists trained at the Institute. Each would have had the knowledge necessary to refine fairy dust. With no legitimate way to make an income after the purges, the pair had turned to the black market to survive. Elias sought safety behind the Institute's walls while Elazar did the same behind those of his villa. Elias likely obtained his supply from the Institute's existing stores, but that still left the question of where Elazar's supply came from. Even from Berengar's limited understanding, no alchemist—no matter how talented— was capable of manufacturing raw fairy dust, which originated in the fairy realm.

Elias stared down at Elazar with contempt. "He was my brother once. Before his cowardice cost me the love of my life."

Rage came over Elazar's face. "I loved her too, same as you. I looked for her everywhere, but she was already gone! You blame me for her loss, but it was you who failed to make it here in time."

Elias crossed his arms. "The riots held me back, as you well know. By the time I arrived, it was already too late. Everyone was gone, and Iona with them."

At the mention of Iona, Berengar and Morwen exchanged glances. "Wait. What's that about Iona?"

The brothers looked at him, their animosity temporarily forgotten.

"A herbalist at the Institute," Elazar volunteered. "We searched for her in the purge's aftermath, but it was no use. She died a long time ago."

Berengar shook his head. "You're wrong. Iona was among those I led from the city."

"You remember her?" Elias looked skeptical.

"I didn't. Not until I ran into her in Munster a few months back. She's set up shop at Knockaney as a healer."

Elias regarded him with utter astonishment. "Iona's alive?"

"Aye," Morwen said. "I can vouch for that. She did a fine job mending my broken leg—for a herbalist, anyway."

Elias took a step back, clearly overcome with emotion, and his eyes fell on his brother. "All these years I spent hating you—all for nothing. Can you ever forgive me, Elazar?"

"I am as guilty as you, brother. I ask your pardon for all that has passed between us."

"You have it." Elias cut the ropes binding Elazar, and the two shared a tight embrace. "I have missed you, brother. You don't know how lonely it's been."

Morwen cleared her throat to get their attention. "Do you think we're just supposed to overlook the fact you've been filling this city with fairy dust? Whatever you've suffered, it doesn't excuse what you've done. People have died. You should both be rotting in a dungeon."

"We'll go away," Elias promised. "We'll leave and go in search of Iona. You have my word. Besides, Dún Aulin is far too dangerous for us."

"Ahem." Azzy's voice interrupted the tearful reunion. "I believe the magician was promised a reward?"

Elias wiped his eyes with his sleeve. "And you shall have it. Come." He led them to the vast atrium with the winding staircases before stopping at an empty wall to raise his lantern. The lantern glowed with a strange green light that reflected off the surface of an invisible seal. Elias pricked his thumb with a knife and pressed the blood against the seal. A faint rumbling sound emanated from the other side as a section of wall descended to reveal a hidden chamber.

"It was here the whole time." Berengar shook his head. "Blasted magicians."

"Alchemists," Morwen corrected.

Candles and torches burst into green flame when Elias crossed the threshold. Morwen and the others filed in after him. Potions, ornaments, scrolls, and all manner of mystical artifacts were packed into the chamber's narrow confines.

Morwen looked on in awe. "The last remnant of the Institute's wealth of knowledge."

"Aye," Elias said. "I saved what I could, but the rioters left little behind. You should have seen it in its day. There was nothing like it in all the land."

Berengar advanced carefully so as not to touch anything by accident. The chamber's mysterious contents held no allure for him. His fondness for Morwen didn't erase his discomfort around magic. Strange amulets and rings—likely bearing all manner of dangerous enchantments—glimmered in the green light.

Morwen stopped dead in her tracks, forcing Berengar to come to a halt to avoid a collision. He followed her gaze to the end of the chamber, where an enormous tree covered the rear wall. Its roots ran into cracks in the stone floor, and its ancient branches spread across the ceiling. The leaves glowed and pulsed with the same green light that filled the chamber as the tree hummed with light. A large, solitary eye in its trunk was closed.

Azzy bit her lip and took a step back, remaining outside the wave of illumination. She instead began searching through the chamber's many scattered relics in accordance with their agreement.

Morwen choked up with emotion. "An elder tree."

"Aye. The last of its kind in the kingdom. I have been its guardian these last years." Elias looked away, distant. "It was the least I could do in remembrance of my fallen companions." He raised his lantern but kept his distance. "Go on. You know what to do. You must prove yourself worthy."

Morwen hesitated.

"What is it?" Berengar asked.

"Nothing. It's just…" She trailed off while continuing to stare at the tree. "This is a hazel tree. My last staff was made of ash."

"So?"

"Ash is a scholar's wood. Hazel is used for bringing change. It's favored by mages." Her voice was full of doubt.

When she was a girl, Morwen had tried to become a mage—a warrior magician—but failed the tests for acceptance into the order. The experience had a deep impact on her, and every now and again Berengar saw that beneath the confidence of youth she still feared she would never quite measure up.

"What are you waiting for? You've spent the last month complaining about not having a bloody staff, and now you're just going to stand there? Get on up there."

Morwen nodded to herself and climbed a small staircase to approach the tree. She knelt before the tree, bowed her head reverently, and held out her hand. "Great tree, I —Morwen of Cashel—humbly beseech you to lend me your strength so that I may spread good and foster peace throughout this land." She stared up at the tree expectantly. When the tree's eye remained shut, she looked to Elias for guidance.

"The tree is very old. It has been asleep for a long time, and it may not soon wake. If it speaks to you, it may show you visions of events yet to come."

Azzy's voice broke the silence. "It's not here!" No longer remotely amused, she knocked aside charms, necklaces, and pendants in her anger. "I don't understand. There should have *been* one here…"

"What's it matter?" Berengar asked. "I'm sure any of these relics would fetch you a handsome price."

Azzy regarded him with a wrathful expression that hinted at an explosive temper usually kept on a leash.

Morwen stiffened suddenly.

"What?" Berengar knew that look. It meant trouble.

"Danger."

Berengar reached for his axe. "How close?"

"Close." Morwen cast a glance back at the tree and reluctantly hurried to join them.

Shadows moved above the atrium, and hisses sounded in the dark. Goblins crawled along the ceiling like spiders and spread across the walls as they descended.

"I thought no one could get in here." Berengar thought again of the secret entrance.

Elias held his crossbow at the ready. "They must have scaled the walls and entered from the tower."

Berengar's grip tightened around his axe as the goblins moved to surround them. His companions gathered around him with their backs to the hidden chamber. Twin knives appeared in Azzy's dexterous hands, and it was clear from her expression she had no love for goblins.

After encircling them, the goblins bared their fangs and rattled their weapons but made no move to attack.

Teelah, the goblins' helmeted leader, stepped forward to face Morwen. "We have no quarrel with you, magician. Give us the stone and you may leave."

"I won't abandon my friends. And I don't have the stone. It was stolen."

"We will see." Teelah pointed a club in Berengar's direction. "This one belongs to us. He has much to answer for."

Berengar raised his axe, prompting a chorus of menacing hisses from the goblins. "Come get me."

"Fool. You're outnumbered three to one."

Berengar grinned. Having spent the last few days hunting for answers with little to show for it but more questions, he finally had a chance to cut loose and use his axe. When a goblin lunged forward, sword raised, Berengar leapt to meet it, and the fight began.

A tremor spread through the atrium, and dust poured from the ceiling.

"Look!" Morwen exclaimed. "The tree!"

The ash tree's eye had opened, and its pulsing lights grew even brighter. Morwen turned and fled into the chamber.

"After her!" Teelah ordered.

Berengar batted his foe aside with ease using his axe's handle and moved on to the nearest goblin. He swung his axe in broad sweeps to hold the creatures back while Elias used his crossbow to distract the archers. Another tremor rattled the hall, and when Berengar looked back, he saw Morwen kneeling once more before the tree, her hand on its trunk.

Teelah sprang forward and kicked him in the face. Berengar was fast, but the goblin was faster, and only his armor protected him from fangs and sharp nails. Azzy, fighting at his side, moved with speed and precision, delivering rapid strikes in concert with his movements. Teelah was thrown off balance, and Berengar seized the chance to strike the goblin's helmet with the butt of his axe. The helmet came flying off, revealing the face hidden underneath. To his surprise, he found himself looking at a female goblin.

"You're a woman," Berengar said, unable to hide his astonishment. *A girl, even.* Although Berengar had no way of reckoning goblin ages, Teelah appeared significantly younger than those that followed her.

Teelah's black hair was worn long in a single braid. She brushed green blood from her lip, sniffed at the air, and her gaze narrowed at Azzy. "You. You're not like the others. You're a…"

Before she could finish, a strong gust of wind ripped through the chamber. Morwen stood at the hidden chamber's entrance with a new staff in one hand and a glowing green rune from her satchel in the other. The hazel wood branch was longer and sturdier-looking than her previous staff. Its surface was still rough and did not yet bear the symbols or charms carved into magicians' staffs, or slots for runes at the staff's head.

Teelah and the other goblins froze, and it was clear they regarded magic with fear and respect. Distant barking broke the tense standoff that ensued, and Faolán—having somehow found her way inside—came bounding up the stairs. Footsteps and raised voices sounded nearby.

"We're not alone," Morwen said.

Berengar gritted his teeth. *What now?*

Men in armor swarmed into the atrium. All wore the insignia of the Acolytes of the True Faith. The monster hunters outnumbered Berengar's companions and the goblins alike. Berengar recognized a few faces among them, including the three who threatened him upon his arrival in Kilcullen. He thought again of the man he caught spying on them the day before. *They must have followed us to the secret door and forced their way inside.*

The mercenary ranks parted for a man in steel armor and a black cloak. The man's eyes glowed with hate in the torchlight. When he opened his mouth to speak, a loud, baritone voice filled the atrium. "Well, lads, look what we have here. Heretics, inhuman vermin, a witch, a thief, and a greater evil than the lot of them." His gaze lingered on Berengar. "It's been a long time, Warden Berengar."

"Winslow," Berengar said.

The Acolytes' leader turned back to his men. "This man cut down your brothers in cold blood and gutted my son like a dog."

"Your son had it coming. I'm glad I took my time with him."

The corners of Winslow's mouth twitched, but he remained calm. "I've been waiting for this for a long time." He gestured to his followers. "Time to do the Lord's work, lads. Exterminate the vermin and the others, but leave the warden for me."

Morwen cast a sideways glance at Teelah. "Given the circumstances, I say we put our differences aside for the moment and work together."

The goblin looked less than pleased at the prospect of allying herself with Berengar. "Agreed."

Berengar and Azzy charged the enemy. Teelah and the goblins rallied to them as Winslow's soldiers converged on them. Berengar's axe connected with an attacker's sword arm and took the limb off halfway up the forearm. He pushed the swordsman out of his way and cut down the next man in his path. Faolán outpaced him and leapt on an attacker before the man could get his sword up. She tore out the monster hunter's throat to silence his cries.

Elias fired at advancing foes with his crossbow while Morwen deflected enemy arrows with defensive wards. Berengar quickly lost track of Azzy, who seemed to be everywhere at once. The thief darted from one spot to another, using her knives to devastating effect.

Chaos broke out across the atrium as the fighting continued in disordered pockets. Arrows from goblin and human archers alike sailed in either direction. Bodies littered the ground, and flames from fallen torches began to spread. Although the Acolytes' losses were greater, they had advantage enough in numbers to bear it. For every man Berengar struck down, two more seemed to take his place. He didn't care. The warden gave himself over to his rage and let the fury of battle take hold. He chopped through an enemy's neck with his axe and fought his way closer to Winslow, who waited ahead, longsword in hand.

"Stop!" Elias shouted among the cries of battle. "If the flames reach the alchemy laboratory…"

Before he could finish his warning, there was a deafening roar, and an explosion tore through the upper levels, sending the tower crashing down from above.

CHAPTER EIGHT

BLOOD TRICKLED DOWN HIS FOREHEAD. The world slid in and out of focus. A voice called to him above the chaos, but the ringing in his ears was too loud for him to make out the words. Berengar coughed, only vaguely aware of his surroundings. The air was thick with smoke. He was lying on the stone floor in dust and debris. Apart from that, the last few moments were a haze.

"Berengar, wake up!"

Fingers grazed his forehead, and a foreign consciousness brushed against his own. Berengar woke with a start and instinctively lunged for the unseen threat, only to find himself gazing upon a familiar face.

"Morwen?" Faolán sat at her side. Berengar moaned and rolled over onto his side. His entire body hurt.

Morwen withdrew her touch. "You have to get up—now." She was worried.

When he coughed again, he tasted blood. Morwen said something in a foreign tongue and reached toward him again, but Berengar brushed her away. "I'm fine." The words came out jumbled. He stumbled to his feet and leaned against her for support. He thought she might buckle under his weight, but she proved stronger than he expected.

His vision sharpened to reveal a scene plucked from a nightmare. The Institute was ablaze. Bodies were scattered across the atrium, barely visible in the dense smoke. Men and goblins alike were crushed under fallen debris or consumed by the flames. Most of those who survived attempted to flee while a precious few continued fighting.

Berengar spotted his axe among the ruins and stooped to retrieve it. A shout echoed above the roar of the flames as a monster hunter emerged from the smoke and swung his sword at him. Berengar's reflexes were slow, and he barely brought the axe up in time to bear the brunt of the blow. He disemboweled the man on the spot.

"Winslow!" The ground shifted under his feet as more rubble fell from above.

"Berengar, we have to go! This place could come down on our heads at any moment."

He wanted to continue his search for the Acolytes' leader, but Faolán barked to get his attention, and he hobbled toward Morwen instead. "Where are the others?"

"Azzy was behind me a moment ago. I don't know what happened to Elias or Elazar." Her tone indicated she feared the worst.

New openings to the outside formed as the Institute continued falling apart. Moonlight stole in through fallen sections of wall. A horn reverberated outside, where the city watch, drawn by the mayhem, approached in full force.

Blast it. The last thing he needed was for his involvement with the goblins and the Acolytes to be made known. Whatever his differences with Teelah or Winslow, they would have to wait.

At that moment, a host of monster hunters headed their way, barring the path forward. Morwen used her staff and the purple rune to manipulate the smoke to shield them from the hunters' sight. Berengar lowered his axe. There were too many to fight in his disoriented state. Besides, the city watch would be there soon.

"Let's go." There was still time to make it out through the underground corridor. With any luck, they could escape and return to the Coin and Crown unseen.

Morwen caught sight of the hidden chamber, all but buried under fallen stones, and ground to a halt. "The elder tree!" Fire spread toward the elder tree, which produced a painful, shrieking cry as its glowing leaves shriveled to ash in the midst of the inferno. "We can't just leave it."

Berengar grabbed her by the shoulders. "It's too late. There's nothing we can do."

Morwen clutched her staff a little tighter and cast a final, remorseful glance back at the chamber. Like the tree, the scrolls and enchanted items were quickly consumed by the flames. The explosion had finished the rioters' work. Soon, nothing would remain of the Institute's vast stores of knowledge.

Together they returned to the passage that led to the trapdoor. Berengar killed two monster hunters they met along the way. Even with Faolán's help, the effort cost more energy than he had to spare, and it was all he could do to keep going.

Exhausted, he didn't bother closing the trapdoor behind him before starting down the ladder. Morwen, whose senses were more attuned than those of an ordinary human, led him through the darkness rather than waste time fishing for her lightstone. Each step seemed harder than the last. He put a hand against the wall to steady himself and fought to remain conscious.

"Stay with me, Berengar. We're almost there."

Moonlight shone from the entrance, and the world again started to blur.

H e woke in his room at the Coin and Crown with no memory of how he got there.

Berengar coughed and sat up in bed. He had a splitting headache, but other than that, everything seemed to be in working order. Faolán watched from the foot of the bed with a look of relief. Morwen was absent from the room. Most likely she was either waiting for him below or still asleep herself.

Natural light seeped in through the curtains. *How long was I out?* Berengar rose from his bed, lumbered to the window, and threw back the curtains. He winced, sensitive to the bright light. It was probably early in the afternoon. He couldn't remember the last time he'd slept so late. Then again, considering the night they'd had, it wasn't surprising.

His thoughts were clear—apart from the headache— but everything that happened after their escape from the Institute was a haze. He put on his cloak and leather armor and retrieved his weapons before leaving the room behind. As expected, Morwen waited below.

"Good morning," she said with cheer after affection-ately greeting Faolán. "Or afternoon, I suppose. I've been working at charms and enchantments for my new staff. I fear it'll take *ages* to finish, though it's still a vast improve-ment over trying to work magic without one." She held a spell book in her hands, and her staff lay across the table beside the purple runestone.

Berengar grunted and took the seat across from her. "Why on earth do you have that thing out in plain sight?"

"Oh, this?" Morwen laid a hand on the staff and glanced over her shoulder. "Anyone who looks at it will see an ordinary walking stick."

"Then why am I able to see it?"

"You already know its true nature. The trick is to charm the staff itself, rather than anyone who might happen to see it—which would be an impossible task for a magician, I might add, even with a rune of illusion. Quite a useful spell, wouldn't you agree?"

Berengar, massaging his temples in a futile effort to relieve his throbbing headache, found her abundance of enthusiasm off-putting. "All the same, you should take more care. You saw what those monster hunters wanted to do to you."

Morwen returned the runestone and her spell book to her satchel. "Are you feeling all right?"

Berengar took a tankard from a barmaid and lifted it to his lips. "It feels like I've got goblin drums banging around in my head."

"I'm not surprised. You're lucky you didn't get hurt worse. Not many people have a tower fall on them and live to tell the tale."

"I'm hard to kill. I don't suppose you have something for this, do you?" Berengar wasn't particularly fond of putting strange substances into his body, but at the moment he would do just about anything to quell his headache. "You know—that potion of yours that tastes like cherries?"

Morwen squealed with delight. "You remember! I'm touched. I think I have the elixir in question, but like you said, it's probably too dangerous to risk drawing attention."

"Morwen, please."

"Well, since you asked so nicely…" Morwen fished

153

around in her satchel until she found a vial filled with a red liquid. She pried the top loose and casually looked around the room before pouring a portion into Berengar's tankard. "Drink up. It should help."

He did as she instructed, and within moments the throbbing pain subsided. Berengar let out a relieved sigh and allowed himself to relax. "Thanks."

"You're welcome—for that, and for getting you back here in one piece. You could hardly stand by the time we made it to the secret entrance. On top of that, the wagon was gone when we got there. I'll give you three guesses who took it."

"Azzy."

"She may not have found whatever it was she was looking for back at the Institute, but the fairy dust is worth plenty. Not that I think she'll sell it, mind you. She seemed aware of its danger."

"She's a thief," Berengar reminded her. "Gold is the only thing they care about. Still, she had her uses, and she was handy in a fight. Not so bad as far as thieves go, all in all."

"There was something about her I never could quite put my finger on, but I suppose we'll never know now. Anyway, I worked a little magic and found us a horse cart that brought us here with the city watch none the wiser. I patched you up before getting some much-needed sleep myself. I don't think your forehead will scar, by the way."

Berengar doubted any additional scarring would make much of a difference. "I owe you." He hesitated. "About the other night…"

Morwen waved a hand in the air. "I've already forgotten it. We both said things we regret. You can be a real grouch sometimes, but it's just your way. I've learned to live with it." Her expression brightened. "And now that I have a new staff, it'll make our search for the thunder rune much easier."

"Aye. Once the ceremony is out of the way, we can leave Dún Aulin and resume our hunt." The two clanked their cups together, and Berengar permitted himself a rare smile. Things were finally looking their way. "Speaking of your staff, did the tree show you anything when it spoke to you?"

"It did." Morwen shuddered and averted her gaze. "It's probably nothing."

"It's not nothing if it has you looking like you've seen a ghost. What did it show you?"

She stared off, as if recalling the details of a troubling dream. "I saw a man surrounded by a great henge, surrounded by stones and skulls. He was dressed in green robes and wore the skull of an elk over his face."

"The man with the face of a monster," Berengar muttered.

"What?"

"It's something Horst said to me. Go on."

Morwen shuddered. "He looked right at me. It felt as if he was watching us. There were monsters nearby, but I couldn't see them. And in the center of the henge, there was a towering tree, like the elder tree—but it was withered and diseased. Blood poured from its bark, and skeletons were trapped within its vines…" She stopped. "That's all I can remember. It was horrible."

"Did the tree say anything else?"

"Nothing of importance." She was clearly holding something else back.

Berengar shrugged and took another drink of his tankard. "Go ahead—keep your secrets. You blasted magicians are all the same."

Morwen grinned. "I wasn't aware you knew any other

magicians." She caught sight of something among her things, and her smile faltered.

"What is it?"

Morwen held up a small piece of rolled-up parchment that bore a black seal. "This wasn't here a moment ago."

"What does it say?"

Morwen broke the seal, and her eyes widened in alarm as she read the letter's contents before passing it to him.

Warden of Fál,

The hour of reckoning is upon you. With the contract fulfilled, you are no longer protected. Our eyes are everywhere, and our hands are a thousand knives. You will never leave this city alive.

The letter was unsigned, but Berengar knew its sender all the same. "Reyna. It seems our business with the Brotherhood isn't finished after all." He crumpled the letter and cast it aside. "The sooner we're out of the city, the better."

"You two certainly seem in good spirits." Friar Godfrey approached with a flagon in his good hand. "What's the occasion?"

"Berengar's been ready to leave since we got here," Morwen replied good-naturedly.

Godfrey slapped his knee with his wooden hand and smiled at her. "You should've seen him at Castle Blackthorn. Prowling around like a restless wolf, waiting to get back to the road."

Berengar was in such a good mood that for once he didn't mind being teased. "What would the two of you do for sport without me?"

Godfrey laughed. "I'm not long for the city myself. With Bishop McLoughlin's funeral over with, I'll stay for the ceremony and then head west to look into the matter we discussed yesterday."

A brief silence fell over the hall as a number of guards filed inside the Coin and Crown. Berengar watched the guards question the bartenders and barmaids for a prolonged interval before departing, and the noise from the crowd promptly resumed.

"I wonder what they wanted," Morwen said.

Godfrey leaned forward in his chair. "Haven't you heard? Someone brought down the ruins of the Institute last night. Some are even calling it divine judgment. The city watch arrived in time to put out the flames but too late to catch the perpetrators."

Berengar and Morwen exchanged glances.

"With the ceremony close at hand, the business has the whole city on edge." Godfrey shook his head. "Word is the Acolytes were involved, and some witnesses claim to have spotted goblins in the area. Can you believe it—goblins, here in Dún Aulin!" He stopped suddenly, as if a new thought had occurred to him. "Say, weren't the two of you tracking a band of goblins here? I don't suppose…" His eyes widened in realization.

"Do you know what happened to Winslow?"

Godfrey shrugged. "Escaped, most likely. The city watch is out in force looking for him, but even if they find him, he'll most likely end up back on the street again. I hear he has powerful friends."

Morwen glanced at Berengar with an amused expression. "Everyone here seems to have powerful friends —except us."

"Friends are overrated." Berengar put a hand on the hilt of his blade. "I've got all I need right here."

"In happier news, Vicar Flaherty emerged victorious from the conclave, even if his margin over Father Valmont was razor thin. Flaherty's one of the old guard, and he plays politics like the rest of them, but he's not a bad sort overall as far as I'm concerned."

Given his disinterest in church politics, Berengar could

hardly have cared less. One was just as bad as the other as far as he was concerned. Still, the prospect that Flaherty might revoke his excommunication was reason enough to give thanks.

"I'll drink to that."

There was plenty of time for a respite before the ceremony. They had earned it.

Things were finally going their way.

Berengar had never seen so many people gathered in one place. The numbers made the crowds that had gathered to witness the bishop's funeral look almost small in comparison. The grand square was packed full, and the swarming masses occupying the streets brought traffic across the city to a complete halt.

The full moon cast a bright glow over Dún Aulin. Torches and lanterns on every corner filled the City of Thieves with light. Guards patrolled the crowds in numbers approaching a small army. Everywhere people craned their necks for a better look at the cathedral. Some conversed in excitement while others looked on in fear. Everyone, from the meanest beggar to the wealthiest lord, had come in hopes of catching a glimpse of the cursed blade.

The cathedral, a beacon of light in the dark, shone brighter than all. But for the path cleared by the guards for the king's arrival, the cathedral was completely surrounded on all sides. Berengar scanned the endless sea of faces as he made his way inside.

Morwen followed at his side. "You're tense—even for you."

Berengar didn't reply. He had witnessed firsthand the damage wrought by the sword. He hadn't forgotten the black contract acquired by a member of the Brotherhood of Thieves. Even with the added security measures, it remained possible someone might make an attempt to steal the blade—either for its worth or its power. He wouldn't rest easy until the ceremony was over and the shard was buried away for the next thirteen years.

"At least I don't have to wear a ridiculous dress like I did for Queen Alannah's coronation." Morwen, far more comfortable in magician's robes or traveler's garb, hated dressing like the ladies at court.

Berengar privately agreed about the need to dress the part. At Ravenna's insistence, he had worn an elegant doublet and tailored pants to her mother's coronation—a decision that cost him when Danes stormed the event and kidnapped the princess. For the ceremony at hand, he had left nothing to chance. He was fully armed and armored, and while his bearskin cloak would give him away, his appearance in the sanctuary might scare off any would-be thieves. By now, the whole city seemed aware of his presence in Dún Aulin anyway.

"Remember what I said. No magic, for any reason."

Morwen rolled her eyes. "Honestly, Berengar, do you really think I'm going to start conjuring tricks with my staff in the middle of the ceremony?"

He kept his tone firm. "Good. Having thousands of witnesses see you work magic is the last thing we need right now."

"Warden Berengar—a word, if you please." The voice belonged to Tavish, who stopped issuing orders to his subordinates long enough to engage them in conversation. "The monster hunters we apprehended outside the Institute told me the most interesting stories. You'll never guess whose name kept popping up."

Berengar remained stone-faced.

"Is it even worth asking what you were up to?" Tavish sighed and shook his head. "I knew you were going to be trouble, but I never dreamed you'd collapse an entire building in the heart of the Scholars' District. I tried my best to keep your involvement quiet, but I can't promise word won't spread. The Acolytes are out for your blood, and they aren't the only ones."

"You'll be happy to know we're leaving after the ceremony. I'll be out of your hair soon enough."

At that, Tavish's expression brightened considerably. "That is good news. I hope you mean it this time." He started to go but stopped short and lowered his voice. "There is one other thing you might like to know. As you asked, I put the word out about the object you've been searching for."

"And?" Berengar glanced back at Morwen, who looked at him with anticipation.

"There are reports an item of value is going up for auction on the black market tonight, not long after the ceremony. I'm not sure, but it could be what you're looking for. A fence affiliated with the Brotherhood is running the auction. His name is Edrick." Tavish nodded respectfully at Morwen and took his leave to return to his duties.

"Edrick?" Morwen frowned. "Azzy's fence? It can't be a coincidence."

Berengar thought back to their arrival in Dún Aulin and the theft of the thunder rune by the hooded thief. "It was her all along. *She* took the rune. Morwen, we've been played for fools."

"If Azzy took the stone, why would she double back and risk giving herself away just to steal our horses?" Morwen's brow furrowed. "Unless…" She trailed off, deep in thought.

"What?"

"She *wanted* us to track her down. She had us marked from the start—from the moment we entered the city. Berengar, this is bad."

Before he could reply, the bell tolled to mark the commencement of the ceremony. "We'll worry about it later. After the ceremony, we'll track down Edrick and recover the stone. Then we'll take care of Azzy."

As the chiming continued, they took their places beside Tavish and Lucien's thane just short of the altar. Berengar surveyed the host of onlookers in the heavily guarded sanctuary. Priests and government officials occupied two rows of pews on either side; the pews at the center were reserved for the nobility. Those of higher rank in the church hierarchy stood opposite Berengar and the others, while the remaining monks and friars watched from the balcony.

Murmurs built into a deafening roar as trumpets blared, announcing the king. Flanked by attendants and his elite guard, Lucien passed through the open doors to enter the sanctuary and walked down the center aisle. He stopped to wave at those in the crowd and flashed an impish grin at the clergy. Father Valmont put a hand on Lucien's shoulder and prodded him forward, and the king adopted a more somber manner while continuing his advance toward the altar. The tall Valmont appeared poised and confident.

The roar of the crowd faded to silence as Flaherty, now clad in white bishop's robes, appeared at the altar. He carried the shard wrapped in a silk cloth in his arms. The candles on the altar flickered as Flaherty unwrapped the shard. Berengar's jaw tightened at the sight of the sword fragment, and Morwen shuddered involuntarily and took a step back. Like the elder tree in the Institute, the shard seemed to radiate an inner energy. Unlike the elder tree, it was a dark, malevolent presence.

The surface of the sword, once beautiful, according to legend, was scarred and corroded—the result of Azeroth's corruption. The steel was blacker than the endless night outside the cathedral. Shadows crept along its shimmering surface. Berengar struggled to tear his gaze away from the shard, which seemed to have a mesmerizing effect. Unnoticed by the crowd, Morwen put her hand around Berengar's wrist and whispered something under her breath. The trance was broken, and he nodded a silent thanks to his companion.

When the procession stopped at the end of the aisle, Lucien stared at the shard with wonder until Valmont nudged him, and the king took a knee at the foot of the altar. Valmont and Flaherty briefly regarded each other with thinly veiled contempt before the bishop stepped forward to surrender the blade.

The moment Lucien reached for the shard, a single high-pitched note broke the quiet inside the sanctuary. Berengar winced, and Morwen, whose senses were more attuned than those of an ordinary human, covered her ears and sank to her knees from the pain. A cracking sound came from above, where the chandelier, along with each of the stained-glass windows, shattered into a thousand pieces.

Everything that followed happened in mere moments. Chaos ensued, and screams rang out as men and women panicked and attempted to flee. In the middle of the confusion, a figure in a hooded cloak stepped out from behind a pillar at the back of the sanctuary.

"There!" Tavish bellowed, and the guards leapt to attention.

The thief, whose face was obscured by a scarf, spun two sharpened knives in her hands and broke into a sprint, moving faster than anyone Berengar had ever seen. She was halfway across the room before the glass hit the ground. The thief effortlessly countered the guards' blades on her way to the altar and jumped over the fallen chandelier as Lucien's elite guards loosed their crossbows at her. She avoided or deflected every arrow as she fell through the air and landed unharmed.

"Stop her!" Tavish drew his sword and leapt to join the king's guards at the altar.

The thief darted past them, and their swords touched empty air. Her hand wrapped around the cloth with the blade. "I'll take that."

Lucien growled like an animal and clung to the sword fragment. "That's mine!"

The thief ripped the blade free of his grasp and aimed one of her knives at him.

Morwen put herself between Lucien and the thief. "Step away from the king."

"He's not the king." The thief aimed the knife at Lucien's heart.

"Boird bhriseadh!" Morwen deflected the throwing knife with a spell, and the weapon went careening across the marble floor. Fingering her remaining knife, the thief looked from Morwen to Lucien, who cowered behind the magician. More crossbows sounded before she could make another attempt, and the thief turned to flee.

"Not so fast." Berengar grabbed at her cloak, and the hood fell away, revealing long black hair and a pair of pointed ears. Even with the scarf covering her face, he knew her at once.

"Azzy?"

Her eyes narrowed in his direction, and she whirled around and delivered a double kick to his chest that knocked him flat on his back. Her cloak pulled free of his grip, and she bolted toward the entrance.

"Bar the doors!" the king's thane ordered.

The massive stone doors slowly began to close, cutting off her path of escape. The thief kept running, even as the sliver of space between the doors grew ever smaller. At the last moment, she slipped through the gap just before they slammed shut.

"Blast it! She got away." Tavish sheathed his blade and approached the guards. "Get those doors open! We can't let her escape."

"Escort King Lucien to safety." Valmont's tone was quiet but firm enough to instill order in those around him. Berengar hadn't noticed it before, but there was an almost hypnotic quality to his voice that inspired obedience in those around him. For some reason, the effect reminded him of the cursed blade. "Spread the word. Bar all the gates to the city. No one comes or goes unless I permit it."

"You heard the man," Tavish bellowed.

Murmurs sounded where the priests had gathered around a crumpled form at the altar. Berengar pushed his way to the front of the pack to get a better look.

"It's Bishop Flaherty," Morwen said. "He's dead."

Flaherty lay on his back, staring up at the ceiling with vacant eyes. Blood stained the white marble beneath him. Berengar turned over the body. One of Azzy's knives protruded from his back.

"Murdered, here in this sacred place," Valmont proclaimed. "By the thief, no doubt." The priests nodded in assent.

Berengar frowned. From her position facing the altar, it should have been impossible for Azzy to stab Flaherty from behind. Then again, everything had happened so fast he could easily have missed something amid all the confusion.

Morwen pulled him aside. "Was that who I think it was?"

Berengar stared at the entrance. Azzy was gone—slipped into the teeming masses gathered for the ceremony. "It was."

"Magic," someone said, and Berengar noticed a man whose finger was pointed at Morwen. "She used magic! I saw it."

All across the sanctuary, onlookers stared at Morwen with fear, and the magician's eyes widened in alarm. In saving the king, she had revealed her powers to everyone in attendance—which included the most powerful men and women in Leinster.

Berengar grabbed her arm. "We have to go. Now."

They rushed from the cathedral and into the night. Berengar whistled, bringing Faolán running to their side.

"That's why Azzy stole our horses." Morwen quickened her pace to match his. "*She* accepted the black contract. She had this planned from the start. She tricked us into leading her right into the king's court in the middle of preparations for the ceremony. I'll bet she had the key to the Institute all along."

Berengar swore. "And now she has half of the most dangerous weapon in Fál. We have to find her and recover the blade before she flees the city."

Morwen glanced back at the cathedral. "What about Tavish and the watch?"

Berengar shook his head. "She's a thief. She'll see them coming from a mile away. Besides, after what you did back there, it's better if we handle this on our own."

"It sounds like you already have a plan."

"Aye. Azzy won't leave the city without stopping to collect the earnings from the sale of the thunder rune. So we get to Edrick first, take back the rune, and catch Azzy when she comes for the money."

Morwen rubbed her hands together. "Good. We'll give her a taste of her own medicine."

A voice called out to him through the chaos. "Warden Berengar!" It was Godfrey. "You must depart the city at once. The priests plan to send monster hunters after Lady Morwen. They say she's a witch."

"I was only trying to help!" Morwen's lip quivered in a show of vulnerability. "You saw—I saved the king!"

Berengar laid a hand on her shoulder. "I know. You did the right thing." He squeezed her gently. "I won't let anyone hurt you. You have my word. Right now, I need you to focus. Can you do that for me?"

Morwen nodded slowly.

"We'll leave tonight, but we have to retrieve the cursed blade first. Godfrey, we'll need your help."

"What can I do?"

"Go to the Coin and Crown and ready our horses. We'll meet you there once we have the blade." Berengar slipped the signet ring from his finger and handed it to Godfrey. "If we don't make it back, send a message to the High Queen telling her what's happened." He noticed guards carrying torches marching from the cathedral. "We should go."

Godfrey pocketed the ring. "Good luck, my friends."

Berengar turned to Morwen. "Come on. We don't have another second to lose."

They left the crowds behind and hurried east, taking a shortcut through the East End District to avoid crossing the Warrens. The streets were all but deserted in the midnight hour; those who hadn't gone to witness the ceremony had long ago returned to their homes for the night. The number of lanterns and lamps dwindled the farther they advanced into the poorer neighborhoods, until at last there was only the full moon's light for illumination.

Eventually, they reached the black market under the overhead bridge. The whole area appeared abandoned. The only sound was the whispering of the wind.

Berengar unlimbered his axe. "I don't like this. It's too quiet."

Morwen shuddered. "The rune is here. I can feel it."

Faolán sniffed the air and stared into the darkness, and Berengar followed her gaze. Faint candlelight glowed in the distance. "There."

The wolfhound led them into the night. Berengar kept to the shadows and approached with stealth. He spotted Edrick pacing nervously in the moonlight as he drew near.

The boy stopped suddenly. "Azzy, is that you?" He held out the candle and peered into the darkness.

Berengar stepped into the light. "Afraid not."

Edrick gave a shout and nearly tripped over his own feet. A growl sounded when he turned to run, and a pair of amber eyes gleamed in the moonlight.

Morwen blocked Edrick's only route of escape. "I wouldn't do that if I were you."

Edrick's eyes darted around, seeking another way out. "What do you want?" Despite his apparent effort to appear confident, his voice broke. He looked a lot less like the hardened youth they encountered before and more like the frightened boy he was.

Morwen took a step forward. "He wasn't lying when he told us he didn't know where the rune was hidden. He left out that he knew *who* had it. I bet you thought you were pretty clever, didn't you? Well, it looks like your luck has run out." She held out her hand. "Hand over the rune. I suggest you do it now."

Edrick sighed and retrieved a small pouch from his stand. "Take it." He tossed the pouch to Morwen, who opened it to reveal the thunder rune, which she promptly returned to her satchel. "You got what you wanted. Now if you don't mind, I'll be on my way."

Berengar shook his head. "Not a chance. Your friend's been busy tonight, and we want a word with her."

Edrick raised an eyebrow but said nothing.

"You don't know, do you?" Morwen asked.

"Know what?"

Morwen looked over at Berengar. "She must've been planning to use the proceeds from the sale of the rune to get herself out of the city."

"What are you talking about?" Edrick failed to hide his surprise. "Azzy's leaving?"

"Do you have any idea where she might go?"

Edrick hesitated and looked away.

"I know you want to protect her, but she could be in danger. There are those who would harm her if we don't find her first."

Edrick bit his lip. "There is one place she used to talk about—the Giant's Foot, a ruin to the west near Tulach Mhór. There aren't many guards that close to the wilds, and the rural constables out that way have their hands full with other concerns." He went quiet and glanced around the deserted area. "Listen to me—we should leave. I was waiting for Azzy, but something's not right."

"What do you mean?" Morwen asked.

"There's no one else here. Just us. No one else came for the stone."

"What aren't you telling us?" Berengar grabbed Edrick and shook him. "Talk!"

A throwing knife sailed past Berengar and embedded itself in the post beside his head. "Let the boy go. Now." Azzy, armed with another throwing knife, stood opposite them in the moonlight.

Berengar tightened his hold on Edrick. "Surrender the cursed blade first."

Edrick's eyes widened at Azzy in astonishment. "You stole the cursed blade?"

Azzy's expression softened. "I have to leave the city, Ed. Leinster's not safe for me anymore. I'm sorry I didn't tell you, but it was for your own protection."

Berengar growled. "You're not going anywhere. Not until I get some answers."

Azzy returned her attention to him. "You have no idea what's happening here. As long as the cursed blade remains in the city, every man, woman, and child is in danger."

Morwen stared at her. "You tried to assassinate King Lucien. Why?"

"I told you. That was *not* the king."

"Why did you kill the bishop?"

Azzy's expression faltered. "What? I didn't…"

Berengar cut her off. "How did you do it? I've never seen anyone move like that before."

"Magic." Morwen pointed her staff at Azzy. "I thought I sensed it before at the Institute, but I wasn't sure. You have magic, don't you?"

Azzy didn't answer.

"What are you saying?" Berengar asked Morwen.

Morwen kept her gaze fixed on Azzy. "At first I thought you simply had some fairy blood. It would explain the things you said on the way to the Institute. There were a few quarter-fairies at Cashel. They were capable of the most unusual things. It wasn't until I remembered the poster in the grand square that I finally put it all together. Your name isn't really Azzy, is it?"

Azzy bared her teeth. "Put that staff away, magician."

"Let's find out," Morwen said, and Berengar noticed

she had one hand hidden behind her back. "You're not the only one who knows sleight of hand." Before Azzy could react, Morwen held out her rune of illusion. "Nocht a nádúr fíor! Let her true nature be revealed!"

The runestone hummed with inner power. Azzy held up a hand as if to shield herself from the spell, but it was too late. Overpowering purple light burst from the stone, flowed down the surface of Morwen's staff, and completely enveloped the thief. When the purple illumination faded, Berengar's jaw dropped in surprise.

The creature that occupied the spot where Azzy stood moments ago bore a striking resemblance to her former self. Her features were sharper and more angular, and the point of her ears was significantly more pronounced, but her hair, size, and clothes remained the same. Her skin, however, had acquired a deep blue hue, and her eyes were solid violet.

Morwen wore a look of triumph. "I *knew* it. You're a fairy, aren't you…Azura?"

CHAPTER NINE

Azura glared at Morwen. "Now you've done it, mortal."

"You're her. The last fairy." Berengar stared at her in disbelief.

Azura rolled her eyes. "I'm not even the only fairy in this *city*. Just because we choose not to be seen doesn't mean we don't exist."

Edrick appeared equally awestruck. "You're a *fairy*?"

Azura gave a mock bow. "Azura of the *Aos Sídhe*." She stiffened suddenly, as did Morwen, whose expression matched the look she gave just before the Institute was attacked.

"We're not alone."

Faolán barked to warn them of danger as figures darted past them in the night. Azura's blue lips pulled into a snarl, exposing teeth that ended in points. Legions of hooded figures stood revealed in the moonlight, which hinted at more concealed within the darkness.

Morwen fumbled in her satchel and held out her light-stone. "Solas!" A wave of white light illuminated the area.

Masks or scarves obscured the intruders' faces, and moonlight gleamed off daggers and knives clutched in their hands.

"Thieves." Berengar took a step back and looked around. They were everywhere. "We're surrounded." This was no mere faction. The entire Brotherhood of Thieves had assembled before them.

Azura flashed them a look of annoyance. "I hope you're happy. You two led them straight to us."

"Warden Berengar!" Reyna moved to the head of the pack. "I said you would regret crossing the Brotherhood."

Berengar, Morwen, and Azura stood back-to-back with Edrick and Faolán as a circle of thieves formed around them. A section of thieves parted to allow a new individual to emerge from their ranks.

"You've been busy, Azzy." The man wore a hooded cloak, and a wooden mask hid his face.

The thief king, Berengar realized.

"Listen," Azura started. "Whatever you've heard, I can explain—"

The thief king held up a hand to silence her. "We're well past all that. You knew the consequences when you decided to take that contract." The thieves under his command remained utterly silent while he spoke, though their knives remained at the ready. "I'm actually impressed. Only a master thief could have accomplished what you did tonight. All this time you've kept your head down, content to remain among the Brotherhood's lower ranks. It was all an act to avoid attracting attention. Or did you think I was unaware of your theft of the thunder rune?"

Azura met his gaze without flinching.

The thief king took a moment to address the others in the Brotherhood. "Let this be a lesson to the rest of you. There's a reason we refuse certain contracts. Our arrangement with the guards allows us to enjoy the spoils of our labors without fear of reprisal. Alone, we are weak, but together? Even the greatest lords in the city respect our influence. That is what you put at risk, Azzy. Your theft of the cursed blade jeopardizes all we've worked so hard to attain."

Berengar faced the thief king. "Let us have her—and the boy. We'll see that the blade is returned to the crown."

The thief king laughed. "I'm afraid it's far too late for that, Warden Berengar. You and your companion know far too much that could prove dangerous to the Brotherhood's affairs." He nodded to Reyna. "Kill them and bring me the blade."

"With pleasure."

Berengar's grip tightened around his axe. There were far too many to even consider fighting. "Morwen, you need to run. I'll hold them off as long as I can."

She held her ground. "I'm not going anywhere."

Reyna and the thieves advanced, further ensnaring them in the circle.

Azura laid a hand on Edrick's shoulder. "Get behind me, Ed." The fairy's violet eyes bore a mischievous gleam. "You two might want to stand back."

The thieves stopped short in their tracks when the moonlight fell across Azura's face. Reyna's confident expression faltered, replaced by astonishment. She glanced back at the thief king, who shrank away moments before Azura let out a deafening roar.

Sheer power flowed from Azura's mouth. In contrast to the high-pitched note she had used to shatter the cathedral chandelier, she spoke with the voice of thunder. The sound, which possessed an ancient and otherworldly quality altogether different in nature from Morwen's spells, was beautiful and terrifying at once. Unlike Morwen,

Berengar had no special sensitivity to magic, but he felt the surge of energy all the same.

The force of Azura's words—if in fact they were words —tore through the area, leveling wood, stone, and brick. Everyone and everything in her way was violently swept aside. Only the thief king, who stood outside the path of destruction, remained standing as the fairy's cry faded.

"I believe that's our cue to run." Azura dived into an alley with Edrick, leaving Berengar, Morwen, and Faolán to follow with the entire Brotherhood of Thieves in pursuit.

Berengar glimpsed movement overhead and saw shadows darting along the rooftops. Three thieves appeared where the alley diverged in front of them, but Azura closed the distance between them with impossible speed before they could attack. Her knives flashed like lightning in the dark, and Berengar could hardly keep up with the quickness of her strikes. The attackers went down in unison, and Azura grabbed Edrick by the shirt and pulled him down another alleyway.

"Where are we going?" Morwen shouted at Azura.

"To the Thieves' Quarter."

Morwen shot Berengar a look of incredulity. "Shouldn't we be running *away* from danger?"

Azura flashed a wide grin. "Trust me."

"Trust you?" Morwen used her staff to cast a spell to turn the dirt behind them into mud to slow the thieves' progress. "You've lied to us from the moment we met!"

Azura deflected a knife hurled at Morwen with one of her blades and cast a wink over her shoulder.

"Fairies," Berengar muttered under his breath. Only a short while ago, they had roused her to anger. Now Azura was in a playful mood once more. Maybe fairies really were as temperamental as the stories suggested.

More enemies waited at the end of the labyrinth of alleyways, which opened to the Thieves' Quarter. With no option left but to fight their way through, Berengar and the others met them head-on. Faolán pounced on the nearest thief, and Berengar followed after, swinging his axe. Morwen forewent use of magic and instead wielded her staff as a club, while Azura proved as deadly as ever with her twin blades. They broke through the ranks of thieves even as more closed in at their backs. The thief king lingered in the shadows, watching from the alley's mouth.

"Come on," Azura said. "We can't stop."

Berengar pulled his axe free from an enemy's back and brought up the rear.

"This way." Azura hurried down a narrow street to a shuttered building that appeared abandoned. "Bar the door."

Berengar did as she said. She led them down the stairs to the cellar, where she pulled an unlit candle from her cloak and breathed the flame into life without the use of flint. A tunnel entrance stood revealed in the firelight.

Azura handed the candle to Edrick. "Follow the tunnel to the river. A boatman will be waiting." She passed her coin purse to him. "This should be more than enough to get you out of the city."

Edrick looked back at her with obvious concern. "What about you?"

"My path leads another way. The Brotherhood will be looking for me, not you." Azura ruffled his hair with affection. "I'm sorry I got you into this mess. I will miss you, my ambitious young friend. Try not to get into too much trouble without me. Now go."

A vacant expression came over Edrick, who obeyed without hesitation, as if her words had taken hold of him.

He cast one final glance at her and disappeared into the tunnel.

"They're in here!" a voice bellowed from outside.

Berengar turned to face the stairs. "What about the rest of us? You've trapped us here with nowhere to go."

"Did I? What makes you think the tunnels are the only way out?"

Above, the door crashed open, and thieves swarmed inside the building. Azura took a step back and vanished through a doorway hidden within a false wall.

Berengar pursued the fairy into a secret passage. "Blast it! After her, Faolán!" It was long rumored the Brotherhood used an underground network to move about the city undetected. Azura's path could lead anywhere. *I've had enough of hidden entrances and secret passages to last me a lifetime.*

They emerged inside the Thieves' Quarter's solitary church, where numerous passages converged. Faolán barked to get his attention, and Berengar caught sight of Azura escaping through the entrance. They hurried outside in time to see her whistle to a nearby horse, which threw its rider and approached the fairy without hesitation. In one fluid motion, she swung herself onto the saddle and seized the reins.

"Did I mention fairies can actually speak to animals?" Morwen asked. "Unlike most magicians, who merely influence animal behavior."

"Save it for later." Berengar spotted horses hitched outside a nearby tavern and hurried to untie one. "She's headed toward the Red Gate. We can't let her get away."

Azura noticed them on her trail and veered off the road before Morwen caught up to her. Morwen and Faolán followed suit while Berengar stuck to the road in case she attempted to circle back. Azura's mount thundered down a stone staircase and dashed across the bridge leading over the river. Even Morwen, one of the best riders Berengar knew, struggled to keep up with the fairy, who deftly guided her horse around all obstacles in her way.

"Halt!" ordered a guard. "Stop where you are!" He threw himself out of the way when Azura and Morwen stormed past, and his companions rang bells to warn the sentries posted at the gate.

"It's the thief! Close the gate!"

Archers loosed their arrows at her, but Azura lowered her head and charged the gate. When Morwen grasped at Azura's cloak in a final, desperate attempt to slow her down, Azura slipped through her grasp. The fairy waved back at Berengar and Morwen just before the gate shut, preventing them from following her out of the city.

Morwen fell back outside the archers' range. "We failed. She escaped."

Berengar caught up to Morwen and pulled his horse to a stop. "It's not over yet. She still has to meet with whoever hired her to steal the blade. If Edrick was right about the Giant's Foot, we know where she'll be." Perhaps more importantly, Azura wasn't aware they knew, which meant that for the first time they had an advantage she didn't.

The Coin and Crown was under guard by armed men when they returned. Berengar and Morwen kept their distance and surveyed the scene from the shadows. The men were most likely monster hunters or guards in league with the Brotherhood. Either way, it was much too dangerous to risk attempting to retrieve their belongings. Berengar had his weapons, and Morwen had her staff—unfinished though it remained—and satchel. That would have to be enough.

"I hope Godfrey has enough sense to avoid alerting the guards." Berengar turned his horse around and motioned for Morwen to follow. "Come on. We should find another way out of the city before the watch closes all the gates."

"What about Nessa? We can't just leave her."

"There's no time. We'll come back for her. I promise."

Azura's theft of the cursed blade had the city watch out in full force. Berengar and Morwen moved quietly to escape the notice of numerous patrols. They stayed off the main roads. With the streets otherwise abandoned in the late hour, two lonely riders were bound to attract attention. They couldn't afford to wait to travel concealed by the safety of the crowds, either. By the time morning came, all exits to Dún Aulin would be sealed.

Berengar wondered if they were already too late when they found the North and Beggar's Gates under careful watch. Finally, they came to the lightly guarded Thieves' Gate, where it appeared Tavish's instructions had yet to reach the sentries, and Berengar and Morwen were able to pass through overlooked.

The following morning, they stopped at the first town they came to for directions to the Giant's Foot. Even with no map to guide their path, the road proved easy. Much of the surrounding lands had been cleared, tamed, and settled, and there were no forests to obstruct their path. Along the way, the two encountered multiple villages, settlements, and farms. As Flaherty had suggested, times were changing. Still, when Berengar thought of Morwen, he wondered what had been lost in the process.

The weather proved fair over the course of their journey. Berengar was grateful to be free of the city at last. On the second day, the companions passed Cobthach's Hold—the fort from which Horst and the other scouts pursued the goblins into the forest.

"If Azura is planning on meeting her client at the Giant's Foot, she'll probably lie low in the nearest village while she waits," Berengar said to Morwen. "Unless she's found a way to disguise herself again, she shouldn't be that hard to spot in a crowd."

"I'm not so sure. Fairies can go unseen if they wish. It's one method they used to play tricks on unsuspecting humans in times past."

Berengar shook his head. "Who would have thought an adolescent girl could cause so much trouble?"

Morwen regarded him with vague annoyance. "In case you've forgotten, I'm an adolescent girl. We're plenty capable of causing trouble."

Berengar chuckled. "You'll get no argument from me on that score."

"Besides, I highly doubt Azura actually *is* an adolescent."

"Morwen, she's almost as young as you."

"Haven't you learned by now that appearances can be deceiving, especially where magic is concerned? Although fairies aren't truly immortal, they age slower than we do, and their lifespans are much greater than ours. I'd wager she's probably as old as you, if not older still."

Berengar had a hard time believing that until he thought back to an encounter with a witch who had taken on the appearance of an elderly woman to enter Cashel unnoticed. "There's something I still can't figure out. What was Azura doing in Dún Aulin in the first place? Her face was posted on bounties across the city. If her aim was to remain hidden, why steal the most dangerous relic in Fál?"

Morwen took a moment to mull over her reply. "Based on what I've read, fairies often have secret motives for involving themselves in the affairs of mortals. To say their sense of morality is difficult to understand is an understatement." She glanced over at him. "Azura might have deceived us, but she also helped us on more than one occasion when she could've chosen to do otherwise."

"She seemed taken aback when you mentioned the bishop. Do you think she was telling the truth about Flaherty?"

Morwen hesitated. "I do."

"You sound uncharacteristically unsure of yourself."

"The fair folk are talented liars—talented enough to fool even some magicians—but her surprise appeared genuine to me. Besides, you saw Flaherty. He was stabbed from behind. Someone else killed him—I'm sure of it."

"Aye, but who?"

Morwen shrugged. "I suspect there's more to this affair than we know. Do you remember what Azura said about Lucien not being the king? I still can't figure out what she meant by it."

Berengar turned the matter over in his mind. "It reminds me of something Horst told me. He mentioned the king and said he knew where 'they' were keeping him. Does that make any sense to you?"

"None at all. Perhaps it's connected to the prince regent's disappearance. If we want answers, we're going to have to find Azura and get her to talk. Preferably *without* maiming her, mind you."

An enormous ruin loomed to the west. A great stone stair ran uphill to the mouth of a towering door mostly obscured by fallen rubble. Vines and weeds devoured fallen archways and pillars weathered and eroded by time.

"The Giant's Foot." There was no sign of the giants who built it—not that he expected to find one. Most wild giants now lived in the north or the mountains, and while friendly giants did occasionally dwell among men, they were certainly not welcome in Leinster. "Tulach Mhór can't be far."

Morwen pointed to the west. "There."

Smoke rose from a village at the foot of a neighboring forest. They had reached the wilds. Berengar kicked his horse in the sides and started toward Tulach Mhór. Most of the villagers were hard at work tending to chores when Berengar and Morwen drew near. He expected the people to greet his arrival with the familiar looks of unease and mistrust that followed him wherever he went, but the men and women of Tulach Mhór seemed not to notice him. Instead, their attention was fixed on a wagon emerging from the woods.

Shouts broke out, drawing more people from their huts, and the church bell began to ring. Berengar's gaze fell on the wagon, which bore two occupants. The first—the driver—gripped the reins in one hand. His other arm dangled uselessly at his side. Berengar noticed a deep gash across his neck.

The driver looked over his shoulder at the passenger, who lay flat in the back of the wagon, and called for help. When the wagon neared the well, it rattled to a final stop, and the man in the back uttered a low moan.

Berengar and Morwen approached for a better look as a crowd formed around the wagon.

"What happened?" a portly villager asked the driver. "Did you kill it?"

The driver ignored the question. Like his companion, he wore heavy armor and was well armed. *Monster hunters.* Judging from the bait in the back, they had probably just returned from a hunt.

The driver released his hold on the reins and stumbled to his friend's side. "Hold on, Baldrick. I'm going to get you help."

Baldrick's mouth opened but produced only rasping, shallow breaths. A blow had caved in his chest plate.

Berengar glanced at Morwen. "Only something big could have done that."

"We need a healer!" The driver searched the villagers' faces in vain. "Are there none who will help us?"

Morwen stepped forward before Berengar could restrain her. "I'm a healer." When Baldrick coughed up blood, her expression said it all—the monster hunter was a dead man. "I'll do what I can for you both."

"You can use my hut," one of the crowd volunteered.

"Help him inside," Morwen said to the others. "Be gentle."

Berengar lowered his voice to a whisper. "I hope you know what you're doing. Those are monster hunters, in case you hadn't noticed."

Morwen put her hands on her hips. "They need my help all the same. I didn't take an oath to heal only those who deserve it. It's not like I'm planning on announcing that I'm a magician to the whole village. Besides, the villagers might be more willing to help if we prove useful."

He scowled at her. "You have a good heart. It'll get you killed one day if you're not careful."

"Duly noted. Why don't you ask around and see what you can learn while I'm busy?" She hurried into the hut before he could reply.

"Come on, Faolán. Let's go." He approached the local constable, who lingered by the monster hunters' wagon. "What's going on here?"

The constable pointed out a bounty posted outside the church. "Something's been prowling about the woods of late—snatching pigs and goats. When the priest went missing some weeks back, the village finally pooled enough money to hire a team of monster hunters."

Berengar inspected the crude drawing, which depicted

a large, brutish creature. "What's this supposed to be?" It didn't look like any monster he'd ever seen.

"An ogre, I think—or else a troll. It's hard to say, really. Not that many have seen it. Most folk tend to keep away from the forest these days."

"You're the village constable. Shouldn't you know what it is?"

"And you think *I* should track the beast to its lair and finish it myself? I'm a constable, not a monster hunter. I leave that sort of work to others." He looked Berengar up and down. "I don't suppose you'd be up to the task? You look like a man who knows how to use that axe."

"You don't know the half of it," Berengar said under his breath. "Is this the only monster that's troubling you?"

The question drew a derisive laugh from the constable. "You're in the wilds now. This creature is the least of our concerns." He nodded at a string of abandoned huts along the forest's edge. Most were in ruins. "Goblins did that, and not too long ago either. Between famine, plague, and all the attacks, it's all most can do just to get by. I suspect it's on account of our proximity to the Giant's Foot. Most believe the ruin is haunted."

"Haunted?"

"Aye. The earth shakes there sometimes. It's said that inhuman whispers can be heard if one sets foot there in the dark of night. But it's been that way since anyone can remember. These monster attacks are new. We've sent emissaries to Dún Aulin to plead for help, but the crown ignores us. It's almost enough to make one long for the days of mages and magicians." He looked around, as if to make sure he hadn't been overheard. "Don't tell anyone I said that."

Berengar stared at the woods. Perhaps Godfrey's suspicions were well-founded. "I'm looking for someone—a small woman with black hair I believe is in the area. She may have arrived recently."

The constable stroked his beard. "I can't say the description is familiar. We haven't had any newcomers that I'm aware of, save for yourselves and the monster hunters. Are you quite sure you don't want to lend a hand with the beast? People here don't have much, but they would see to it you were compensated for your trouble."

"Sorry. I have other matters to see to at the moment."

The constable made no effort to hide his disappointment. "In that case, I must take my leave. I have to convince Gretta Cruickshank her son Irvine isn't under a spell."

Berengar frowned. "What sort of spell?"

"The lad's taken to sleepwalking to the old granary. His mother found him with a plate of food in his hands. When she woke him, Irvine claimed he was lured out of his bed by a beautiful song. Naturally, his mother thinks some magical creature has bewitched him." The constable waved his hand, as if to dismiss the notion.

Berengar suppressed a smirk. Given her blue skin, pointed ears, and other features, it made sense Azura would want to hide herself from the villagers while she waited to meet with whoever hired her to steal the blade. Using her voice to enthrall Irvine to bring her food would allow her to remain out of sight by day.

He left the constable to his work and led his horse to the granary, another of the forsaken buildings along the village's periphery. Shadows danced at the granary's entrance, where one door had fallen off its hinges. No sound came from within. Berengar cautioned Faolán and approached slowly with his hand on the hilt of his blade.

Horses' hooves shattered the calm, and Azura charged from the barn on horseback, headed for the woods.

Berengar threw himself aside, swung himself onto his mount, and took off after her. He pulled up to within an arm's length and nearly grabbed her cloak before having to veer from his path to avoid hitting a tree. When he looked up, Azura's horse was fleeing deeper into the woods without its rider.

Berengar jerked back on the reins and brought his horse to a standstill. *Where did she go?* He glanced from side to side, but Azura was nowhere among the falling leaves.

Laughter came from above, where Azura sat perched on a branch. A pair of translucent wings protruded from her back, and Berengar realized how it was Azura had disappeared into thin air after stealing the thunder rune.

"Did you really think you could sneak up on me?" Azura cocked her head to one side and playfully tapped one of her pointed ears. "These aren't for show, you know."

"Get down from there."

Her smile widened but conveyed no ill will. "I thought you would have tired of chasing me by now, Warden Berengar. I don't suppose I could convince you to let me be? I have somewhere to be very shortly."

"I'm not leaving here without the blade. I'll cut down the bloody tree if I have to."

Azura sniffed at the air, and her brow furrowed suddenly.

"What is it?"

Faolán began to growl. At that moment, an arrow whizzed by Berengar's head. Azura flew from the branch and tackled him off his horse before a second arrow found its mark.

"Goblins."

Berengar and Azura stood side-by-side as goblins emerged from the brush to surround them. He whistled to

Faolán, who drew the archers' fire while he sprinted toward them. He split the closest goblin from head to toe and brought his axe around to gut a second only to find himself facing down a goblin archer with his bowstring pulled back. One of Azura's knives hit the creature's hand, causing the shot to go awry. Berengar closed the distance between them and beheaded the archer before he could nock another arrow.

Azura bent down to retrieve the knife and cleaned goblin blood from the blade. "Disgusting creatures." She clearly had no love for goblins.

Berengar turned over the corpse with his foot. It looked like one of the goblins who attacked them at the Institute. "These are only scouts." Faolán, who remained uneasy at his side, continued growling. Berengar froze. It wasn't him the goblins were looking for. "Morwen."

A horn resounded somewhere deeper in the forest. Berengar hurried to his horse as more arrows streamed past them. A whistle from Azura brought her mount running back to her, and they galloped through the forest with the goblins on their trail.

"You must have led them here," Azura called to him.

"How do you know it wasn't you they followed?"

Azura glanced at him with a mix of amusement and pride. "As if a band of goblins could track a fairy." She ducked, avoiding an arrow, and made a chirping sound. Sparrows flocked from the trees and swarmed the goblins behind Berengar. Tulach Mhór appeared ahead through gaps in the trees, and they emerged from the forest with more goblin horns blaring at their backs.

"Goblins!" someone shouted at the sight of the creatures.

The church bell rang out in warning, and villagers fled in all directions as a second group of goblins descended on

Tulach Mhór. *The blasted things are everywhere.* There were more than he remembered from the Wrenwood and the attack on the Institute. *Where did they all come from?*

Amid the confusion, he spotted Morwen outside the hut where she had treated the injured monster hunters. She and the monster hunter with the broken arm were surrounded by three goblins on foot. Berengar took the reins in one hand, reached for his axe, and galloped toward her. A goblin with a spear blocked his path, but Berengar continued undeterred and trampled the creature beneath his horse's hooves. A pained sound from the horse let him know the goblin's attack had been at least partially successful. The monster hunter took one of the goblins with him when he fell. Berengar cut through another with his axe and pulled Morwen up onto the saddle. The trees began to sway when he cast a look back at the forest. Something was headed their way. Something big.

"Azura's escaping." She was headed to the Giant's Foot. Berengar spurred his injured horse forward.

Morwen gripped his shoulders. "What about these people? We can't leave them!"

"It's you they're after. They want the thunder rune, remember?"

As Berengar promised, the goblins left Tulach Mhór in pursuit of them. He shifted his focus to Azura, who leapt off her horse and disappeared into the ruins. Their mount buckled under their weight, throwing them to the earth, and collapsed with a final shudder. Faolán barked to warn them as the goblins closed in on them. Berengar reached for his axe and helped Morwen to her feet. They scrambled up the broken stair after Azura and toward higher ground. Thorns and vines grew over the walls remaining at the summit, where tall grasses poked through overturned stones.

Azura was muttering to herself at the pile of rubble obscuring the entrance to the ruins. "Something's wrong. The client should have *been* here by now…"

Berengar shifted the axe in his hands. "There'll be time for that later. Those goblins are almost upon us."

Azura clutched her twin knives and spun around. "Let them come."

Morwen opened her satchel to retrieve the thunder rune, which pulsed with bright light.

"Do you know how to use that thing?" Berengar had seen before the damage the stone could do, and Morwen's staff still wasn't finished.

Morwen, clearly uncomfortable at the prospect of using the stone, clenched her teeth. "We don't have a choice."

The three stood back-to-back, each facing one of multiple empty archways ringing the hilltop. Hisses sounded nearby, and goblins crawled down pillars until they were encircled.

The ground shook again, and loosened stones fell as a fearsome troll crashed through an archway on its way up the hill. The troll stood three times as tall as a man, and its hulking frame cast a shadow over the earth. It roared with fury and demolished the remnants of the archway with its club. Two ogres—great orange brutes with protruding, flabby bellies—appeared on either side of the troll, also wielding clubs.

Berengar stood his ground. Trolls and ogres were usually solitary creatures. What were they doing working with goblins? Judging from Morwen's expression, she was thinking the same thing.

The troll and ogres stopped short at the command of Teelah, who no longer wore her helmet. Her eyes narrowed with contempt when they fell on Azura. "Fairy."

Azura's brow knotted in anger. "Goblin."

Teelah ignored Azura and held out her hand to Morwen. "Give us the rune."

Berengar brandished his axe. "Come and get it."

He expected the goblins to attack, but instead, many scurried back up the pillars. The sky darkened, and thunder reverberated across the heavens as black clouds gathered above. Sweeping winds bent the scattered trees that grew along the hillside and tore away their leaves.

Morwen clutched her staff and held a hand in front of her face as if to shield herself from an invisible threat.

"What do you feel?" Berengar asked her. "More monsters?"

"Something worse."

A hush fell over the ruins as the ogres parted to reveal a figure in dark green robes who loomed under an archway.

The robed figure stepped from the shadows. Leaves, vines, and moss grew on his bark-like skin. He carried a scythe in one hand, and a sinister dagger hung from his belt unsheathed. His face, hidden behind an antlered elk skull mask, was blackened and burned.

The man with the face of a monster.

"It's him," Morwen said. "The man from my vision."

"Warden Berengar," a monstrous voice said from within the skull. "It's been a long time."

Something about the voice was familiar. Berengar narrowed his gaze at the figure. "Who are you?" The hate-filled eyes looking back at him hardly seemed human.

"Surely you haven't forgotten me after all this time." The figure slowly removed his mask, revealing the scarred flesh underneath. "After all, it was you who gave me this face."

Berengar stared at him with growing realization. "Cathán."

CHAPTER TEN

Morwen looked from Berengar to Cathán and back again. "The druid responsible for the purges?"

Berengar's gaze remained fixed on Cathán's inhuman visage. "This must be some kind of trick. He's dead."

"You of all people should know better than that, Warden Berengar. Do you remember how I pleaded for death after you crushed my hands and held my face to the flames? But you wouldn't grant me even that small mercy, would you? You left me to live with the pain of my loss." Cathán returned the skull to its proper place over his face. "You should have finished the job."

"How did you survive?" If the crowds didn't kill Cathán, his wounds should have.

"Even without the use of my hands, I had strength enough to escape the city. I fled west, deep into the Elderwood, to die. Then I heard it. The voice of something other."

"What did you say?" A shiver ran down his spine. He had heard those words before.

"You know of what I speak. A giant with one terrible red eye."

Berengar's blood ran cold. "Balor."

"The King of the Fomorians spoke to me at the point of death. He offered me new life in return for my service. I drank the blood of the Wither Tree and was reborn in this form, more powerful than any druid before me."

Azura's eyes widened in alarm. "The Wither Tree is evil. Its cursed blood comes at the price of your soul."

"I surrendered it willingly." The druid's attention lingered on her. "One of the fair folk. How unexpected. You were hidden from my sight in Dún Aulin." He turned his attention to Morwen. "You, I saw. You have some skill for one so young. There is power in your blood."

Morwen brandished her staff as a defensive weapon. "It's not my blood you should concern yourself with."

Teelah shot Morwen a look clearly meant to dissuade her from antagonizing Cathán any further. "The magician is not like the others. She should not be harmed."

"Of course. We needn't be enemies, girl. Magical blood is much too valuable to shed idly. Give me the rune, and I will teach you long-forgotten knowledge and raise you to power hitherto undreamed of."

"Sorry. I make it a point not to trust anyone who hides his face behind a skull—*or* anyone who uses the word 'hitherto' in a sentence. I'm fine where I am, thank you very much."

Cathán's voice became a hiss, frightening even some of the goblins. "We are more than human. This world is ours, not theirs, and yet the two of you stand with *him*? He who butchered goblins by the hundreds and slaughtered my companions at Dún Aulin. The others only wanted to protect magic and nonhumans, and he murdered them for it."

Berengar pointed his axe at Cathán. "I was there. I saw the alchemists crucified outside the gates. The herbalists hung from the walls. The magicians stoned in the streets. The very people you claimed you wanted to protect. How many innocents died because of you and your friends?"

The ground trembled under Cathán's rage, and Berengar and Morwen exchanged glances. Maybe Cathán was as powerful as he suggested.

"No one is innocent. You showed me that. I would have given you peace, but your kind understands only death. Humans are a pestilence—a blight upon the earth."

Azura shook her head. "Humans aren't perfect, but they are capable of more than you give them credit for, druid."

"Their very existence is an offense against nature. They raze the forests and strip the land of its resources to expand their cities and settlements. They make war against all who are different from themselves. They threaten the practice of magic, which I took an oath to protect. I would see every man, woman, and child put to death."

Morwen's expression hardened. "You're a monster."

Cathán pointed a long, claw-like finger at Berengar. "*He* is the monster. He and his kin. How many 'innocents' did he cut down in the purges? Surely you don't imagine all were rioters."

Morwen regarded the druid defiantly. "He's made his share of mistakes, but he's nobler than you'll ever be."

Sinister whispers reverberated through the clouds above. Berengar looked around, mindful of Cathán's followers. He had beaten Cathán before, but even with Morwen and Azura at his side, he was outnumbered by a large margin. The troll and the ogres shifted restlessly, spoiling for a fight, while the goblins remained nearly motionless, their shadows moving in the dim light.

Unnoticed by the others, Azura fingered one of her throwing knives. Berengar stepped toward Cathán to keep the druid's attention on him while Azura carefully inched toward a better position.

Cathán turned back to Teelah. "What of your other task in Dún Aulin?"

"I found the scout who escaped. The warden led me straight to him. The scout told me everything. Soon King Lucien will be within our grasp."

"It was you from the start," Berengar said. Cathán had been watching them the whole time, probably from the moment they entered Leinster. "You hired the Black Hand to retrieve the thunder rune—and the goblins after I took it from them. So much death, all for a stone."

"This is about far more than the stone." Cathán spread his arms wide. "Do you know what this place *really* is? The ancients called Tulach Mhór the 'great mound.' It is no giant ruin. It's a prison."

As he spoke, something stirred deep within the earth, and Morwen's face whitened in response to an unseen threat.

"I sense it too," Azura said.

Cathán lowered his arms. "This is where Padraig banished Caorthannach, the mother of demons, when he defeated the last of the Fomorians. And here she has slumbered ever since, waiting to be released to pour out her wrath upon the land and cleanse Fál of the unworthy. I need only an elemental stone and a sacrifice of royal blood to release her from her prison. Once she has collected enough souls, I will resurrect Balor, and the Fomorians will eradicate humanity from the land and usher in a new age of darkness."

"What?" Teelah's brow furrowed, betraying her surprise. "That's not what we agreed. We joined you so we might have our revenge on King Lucien, not eradicate the entire human race. The Fomorians enslaved our ancestors and brought only misery to the world. I'll play no part in their return."

Berengar stole closer still. With any luck, he could reach Cathán before the troll or ogres could intercept him. He cast a look at Azura, who kept the throwing knife held behind her back, and gave Morwen an almost imperceptible nod.

"The time has come to pick a side," Cathán declared. "Your kin don't seem nearly as hesitant to join my cause." All across the ruins, goblins hissed in assent. "Perhaps you do not enjoy the loyalty you thought. Now bring me the stone."

Teelah remained where she stood.

Berengar sprinted forward. "Now!"

Morwen cast a ward that deflected black arrows as Berengar cleaved a goblin in two and charged at Cathán with his axe held high.

"Stailc gaoithe aeir." Cathán formed a fist, and a blast of wind struck Berengar head-on. The force knocked him to the ground. "Fool. Have you forgotten that nature herself is my servant?" He looked up at the goblin horde and pointed at Berengar and the others. "Kill them and bring me the stone."

The troll and two ogres lumbered forward, swinging their clubs while the goblins scurried to join the fray. Berengar dodged an arrow, ducked under a blow from an ogre, and beheaded a goblin before falling back to join Morwen and Azura. Enemies closed in around them as Cathán looked on.

Azura cut through one goblin after another without tiring. Even with the damage wrought by his axe, Berengar could hardly match her pace. The goblins, which moved faster than most humans, couldn't land as much as a single blow on her. Morwen alternated between battering goblins with her staff and casting spells, though it was obvious her new staff was more difficult to wield unfinished.

Goblins scrambled from the troll's path as it headed straight for Berengar. He kept his axe at the ready and braced himself for impact. "Stay together. Don't let them pick us apart."

Azura used her voice to target the troll, and a current of power blasted across the hilltop. The impact threw goblins aside and struck the troll head-on. Although the creature's momentum carried it forward, the force of Azura's words altered its course enough to cause it to miss them entirely and fall down the hill.

Azura's moment of triumph was short-lived, and she found herself cornered by an ogre. When she attempted to knife it, a stray arrow knocked the blade from her hand. She took to the air to fly over it, but the ogre seized one of her legs and swung her back and forth in the air.

Berengar brushed past the goblins in his path and charged the ogre. The creature was too slow to bring its arm up to defend itself. The axe drew blood, and Azura slipped from the creature's grasp. The ogre rounded on Berengar, who rushed to meet it. The collision sent them both to the ground, and Berengar's axe fell away. He rolled out from under the ogre's fist, which shattered stone beneath it. Faolán pounced on the monster's back long enough for Berengar to free his sword and cut the ogre down the middle.

Before he could rejoin the others, the second ogre struck him with its club. The impact lifted him off the ground. He lost his grip on his sword and landed hard against a stone pillar. The ogre lumbered toward him, its club held high. Berengar attempted to go for his fallen sword, but a goblin leapt on him from above and sank its teeth into his neck, drawing blood. While he wrestled with the goblin, the ogre drew nearer.

"Morwen, do something…"

Lightning fell from the sky and struck the hilltop, and the ogre and most goblins were knocked off their feet. A scream came from Morwen. Smoke rose from the burned hand holding the thunder rune. She dropped the stone, which rolled away and landed at Cathán's feet, and sank to her knees.

The runestone vibrated and glowed when Cathán picked it up. Sparks ran across his robes, and his eyes shone with white light. He trained the thunder rune on Berengar and his companions. "Farewell, Warden Berengar." A blast of pure energy shot from the stone to incinerate them.

A growl came from Morwen, who, despite her injury, forced herself to her feet with an expression of pure determination. "No." Fierce winds swept the hilltop as she grabbed a golden amulet that hung around her neck. "This amulet is enchanted with light magic, and you cannot overcome its power."

When Azura saw the amulet, her eyes widened in recognition. "Ramsay."

Morwen gave a great cry, and the amulet shone with light. A golden sphere formed around them, shielding them from the lightning. "Leagan amach!" The sphere detonated outward, and a wave of energy knocked all the goblins in the area aside. Morwen crumpled to the ground, weakened by the energy required to wield the amulet's power.

Berengar scooped up his axe and rushed Cathán with a roar. "Now!"

The druid countered the strike with his scythe and aimed a weaker bolt of energy at him. To Cathan's surprise, Berengar's axe absorbed the blast and deflected excess electricity.

"Surprised?" Berengar shrugged off the lightning and continued his advance, even as Cathán held the rune on him. "You should have paid closer attention to my axe."

His axe bore a silver rune of its own. Morwen had enchanted the axe with a spell of resiliency that drew on the rune's power to repel magical attacks. It had worked against Ravenna's shadow magic, and it appeared just as capable against the electrical force wielded by Cathán. Although the weight of the energy flowing from the thunder rune threatened to drive him back, Berengar forced himself to keep going until he was within striking distance of Cathán. The lightning rebounded on his foe.

The fluttering of wings sounded above the thunder, and Azura landed next to him. "Let's take him together."

Cathán looked from one to the other, his eyes full of uncertainty for the first time.

An arrow whizzed by the druid's head as a horn reverberated in the distance.

"Humans!" a goblin cried before an arrow struck him dead.

Men in armor stormed the hilltop in numbers equal to Cathán's followers. They wielded swords, bows, and other weapons with lethal efficiency.

Monster hunters, Berengar realized. Given the odds against him, he might have been relieved by the monster hunters' sudden appearance—if not for the insignia they wore. "The Acolytes." *How did they find us?*

He looked back at Cathán, but the druid had vanished, taking the thunder rune with him. Before Berengar could pursue his foe, goblins ran at him through the archway, though most ignored him in favor of the monster hunters.

The monster hunters' captain reached the top of the

stair. "Find the cursed blade and the one who carries it—along with the warden and his companion."

The skirmish quickly turned into an all-out battle between Cathán's forces and the Acolytes, with Berengar and his allies caught in the middle. Azura spread her wings to fly away, but the monster hunters threw a net over her. Berengar waylaid a goblin in his path and looked from Azura to Morwen, who was fighting with her back against a stone wall. He couldn't help them both at once.

Two attackers ran at him with their swords raised, and Berengar took them on together. One managed to score a slash across his armor before Berengar bashed in his head. The other rattled his teeth with the hilt of a blade before falling victim to a goblin's arrow. When the troll smashed through another archway, the monster hunters were forced to divert their attention to the rampaging brute. Berengar continued toward Morwen, now almost completely surrounded.

Just before he reached her, the ogre he thought he killed earlier came running at him. The collision sent them both over the hillside. Berengar fell several feet and landed hard beside a pile of rubble. He pushed himself up, staggered to his feet, and looked for his axe. It hurt simply to stand. The sounds of battle carried from above, and his gaze fell on the stair leading back to the summit.

He saw the ogre's fist a half second too late. The blow struck his chest, and the next caught him on the chin. When the ogre bashed him against a stone wall, Berengar tasted blood, and his vision swam. He fought to remain conscious and searched for a weak spot. Blood flowed from the open wound where Berengar's sword had sliced through the ogre's abdomen. Mustering all his strength, he planted his feet against the wall and drove himself forward, taking the ogre by surprise. He thrust his hand into the ogre's exposed abdomen and ripped out its viscera in a heap. The ogre dropped to its knees, and Berengar bashed its head in with a rock until it stopped moving.

He limped toward the staircase. His leg threatened to give way under him, but he forced himself to keep going.

"There he is!"

A group of monster hunters encircled him. Unarmed and barely conscious, Berengar lashed out in anger. Someone hit him on the back of the head, and suddenly he was on the ground looking up at a sea of unfamiliar faces.

"Put him with the others. The boss wants this one alive."

A boot hurtled toward his face, and his world faded to black.

The world shifted under him. Berengar stirred. His body ached all over. A blindfold covered his eyes, and ropes bound his hands and feet. He was still too weary from battle to even attempt to free himself.

I should be dead. The Acolytes wanted him dead, so why was he still alive?

No answers came. His thoughts were a clouded mess. Whatever the reason the monster hunters had spared him, it couldn't have been for anything good.

The earth moved beneath him again. His body lay sprawled across a wooden surface. A wheel rolled over a rock below, tossing him about. He was in the back of a wagon. The sound of horses and men's voices carried from outside. They were in transit.

Where are they taking us? He coughed and felt searing pain. The ogre had cracked—or broken—some of his ribs.

He was lucky it hadn't punctured a lung. He was in a sorry state either way.

"Morwen?" The word came out jumbled. It occurred to him he might have been unconscious longer than he thought. "Azura?"

There was no answer. The last he had seen, Morwen and Faolán were cornered, and Azura was trapped in a net. He hoped Morwen at least had managed to escape in the midst of the fighting, but he feared the worst. The wagon rolled over another rock, causing him to hit his head against the wagon's side, and again the world faded away.

He drifted in and out of consciousness for the duration of the journey. Time lost all meaning, and he was only vaguely aware of his surroundings. Past and present converged in fragmented dreams where he saw the faces of those he had killed waiting for him to join them in death.

When he came to again, the wagon was rolling over a paved road. His head still hurt, but his thoughts were clearer. A bell tolled in the distance, and he heard the sounds of crowds outside the wagon. They were back inside the city. Eventually, the wagon came to a stop when the company reached their final destination, and the door to the back of the wagon was thrown open.

"He's awake," a voice said.

"Knock him out," said another. "He'll be easier to manage."

"Look at the shape he's in. He hasn't eaten in days. Besides, there are hundreds of guards within these walls."

"Do you know who he is? I'll not take the chance. Do it."

Another blow to the head left him in a haze. Strong arms hauled him from the wagon and dragged him indoors.

The next thing he knew, someone was saying his name.

He hung in midair, suspended by chains. His blindfold had been removed. The guards had taken his cloak, armor, and boots, leaving him clad only in a pair of pants. Berengar blinked and let his eyes adjust to the pale light that crept into a wide stone chamber. Held at bay by torches, shadows lurked hungrily about the periphery of the room. Iron bars covered the windows.

"Berengar?"

Morwen was similarly restrained, as were Azura and Teelah. Berengar extended his hand toward her, but his shackles held him fixed in place, and she loomed just out of his reach. The sight of her in chains woke something dark and angry in him.

"Are you all right?"

Her right hand appeared badly burned from her attempted use of the thunder rune. "Better than you, in any event. It's not as bad as it looks."

"Where are we?"

"Listen." Azura craned her neck toward the chamber's locked door. "We're in a tower cell in the palace. There are guards posted outside."

Berengar listened carefully. "I don't hear anything."

"That's because you're listening with human ears."

"Show-off," Teelah said ruefully.

"Can't you get us out of here?" Berengar asked Azura. She shook her head. "These chains are iron."

"So?"

"Iron repels fairies," Morwen explained. "The monster hunters of old used iron weapons to kill the fair folk."

"Figures. How did the Acolytes find us?" *And what are they doing working with the palace guards? They're supposed to be outlawed by the church.*

"It wasn't us they were following." Like his armor and

weapons, Morwen's staff and satchel were missing. "It was the cursed blade they were after. They took it."

"So the blade's back where it belongs. What of it?" Berengar willed away the pain and forced himself to think. "Something doesn't add up. I can see why the palace guard would want *her* locked up, but what are *we* doing here?" He was a Warden of Fál. If the High Queen learned he had been strung up like a common criminal on Lucien's orders, Leinster's boy-king would bear the full brunt of her ire.

"You should have let me go when I asked," Azura said. "Now the whole kingdom is in danger."

Berengar felt his anger rising. "If you hadn't stolen the cursed blade, none of this would have happened. Enough games. I want answers. Who hired you to steal the blade?"

"I don't know. They offered me a wand in return for the theft of the blade."

"A wand?"

"A fairy wand. It's what I hoped to find at the Institute."

"I've seen you use that voice of yours. What do you need a wand for?"

Her lips pulled into a frown, revealing her pointy-edged teeth. "All fairies have magic, but wands help us hone our power into spells in the same way most human mages rely on staffs."

"Some human magicians use wands as well," Morwen offered.

"Fairy wands are not like those used by humans. They are very rare and hard to come by. Mine was taken from me when I was banished from the fairy realm." Azura lowered her head. "I agreed to meet the client at the Giant's Foot to make the exchange, but I never intended to surrender the blade. I know the dangers it poses. That's why I stole it in the first place—to keep it from falling into the wrong hands."

Morwen's brow furrowed. "You mean King Lucien? Why did you say he wasn't the king?"

Azura's expression softened. "Finally—someone asking the right questions. The thing that sits on the throne isn't King Lucien, but a changeling impersonating the king."

"A changeling?" Berengar didn't try to hide his skepticism. Although he had heard the cautionary tales about fairies kidnapping children and replacing them with changelings from the time he was a boy, it seemed highly improbable they could have taken the king. Then again, until recently, he had believed fairies were extinct throughout the land of Fál.

"It makes sense," Morwen said. "It would explain the sudden change in the king's behavior. When we first set foot in the throne room, I sensed magic coming from the throne. At the time I thought it was fairy dust, when it must have been the changeling I sensed. But if the Lucien we saw was an imposter, what happened to the true king?"

Azura nodded to Teelah. "Ask her. You heard what she told the druid. She knows where they're keeping him."

"Where *who* is keeping him?" Berengar asked Azura when Teelah refused to elaborate. "You still haven't said who's behind all this."

"I'd have thought it rather obvious. Who controls the pretender to the throne?"

The answer came to him at once. "Valmont."

"The man you know as Father Valmont is not as he appears. The magic Morwen sensed came from him."

"You said you weren't the only fairy in Dún Aulin," Morwen said. "Valmont is the other, isn't he?"

"Aye. His true name is Völundr. He murdered his

predecessor to gain influence at court so he could replace the king with a changeling."

"To what end?" Berengar asked.

"Völundr is one of the *Unseelie*—a dark fairy. Years ago, he fell in love with one of the fairy king Annwyn's daughters, Princess Aurora. King Annwyn forbade them from marrying, so the two arranged to run away together. Before she could meet Völundr, Aurora was ambushed by goblins. She escaped the Otherworld and fled here, where she encountered a group of men who took her for a monster. They cut out her tongue to prevent her from using her voice and tortured her to the point of death. When Völundr found her, it was already too late.

"King Annwyn blamed Völundr for his daughter's death and exiled him. Fueled by his thirst for vengeance, Völundr made a pact with the dark forces for power. He believes all other races are inferior species and seeks dominion over all life. He hopes to reunite the two halves of the cursed blade to accomplish this foul purpose."

Morwen watched Azura with interest. "How are you involved in all this?"

"After the Shadow Wars, King Annwyn and your High Queen signed an armistice sealed in blood that forbids the king and his subjects from intervening in human affairs. Annwyn, who has no love for humanity, knew the treaty would not apply to the fairies like Völundr not under his rule. I refused to sit and watch while Völundr attempted to conquer and enslave mankind, and for that I was stripped of my wand and cast out. I followed Völundr to Dún Aulin, assumed the identity of a thief, and have worked to thwart his aims ever since."

Morwen stared at her, confused. "You've seen how most of the people here regard magic and nonhumans. Why give up everything to help those who hate you?"

Azura gave a sad smile. "'Tis a long story—one best saved for another time. Our captors draw near."

The door opened, and guards with torches swept inside the chamber. The guards remained stationary along the walls as three monster hunters followed them into the tower cell.

"Winslow," Berengar muttered.

The Acolytes' leader carried Berengar's axe. "A weapon of legend. You used it to gut my son, did you not? I think I'll enjoy taking your head with it." He nodded to his subordinates. "Hold him steady."

The monster hunters seized him and jerked on his hair to pull his head back. Berengar stared into his enemy's eyes, issuing an implicit challenge. "These chains aren't enough for you?"

Winslow struck him across the face with a gauntleted fist.

Berengar laughed and spit out a tooth that landed at his enemy's feet. "I hardly felt that. Surely you can do better than *that*."

"I've spent years thinking of how best to break you. Go on—resist. It will make your final moments all the sweeter." Winslow hit him again, this time in the abdomen with the axe's handle.

Berengar continued to laugh, even as his eyes stung from the pain. "That all you got? Even your son put up more of a fight."

The monster hunters glanced at each other uneasily, but Winslow continued the beating undeterred. Just before Berengar lost consciousness, his tormentor stopped to wipe the blood from his sleeve.

"You're tough, I'll give you that. The High Queen's Monster. A man with no love for anything or anyone. But that's not exactly true, is it?"

Berengar followed his gaze to Morwen.

"I know that look. Only a parent can understand it. I always thought you cared for nothing. How do you hurt a man like that? Then I saw the way you looked at her." Winslow took out a dagger and traced the point along the side of Berengar's face, stopping just beneath his eye. "I considered taking your remaining eye, but I want you to see what we're going to do to her."

Berengar let out a primal scream, broke free of the monster hunters' hold, and drove his forehead into Winslow's face.

Winslow held a hand to his bloodied, broken nose. "Have you ever witnessed a witch burning? It's a thing of great beauty." He walked over to Morwen and cupped her chin in his hands. "Such a pretty face. I wonder what it will look like turned to ash."

Berengar's blood boiled with uncontrollable fury. "Lay one hand on her, and I'll take you apart piece by piece." He threw himself at Winslow, but the chains pulled him back.

"I was never a pious man in my youth. I was a soldier, like you. It took me years to find the Lord's will. My son was different. He was special. I would have done anything to protect him. When you took him from me, I felt helpless for the first time in my life. Do you know what that feels like?" Winslow turned back to Berengar. "You will. I promise you that."

Morwen bit Winslow's ungloved hand, and he slapped her across the face with his gauntlet.

"You bastard!" Berengar strained against the chains. "I'll kill all of you!"

"Enough." Valmont entered the chamber. He now wore white robes and a gold cloak with green trim to signify he had emerged as Flaherty's successor. "I promised you the warden, Winslow. The others are mine until I decide otherwise." Although quiet, his voice compelled obedience from Winslow, who backed out of his way. "Who was the druid in green robes?"

Teelah spat at him rather than answer.

Valmont wiped the spittle away with a look of revulsion. "Disgusting creature. Perhaps torture will loosen your tongue." He gestured to the guards. "Take her away."

"Release us at once," Berengar said. "I am a Warden of Fál. When the High Queen learns of this, she will—"

"Nora will do nothing, I assure you. As far as your High Queen is concerned, you were slain by goblins at Tulach Mhór while in pursuit of the cursed blade. When the king's men arrived to recover the blade, you were already past all help. The truth will never leave this room."

"You're meddling with forces beyond your control," Morwen said. "You're mad if you think you can wield Azeroth's sword."

Valmont returned the shard to a black sheath. "I am far more knowledgeable about the blade than you, magician—including how to reforge it, once the other half is in my possession. As for you…the ceremony's attendees witnessed your role in the fairy's escape, as well as your complicity in Bishop Flaherty's murder. I should thank you. Once I was elected bishop in Flaherty's place, I was able to rescind the edict disavowing the Acolytes of the True Faith."

"You killed Flaherty—murdered him with one of Azura's knives." Berengar cast his gaze on Winslow. "You've been working for a fairy this whole time."

But Winslow, his men, and the guards had gone utterly still. Each stared ahead with a blank expression. Berengar noticed a crystal wand in Valmont's hand. Valmont waved the wand, which glowed with purple light, and his appearance shifted before their eyes. The long, white hair clasped behind his back remained the same, but his skin took on a dark gray hue, his ears grew pronounced points, and his hands became claws. Two monstrous bat-like wings spread out behind his cloak. It was like looking at a twisted, monstrous reflection of Azura's beauty.

"I trust the iron is to your liking, Azura? I wouldn't want you escaping—not after all the trouble I went through to capture you."

Azura grimaced in discomfort. "Let these two go. Your quarrel is with me."

Valmont regarded her with a pair of indigo eyes that seemed to burn in the pale light. "I find your peculiar affection for mankind perverse. You are of the Aos Sídhe, and yet you choose them over your own kin—all because you gave your heart to some human sorcerer. Pathetic. If you truly cared for these two, you wouldn't have involved them in our affairs.

"The Bear Warden is nothing more than a tool of his queen. Like most of his kind, he loves only violence. He is beneath my attention. As for the magician…" His gleaming eyes fixed themselves on Morwen. "She has only middling talent, if that. Still, it should prove useful to have a human magician in my service."

Morwen stared at him in defiance. "I will never serve you."

"You will have no choice in the matter. I will fill your head with words until your will is mine to shape according to my desires." He returned his attention to Azura. "Don't think I've forgotten you. You have worked against my interests since I first came to this wretched city, all while hiding under the guise of a common thief. Even as my influence grew, you avoided my hunters and spies. Impressive, given the bounty I placed on your head. Then again, you are of the Aos Sídhe. You are clever—just not as clever as you think.

"It was I who arranged for the offer of the black contract." Valmont pointed the wand at Azura. "You played perfectly into my hands. I knew you would attempt to steal the blade to keep it from falling into my hands, and the prospect of obtaining a wand in the process would be too tempting to forgo."

So that's how his men knew to look for us at the Giant's Foot, Berengar realized. *He set up the meeting to lure Azura into a trap.* "Elazar's supplier of fairy dust—it was you, wasn't it?"

"Perhaps you're not as dimwitted as you appear, Warden Berengar. I used the revenue generated by the sale of fairy dust to buy off the city watch and curry favor with corrupt courtiers and church officials. Humans are remarkably easy to manipulate even without the use of magic."

"And the Acolytes?"

"Fanatics make for useful pawns. So long as I allow them to indulge in the persecution of nonhumans, they are content to enforce my will, all the while unwittingly acting in the service of a fairy."

Anger lined Azura's face. "You would allow those monsters to butcher countless creatures, so long as they do your bidding?"

"How very *human* of you. It was mankind who invaded our forests and hunted us from the lands they stole. They have forgotten the old ways even as they expand their settlements across the land. King Annwyn is content to forget their slights, but he is old and weak. There are other, wiser leaders who would succeed him.

"The time has come to take back what is ours. Even in the time of Áed, there were fewer and fewer magicians. With your beloved thane slain alongside his king, there are no sorcerers left to oppose us. The cursed blade is but the first step. I plan to reunite all four of the lost treasures of the Tuatha dé Danann and cast down the humans' false queen."

"Azura was telling the truth," Morwen muttered to Berengar. "This just went from bad to worse. Cathán wants to destroy humanity and Valmont wants to conquer us."

"And we're stuck here." Valmont had used his influence to get close enough to the throne to replace King Lucien with a changeling. *Prince Tristan must have realized something was amiss and fled Dún Aulin before Valmont had him dealt with.*

With the prince regent missing and Niall gone in search of him, there was no one left to stand in Valmont's way. With the crown and the church under his control, the most powerful man in Leinster wasn't actually a man at all. If Valmont succeeded in his quest to reunite the shards of the cursed blade, he could bring about a second great war for dominion of Fál. *Someone has to tell Nora.* Berengar struggled against his restraints, but it was no use.

"Attempted regicide. The theft of the cursed blade. The murder of Bishop Flaherty. I wonder if the humans you've grown so fond of will lift a finger when your sentence is carried out, though I suspect they'll all gather to watch you burn." Valmont tapped his wand twice before returning it to his robes. When he turned back to face Winslow and the others, his appearance was human once more. "I must see to the king. Remove the magician to another cell. I wish to question her further. These two I leave in your hands." He lingered a moment longer at the chamber's entrance. "Farewell, Azura."

"Get back here," Berengar shouted as the guards led Morwen away. Although she tried to appear brave, the fear in her eyes was plain. Winslow and the others withdrew, leaving him alone with Azura.

"This is on you. If they hurt her, I'll flay you alive."

"Charming. It's actually rather sweet, you know—the way you care for her."

"Shut up. I'm trying to get us out of here." He strained against his chains, but only one of the nails anchoring him in place budged even a little. He kept at it until his strength ebbed, and he collapsed, relying on his shackles for support. *Don't give up, you bastard. You promised you'd keep her safe.* With a pained cry, he pulled again. The nail came loose, and the chain came free of the wall. *One down. Three more to go.*

"Impressive. At this rate, we'll be free sometime tomorrow—after they've killed us."

"I don't suppose you have a better idea."

"As a matter of fact, I do." She pursed her lips to reveal a lockpick protruding from her teeth.

"You had that lockpick the whole time?"

"A good thief is always prepared to make her escape." Azura bent her neck and contorted her body to bring her face in proximity to the shackle on her right arm. The increased slack on her chains on account of her small frame lent her greater mobility, and she deftly worked the lockpick into the shackle.

"What's taking so long?"

Azura kept working until the shackle opened with a click. "It's not as easy as it looks." She winced and bit her lip.

"What?"

"That iron took more out of me than I thought." She opened her mouth to allow the lockpick to fall into her nimble fingers, pried open the shackle on her left arm, and started on the restraints binding her legs. "You're not actually going to flay me alive if I set you free, are you?"

Berengar growled at her. "Only if you don't hurry up and get me out of these chains."

Azura froze, and her gaze fell on the door. "Someone's coming."

"No one said you were coming," the guard who opened the door to their cell said to an individual behind him.

"The Bishop sent me," a familiar voice replied. "I'm to hear the warden's final confession."

The skeptical-looking guard removed the key from the door to the cell and appeared poised to ask another question when he was hit on the back of the head with a walking stick and crumpled to the ground.

Behind him stood Friar Godfrey, next to Faolán.

CHAPTER ELEVEN

EVEN IF HE didn't show it, Berengar couldn't remember the last time he'd been so glad to see a man of the cloth. "Took you long enough."

"On the contrary, it appears I arrived just in time. You're in quite a state, if you don't mind my saying so." Godfrey caught sight of Azura, and he stammered, suddenly at a loss for words. "You're a…"

"Fairy." She showed him her teeth. "Keep that crucifix away from me and we'll get along just fine."

Berengar cleared his throat to get their attention. "Hurry. It won't be long before more guards arrive."

Godfrey tore his gaze away from Azura and stooped to retrieve the guard's keys. "Your hound found me at the Coin and Crown and led me here." He hastened to free Berengar from his chains while Azura removed her remaining shackle. "I have a wagon waiting outside. We'll have to move quietly, though—the palace is crawling with guards. Once we're beyond the walls, you can tell me what a Warden of Fál is doing locked in one of King Lucien's tower cells."

Berengar came free of his restraints. Faolán approached and licked his face.

"It's good to see you too, girl. We're going to have to fight our way out of here."

Although a stout man himself, Godfrey nearly buckled under Berengar's weight. "Fight? You can barely stand."

"I'll live." Berengar pushed Godfrey away. "They've taken Morwen. We're not leaving without her." Fury kept him upright. He didn't need his armor or his weapons— only his rage. It was all he had ever needed. It was time to remind Winslow and his men why he was called the High Queen's Monster.

Azura's gaze moved to the door. "They're coming."

Two monster hunters came running into the cell. When they saw the guard slumped unconscious on the floor, they regarded the prisoners with complete astonishment. Azura hurled her lockpick at one's throat to prevent him from alerting others in the area. Berengar was on the man's companion before he could get out his sword. He shoved the guard into the wall hard, but—still weak from confinement—lost his balance with his foe still in his grip. When they hit the floor, he pinned his opponent under him and wrapped his hands around the man's throat. The monster hunter clawed at Berengar's face in a desperate but futile attempt at escape before finally succumbing.

Panting for air, Berengar rolled off the corpse, and his attention fell on the dead man's companion crawling along the floor. He pried the corpse's sword free of its sheath, pushed himself to his feet, and approached with sword in hand.

The monster hunter threw his hands up to shield himself. "Mercy, please!"

Berengar drove the sword down through his heart, an act that earned him a reproachful look from Faolán.

"Don't worry. There'll be plenty for you before we're through." He beckoned the others through the doorway. "Come on."

Godfrey cast a look at the corpse as he stepped over the body. "That was murder. That man was trying to surrender. The Acolytes may be butchers, but the guards are just following orders."

Berengar limped forward. "If they want to live, they should stay out of my way." He could worry about his conscience when Morwen was safe. "Faolán, find her."

Azura stooped to retrieve the lockpick on the way out. Faolán led the way, and the group quietly advanced through the tower. The smooth stone floor felt cold against Berengar's bare feet. When they caught an unsuspecting patrol unawares, Berengar made quick work of one while Faolán mauled the other. They hid the bodies in empty cells and continued on their way. The tower was well guarded with the added security provided by the Acolytes, but there was more than enough room to maneuver. Although Berengar would have slaughtered them all in a rage if he could, he kept silent for Morwen's sake, mindful of his weakened state. Leaving too many bodies in his wake meant alerting the guards all the sooner, and they would need precious time to escape the palace after recovering Morwen.

Faolán came to a stop at the end of a corridor. Voices came from nearby. *She's close.* Berengar's fist tightened around the grip of his blade. He readied himself to spring into action.

Azura gently touched his shoulder and spoke in a whisper. "Wait."

A moment later, he heard a door open, and numerous guards emerged from a cell they locked behind them. Once they were no longer in earshot, Berengar stole forward and prepared to hack away the lock with his sword.

Azura held a finger to her lips. "There are others nearby. We don't want to draw more attention." Using the lockpick, she picked the lock in short order.

Morwen was inside, strapped to a chair. Her staff and satchel lay on a table nearby. "Berengar!"

"Did they hurt you?"

She shook her head. "Valmont planned to test my powers first."

Berengar's anger diminished, if only a little, at the sight of her unharmed. "I told you this city was dangerous." He severed the ropes holding her, pulled her to him, and patted her head. "Don't do that to me again."

She went to reclaim her staff and satchel. "We must hurry. Valmont could return at any moment. Teelah is in the next cell. We can't leave her here to suffer at the torturers' hands."

Azura appeared offended by the very suggestion. "In case you've forgotten, that goblin has tried to kill us twice now. Besides, there's no time. We must recover the cursed blade before Völundr realizes we've escaped."

Morwen put her hands on her hips. "She's the only one who knows where King Lucien is."

Godfrey appeared confused. "Am I missing something? The king is here in the palace, isn't he?"

"We'll fill you in later." Berengar let out a reluctant sigh. "Morwen's right. We need her."

Azura uttered what was very likely profanity in the fairy tongue. "Foolish mortals. Now I'm to risk my life to rescue a *goblin*…" Lockpick in hand, she marched to the door to the neighboring cell.

When the door swung open, Berengar charged into the cell. By the time the monster hunters turned to face him, he was already halfway across the room. Faolán tackled one man off his feet, Berengar cut down two more, and Godfrey bashed a fourth over the head with his walking stick. Morwen used a spell to stick the final guard's blade in its sheath, and Berengar cut his throat.

"You." Teelah had clearly been treated more severely than Morwen. Dark green blood ran from cuts, and her skin was bruised. "Why come back for me?"

Morwen approached. "I want your word that you won't attempt to harm me or my companions if I let you go."

Azura's mocking laughter filled the chamber. "The word of a goblin? She'll murder you the first chance she gets."

Teelah regarded Azura with contempt. "And I suppose you're worth trusting, fairy? It's your kind who delight in ensnaring humans in wishes and deals."

"Your word," Morwen insisted. "You know where they're keeping King Lucien. Tell us where he is."

"You're a strange human, even for a magician. Very well. Help me escape, and once we're beyond the city gates, I will tell you all I know."

"That's good enough for me. Hold still." Morwen set her free.

Berengar stared Teelah down. "Don't make us regret this, goblin."

Before she could reply, raised voices sounded outside the cell.

Godfrey started toward the door. "I take it they've found the bodies. I suggest we take our leave before they find us as well."

They withdrew from the cell and began their descent through the tower. Torchlight shone below the winding stair, where guards approached in greater numbers. Berengar started toward them, sword ready.

Morwen stayed his hand. "There are too many." They retreated up the tower.

Godfrey shepherded them through a narrow passageway. "This way. Hurry!"

The corridor led out into the sunlight. The companions raced along a stone bridge. The cool wind caressed the warden's face, lending him new strength. The outer gate remained open, at least for the moment. If they failed to reach the wagon before the alarm went out, the guards would seal the entrance, trapping them within the palace walls.

Fortunately, the neighboring tower was sparsely guarded, and they made their descent without encountering opposition. Their path took them to a high balcony that overlooked the throne room.

At the sight of Valmont conversing with a number of the king's advisers below, Azura ground to a stop, and her voice rang through the chamber. "Völundr!"

Valmont looked up at her, and their eyes met. Azura's wings fluttered, but Berengar restrained her before she could take to the air.

"What are you doing? He has the blade!"

"There's no time!" Berengar understood her urgency. If they left now, they likely wouldn't enter the palace again without an army at their back. Still, they couldn't very well recover the cursed blade if they were dead, and the throne room was too well guarded for her to make a stand.

Valmont ordered the guards after them, and Azura reluctantly followed the others. They ran down another set of stairs and escaped the palace through a servant's entrance, where an archer stood guard. Berengar clamped a hand around the man's mouth and restrained him until he stopped kicking, and Teelah armed herself with the archer's bow and arrows while he concealed the body. After waiting a tense interval for the patrol to pass them by, they ran to Godfrey's wagon and concealed themselves in the back.

Godfrey took the reins, and the wagon slowly rolled toward the gate. Berengar watched the sentries on the walls through gaps in the wagon's covering. The gate remained open. So far, so good.

"Peace, brothers," Godfrey said when he arrived at the gate. "Bishop Valmont sends his regards."

A sentry started to usher them through the gate when bells tolled to sound the alarm. "Halt!"

Godfrey steered the wagon forward and charged the gate before the guards could close it. Arrows cascaded from above, littering the wagon's covering. The walls dwindled behind them as the wagon gathered speed. The sound of hooves came from a host of approaching horsemen. Escaping the palace was only the first step. They weren't safe until they were beyond the city walls.

"Hold on!" Godfrey turned the wagon onto a crowded road, and the chase was on.

Pedestrians fled before them as the wagon hurtled down a busy street. Jostled about, Berengar tightened his grip on the wagon. An arrow from Teelah struck the closest enemy rider in the chest, and the goblin unleashed three more arrows in rapid succession. Each arrow found its mark, but for every horseman downed, two more took his place. The watch had eyes everywhere. They weren't making it out of Dún Aulin without a fight.

One horseman drew near enough to grasp at Morwen's ankle. He nearly succeeded in pulling her off the back of the wagon, but she kicked the man in the face, and he fell away.

"Can't you go any faster?" Berengar called to Godfrey over his shoulder.

"I'm a friar, not a horseman! We spend most of our time on foot."

They took a sharp turn, rounding a corner, and pedestrians scrambled to get out of their path as the wagon veered to one side of the road. The effort failed to throw off their pursuers, who continued to close in on the wagon.

"Keep it steady, Godfrey!"

"I'm trying my best!"

Morwen tugged on Berengar's sleeve. "Don't look now, but there's trouble ahead."

They were headed straight toward a watch outpost. Archers began taking aim at the wagon and its driver.

Berengar swore. "Go help Godfrey. We'll handle this lot."

Morwen grabbed her staff and climbed up beside Godfrey at the front of the wagon. Berengar hoped her wards would be enough to deflect the archers' arrows. Meanwhile, the approaching riders threatened to overwhelm them.

A gust of wind came from Azura's beating wings, and she shot off the wagon. The fairy landed behind a rider on his saddle, and her fingers closed around the dagger sheathed at his side. "I'll take that, if you don't mind."

Before the man could react, she pulled the dagger free and threw him from the saddle. Azura fell back alongside another horseman, and a well-placed kick sent him over the side of his horse, which continued dragging him behind it. When one of Teelah's arrows struck another rider, missing Azura's head by inches, Azura shot her an ugly look, drawing the closest thing to a smile Berengar had seen from Teelah.

Godfrey turned off the street onto the main road. "The

gate's just ahead!"

Teelah nocked another arrow and scurried to the front of the wagon. Berengar cast one more look at Azura and went after her.

Looks like trouble. Archers lined the walls. Worse still, guards armed with swords and spears had assembled on foot to block their passage.

"Shut the gate!" a sentry cried out.

Teelah shot at the first man to reach the lever, and he toppled over backward. Fire from the archers forced her to pivot and shoot in their direction. It wasn't long before another guard reached the lever.

If that gate shuts, we're dead.

Azura flew to the wall and fended off sentries to keep the gate open long enough for them to squeeze through.

Berengar turned his attention to the guards blocking the wagon's path. "Brace yourselves." The wagon gathered momentum, speeding toward a deadly collision.

Azura whistled to the riders' horses, causing them to divert from their course and stampede. Some guards fled in panic; others were trampled underfoot. The wagon and its occupants passed through the gate unharmed, and before Berengar knew it, Azura was sitting beside Morwen in the driver's seat, wearing a self-satisfied smile.

They were free—for the moment.

O nce they were beyond the reach of the sentries' arrows, they took the horses and left the wagon behind. Morwen squealed with delight when she realized Godfrey had fetched Nessa from the Coin and Crown. Berengar was equally pleased to discover the friar had loaded their belongings into the saddlebags.

They did not linger. It would not be long before

Valmont sent more hunters in pursuit, and they needed to put as much distance between themselves and Dún Aulin as possible in the meantime. After the others selected new mounts from among the guards' horses that had accompanied them from the gate, the companions set out in haste.

Berengar knew Valmont would have the road to Tara watched, so they headed west instead, riding as if Balor and all the Fomorians were at their backs. Azura and Teelah were excellent riders, and Godfrey quickly proved himself more than capable of holding his own in the saddle. The route was not without danger, as venturing so close to the wilds brought them into proximity with Cathán's army of monsters.

The company sought refuge at Cobthach's Hold, which they reached just before sunset. An eerie silence hung over the abandoned outpost. As the constable at Tulach Mhór had suggested, there were few soldiers stationed near the wilds to begin with. Horst and the other scouts were probably the fort's only inhabitants before they were attacked in the Elderwood, leaving the hold unmanned. With all the recent happenings in Dún Aulin, it was unlikely the watch had bothered to allocate replacements.

Given the defensive fortifications in place, the hold was the safest place for them to find lodging. It remained a foreboding site to take up residence, even if only for the night. The fort was built by Cobthach Cóel Breg, who murdered his brother, Lóegaire Lorc—one of Leinster's first kings—to seize the throne. Years later, when Lóegaire's son Labraid defeated his uncle's armies, Cobthach retreated to the hold, but Labraid had it burned with Cobthach and his men inside. In the centuries that followed, scouts stationed at the outpost occasionally reported witnessing Cobthach's ghost wandering its grounds.

After finding shelter for their horses, the companions quickly set about exploring the fort. Berengar was careful not to let Teelah out of his sight in case the goblin went back on her word now that they were free of Dún Aulin. He needn't have bothered. Azura watched her even more closely. The dynamic between the two bore witness to the enmity fairies and goblins shared in the old tales.

They settled in the main hall for the night. A chill lingered in the air even once they got a fire going. Berengar tried on a pair of boots left behind by one of the outpost's previous inhabitants. They were as close to his size as he was likely to find, if a tad on the small side. A similarly abandoned tunic proved a better fit. The scouts hadn't left much in the way of armor, but he managed to find a shield to go along with his sword.

Aware of Morwen's gaze, he tried not to show his residual discomfort from the beating Winslow had inflicted. He didn't argue when she forced him to drink a healing draught and a potion to help with the pain.

Recent ordeals had left them all tired and hungry. Fortunately, the outpost was fully stocked with enough rations to last for months. They discovered a storeroom filled with brined meat and fish, dried grains, candied nuts and fruits, and other varieties of preserved foods. Berengar, ravenously hungry after days without food, devoured one heaping portion after another. Grateful for the reprieve, he eased himself down beside the fireplace and held out his hands to the flames. Although battered and bruised, he wasn't seriously injured. With a little rest, he would be back to his old strength soon enough, even if he remained acutely aware of his axe's absence. Without his cloak, armor, or battleaxe, he hardly felt himself.

Morwen brushed the burs from Faolán's coat. "Where will we go in the morning?"

Berengar stared into the flames. "Tara. The High Queen must know of Valmont's treachery."

Teelah bristled at the suggestion. "Then you go alone. I'll not trade one cell for another."

"What makes you think you have any choice in the matter?"

The goblin flashed her fangs in a sign of displeasure.

Azura shook her head. "There is no time to seek your queen's aid. Now that we have eluded his grasp, Völundr will send others to eliminate King Lucien while he continues his search for the remaining half of the cursed blade. We must reach Lucien first and restore the true king to the throne."

Berengar held her gaze. "I'm in charge here."

"Then it is fortunate I do not require your permission. You are free to go in search of your queen. The magician, however, stays with me until she has fulfilled our bargain."

"Bargain?" Morwen's brow arched in confusion. "What bargain?"

Azura smiled widely. "You haven't forgotten our ficheall game, have you? An unspecified favor—I believe that was our deal."

Teelah regarded Morwen with an expression of incredulity. "You made a pact? With *her*? I thought you were cleverer than that."

"I didn't know she was a fairy at the time…"

"I don't care what she promised you," Berengar snapped. "Where I go, she goes too."

Azura rubbed her hands together. "Then it appears you will be joining us on our quest. She could not refuse even if she wished. Magic would compel her to honor her word."

Berengar looked to Morwen. "Compel?"

Morwen shifted uncomfortably. "It's true. There's a

reason it's unwise for humans to enter into bargains with fairies."

Azura patted her on the back. "Cheer up! It'll be over before you know it. Once King Lucien again sits on the throne and the cursed blade is back where it belongs, you might even find yourselves thanking me."

Berengar narrowed his gaze at her. "You've caused us nothing but trouble so far. I don't trust you any more than I trust the goblin."

Azura's sunny expression didn't falter. "Is he always like this?"

Morwen laughed. "More or less. You caught him on a bad day."

Berengar shot her a reproachful look.

"What? It's not a bad plan, all things considered. If we return to Dún Aulin with the *real* Lucien, the city watch will turn on Valmont and the pretender."

Still angry at having been tricked by Azura once again, Berengar just grunted. Maybe she was right, but he didn't have to acknowledge it. He turned his attention to Teelah. "Time to make good on your word. Where's Valmont keeping the king?"

The goblin's reptilian eyes flitted toward him. "The fairy has him in a barrow hidden deep in the Elderwood. The scouts here helped conceal the location. You are not alone in your search—Cathán also seeks your king."

"You ought to know. You've been working for him from the start."

"I didn't know he planned to sacrifice the king to awaken Caorthannach. I thought he was only after vengeance, as am I."

"Will you show us the way?" Morwen asked. "We must find him first."

"I have no love for Lucien. The church's monster

hunters have caused the deaths of countless goblins. But the return of the Fomorians would mean death and despair for all races—goblins included. The others are too far gone in their hatred of mankind to see it."

"So you'll help us?"

Teelah paused for a moment, and the roar of the flames broke the silence. Finally, she nodded. "I'll lead you to him, but then my debt to you is settled. If you want more than that, you'll have to pay me for it."

Berengar felt a grudging sense of respect for her. Unlike Morwen, she was not bound by some magical pact to honor her commitment. Goblins were not generally considered truthful creatures, and he had known plenty to go back on their word.

"Look what I found!" Godfrey appeared, rolling a cask of ale. When he noticed the dark mood that had settled over the company, his expression faltered, but only for a moment. "Anyone care to join me?"

Berengar, still so full he could hardly move, nevertheless nodded in assent. Godfrey handed him a tankard, and Faolán left Morwen and settled beside him. He scratched her behind the ears, and his eyelids grew heavy.

He woke again sometime later in the night. Winds howled outside the fort. He wasn't sure if it was due to the tense atmosphere or the uncomfortable stone floor, but the others were still awake. Berengar rubbed his eye and glanced around the room. Godfrey stooped to feed the dying fire. Teelah lingered in a corner some distance from the others while Morwen labored on her new staff at a table. When she grimaced in discomfort from the pain caused by her burned hand, Teelah approached to take the seat across from her, and Berengar reached for his blade in case she was up to something.

Instead, Teelah reached into her belt and offered

Morwen a vial containing a salve. "Rub this on the burn. Wrap your hand and check the bandages in two days' time."

Morwen accepted the gift without hesitation. "Thank you."

Teelah shrugged. "My mother was a healer. She always expected I would follow in her footsteps. I wonder sometimes what she would think if she saw my face on bounties posted across the kingdom."

Faolán whined, and Berengar noticed her staring at Azura, who produced a similar noise. Were the two actually *talking* to one another?

Azura seemed to respond to his thoughts. "She's quite remarkable. Much older and more intelligent than an ordinary hound. You must have done something very special to have earned her loyalty."

"We've been through a lot together."

"I'm sure you have. No animal sees the other side and returns unchanged."

Morwen, who had finished bandaging her hand, shot him a curious glance. "What did she mean by that?" When Berengar didn't answer, she turned her focus back to Azura. "Might I ask a question? You mentioned before that you lost your wand for involving yourself in human affairs. Why help us?"

The question put Azura in a somber mood. The mirth Berengar had come to expect from her seemed diminished, hinting that she carried deeper emotions beneath the surface. "I was always fascinated by humans. Many fairies are. There are those who delight in bringing misfortune to your kind, but most are simply after amusement. Our lives are much longer than yours, and we bore easily.

"When I was a girl, I was alone. I had no one. More than anything, I wished for a friend. And so I left the

Otherworld and came to your realm in search of one. There was a mortal who lived in a castle. Like me, she longed for adventure. Her name was Anya."

Berengar raised an eyebrow. "King Áed's daughter? Áed reigned years ago—before the Shadow Wars."

Morwen glanced at him sidewise. "I told you. Fairies age more slowly than we do."

"I took the princess from her home." Azura's eyes fixed on Morwen's amulet. "That amulet you carry—do you know where it comes from?"

Morwen nodded. "It was a present from my father. It was enchanted by Thane Ramsay himself."

"It was a kingly gift, for that is no mere relic. In those days, magic was not hated as it is now. Magicians, mages, and druids protected the land. But the greatest of these was King Áed's thane, the sorcerer Ramsay of Connacht —a hero whose legend stands beside Padraig himself. Time and again, Áed and his thane delivered Fál from evil and kept the peace between the five kingdoms.

"Anya was Ramsay's adopted sister. When she was taken, he came after her." Azura smiled once more, but it was a sad smile. "He was just as great as the stories say he was. But greater still was the size of his heart."

Morwen studied her intently. "Valmont said you gave your heart to a mortal."

"He spoke truly. I loved Ramsay—love him still."

"All know of the doom of Áed." Berengar had heard some of the story from Nora herself, who was there when Áed's castle fell.

"Aye. When Áed perished, his family died with him. Your High Queen is the last of his line. I sought Anya and Ramsay in the chaos that followed but could not find them. Most believe they perished at Áed's side in the final battle.

"Since that time, I have done what I can to help

mankind, all while searching for answers. No matter how lonely it gets, no matter the cost—I still believe that one day I will find him, and he me."

Silence hung in the air, and Berengar and Morwen exchanged glances. Thane Ramsay was a storied hero, it was true, but he had passed into legend many years ago. He was gone, along with Anya, Áed, and the others. Áed's fall brought about a time of chaos between the kingdoms from which the Lord of Shadows emerged to begin his conquest of Fál, until Nora took up her uncle's crown and drove him from the land. Still, while Berengar knew Ramsay was dead, he couldn't bring himself to shatter Azura's belief to the contrary. Cynic though he was, there was something pure about her unabashed faith—something true. Even Teelah seemed touched by the story, though she said nothing on the subject.

"We have a dangerous road ahead. You all should try to get some sleep. I will keep watch." Azura began to sing —a lullaby that slowly clouded Berengar's thoughts.

Morwen stifled a yawn. "What about you?"

"We fairies require very little sleep. The magic that runs through our veins gives us energy. Do not worry about me. Rest and dream of happy things." With that, she resumed her song.

Berengar was too tired to do otherwise. Before he again succumbed to his fatigue, he leaned over and whispered to Morwen. "About what you said before—you're not my pet magician, you know." He heard only a snore in response. Morwen was already asleep. He sighed and closed his eyes.

When they woke in the morning, Azura had finished Morwen's staff.

CHAPTER TWELVE

THEY SET out from Cobthach's Hold at first light. Berengar didn't want to take the chance that Valmont's hunters might find their trail—not when they were already headed further into danger. They made sure to pack enough rations for the journey. The scouts certainly wouldn't be needing them, and there was no point in letting good food go to waste.

The company traveled north to avoid Tulach Mhór and the Giant's Foot. Berengar kept ahead of the others while Faolán trailed at a distance to keep watch. Morwen and Azura rode side by side, and Godfrey, bringing up the rear, attempted to engage Teelah in conversation only to find himself repeatedly rebuffed. True to form, the good-natured friar persisted. Eventually, Teelah relented enough to answer him in short, one-word responses, though her demeanor remained as solemn as ever. A magician, fairy, goblin, and friar certainly made for strange traveling companions, even in the company of the Bloody Red Bear.

Morwen spent the first hours in awe of Azura's handi-work. Charms and symbols etched into the staff's wooden surface now ran its length. "I *love* it. How on earth did you manage all this overnight?"

Azura regarded her with obvious amusement. "All fairies speak the language of magic with ease. We do not require years of study or heaps of books to understand it."

Morwen ran a hand along the staff. "These defensive charms will come in handy. It's perfect." She delved into her satchel and placed her lightstone and a blue runestone into two slots near the staff's head.

Azura laughed. "Now maybe you'll avoid draining or burning yourself from attempting to wield those runes with your hands."

Morwen flushed, embarrassed, and Berengar suppressed a smile. As she was so fond of teasing him, it was nice to see the shoe on the other foot for a change.

"Beware of fairy gifts," Teelah called from behind. "Especially when they come with strings attached."

Azura looked over her shoulder and bared her teeth. "No one asked you, goblin. What have your kind ever given humans but war and strife?"

Teelah snorted derisively. "In times past, there were great goblin kingdoms—kingdoms that lived in peace with humans, even if they have forgotten it. It isn't our fault that they see our claws and teeth and judge us monsters—or that they see your great beauty and forget your many sleights against them in hopes of a free wish."

"And I suppose your raids on the countryside are the acts of a friend?"

Teelah pointed at Berengar. "Men like *him* burn down our homes, kill our families, and try to exterminate our entire race. Can you blame us for defending ourselves?"

"Leave me out of your squabbles." Berengar came of age slaying goblins to the north. He refused to apologize for doing what was necessary to protect his home. In truth, he had learned a long time ago that goblins—like people—were capable of both good and evil, but he didn't feel the need to justify himself to anyone—least of all someone who had attempted to kill him on more than one occasion.

Teelah fixed her withering gaze on him. "See? He doesn't even try to deny the blood on his hands. He's as much of a butcher as any of my kin."

"You are wrong about him," Godfrey volunteered on his behalf. "When I first met him in Alúine, Warden Berengar put himself in grave peril to save the last hobgoblins from Laird Margolin's forces. He even let them keep the thunder rune they had stolen from him so they could start a new life in Munster."

"That's enough, Godfrey." The last thing he wanted was Godfrey spinning him into some sort of hero. If the friar kept it up, it wouldn't be long before Morwen joined in.

"That's right," Morwen added, prompting a groan from Berengar. "It was to avenge their deaths and recover the stone that he returned to Leinster in the first place."

Berengar shot them both a warning look. "I said enough." Teelah was right. There was a reason the goblins called him Berengar Goblin-Bane. It was unlikely any man alive had slaughtered more goblins. He was no friend to them, and he was certainly no hero.

For her part, Teelah appeared unconvinced, though she chose not to press the matter further. Berengar didn't blame her. After a lifetime spent hearing stories about the atrocities he had committed, she had good reason to doubt him. In that respect, she wasn't that different from most others.

He went farther ahead to avoid being drawn into conversation. To his surprise, he felt remarkably well-rested. He couldn't remember sleeping so well in a long time. Even his soreness was notably improved from the previous day. He wondered if the change had anything to do with Azura's lullaby. He again caught himself humming the tune but could no longer recall the words.

When they arrived at the Elderwood before midday, Teelah instructed them to keep close together. "Move carefully. Cathán will have spies looking for us in hopes we will lead them to your king. He has many animals and trees under his command."

"I have friends in the forest too." Azura called to a sparrow, which landed on her outstretched hand. After a brief exchange, the bird flew to a branch and hopped to another. "She will show us a safe route."

Berengar nodded to Teelah. "I believe you know the way."

She started down the path without reply. They continued for most of the day. According to Teelah, it would take at least another day to reach the barrows where Valmont had hidden Lucien. The Elderwood's size, which spanned the borders of multiple kingdoms, made it the perfect place for the dark fairy to conceal Lucien from prying eyes. The forest had a well-earned reputation as a place of magic and dangerous creatures, and many believed it was cursed. Even the monster hunters might think twice before following them inside.

The sparrow proved a valuable ally. They encountered no enemies on the first leg of their journey, though Berengar suspected the true danger lay ahead. Late in the day, they passed a farm tucked away in an isolated clearing. Smoke rose from the farmhouse's chimney, and a modest barn nestled under the trees. Well-fed chickens wandered freely while pigs roamed about their pens.

A middle-aged woman with five small children was finishing her chores outside the farmhouse. Azura and

Teelah remained out of sight while Berengar and the others made their way to the farmhouse. One of the woman's children pulled at her sleeve to get her attention at their approach.

"Welcome. It's not often we get travelers here. I am Nairne, and these are my young ones." Her gaze fell on Berengar's sword. "What brings you this way?"

Berengar ignored the children, who hid behind their mother at the sight of his scars. "Just passing through."

"We are simple folk," Godfrey volunteered. "We mean you no harm."

The friar's crucifix seemed to set her at ease. "You are welcome to shelter here for the night, provided you leave your weapons outside."

Berengar did as she requested. "Faolán, stay." The wolfhound stared hungrily at passing chickens but obediently remained where she was.

Berengar ducked under the farmhouse's doorway and filed in behind Morwen, who winked at each of Nairne's children in turn. Were they in another kingdom, she might have entertained them with magic, but she kept her abilities to herself.

It wasn't long before they were all packed around the hearth, sharing mutton stew prepared over an open fire. Berengar was content to let Godfrey do most of the talking while he ate in peace. Nairne was curious about their travels; the frontier received little news about current affairs. The friar explained the purpose for their journey only in the vaguest of terms as the children stole glances at his wooden hand.

Their host was a widow. Her husband and their eldest daughter had passed on from plague the previous year. She had managed well enough in her husband's absence, but times were hard, and she was not sure there were stores enough to last through the coming winter.

"You should be careful if you're planning to venture deeper into the forest. Lots of strange happenings in these parts, especially of late. Ghost sightings and goblin raids— that sort of thing. The entire community of Ferbane vanished overnight."

Berengar already knew the area was dangerous, but her words boded ill all the same. He wondered what would become of Nairne and her children after their departure. If the monsters didn't get them, the family faced cold and starvation when winter arrived.

In the morning, the company left the farm, and Azura and Teelah joined them at the forest's edge. One look was all it took to know the two hadn't yet put aside their differences. There were fewer signs of human influence the farther west they traveled. It was a sign that however civilized the world had become, there were still dangerous, untamed places better left alone. The Elderwood shifted and changed as they continued on their way. Towering trees drowned out the sunlight and cast fallen leaves over the earth. More than once, Berengar had the feeling of being watched.

Eventually they came to Ferbane. The abandoned settlement was a shambles.

Berengar slowed his pace and inspected the scene. "Monsters were here. A lot of them, from the look of it." It appeared the settlement's defenders had been overrun.

Morwen eyed a decomposing corpse near the well. "What do you think became of the others?"

"Who can say?" He didn't imagine it was a pleasant fate. Monsters had ravenous appetites.

Godfrey, no stranger to death, looked uneasy. "We should keep going."

Berengar turned to Teelah, who surveyed the remnants of Ferbane with an indiscernible expression. "Lead the way."

She returned to the trail without a word and led them deeper into the forest. They followed her along a winding path into a marsh. The pale light took on a greenish hue that matched the water's murky color. Strange-looking fungi grew on deformed, sickly-looking trees whose bare roots ran deep underground.

Berengar swatted a mosquito and kept his gaze fixed on the road ahead. Menacing crows stared down from twisted, appendage-like branches at the travelers passing underneath. "The horses are spooked." He reined in his horse to prevent the stallion from stepping off the path and peered into the marsh, where human skulls were visible among moss-covered stones. Flies swarmed around decaying animal corpses.

Godfrey stared at an enormous spider's web between two trees, and his grip tightened around the cross hanging from his neck. "I don't like the look of this place."

Teelah pressed a finger to her lips. "Quiet. We're close now."

Fog spread from the banks of the marsh, and the path soon disappeared. Tiny winged creatures, glowing like candles, flitted through the air. When Morwen reached toward one, it quickly retreated, followed by the others.

"What are they?" Godfrey asked. "More fairies?"

"Pixies," Azura corrected. "They were trying to warn us away. The walls between your world and the fairy realm are thin here. This is the place."

Large grassy mounds loomed ahead, and the companions dismounted and advanced with weapons drawn. Thorns and briars covered the soft earth. Fog clung to scattered pillars and overturned stones as if moving with a life of its own. Many stones bore strange markings reminiscent of the symbols on Morwen's runestones. A soft, rasping sound prompted a growl from Faolán. They weren't alone.

Berengar lowered his voice. "Stay close."

"Look." Morwen held her staff high, and her light-stone illuminated a hidden entrance under one of the mounds.

Vines and fallen leaves rendered the mounds' entrances nearly invisible. Although a stone frame formed each entrance, there were no doors to bar the way inside. Shadows lurked beyond the empty doorways.

"So Lucien's in one of these holes?" Berengar started toward the closest entrance.

Azura blocked his path. "Völundr has hidden King Lucien among the dead. These barrows are protected by far more than doors. If we enter the wrong mound, we will find only death."

Berengar made no attempt to hide his frustration. "Then what do you suggest we do—wait here for Cathán's spies to discover us?"

"Let me try." Morwen closed her eyes and stretched her hand toward one of the doorways. "Teacht ar do ruin." The rune of illusion glowed with purple light, but nothing happened.

Azura shook her head. "You underestimate the trickery of fairies. Völundr would never make such a choice that simple. We must look closer. He will have left some clue to the correct choice."

The company spent the better part of an hour searching for a hint that might point them in the right direction. They inspected markings on the pillars, turned over stones, and even counted the number of skulls adorning each entrance—all to no avail. Berengar was about to give up hope when he caught Morwen staring into the marsh.

"It's the reflection," she mumbled to herself.

Berengar followed her gaze to the water's edge. "What?"

She spoke louder, more sure of herself. "It's the reflection! Look!"

Only one entrance was mirrored by the marsh water. The others cast no reflection.

"Clever." Azura beamed at Morwen. "Perhaps the tales concerning the decline of Fál's magicians are premature."

A cold wind brushed by like a whisper as they passed through the entrance. Nothing happened when they entered, which was one good sign, at least. The light from Morwen's staff revealed a long stone stair stretching down into darkness. When they reached the end, torches below burst into flame of their own accord, and their light cascaded over a sprawling stone chamber.

Morwen shuddered. "Be careful. There is strong magic at work here."

Although hidden treasures and heaps of precious stones were strewn throughout the room, Berengar's eye was drawn to one of several lidless, dust-covered coffins. A set of bony fingers curled motionlessly over the side. Beyond the reach of the torches' light, a set of skeletal remains was visible tucked away in a hole carved into the wall. "This is a tomb."

The added illumination provided by Morwen's light-stone revealed scores—if not hundreds—of similar remains. "I have a bad feeling about this place." Faolán growled in agreement. On the other side of the chamber, a narrow bridge led to a slab where a sleeping fair-haired youth lay on his back. A silver crown rested upon his head. "Lucien. Valmont has him under some sort of spell. We'll have to wake him before we can remove him from the barrow."

Teelah stopped Berengar from proceeding forward. "Wait." A crease formed on her brow as she regarded the floor panels, which bore strange symbols similar to the markings found outside. "The floor is trapped."

Azura agreed. "She's right. Völundr expected intruders would take the simplest path to the king."

Nervous, Morwen stared at the floor. "What will happen if we step on the wrong panel?"

Azura left the question unanswered. She scanned the chamber until her gaze fell on symbols adorning the various pillars throughout the room. The symbols matched those on the floor. "It's a puzzle. We're meant to follow the path laid for us by the pillars."

When she stepped onto the first panel, Berengar tensed, prepared for the worst. Nothing happened. Azura laughed with glee and motioned for them to follow her. Morwen used the rune of illusion to highlight the safe sections of floor with purple light. The winding course took them the long way around the chamber. When they finally reached the bridge that led to the king, Morwen and Azura exchanged glances.

"What?" Berengar stared at the precipitous fall that awaited any who strayed from the path.

"There is an artifice upon the path." Azura looked to Morwen. "Will you do the honors?"

Morwen raised her staff, held out her palm, and closed her eyes. "Taispeáin an litriú!" The rune of illusion again glowed with purple light, and writing appeared on the stone wall behind the king.

To Berengar, the markings were an indecipherable mess. "Morwen, what does it say?"

"I don't know. I can't read it."

"It's written in the fairy language. It says only one can cross the bridge and safely return." Azura unfurled her wings. "Thankfully, I have other ways of moving about." She waited for Morwen to make the journey on foot before gliding across the expanse, and the pair began working to stir King Lucien from his enchantment while Berengar and the others watched.

As time stretched on, Berengar found himself growing restless. "What's taking so long?"

Morwen cast a reproachful look back at him and fished through her satchel for another spell book. "It's not as simple as it looks. We don't know the nature of the enchantment he's under."

Azura showed signs of losing her temper. "Nothing. I've tried every method to lift a sleeping curse I can think of and nothing has made the slightest difference."

Morwen glanced away from her spell book as if a new thought had occurred to her. "What if it's not a spell?" She put the book away and leaned in closer to Lucien's motionless form. "What if it's a sleeping potion?"

"I see. Völundr means for us to waste our time trying to lift a curse that doesn't exist. How irritatingly clever. Any ideas?"

Morwen grinned. "Fortunately, potions are a magician's domain." She reached for another book from her satchel. "I have some potions and alchemy ingredients on hand, but I can't attempt to administer an antidote until I know the potion used to put Lucien to sleep. Otherwise I could kill him."

Berengar turned away to survey the barrow's hidden recesses in time to notice Teelah silently reach for an arrow from her quiver. "What are you doing?"

"I promised to lead you here. Nothing more."

She plans to kill the king. Berengar trained his sword on her. "Put down the bow."

"I will not. Leinster's soldiers slaughter nonhumans by the hundreds, all in his name. With this arrow, I will avenge my fallen kin and send a warning to all who would harm us."

"Killing him won't save your people. It will only further enflame humans against you. Don't make Cathán's mistake." By now, the others had taken note.

Teelah pulled back on the arrow. "Do you know what it's like to watch your family die, Berengar Goblin-Bane?"

Berengar's jaw tightened involuntarily. "Put down the bow. Last warning."

When Teelah raised the bow, Berengar whistled to Faolán, and they charged her together. The goblin slipped out of his grasp and managed to avoid Faolán's teeth, but before she could take aim at Lucien, a floor panel shifted under her feet. Teelah instantly stepped off the floor panel, but it was too late, and the panel stuck in place. A rasping whisper emanated from somewhere in the dark, and the torchlight flickered as a gust of wind blew through the chamber.

Berengar took a step back, and his hand tightened around the hilt of his blade. For a moment, he thought he caught a glimpse of movement in the shadows. Faolán barked loudly at a black cavity filled with skeletal remains. One skull was visible among the various bones embedded within the wall. Darkness seemed to pour from the skull's vacant eye sockets. Without warning, its jaw snapped shut, and the skull let out a hair-raising shriek. Skeletal fingers clenched and unclenched, as if waking from a deep sleep, and the wight slowly pulled itself free of the wall.

When it staggered toward Berengar, one swing of his sword cleaved its head from its body, and the bones fell in a

241

heap on the floor. For a moment, there was silence. Then a groan came from across the room, where a bony hand shot out from a casket. A chorus of inhuman moans joined the first, and one by one, skeletal figures came to life all over the chamber. Some wore the tattered remains of armor. Many wielded rusted swords and splintered bows from a time long forgotten.

The pile of bones at Berengar's feet began to coalesce, and the wight's hand grasped at his boot. He stomped the hand, shattering bone, but again the wight reformed. Teelah felled another with an arrow, but like the wight Berengar destroyed, it too pulled itself back together. Guided by whatever foul magic animated them, they dragged themselves toward Berengar and his companions.

Godfrey kissed his crucifix. "May the Lord protect us."

A second arrow from Teelah disappeared through an empty eye socket. She hissed, nocked another arrow, and fired again. The wights continued undeterred, forcing Berengar and the others to retreat to the chamber's center.

Azura glanced at Morwen. "Keep working. I'll help the others." She landed beside Teelah and shot her a dark look, which the goblin returned in kind. "Look what you've done. Those wights will keep coming until we're dead."

Berengar glanced back at Morwen. "You might want to pick up the pace."

"I'm working as fast as I can! It's not as if I'm reading under candlelight in my library at Cashel!"

Berengar bit back a retort and stepped forward to meet the closest wight. He lodged his sword in its rib cage and crushed its torso with a boot. He brought the sword around in an arc that dismembered all wights within reach and raised his shield in time to intercept an arrow from a skeletal archer. Teelah knocked the archer from its perch with a well-placed shot and spun around to fire at another.

Godfrey held incoming wights at bay with his walking stick. The touch of his crucifix instantly shattered those that came within reach.

Berengar cut loose and rampaged across the chamber without restraint, smashing wights to pieces with each stroke of his sword while Faolán picked off those that eluded him. Yet for each wight he destroyed, two more took its place. The growing horde drove the companions back, closer to the precipice. The archers' arrows vanished into the abyss, falling closer to Morwen with each volley.

Berengar battered an enemy swordsman with his shield and cast the wight off the ledge. "Keep them away from Morwen!" He went on the offensive to buy the others more time. Although the wights were weak and slow, their numbers made them dangerous, and it was all he could do to stave off multiple attacks. When two wights leapt on his back, he was forced to drop his sword to tear himself from their grasp.

A cry sounded behind, where Teelah had dodged an incoming spear and lost her balance. She toppled backward over the ledge and managed to clutch the side, where she hung helpless and exposed as more wights shambled toward her. At the last second, Godfrey—having lost his walking stick—reached out and pulled her back over the side, and Berengar fell back to join them.

"I've got it!" Morwen waved to them with a look of triumph. "It's the Dreamer's Delight! Now I need only prepare an antidote."

Berengar groaned and turned back to face the army of wights. He was tiring, and the blasted things just kept coming. He sucked in a deep breath and readied himself for another bout, and the companions made one final stand as the wights closed in on them. He lunged past Teelah—who couldn't fire arrows fast enough to keep the enemy at bay—and lost his grip on his shield to an axe strike. Legions of bony fingers wrapped themselves around him, and before he could free himself, more threw themselves on him from all sides. Completely enveloped and unable to breathe, Berengar clawed desperately for a way out, but the wights' numbers were too many. At the last moment, Faolán bit his boot and dragged him out from under the wights, and Berengar gasped for air.

"Stand back!" Azura shouted a word of power, and the force of her voice leveled the area and reduced the approaching wights to scattered bones and ash. She bent over and put her hands on her knees. It was clear the display of power had taken its toll. "I don't know how long that will hold them for."

Berengar stooped to retrieve his sword. "Fall back to Morwen. If any more come for us, we'll fend them off one at a time."

They hurried across the bridge, where Morwen was administering a decoction to Lucien. A shudder passed through his body, he coughed up a dark, purple liquid, and the king's eyes fluttered open. When he saw Teelah looming over him, he screamed and fell back with a start.

"Monster! Keep that thing away from me!"

Teelah hissed at him but made no attempt to attack.

"It's all right." Morwen put her hand on Lucien's arm. "You're safe now, Your Highness."

Lucien calmed to her touch. He took note of her staff and spell books and shrank away from her. "What are you —a witch of some kind?"

"I'm no witch! I am Morwen of Cashel, former court magician to King Mór of Munster."

Lucien raised an eyebrow. "The one that got him killed, you mean? Of course, he brought it on himself by involving himself in witches' affairs."

"I should have left him asleep," Morwen muttered under her breath.

"That's no way to greet your rescuers," Berengar said.

Lucien looked him up and down with skepticism. "And who are you? You look even less trustworthy than the goblin."

"Warden Berengar. You might have heard of me."

Lucien reacted poorly to the mention of Berengar's name. "Bishop McLoughlin sent the *High Queen's Monster* to rescue me? Where is Warden Niall?"

"McLoughlin's dead. Niall's out searching for your cousin, the prince regent."

The king did not take the news well. "I should have known. What kind of trouble has the errant fool gotten himself into now?" Lucien held up a hand, as if to dismiss the question. "Never mind that. Where am I? I command you to tell me."

"You're in the Elderwood," Morwen answered. "Put in a trance by a sleeping potion."

"Valmont." Lucien's expression darkened. "That treacherous fairy. When I return to Dún Aulin, I'll have him burned at the stake."

"We shouldn't linger here. It's not safe." Morwen offered her hand to help the king to his feet.

Lucien ignored the gesture. "I'm not going anywhere with you, witch. None among your company look particularly trustworthy, save perhaps the priest. For all I know, you're in league with Valmont, especially if you travel with *her*."

Azura merely laughed in amusement when he pointed to her.

Berengar took a step toward him. "You're coming with us, one way or another. Even if I have to carry you back to Dún Aulin myself."

Lucien's brow furrowed in anger. "I am the king of Leinster! I will not be ordered about like a child!"

A violent tremor shook the chamber. Berengar turned around, the king temporarily forgotten. Bones rolled across the floor, amassing in an ever-expanding heap. Remnants of individual wights stitched themselves together to form a multi-limbed monstrosity that towered nearly to the ceiling.

"Run!" Morwen said.

This time, Lucien didn't argue. The group took off running along the bridge with the ground shifting under their feet. The living bones lashed the bridge, which gave way just as the last of the company made it to the other side. When a bony tendril reached out for Lucien, Berengar chopped through it with his sword, and Morwen cast a ward to deflect another tendril aimed at Godfrey.

The mass of bones rushed to block their path to the staircase, but Azura unleashed a verbal assault that blasted a hole down the creature's center, and the company rushed through the gap before it could reform. Faint light shone ahead at the barrow's entrance. *Almost there.* A roar came from behind, where the monstrosity squeezed itself into the narrow passage to continue its pursuit. As the others spilled out of the entrance, a tendril wrapped itself around Berengar's ankle just before he crossed the threshold. The tendril threatened to drag him back inside the barrow, but Godfrey, Teelah, and Azura pulled him free at the last moment.

Morwen thrust her staff at the barrow before the monstrosity could emerge behind him. "Buille a bhriseadh!" A crack formed along the entrance, and the barrow caved in on itself, burying the remnants of the dead beneath.

For a moment, no one spoke. Then Lucien dusted himself off and nodded to himself, as if resolving some inner dispute. "Very well. I shall allow you to escort me to Dún Aulin." He started on the path that led from the marsh and looked back impatiently. "What are you waiting for? We've no time to tarry."

Berengar exchanged a glance with Morwen, shook his head, and trudged after the king.

CHAPTER THIRTEEN

AZURA'S SPARROW friend was waiting for them near the barrow's entrance. After a brief exchange with the bird, Azura addressed the others. "The path we took to reach the marsh is being watched. We must return to Dún Aulin by another route."

Although they had escaped the barrow, Faolán remained uneasy, a sign they weren't out of danger yet.

"Blast it." Berengar stared at the sky. They were losing the light, and he had no intention of learning what other horrors lurked within the marsh. "Where will we go now?"

Azura posed the question to the sparrow, which took flight after answering. "She says there are men not far from here."

Lucien rubbed his hands together in anticipation. "Excellent. Let us be on our way. My loyal subjects will greet us with open arms."

Berengar would rather they seek shelter than spend the night outdoors, but that didn't mean they could forsake caution altogether. "Not so fast. Cathán has spies everywhere, and so does Valmont. We should keep our heads down until we're out of the Elderwood."

He quickened his pace. It was a short walk to where they left their horses. Lucien mostly kept to himself. Teelah, however, appeared to have warmed to Godfrey considerably following their shared ordeal in the barrow. The good-natured friar even shared his drinking horn with her in a sign of friendship. Although she showed no sign of thawing toward Berengar, she nevertheless agreed to help escort the king from the Elderwood in exchange for gold. That at least, he hoped, would keep her from making another attempt on Lucien's life.

When they reached their horses, Azura offered the king a portion of the rations they took from Cobthach's Hold. "I'm sure you must be hungry after your long rest."

Lucien turned the food away.

"You would refuse my hospitality?" Azura's smile fell.

"I've had enough dealings with treacherous fairies to know better than to accept a gift from one of your kind, girl."

Azura's amusement at his antics quickly faded. "You should choose your words more carefully. I am much older than you, my young friend."

"I'm not your friend, monster," the king snapped.

Morwen laid a hand on Lucien's shoulder. "It isn't wise to insult one of the fair folk, Your Highness."

"Fair folk? Bah! Winged devils, more like."

Azura's eyes widened, and she bared her teeth as if a grave offense had been committed. "You wicked little imp." Before Morwen could stop her, she snatched the rune of illusion from the magician's staff and held it over Lucien. "Until you learn to act like a king, an imp you shall be."

The king swallowed hard and took a step back. "Stay

back!" He looked to Berengar and the others for support. "Keep her away!"

There was a flash of light, accompanied by a shriek from Lucien. The king checked himself before casting an angry gaze at Azura. "Ha! Your spell failed, fairy."

Azura's lips curled into a mischievous grin. "Did it?"

The king gave a start, and a barbed tail poked out from behind him. Lucien screamed as patches of brown fur covered him from head to toe and his pupils became slits.

Stunned, Morwen looked from Lucien to Azura. "You turned him into an imp."

Azura doubled over laughing, and it was Lucien's turn to be unamused.

"Change me back! I order you to change me back!"

Azura playfully wagged a finger in his direction. "I'm afraid you're the only one who can do that. You might start by behaving in a more kingly fashion."

"So you *can* use magic without a wand," Morwen said.

"I *am* a fairy, after all." Azura invoked the rune's power again to restore her human form. Only her pointed ears hinted she was more than she appeared. "That's better. Now when we reach the town, I'll fit right in. Can't say the same for you, I'm afraid, Your Highness." She tossed the stone back to Morwen.

"Morwen…" Berengar started.

"Don't look at me. I don't know how to lift the spell. It might work to our advantage. Cathán's spies will be looking for the king, not an imp. Besides, it might teach the little brute a lesson. You heard what he said about my father."

"Fine." Berengar pulled a cloak from his bag and tossed it to Lucien. "In the meantime, I suggest you use this to hide that mug of yours."

Lucien stared down at his fur-covered hands. "What? I command you to make her change me back."

"I don't take orders from you." Berengar put one foot in the stirrup and swung himself onto his horse. "Now get on a horse before I bind and gag you."

"Here, Your Highness." Godfrey reached out to the king from his horse. "I am Friar Godfrey."

"One honest man among you, at least." Lucien shot Berengar a rueful expression and climbed onto the back of Godfrey's horse.

The company started south. They reached the marsh's edge as the last vestiges of sunlight ebbed. Night descended upon the Elderwood, and just when it seemed they would have to stop or risk losing their way, firelight glowed ahead through the encroaching darkness.

Smoke rose in the distance. "We're close." Berengar spurred his horse forward, and the others followed.

It wasn't long before a town came into view. The frontier community was far removed from civilization, as if someone had taken an ordinary town and dropped it in the middle of a dense forest. No roads led in or out. Neither were there walls to keep out intruders, despite the proximity to the marsh.

"Halt!" The bellowing voice belonged to a night watchman at the town's entrance. "Who goes there?"

Godfrey made sure Lucien's hood was up before riding to the company's head. "Greetings, brother. We're only passing through, and we need a place to stay for the night."

"It's a late hour to be traveling about, especially in these parts."

"We lost our way in the marsh. Where are we, exactly?"

"Newtown, of course." The watchman raised his torch and looked at each member of the company in turn. His

251

gaze lingered on Berengar's sword a moment longer than necessary. "You're a strange-looking group."

"We're monster hunters," Morwen answered. "Sent by the church to deal with the increased attacks."

At that, the watchman's expression betrayed obvious relief. "Why didn't you say so?" He stepped aside to allow them passage. "You'll find lodging at the Gray Lady. The proprietor can point you in the direction of some work while you're at it. There's lots that needs doing around here."

The company started down a soft dirt path. Bright moonlight peeked through gaps in the neighboring trees. A forceful wind shook dry leaves from the branches to join piles of others below. Judging from appearances, Newtown probably got its start as a trading outpost, given the abundance of natural resources in the area. The church's prominent location was the only sign that the town, which seemed to sit at the edge of the world, belonged to Leinster at all.

Despite the hour, a fair number of townspeople were busy about their affairs. Berengar kept his head down in case Valmont's spies were among them. He slid from the saddle and hitched his horse outside the tavern, and the others did the same. Like Lucien, Teelah hid her face behind a hooded cloak. A scarf from Azura concealed most of her face, and the darkness did the rest.

After what he'd encountered in the barrow, Berengar was ready for a hot meal to fill his belly and a warm bed to lay his head, if only for a night. He stopped outside the tavern's entrance and lowered his voice. "Remember what I said. Stay together. Don't speak to anyone unless you have to." He stared hard at Lucien to emphasize the point before venturing inside.

The tavern was more crowded than he had anticipated.

The patrons—workers, mostly, unwinding after a day's labors—were a loud and raucous bunch. Lively music came from a small band comprised of fellow patrons. Listeners gathered nearby raised their tankards and joined in a bawdy song. The display seemed unusual for rural Leinster, normally renowned for its piety. Then again, considering the danger in which they lived, the tavern's occupants were hardly at fault for wanting to enjoy themselves.

Berengar advanced into the room. Lucien and the others filed in behind him. In contrast to the Coin and Crown, the hall was dimly lit, and not nearly as clean. The song broke off, followed by a round of applause. Azura bumped into a musician and bowed by way of apology. When she came away, Berengar noticed the musician's flute tucked away in her cloak.

The others settled at a table near the hearth while he sought the tavern's proprietor, a stocky man who looked more than capable of settling disputes between patrons.

"My friends and I are looking for a place to stay. That's them over by the fire." He nodded in his companions' direction.

"You'll have to bunk together then. We're not an inn. Our rooms are few." The proprietor chuckled softly, amused by some private thought. "You're lucky that our last guest moved on. You'd have to settle for the stables otherwise."

Berengar followed him across the hall. "Do you get many travelers out here?"

The proprietor bent low to retrieve a room key from behind the counter. "More than you'd think. Mostly miners and woodcutters. Folk tend to move about in this part of the country."

Berengar handed over the few coins he had left in his

possession. The Acolytes had stripped him of his coin pouch along with his armor, and his companions had little in the way of coin. The exchange left him nearly penniless, but at least they had secure lodging for the night. "Given the danger in the area, I'm surprised so many choose to live here."

The proprietor's mood quickly improved once the coins were in hand. "We must do our part for king and country, friend. Besides, there is a great deal of money to be made at the frontier, even if we have more than our share of hardship out here."

"We saw Ferbane on our way."

The proprietor let out a sigh. "Aye. A tragedy, it was. I had a cousin there."

"Do you know what happened to the people there?"

"No, and I'm glad for it. I don't want to dwell on whatever horror was responsible. We tried sending a search party, but the area's dangerous enough, and we've problems of our own. A fear dearg was giving the miners some trouble recently. Lucky for us, the warden was on hand to drive it off."

Berengar stopped. "What warden?"

The question earned him a laugh. "*The* warden. Warden Niall, of course."

"Niall was here?"

"Aye. Searching for the prince regent. Apparently, Prince Tristan's in the area, though for the life of me I don't know what would bring him all the way out here. If I had one-tenth of his gold, I'd never leave Dún Aulin."

"What way was Niall headed?"

"West, I think."

So Niall and Tristan were close. Before Berengar could process this new information, a commotion sounded behind him. He turned around in time to witness Lucien

254

climbing onto a table near the hall's center. *What's that fool doing now?*

The king kicked over several tankards in the process, spilling their contents over angry patrons. "Hear me, good people of Leinster! It is I, Lucien—your rightful king." The hall's inhabitants stared at him in complete befuddlement. Lucien pointed at Azura and the others. "An imposter has stolen my throne, and these rogues have kidnapped and enchanted me. I demand you seize and imprison them at once."

The declaration was met by a round of loud laughter. Across the room, Morwen buried her face in her hands.

"Get down from there!" someone shouted.

Another threw a loaf of bread at the king. "Cease your nonsense, boy!"

Lucien regarded them with a mixture of disappointment and irritation. Godfrey attempted to intervene, but the king persisted. "Very well. If it's proof you desire, look upon the face of your king!" He threw back his hood to a collective gasp from the crowd. "There! Do you not see my crown?"

Azura roared with laughter. In place of Lucien's silver crown, a thatch of twigs lay atop his head.

"What the devil are you? Some kind of half-breed hell spawn?"

Others beholding the king's impish form quickly reached a similar conclusion. "Monster!"

Berengar pulled the king down from the table and cuffed his ear. "Keep your mouth shut before you get us all thrown out of here, you insolent little whelp."

"He's the Bear Warden!" Lucien protested. "She's a fairy, and she's a witch!"

Patrons mocked the king with laughter. "If he's the Bloody Red Bear, where's his cloak and axe?"

Azura patted Lucien on the back. "Don't mind him. He's our imp. He's got a fiendish tongue, especially when drunk, but he comes in handy tracking monsters."

The tavern's proprietor shook his head. "That may be, but we don't allow his kind in here."

Berengar released his hold on Lucien's ear and shoved him toward the door. "As you wish."

When Lucien refused to budge, the tavern's proprietor seized him and dragged him away by his shirt. "Unhand me! I am your king!" The man ignored his protests, threw open the door, and tossed him outside. Lucien landed on his backside in the mud.

"I'll see to him," Morwen volunteered before a worried look crossed her face.

"What is it?"

She stared past him to the spot where a hooded figure had watched the spectacle unfold. "That man worries me. I sense dark intentions." Morwen quickly averted her gaze, but it was too late—the stranger noticed her. He immediately began making his way through the crowd toward the back entrance.

Azura was already on her way after him. "Leave him to me."

"Good. Meet us outside when you're done with him." Berengar motioned for the others to follow. Once they were out of earshot, he relayed what he had learned about Niall and the prince regent.

Teelah approached Lucien, who was sobbing in the mud. "Are you all right?" Her voice contained a measure of pity.

He wiped his tears and looked up at her with red eyes. "You want to gloat, is that it? Come to mock the monster like the rest of them?"

"I know why you cry."

Lucien fought back another wave of sobs. "Kings don't cry. It's not regal."

"Now you know what it's like to be called a monster. It hurts, doesn't it?" Teelah hesitated and offered him her scarf. "For your tears."

Lucien stared at the scarf with suspicion, as if afraid he was the butt of some joke. Finally, he took the scarf from her and blew his nose. "Thank you." His words were so quiet they were barely audible.

Azura appeared, leading the stranger from the tavern at knifepoint. She marched him to the wood's edge and waited for the others to join her.

"Good work." Berengar loomed over the stranger. "You had better start talking."

"It is you. The Bloody Red Bear."

Berengar put his hand on the hilt of his blade. "Aye. And who are you?"

"No one of importance."

"He's lying," Morwen said casually.

Azura knelt beside the stranger and looked him over in the moonlight. "I recognize his face. He's in the Brotherhood."

Berengar grabbed the man and shoved him against a tree. "What's a thief doing in Newtown?" When the stranger failed to answer, he struck him hard across the face. "I can keep this up all night." He peered deeper into the forest, where strange sounds echoed in the night. "Or perhaps we'll just leave you in the marsh."

That seemed to do the trick. "Wait! I was sent here for word of Prince Tristan. There are others throughout the Elderwood with the same task. We have orders to find you as well."

Berengar pressed him against the tree. "Orders from who?"

"Bishop Valmont."

"The Brotherhood of Thieves is working for Valmont?"

"Of course," Azura said. "Völundr has them searching for the four jewels of the Tuatha dé Danann. It all makes sense now."

"What's he planning?" Berengar demanded. He hit the thief, who laughed and spat out a tooth.

"You're too late. We've located the other half of the cursed blade. Soon it will be in the Brotherhood's possession."

Before they could process the news, Morwen's eyes widened in alarm. "There's danger. It's close."

Berengar pushed the thief away and reached for his sword. The wind shifted, prompting a growl from Faolán. He glimpsed movement in the trees through the moonlight, and multiple eyes gleamed back at him in the darkness. Eight hairy, segmented limbs crept along the branches.

Morwen trained her staff on the trees. "Solas!" The lightstone glowed with white light, revealing a spider as large as Faolán.

The creature bristled in response to the light. Before Berengar could react, it leapt from the branches onto Morwen. The spider pinned her to the ground and opened its mouth to reveal a set of venomous glands, and Morwen strained against the spider's weight with her staff. The charms Azura had carved into the staff grew red with firelight, burning the spider. Morwen rolled out from under it and attempted to scramble away, but it scurried toward her. Just before it could sink its fangs into her neck, Berengar drove his sword into the spider's abdomen. When he pulled the blade free, blue blood covered the steel.

Shrieking, the spider thrashed about and retreated into the woods.

"Are you all right?"

Morwen dusted herself off. "I think so. Where did the thief go?"

The man was gone. "Blast it! If he brings word to Valmont…"

Just then, all hell broke loose. Screams came from the town as torchlight filled the night.

Berengar turned to face the town, where bells tolled to warn of the threat. "The people are under attack."

Faolán, still facing the forest, continued barking, and Morwen's lightstone revealed more spiders approaching through the trees.

"Go!" Berengar waited for the others to pass before sprinting after them.

Newtown's inhabitants rushed to the town's defense. Archers hurried up the steps to man the church's bell tower while laborers wielded their hammers and pickaxes as weapons. Any community living in the wilds had to be prepared to respond to potential raids at a moment's notice. Berengar expected they had endured attacks before.

Watchmen shouted to alert the archers to spiders along the town's perimeter. A few spiders made it past the volley of arrows that followed, but others shrank back, waiting. Black arrows streaked from the forest, and one of Newtown's defenders toppled from the bell tower.

"Goblins!"

With the town's archers distracted, the spiders crawled up buildings and forced their way into huts. Godfrey grabbed a torch and burned a spider's carapace while Faolán kept another occupied long enough for Berengar to hack off its limbs.

Unearthly wails emanated from the forest. Ghostly figures glided into Newtown like living shadows. Spears and arrows thrown in their direction passed right through them.

Berengar turned to find one blocking his path. Its skin moved and flowed, and darkness swam in the spots where its eyes had once been. He tensed, bracing himself. *Sluagh.*

Godfrey held up his crucifix to ward against the shade. "Begone!" The creature hissed but shrank away.

"Fall back!" a voice cried. "Fall back to the church!"

Although the town's defenders had seemed capable of beating back the initial wave of attackers, Newtown quickly succumbed to chaos as more monsters emerged from the forest. Fighting broke down into discrete pockets scattered throughout the area, and fires from fallen torches spread, devouring huts and buildings.

"The blasted things keep coming!" Berengar cut down another spider and retreated to the town square as the ground shuddered under his feet. *What is it now?* An enormous troll burst from the forest with a roar and struck the bell tower with its club. The tower fell and crashed to the earth, burying the last remaining archers. Morwen barely leapt out of the way in time. She landed on her back in front of the troll, which raised its club to deliver the killing blow.

"Get away from her!" Lucien clutched a fallen spear in his grip. When the troll turned to face him, the king stared up at its towering bulk and stood rooted to the spot. Overcome by fear, he dropped the spear.

An arrow from Teelah struck the troll in the shoulder. It bellowed with anger and spun around to face her, but Morwen forced it back with a wave of illumination from her lightstone. Azura deftly weaved through the air to distract the troll long enough for Teelah to scurry up the side of a hut and loose more arrows. Berengar severed one of its heel tendons with his blade, finally bringing the beast down, and a well-placed goblin arrow finished it.

He didn't have long to celebrate the victory. The warden peered through the smoke and saw Cathán looming beyond the flames, holding his scythe aloft to order the army of monsters forward.

Berengar shook his head to warn Teelah against taking aim. "We have to go—now."

Morwen grabbed his arm. "What about the townspeople?"

"There are too many." The last of Newtown's defenders fell, leaving its people at the mercy of Cathán's growing legions. The townspeople fled in a blind panic, but the creatures were everywhere. The lucky ones were felled by goblin arrows. Those who weren't so lucky found themselves devoured by spiders or crushed by ogres.

"We have to do *something*!"

"There's nothing we can do for them now." Berengar tore his gaze away from the nightmarish scene and eyed the tavern. If they waited any longer to make their escape, it would be too late. "Quick—to the horses."

They made their way through the fighting to the Gray Lady, where their horses waited. Azura called a fleeing horse to Lucien, who managed to climb onto its back, and the companions slipped out of Newtown unnoticed. They fled into the darkness, listening to the cries from those left behind as fire licked the sky.

CHAPTER FOURTEEN

THEY RODE FAR into the night. When they finally stopped, no one dared speak above a whisper. Despite the cool autumn air, they slept without a campfire. Berengar kept watch with his sword across his lap just in case. Each time fatigue crept in, unnatural sounds from the dark jolted him awake.

They set out again at first light. It didn't appear anyone had slept easily. According to friendly birds in the area, the way east remained under watch. It was important to put as much space between them and Cathán's forces as possible. Many monsters—trolls especially—preferred to move about at night. Even if the dense forest sheltered the creatures from much of the weak sunlight, it was still safer to travel by day.

They were lucky to have escaped at all. The creatures that attacked Newtown were far greater in number than those Berengar and Morwen encountered at the Giant's Foot. While the crown's attention was otherwise occupied with the Ceremony of the Cursed Blade, Cathán had amassed an entire army of monsters in the Elderwood.

The forest was no more welcoming the farther they traveled. Briars and thorn hedges grew everywhere, and menacing crows replaced the friendly sparrows. Azura disappeared occasionally to scout the path ahead and behind from the air. Although the way forward was clear, the quiet between them continued. Berengar, who preferred silence to conversation, welcomed the change. Lucien remained sullen and reserved, speaking only to Godfrey. At least he appeared to have finally resigned himself to his traveling companions. While the boy-king was clearly having difficulty with the prolonged length of time spent in the saddle, he didn't complain, much to Berengar's surprise.

When they stopped to make camp that night, Berengar decided it was safe enough to start a campfire, and Faolán watchfully patrolled the camp's perimeter as Berengar and the others gathered around the flames for warmth.

Morwen noticed Lucien sitting off by himself and approached him. "I wanted to thank you for distracting that troll earlier."

Lucien shook his head dismissively. "I did nothing. I just stood there like a frightened child when the beast drew near."

Godfrey chuckled. "It was your first battle. It's only natural, Your Highness."

"Not for me. A king should be brave. All my life I've been forced to watch my oaf of a cousin diminish the crown's influence. That fool has allowed the *Rí Tuaithe* and lesser lords to steal power for themselves, indulging in licentious pursuits, while I have studied tomes and scriptures to prepare myself for the day when I come of age."

"Bravery often comes from unexpected places, my king. You may find it where you least expect it."

Morwen sat next to Berengar. "Do you think we'll find Prince Tristan or Warden Niall if we go farther west?"

Berengar shrugged. He still wasn't sure what either was really after.

"It's a mistake to go that way," Lucien declared. "We should be headed east to take back my throne instead of riding around the wilds in a circle."

Berengar spared him a brief glance of irritation. "And you're not concerned by the army of monsters in our path?"

Lucien glared at him. "The only monster I see here is you."

Berengar held the king's gaze. "Do you have something you want to say to me, boy?"

Lucien shot up from where he sat. "Leinster is no place for murderers. Excommunicating you for what you did at St. Brigid's was a kindness. I'd have thrown you in the dungeon to rot for the acts you committed during the purges. A killer like you has no place among the good people of Leinster."

Berengar let his anger get the better of him. "I saved your rotten city because it was my queen's command. If it were up to me, I'd have let the whole place burn. You talk about the good people of Leinster? I watched them turn on each other for nothing. Where were the palace guards when the Acolytes cut down those accused of following the old ways? When the mobs stoned innocent women and children in the streets?"

Lucien shifted uncomfortably. "The purges were before I was born."

"And what's your excuse now? Things have only gotten worse. The criminals and the corrupt thrive while your people cry out for help and no one answers. No wonder it was so easy for Valmont to take power." Lucien made no reply, a sign the remark struck close to home. "That's what I thought. We're not going east until we find a clear path, and that's the end of it."

Lucien turned to face Azura. "Very well. Fairy—I wish for you to transport us to the palace at once." When Azura made no move to accede to the king's request, he crossed his arms in a show of displeasure. "Well? I thought fairies granted wishes."

"That's not how it works."

Morwen gave Azura a curious glance. "How does wish magic work exactly?"

"I would need a wand, for starters. Wish magic is incredibly complex. Belief plays a role, as does the intention of the individual making the wish. A pure heart is best, but as fond as I am of you, I can count the number of humans I've seen use their wishes to help others on one hand. Most people approach their wishes with selfish hearts and then have the temerity to wonder where it all went wrong."

Teelah, busy sharpening an arrow, scoffed at her. "Please. You fairies delight in using the promise of wishes to seduce your prey. You can't blame them for taking it out on you when they figure out your game."

The pair exchanged dark looks, and no one spoke for several moments.

Morwen was first to break the silence. "If you don't mind me asking, why *do* goblins and fairies hate each other?"

Teelah set the arrow aside and began work on another. "Every goblin knows the story. There was a time, when this world was still new, that our races lived together in peace. We goblins were legendary conquerors and warriors, feared above all others. In their pride, the envious fairies tricked us into angering the elder gods. The gods cursed us, stripping us of our most powerful magics and great beauty and making us ugly in the eyes of others."

"I don't think you're ugly." The words came from Lucien, who appeared to have uttered them without thinking. No one seemed more astonished by his pronouncement than Lucien himself, who refused to meet Teelah's gaze. "For a goblin, anyway."

Azura, her attention still fixed on Teelah, appeared not to have noticed. "Surely you don't actually believe that rubbish. The elder gods aren't even truly gods. They're exceptionally powerful immortals and nothing more."

Morwen looked surprised. "I thought fairies worshipped the Tuatha."

"A common misconception."

"Then what do you worship?"

"Nothing—and everything."

Teelah shook her head. "Now who's speaking rubbish?"

"Fairies venerate magic, much in the way druids revere life—certain madmen excepted, of course."

"But druids also worship the elder gods," Morwen reminded her.

Lucien interrupted. "There is only one true God. The Lord of Hosts. He is the way, the truth, and the life—the source of light in this world. He offers salvation freely to those who would receive it."

Morwen looked skeptical. "What of nonhumans? I've seen how your church treats them. Winslow and the Acolytes would have burned me at the stake for being a magician."

"You can't judge an entire belief system based on the actions of fanatics!"

"Yet the people of Leinster treat all magicians as monsters because of the Lord of Shadows' conquest of

Fál. They treat goblins and fairies the same way for similar reasons, I might add."

"That's different!"

It was Morwen's turn to cross her arms. "Not from where I'm sitting."

Berengar hadn't expected her passion on the subject. Worship of the Lord of Hosts was the dominant practice in Munster, even if religion played a more ceremonial role there than in Leinster. He supposed Morwen's sympathy for the older ways shouldn't be that surprising considering her background as a magician.

Lucien looked to Godfrey for support. "You're a man of the cloth. What do you say?"

"The scriptures say 'The Lord is the Maker of all.' Just as I believe we are all His children, I do not believe all forms of magic are evil. Where did such abilities come from, if not Him?" He stopped to take a swig from his flask.

Lucien sniffed the air and frowned. "Is that whiskey? You're a terrible priest."

Godfrey chuckled. "Friar, actually—but you're not wrong." He put the flask away and wandered to the forest's edge to relieve himself.

Lucien buried his head in his hands. "I do not know why He has chosen to test me so."

"Take heart, my king." Godfrey slapped the king on the back on his return to camp, earning him a look of ire from Lucien. "It is also written that the Lord will not test you beyond your capabilities."

"You're awfully quiet, Berengar. What do you think?" Morwen peeled back her bandages to discover the burns from the thunder rune had healed. She flashed Teelah a grateful smile, which the goblin acknowledged with a nod.

"You're not dragging me into this." He was born far to

the north, where worship of the elder gods remained strong. For a long time he had believed in nothing at all. That changed when he met Nora. Now he was no longer sure what he believed. If there was a just God, it seemed unlikely that He would look favorably on Berengar's many misdeeds.

"I see too many unpleasant faces for such a beautiful night." Azura reached into her cloak and removed the musician's flute she had stolen. "This is a night for songs." She lifted the flute to her lips, dancing as she played, and the fire seemed to dance with her.

Slowly, the melancholy mood about the camp began to lift. Godfrey and Morwen joined in the dancing, and both lent their voices to more than one familiar tune. Despite her apparent efforts to appear otherwise, Teelah too seemed to enjoy the music, and even Lucien tapped his foot to the melody.

After watching the merriment for some time, Berengar stalked away from camp. Faolán joined him, and they continued listening from a short distance away.

Eventually, Morwen found him, her face flushed from song and dance. "What are you doing out here by yourself?"

Berengar shrugged. "Someone has to keep watch while you lot enjoy yourselves. We're surrounded by danger on all sides, remember?"

She laughed and sat down beside him. "It wouldn't hurt you to try and enjoy yourself every once in a while." She followed his gaze to the dancers. "I see. You wanted to get away from the others. They're not so bad. You might try giving them a chance."

"I prefer to work alone."

"That's what you said when we first met. It's okay to

THE CITY OF THIEVES

have friends. It doesn't make you weak. You know what I think?"

"You're going to tell me anyway, aren't you?"

Morwen punched his shoulder. "I think you're so used to being the outsider you've forgotten what it's like to have real friends. Look around. I see misfits and outcasts, just like you and me." She smiled at him and climbed to her feet. "Maybe you're not as alone as you think you are."

Faolán watched her go and gave a low whine.

"Fine." Berengar picked himself up and trudged back to join the others.

The merrymaking didn't last much longer. With the exception of Azura, who looked as if she could dance all night, the companions were still tired from their flight from Newtown. Soon the crackling campfire and howling winds were the only sounds.

Left alone with his thoughts, Berengar turned Morwen's words over in his head. He hadn't always been alone. He had a wife once. That was before the war—a lifetime ago now. Morwen was right about one thing. He *was* an outcast. His reputation, spread by tall tales and bards' songs, was well-earned, and his frightening appearance didn't help matters.

The loneliness didn't bother him. He'd grown accustomed to it—even learned to prefer it. That was one reason he kept to the road, always moving from one task to another. He couldn't quite put his finger on when that had started to change. Perhaps it was when he met Morwen. Already he felt as if she had changed him more than the other way around.

Then again, Berengar would never have allowed her to get close to him if not for the events that brought him to Leinster the last time. He had been at his lowest point. No matter what he did—no matter how many monsters he killed—the world never seemed to get better. He had helped the hobgoblins but they died anyway. He had put Imogen on her uncle's throne only to watch her become a tyrant. Then there was Rose, who with her dying breath told him it wasn't too late for him.

Was it? He wasn't sure. He had felt something for Ravenna he hadn't for anyone since his wife's death. Something he didn't even think he was capable of experiencing anymore. In the end, he wasn't able to save her either. Despite keeping Cashel from destruction, he had failed Mór and Alannah, and chaos now gripped Munster.

The wind picked up, and he heard teeth chattering. The sound came from Lucien, who was shivering, having moved away from the fire and stubbornly refused to return in his effort to distance himself from the others. The sound of his moans woke Teelah, who approached the king's sleeping form without making a sound. Berengar tensed, ready to intervene, but to his surprise, Teelah laid a blanket over Lucien and returned to her bedroll. Lucien stirred, glanced at the blanket, and stared at her for a long time before returning to sleep.

B erengar woke at dawn. Pale gray light crept through branches down to the forest floor. A dream lingered in the back of his mind, like lost words on the tip of his tongue. A memory of Ravenna came to him, unbidden, and a kiss, beautiful and tragic.

"Father?" Morwen muttered when he woke her. It appeared he wasn't the only one dreaming.

"Ready yourself for the road. We're leaving soon."

She stretched out with a yawn, and he went to rouse the others, who proved equally difficult to wake. He wondered if the strange dreams were brought on by

Azura's songs or the magic of the Elderwood. Before long, the company shared a simple breakfast around the fire.

Lucien, sitting underneath a tree, glanced around suspiciously. "Where's the fairy?"

Azura hung upside down from a branch directly above him. "Here!"

When Lucien looked up, he found himself staring into her shimmering violet eyes and let out a shriek. Morwen bellowed with laughter, and even Godfrey had a hard time concealing his amusement.

Although Lucien quickly recovered, his embarrassment was plain. "Impudent fairy. I've had enough of your mockery."

Azura dropped from the branch and landed beside him. "You take yourself far too seriously. You should learn to laugh at yourself."

Lucien stormed away to fill his water horn at a nearby stream. Moments later, a growl sounded above the running water. Berengar followed the king's gaze to an enormous wolf across the stream. At the sight of Lucien, the wolf snarled and bared its fangs. Berengar reached for his sword, but the space between them was too great to cross the distance in time.

The wolf crouched, as if to pounce, but a black arrow felled it before it could leap. The wolf let out a howl before a second arrow silenced it, and Lucien looked back to see Teelah clutching her bow.

Lucien opened his mouth to speak, but few words came out. "I…"

"It's a scout." Teelah knelt to inspect the wolf's corpse and sniffed at the air. "The pack is nearby."

As Berengar and the others hurried to their horses, a flock of crows burst from the trees. The riders started out of camp with the swarm at their backs. Berengar clutched the reins tightly, lowered his head, and rode ahead. More howls rang out behind them, and the crows enveloped them, pecking and clawing as they passed overhead. Teelah's horse reared and threw her to the earth. When Berengar looked back at her, the wolves were almost on her.

Just before the pack descended on her, Lucien turned his horse around and galloped toward the goblin. Ignoring the danger, he charged at the wolves. "Take my hand!" He reached out to Teelah, and her hand closed around his at the last moment. Lucien pulled her onto the saddle, and they raced to rejoin the others with the wolves nipping at their heels.

Morwen glanced back at them over her shoulder and looked to Berengar in alarm. "They're not going to make it!"

Suddenly, a horn reverberated through the forest. Hooded archers appeared among the trees. Berengar expected the worst, but the archers trained their fire on the wolves, allowing Lucien and Teelah to escape unscathed. The swarm of crows cawed as one, took to the sky, and flew away.

More archers appeared to block the path ahead, and Berengar pulled back on the reins to bring his horse to a stop.

"Halt!" The cloaked figures emerged to surround them.

Berengar put his hand on his blade's hilt. "Let us pass."

"We give the orders here, stranger. Who are you, and what are you doing in these woods?" The archers took aim, and Berengar let his hand fall away.

Morwen rode up beside him and shot him a look that suggested he let her do the talking. "Many thanks for your help. We are peaceful travelers, seeking safe passage to Dún Aulin."

The archer remained unmoved. "They don't look peaceful to me, lads. The one with the eye patch looks like a brigand to my reckoning."

"Can't be too careful," another replied. "I say we lock them up and be done with it."

"You will do no such thing." Lucien prodded his horse to the front. "You will let us pass unharmed."

"And who are you to command us, imp?"

"I am Lucien, sovereign of Leinster—your king."

The archers exchanged looks and laughed like the men in the tavern at Newtown.

"Wait." One archer trained his bow on Berengar. "I know this man. Esben Berengar, he is!"

The laughter died as quickly as it started.

"Lower your bow, you fool. There's someone who'll want to see this one." He nodded to Berengar. "If you truly are the Bear Warden, you should come with us."

The archers led them to a cave nearly hidden from sight. Torchlight illuminated the narrow entrance, which widened as they followed its course. Finally, they emerged into an immense cavern where sunlight stole inside through an opening above to mingle with lantern and candlelight.

"Incredible." Morwen's voice betrayed a sense of awe.

An entire community lay before them. There were people everywhere, too many to count. They followed the archers up a stair and over a bridge while those below fetched water from the stream. The sound of hammering echoed through the cavern as teams built homes from sturdy wooden boards. Others harvested vegetables from the topsoil and carted them off in wheelbarrows.

"These must be the villagers from Ferbane," Morwen said to an archer.

"Aye. As well as those from Tulach Mhór, Durrow, and the surrounding lands."

Despite the dangers within the Elderwood, the people appeared happy and unafraid. Children ran by, laughing and playing, while men and women told stories or sang songs.

"There are goblins among you," Lucien noted in surprise.

The remark drew chuckles, and a few archers lifted their hoods to reveal goblin faces underneath. Sure enough, Berengar noticed several goblins toiling alongside the men and women about their labors. "This was a goblin village long before men set foot here. They gave us shelter when the raids on our settlements began. All who wish to live in peace are welcome here."

Lucien observed the creatures they encountered in disbelief. "I didn't know there were so many nonhumans in all Leinster."

"We have broonies, clurichaun, pechs, pixies, and even a friendly giant who have chosen to make this their home."

"But giants are cannibals! They eat the flesh of their enemies!"

The archer laughed heartily. "Where did you hear a silly thing like that? Ours only eats vegetables and fruits." The ground shook when a gangly giant with long, thin limbs shambled past them, carrying stones for the builders. "He's very gentle, really. The little ones love him."

Teelah appeared equally surprised. "You live together in peace?"

"The forest is beyond the protection of Leinster's scouts," a goblin archer answered. "We must look out for one another if we are to survive."

For the first time since Berengar had known her, Teelah smiled.

Lucien shook his head and muttered to himself in disbelief. "I don't understand. I thought they were all monsters."

Godfrey put his hand on the young king's shoulder. "Your forebear, King Lorc, had a peace with nonhumans."

"He was a heathen."

"Perhaps he was wiser than you think."

Lucien fell silent, deep in thought.

They came to a lone tree where a group assembled around them. Men and women whispered among themselves until two figures stepped forward to greet them. The first threw back his hood to reveal a jovial face framed by brown curls.

Berengar recognized the second at once. "Niall."

"I take it the Ceremony of the Cursed Blade didn't go as planned. Still, I'm glad you two managed not to get yourselves killed in my absence."

Niall's companion fixed a pair of mirthful eyes on Lucien. "I must say, you're looking rather *hairier* these days, cousin."

Lucien glared at him. "Tristan."

"It's good to see you're free of Valmont's hold, though I suppose we have Warden Berengar to thank for that." Tristan stopped short when he noticed Morwen. "And who is this charming creature?"

"Don't even think about it," Berengar warned.

Lucien eyed Tristan suspiciously. "Where have you been? Drinking and whoring, no doubt."

"Retrieving *this* before Valmont's thieves could get their hands on it." Tristan unwrapped an object covered by a shroud to reveal the missing half of the cursed blade.

Lucien regarded him with utter disbelief. "How did *you* manage to acquire the missing piece?"

"Don't look so surprised. I've made quite a name for myself as an adventurer."

Lucien folded his arms across his chest. "An adventurer? A trouble seeker, you mean. You're always needing a *real* hero—like Warden Niall—to rescue you from your mistakes. You may be regent for now, but once I come of age, I'll make sure the kingdom knows you for what you are—a drunkard and a fool."

"You should show him a little gratitude," Berengar said. "While you were off getting yourself captured by fairies, that drunkard risked his life to try to find the cursed blade."

"No harm done. I *am* a drunkard and a fool, though not always at the same time." Tristan ruffled his cousin's hair, earning him a reproachful look from the boy-king. "Come, let us share food and drink, and you can tell us all about your adventures."

They settled at a long, unfinished banquet table under the solitary tree's shade. A wide assortment of grain, fruit, cheese, and vegetable baskets lay spread out for them. Servers came and went, bringing new plates of food and refilling wooden goblets with wine or ale. Everyone gathered around the crowded table, and there was laughter, music, and dancing in abundance.

After all they had endured since setting foot in the Elderwood, the others seemed glad for the opportunity to relax. Even Azura was unconcerned by the presence of goblins, and while she kept a reserved distance from them, she readily conversed with various other creatures, most of whom treated the fairy like royalty.

A goblin woman laid a steaming plate before Lucien, who made no move toward the food.

"Eat up, cousin!" Tristan exclaimed from across the table. "Here—have some wine."

Lucien ignored the wine. "A king should be sober-minded." He regarded the unfamiliar food with skepticism, obviously more than a little reluctant to try anything prepared by goblin hands. Finally overcome by hunger, he took a small bite. The king chewed the food for a moment, and an expression of pleasant surprise came across his face. "This is good." He grabbed a handful from another plate. "*Very* good." Soon, his plate overflowed with heaping portions. "This is fine fare, especially for food prepared by..." He stopped short when he caught sight of Teelah. "Forest dwellers."

"Do you ever say something that's not meant as an insult?" Berengar asked, and Lucien went quiet.

"You shouldn't be so hard on him," Morwen said. "I don't think he's mean-spirited. Not really. I sense he carries a great deal of sorrow and loneliness, but also courage and virtue. I grew up in a royal court, and I know how lonely it can be. He probably has few friends."

"I think your magician's intuition might be off this time. Lucien's a noble—and a royal at that. I've only met a handful that ever cared about anyone but themselves."

"He did rescue Teelah. Why is it you're incapable of seeing the good in him?"

Berengar sighed. "Every time I look at him, I'm reminded of Lady Imogen."

Morwen's brow knotted in curiosity. "What do you mean?"

"Imogen was nothing like Laird Margolin. She was decent—kind, even. The people loved her. Good people died to put her on her uncle's throne, but once she had it, she became just like him. She promised to bring peace, but she brought only more violence."

"You should try giving people a chance. They just might surprise you every now and then."

Teelah turned away from a conversation with another goblin to face Lucien. "Why did you help rescue me? You could have left me to the wolves."

"A king should defend the helpless and the weak." Lucien seemed to note the response disappointed her. "Why did you aid me at the stream?"

She shrugged. "They're paying me to help keep you alive."

Lucien also appeared disappointed by her reply. "Gold. I should have expected nothing less from a common mercenary."

"I do what's necessary to survive. Do you know what life is like for a goblin in Leinster? We once shared these lands with you. Now we're hunted like animals. I lost my entire family before I came of age, all because of your laws. I've learned to look out for myself."

"They're not my laws. They were written before I was born." Lucien's expression softened. "My mother died in childbirth, and my father not long after. I'm an orphan too."

While more than a few of their hosts observed them with interest, others in the community continued with their tasks and conversations. Berengar, busy filling his belly, relied on Morwen to relay all that had occurred from the time they encountered Niall at the Coin and Crown. Once she finished, Niall and Tristan recounted their exploits in turn.

"Some time ago, Vicar Flaherty came to me, concerned about a change in the king. Imagine my surprise when I learned my pious cousin had suddenly become a mischievous little fiend. Naturally, I took it upon myself to investigate further. As it happens, I have some friends in very low places who helped me uncover the truth. Once I learned what Valmont was planning, I fled the capital, telling no one to avoid alerting his spies.

"Little did I know the reports coming from the Elderwood were true. It seems the druid Cathán survived the purges and has set about terrorizing the wilds. I would have lost my head more than once if Niall hadn't come after me." He lifted his goblet toward Niall, and the two clanked their cups.

Niall picked up the story from there. "According to legend, the four treasures are scattered across Fál. We sought out the Seer of the Black Pool to find the monastery at Dál Birn and fought off monsters and thieves alike to acquire the cursed blade's twin. Valmont may have half of the cursed blade, but it's of little use to him without its mate. The stone of destiny is at Tara, but the Dagda's cauldron and Lugh's spear remain unaccounted for."

Berengar gritted his teeth. "I have some bad news on that front. A thief we interrogated at Newtown told us the Brotherhood has located the missing piece. They must know you're here."

"That is unwelcome news. Valmont is more dangerous than you know. It seems he has an agreement with Prince Mordreth."

"Mordreth?" Morwen asked.

"Mordreth the Merciless," Azura explained. "One of Annwyn's sons. His wickedness and cruelty are legend among my kin."

"If Valmont reforges Azeroth's sword, Mordreth will send his armies to invade Fál and claim her by force," Niall said.

Berengar lowered his tankard. "War."

"Aye. Our time is short. If your thief escaped Newtown, he'll bring word to Valmont. With the Brotherhood and the Acolytes in his employ, the odds are stacked in his favor."

"That's never stopped us before."

Niall allowed himself a sideways smile. "No. It hasn't."

"Warden Berengar?" The question came from a goblin woman. There was something familiar about a youngling beside her who regarded Berengar shyly.

"Do I know you?"

"This is Magg," the woman said. "When the hobgoblins caring for her were slaughtered, you found shelter for her. She is alive because of you."

Berengar shifted uncomfortably at the expression of gratitude. He was more accustomed to receiving accusations than praise. "It was the least I could do." He stared at the young one, the only survivor of Gnish's tribe. Hard as it was to believe, despite everything that had happened with Margolin, Imogen, and the whole sordid affair, maybe something good had come from it.

Teelah's brow arched upward, and although she said nothing, it was clear she finally accepted that the friar's story about how Berengar had helped the hobgoblins of Alúine was true.

An arrow whizzed past Berengar's head and struck the tree behind him. Another man looked down at his chest in shock, and his smile faltered as blood covered his white tunic. More arrows landed, turning over goblets or striking the table. Berengar tackled the goblin woman and youngling out of the way and shielded them with his body.

"We're under attack!" He looked to the cavern's entrance, where men clad in armor appeared.

"Send word to Winslow," one declared. "Tell him we have found his prize. Find the warden. Kill the rest."

The Acolytes. They must've tracked us here.

A thief in a hooded cloak accompanied the company's

leader. "The fragment is here. Find it." More thieves appeared behind him and spread out across the cavern.

Morwen crouched behind the table to avoid incoming fire. "Is there another way out?"

Tristan nodded. "There's a tunnel that leads to the surface."

Berengar drew his sword. "Get everyone out. We'll hold them off."

Niall unsheathed his blade and one of two twin daggers at his side. "Just like old times, eh?"

"Try to keep up."

They charged into battle alongside the sentries stationed near the cavern's entrance. Goblin and human bowmen exchanged arrows with the Acolytes' archers while monster hunters armed with torches and swords poured inside. The cave's occupants ran for their lives as the monster hunters set everything in their path afire, and before long the community was ablaze. Berengar cut down every man in his path to stem the flow of hunters into the cavern. Niall fought alongside him with the grace and speed of a trained swordsman, using the combination of his sword and dagger to bloody effect.

Tristan shouted for Lucien to accompany him, but instead the king hurried to fight beside Teelah.

"Kill the imp!" an enemy fighter bellowed.

Morwen and Faolán did their best to provide cover for retreating villagers, though the community's large size made it a difficult task. Fortunately, nonhuman creatures joined in the struggle to hold the enemy fighters at bay. The giant stepped in front of Lucien to shield him from arrows. Broonies, too small and agile for the hunters to catch, scurried between the fighters' boots, slowing their movements and causing them to stumble. Likewise, pixies flew around the monster hunters, who missed the tiny creatures with wide sweeps of their blades. Even the clurichaun pelted the enemies with ale and wine, cackling as they did so.

Niall slipped his dagger under a man's helmet and severed an artery before bringing his sword up to defend against an enemy swordsman. "Fall back to join the others!"

Berengar knocked Niall's foe off his feet, allowed his friend to deliver the killing blow, and dropped back. The cave's inhabitants were almost out. *Just a little longer.* Defenders and attackers fell left and right until their bodies covered the ground. Fire spread through the cavern, devouring homes, tables, and food stores. Everything the people had worked so hard to build vanished, lost to the flames.

"Berengar!" Morwen called. "We have to go! Now!"

He took an enemy's sword arm off at the elbow, turned, and pursued her into the tunnel as the stairs collapsed behind him, burying the entrance. It was a short jog out into the fresh air, where the others waited.

Tristan sat on the ground, head held in his hands. "They took it."

Berengar narrowed his gaze. "What did they take?"

"The fragment of the cursed blade. The thieves stole it off me."

Berengar made no attempt to hide his anger. "Blast it! Now Valmont has the means to reforge the sword."

"There's nothing we can do about it now." Niall put away his blade and returned his dagger to its sheath. "We should move on before the hunters find us."

"Wait." Morwen's voice was full of alarm. "Lucien's missing."

Berengar stared at the tunnels. "Did the Acolytes capture him?"

282

Teelah shook her head. "No. He was here a moment ago."

"Not anymore," Niall said.

Berengar looked around, but there was no sign of him.

Lucien was gone.

CHAPTER FIFTEEN

A BLIGHT LAY upon the forest. Berengar spotted footprints left behind in the soft earth. "He's close." He stared past the crooked trees into the shadows beyond. A set of matching tracks led farther away. "Leave the horses. We go on foot from here."

It hadn't taken long to pick up Lucien's trail. Rather than continuing their pursuit, the Acolytes had withdrawn, allowing the companions to retrieve their horses. Berengar knew better than to take the retreat as a good sign. More likely than not, the monster hunters were scouts gone to rendezvous with a larger force. It wouldn't be long before the Acolytes returned in greater numbers.

The survivors they rescued were safe, but for how long? With their home in ruins, the community's members had nowhere to go. Cathán's corruption left much of the forest uninhabitable, and Leinster's laws made leaving the Elder-wood unthinkable for the nonhumans. It was decided the survivors would retreat to the ruins of Ferbane while Berengar and his companions went after Lucien. Berengar and Teelah were seasoned trackers more than capable of following the king's trail.

Faolán growled at something ahead, and Berengar motioned for the others to hide themselves. A living shadow detached itself from the trees, glided across the path, and vanished from view.

"Sluagh," Berengar said when it was gone. "Why the devil would the king venture into such a place?"

Azura held a finger to her lips. "Hush now. Here the trees have ears."

A sudden movement came from the brush. Berengar quietly reached for his blade but stopped short when a fox poked its head out from a bush. After Azura bent low and whispered into its ear, the fox slipped back into the brush with a silent nod.

"What was that about?" Much to Berengar's annoyance, Azura gave no answer.

The sky grew bleak as they went on their way. Sluagh roamed freely, darkening the forest with their sinister presence. The specters weren't the only potential dangers, as unfriendly goblins patrolled the area while crows watched from trees.

Teelah came to a halt. "Listen." Dry leaves crunched underfoot somewhere nearby. She sniffed the air and quickened her pace. Ahead, they spotted Lucien wandering through the forest. When they called to him, the king gave no sign of acknowledging their presence.

"What are you doing, you little fool?" Berengar hissed. "You'll be seen."

Again Lucien failed to respond. Niall rushed forward and pulled Lucien into the brush before he could draw more attention to himself. The moment Niall released his hold, Lucien attempted to return to the path, forcing them to restrain him.

Morwen snapped her fingers in front of him, but Lucien merely stared ahead with a vacant expression. "He's in some kind of trance." When she closed her eyes and held her staff toward him, the blue runestone pulsed with faint light. "Blood magic."

"Cathán. Snap out of it, boy." Berengar tried shaking Lucien awake, but the king's eyes remained blank and empty.

"Only breaking the trance will wake him." Morwen selected a spell book from her satchel and flipped through its pages until she came to one she had marked. "I marked these pages when we were looking for a way to lift the sleeping curse. There are a few spells that might do the trick."

Godfrey regarded the magician's satchel curiously. "How do you manage to fit all those books and potions into such a small bag?"

"It's enchanted with a charm of holding. I did it myself." Morwen opened the bag to show off her handiwork before returning to the task at hand. "Ah, I think this incantation will do nicely."

A twig snapped nearby where a goblin scout watched. Teelah took aim with her bow but hesitated rather than releasing the string, and the goblin scurried off.

"Blast it!" Berengar shot Niall a warning look. "That scout will bring the others down on our heads. We can't stay here."

"Wait." Morwen pressed her outstretched palm against the king's forehead. "Teacht ar ais chuig an solas. Scaoileann tú ón rud atá i do sheilbh. Teacht ar ais chuig an solas. Open your eyes."

Lucien blinked several times in rapid succession, and his brow arched in confusion. "Where are we? What am I doing here?"

"The druid attempted to lure you to him."

Azura cocked her head to one side. "They're coming!"

Black arrows fell from branches as the goblins returned in force.

Berengar drew his sword, and the others did the same. "Run!"

The company raced through the forest with the goblins at their backs. Above, spiders jumped from tree to tree in pursuit. When one leapt at Lucien, Berengar stepped in his path and cut it down the middle. Howls came from wolves, which quickly outpaced the goblins. Sluagh appeared on all sides, forcing the company to weave through the forest to avoid them. Everywhere they looked there were monsters.

They stumbled past the trees, and without warning the forest was behind them. Ahead loomed a great, ring-shaped henge. A stone circle surrounded the henge's bank. Ritual symbols and markings were painted in blood on the standing stones. Inside an inner circle of skulls, Cathán sat crossed-legged, chanting with his scythe laid across his lap. Behind him towered a monstrous tree with blackened and charred bark. Blood oozed from its surface to form pools on the ground.

Morwen whitened. "I've seen this place before, in my vision from the elder tree."

The monsters herded them toward the henge. Surrounded, the companions stood back-to-back with their weapons at the ready, but their enemies made no move to attack.

Cathán climbed to his feet and took up his scythe. "You have returned, Warden Berengar." He looked around, searching for Lucien. "But where is the king?"

"The boy is *here*," the tree rasped. "Look closer."

Cathán muttered a string of words in a black tongue,

and his eyes fixed on Lucien's impish form. "Fairy magic. Clever, but not clever enough." He held out his hand to Lucien. "Come to me, and together we will wake Caorthannach from her slumber."

Lucien resisted. "I do not fear you, druid. These lands are under my protection."

"Little fool. Your death will help usher in that of mankind itself." As he spoke, a vast wraithlike presence covered the earth and took on the form of a giant that snaked across the ground and stretched its hands toward Lucien.

Berengar recognized the shape. Its nightmarish features still haunted his thoughts. "Balor."

"Margolin succeeded in giving Balor shape in this world, but you thwarted the ritual before it could be completed. Once I have collected enough souls, I will finish what he started and resurrect Balor."

"Your plan is obvious," Morwen said. "You intend to use Caorthannach to birth a new army of monsters so you can destroy Dún Aulin and claim the souls of all its inhabitants."

"Clever girl. I need only a sacrifice of royal blood, and you've foolishly brought me the king of Leinster. How fitting, as it was King Lucien's father who forced my hand all those years ago. Even more fitting that it is your doing, Warden Berengar. In the end, you couldn't save the people of Dún Aulin after all."

Berengar tightened his grip on his sword. "We'll see."

Cathán trained his scythe on Lucien. "Bring me the king. Kill the others, but save the warden for last."

Berengar readied himself to make a final stand, but before the monsters could attack, the ground started to tremble. Cathán stared past them to the forest's edge, where the fox Azura befriended leapt from the trees.

Animals of all varieties followed in a stampede that caught the monsters unawares. Birds flocked from the sky by the hundreds, overwhelmed the crows, and descended on Cathán and his forces.

Azura smiled triumphantly. "Now would be a good time to run."

Berengar cleaved through a spider in his way and broke into a sprint. "To the horses! Quick!"

Cathán held his arms high, and vines shot out of the ground to block their path. One vine wrapped itself around Lucien's foot to drag him back, but Berengar severed the vine with his sword and pulled the king free. At Cathán's command, dark clouds swarmed across the sky, powerful winds roared with fury, and lightning fell in bursts across the field.

Berengar and the others fled into the forest. The chaos unleashed by the storm scattered animals and Cathán's forces alike, giving the companions the opportunity to slip through the woods unharmed.

A strange look came over Prince Tristan's face when they reached their horses, and he turned to face his cousin. "I might have done a poor job showing it, but I was always fond of you, cousin." He unstrapped his sword and handed it to the king. "I was always rubbish with the blade. Perhaps it will serve you better than I."

"What are you doing?" Lucien accepted the blade with evident bewilderment.

"You heard the druid. He needs a sacrifice of royal blood—blood that flows through my veins as well."

"You can't mean…"

"You can't outrun them. Not unless I lead them away." Tristan clasped Niall's hand. "Get Lucien back to the capital. If he catches me, Cathán will take me to the Giant's Foot for the ritual. That will give you time enough to flee these woods, expose Valmont, and put the true king on the throne."

For the first time, Lucien stared up at his cousin without contempt. "I don't understand. Why are you doing this?"

"You were right about what you said before. I know I haven't always been the kind of man you would've liked me to be. Try not to judge me too harshly. People aren't always one thing or the other." Tristan ruffled Lucien's hair affectionately. "Farewell, cousin."

"We'll come back for you," Niall promised. "We won't leave you to be sacrificed."

"It appears it's finally my turn to play the hero, old friend." Tristan put a foot in the stirrup and looked back at the others one last time. "I always wanted a ballad in my honor." With that, he spurred his horse forward and galloped down the trail with wolves following at his heels.

The companions rode east until they were out of harm's way. They fell back to Ferbane, where the survivors who fled the cave awaited their return. The people gathered around the ruins when they approached. Some searched for Tristan.

"We can't stay here," one said. "The Acolytes will hunt us down if we do."

"But where will we go?" another asked.

Berengar didn't have an answer.

Azura started forward. "We cannot linger. We must set out while the way to Dún Aulin remains open."

Morwen shook her head. "What about the people here? We can't just leave them."

"We don't have a choice. Völundr must be stopped before he reunites the halves of the cursed blade."

"If Cathán succeeds in freeing Caorthannach, Dún Aulin will fall all the same."

Berengar nodded. "Morwen's right."

While the companions debated their next course of action, tempers flared among the survivors. With everyone on edge, it didn't take much to push the community past its breaking point. Troubled murmurings quickly escalated to arguments and accusations, and it wasn't long before humans and the various creatures were at each other's throats.

"That's enough!" Lucien forced his way to the crowd's center and climbed atop a well. The king looked over the creatures gathered in his midst, and a hush fell over the crowd. "I used to think all nonhumans were monsters. But I was wrong." As he spoke, Azura's enchantment fell away, and he returned to human form, once more wearing a silver crown. "A dark fairy has stolen my throne and threatens to reunite the halves of the cursed blade. If he succeeds, Leinster will fall into darkness, and men and nonhumans alike will suffer and die. I must stop him, but I cannot do it alone.

"I know I have no right to ask for your help. We have an ugly history. My people cast you out. We drove you from your homes and the lands you once held. You've been persecuted, hunted, and made to watch your way of life destroyed. I make this vow to you now, in the sight of the Lord of Hosts—stand with me, and when the time comes, I will not forget it. Fight for Leinster, and I pledge to forge a new peace between all our peoples."

While Morwen greeted the king's proclamation with enthusiasm, Berengar remained skeptical. Imogen had promised something similar. So often the powerful used others as pawns only to discard them when they were no longer of use. The people of Dún Aulin would not take kindly to monsters in their presence. Would Lucien remember his vow then, when the fighting was done?

Lucien drew his sword and held it high. "Who will stand with me?"

For a long moment, no one spoke, and the only sound was the wind shaking free autumn leaves from the trees. Then Teelah stepped out from the crowd, raised her bow, and nodded to Lucien. The goblins did the same, and one by one the remaining creatures cheered and raised their weapons or fists in solidarity with the king.

Berengar turned his attention to Azura, who watched the scene unfold with a knowing smirk. "Did you plan for this to happen?"

"I wanted only to teach him a lesson. Perhaps he's learned it."

"Perhaps."

"What now?" Godfrey asked as Lucien and Teelah rejoined the company.

Niall readied his horse. "I'm going to the Giant's Foot to stop Cathán."

Berengar stepped toward him. "Not without me, you're not. The druid and I have unfinished business."

"I'll come too," Godfrey said. "But the odds are against us. Cathán has an army with him. And what of the people here? There are many who are too weak or young to fight. If the others leave for Dún Aulin, who will protect them from the Acolytes?"

Niall stroked his beard. "The monsters want to kill us. The Acolytes want to kill us. I say we pit our enemies against each other. We'll draw the Acolytes out and lead them away from here to the Giant's Foot. That will leave the city watch and the Brotherhood of Thieves for the rest of you to deal with."

"Völundr will know we're coming. It will take cunning and skill to find our way inside the city unseen—a task a thief and a goblin are uniquely suited for." Azura nodded to acknowledge Teelah, a gesture the goblin returned.

"That still leaves Valmont and the false king," Morwen said.

Azura smiled. "Which is why we will require a magician's assistance."

Berengar crossed his arms. "The girl stays with me."

"We need her. Völundr is powerful. Without a wand, it will be difficult for me to stand against him alone."

"You won't be alone." Morwen turned to Berengar. "She's right."

"Fine, but that doesn't mean I have to like it."

"I don't like it any more than you. You need me watching your back against that druid."

"I've handled Cathán before. I can do it again. This time, I'll make sure he stays dead." He reached down and cupped her face in his hands. "You know how dangerous the city is. Be careful. Once Cathán is dealt with, I'll come back for you."

She squeezed his hand and gave him a smile. "You'd better."

CHAPTER SIXTEEN

A DARK FAIRY, a stolen throne, and a city of thieves. Even better, she had a chance to show Berengar that she was more than capable of looking after herself.

This is more like it. Morwen couldn't understand why Berengar was so somber all the time. She had never felt so alive. This was the life of adventure she had dreamed of from the time she was a girl. She belonged in the world, not shut up in some castle with her books and potions. True, her studies had suffered of late, but there would be plenty of time for that once they emerged victorious. Besides, as her father had often remarked, there was no substitute for experience.

Lucien anxiously drummed his fingers against the table. "Where is she?"

Morwen sat with Teelah and the king inside an inn at Kilcullen. She understood Lucien's concern. Waiting in such a visible place was not without risks. She would have preferred to shelter at the monastery, but Godfrey had warned them that with Valmont in control of the church, the monastery was no longer safe.

The door opened, and the trio turned their heads in unison as orange autumn light crept into the hall. A group of friends entered the inn, and the door slammed shut behind them. Lucien sank back in his chair and ground his teeth together in annoyance.

Morwen lowered her voice. "Give her time. Azura will be back soon enough."

"I don't like it. What if they've caught her?"

"She's not that easily caught. Take it from someone who's tried."

After their arrival at Kilcullen, Azura had gone in search of contacts from her time in the Brotherhood.

"I don't see why we can't just storm the palace and be done with it." Having discarded his crown and royal finery in favor of nondescript traveler's clothes, Lucien looked like an ordinary youth, though he kept his cousin's sword hidden under his cloak.

"We must secure the cursed blade first. If we tip our hands too early, Valmont could vanish with the blade."

In addition to her cloak, Teelah concealed her face behind a scarf. "We must move with caution. The city watch outnumbers our forces twenty to one."

Lucien crossed his arms. "The city watch will answer to their king."

Morwen shook her head. "It's not so simple. We don't know which guards are in the Brotherhood's pocket. If we go around announcing ourselves, Valmont will have our throats cut before we ever reach the palace."

The king went quiet, occasionally stealing furtive glances toward the door. "Do you think they'll rescue him? My cousin, I mean."

"If anyone can, it's Warden Berengar."

Lucien's voice was soft. "When fits of the kink took me and I could barely breathe from the coughing spells,

Tristan stayed up all night at my bedside. I must've been five or six. It was the only time I've ever seen him pray. Funny I haven't remembered it before now." He met Morwen's eyes. "You were King Mór's court magician. Were you close to him?"

He was my father. She left the words unsaid. "Aye."

"I'm sorry about what I said about him earlier—and for calling you a witch. I'm sure you served him well."

Leaving Cashel to go with Berengar had helped ease the sting of her father's loss. Morwen couldn't bear to remain at the castle in the face of constant reminders from the past. In the beginning, she thought of her father every day. Her adventures with Berengar kept her from dwelling on the subject—she found it hard to dwell on much of anything while fighting for her life on a regular basis. She still thought of her father, and he often popped into her head when she least expected it. The pain never went away, but it had dulled as the days went on.

"What's this?" The friends who entered moments before now loomed over their table with flagons in hand. One inspected Teelah with a leering grin. "I wonder what this one's got hidden under that scarf." Encouraged by his friends' laughter, he reached toward her scarf.

"Touch me and lose the hand."

"Got a bit of a mouth on you, do you? You should show more respect to your betters, wench."

"Enough." Lucien's anger was palpable. "You heard what she said. Leave her alone."

The man's attention moved to him. "Or what, boy? I bet these two girls could take you in a fight." He looked to his friends for support. "What do you say we teach him a lesson?"

"I say you should move along." The voice belonged to

Azura, who pressed a knife to the man's back. "Unless you want trouble with the Brotherhood."

The man whitened a shade, and he turned to find his friends had deserted him. "Forgive me if I have given offense, my lady." He bowed and mumbled a hasty apology before hurrying away. The Brotherhood was not a name to be taken lightly, especially in the City of Thieves.

A brief look passed between Lucien and Teelah. Morwen fought the urge to chuckle when Azura slid into an empty chair between them, and the pair quickly glanced away from each other. Although Teelah was harder for her to read, Morwen didn't need to be a magician to recognize the king was taken with her. Teelah was perhaps a few years older, but the two *were* close in age.

"Took you long enough." Lucien, who had warmed to many in the company, nevertheless remained wary of Azura, and with good reason. She had turned him into an imp, after all.

"The Brotherhood has eyes and ears everywhere." Just like that, the anger Azura displayed toward their harassers vanished, replaced by a wide smile. "I missed you too, little one."

Morwen had grown accustomed to Berengar's temper, but Azura's mood was almost impossible to anticipate. At any given moment, she could be thoughtful and wise, playful and mischievous, or irritable and temperamental—sometimes all within the span of minutes.

Maybe fairies really are as volatile as the stories suggest. Unpredictable though she was, Morwen couldn't help liking her. Azura's intentions were good, even if she caused more than her share of trouble. Morwen could hardly imagine what harm a fairy less favorably disposed to humanity might wreak. They were lucky Azura was on their side. Morwen certainly wouldn't want her for an enemy.

"Well?" Lucien didn't bother hiding his impatience. "What have you learned? Can you get us into the city?"

"That'll be the easy part." There was a hint of amusement in Azura's voice.

"What do you mean by that?"

"You'll see soon enough."

"I've had enough of your fairy games. I think you enjoy speaking in riddles."

Azura smirked. Despite the hearth's warmth, she kept her hood on to conceal her identity—and her pointy ears. "Although the Acolytes have left the city, the watch, the palace guards, and the Brotherhood remain at Völundr's disposal."

Two guards entered the inn and surveyed the hall before approaching the innkeeper. Teelah kept her head down to avoid drawing their attention. "Once we're within the walls, what then?"

"One of my old contacts knows someone who claims he can get us inside the palace for the right price. We're to meet with him around noon."

Teelah waited for the guards to leave before speaking again. "What of the others?" The forces they had gathered in the Elderwood remained a secure distance from the city, as there was nowhere in Kilcullen safe to conceal them.

"The sentries will never let them near the city by day. The Rat Gate is the least heavily guarded. We'll need to move quietly to avoid alerting the rest of the watch. Stealth and cunning are required, which sounds like a task for goblins to me."

Teelah nodded to acknowledge the compliment. Although the two seemed unlikely to become friends anytime soon, an unspoken understanding had developed between them. "I'll lead a party over the wall after dark.

Once we've dispatched the guards, we'll open the gates to the others."

"Good," Morwen finished. "Send word to the others. Tell them to be at the Rat Gate tomorrow night. If all goes well, we'll enter the palace under cover of darkness."

They waited for Teelah's return without incident before departing the inn. It was a brisk walk from Kilcullen. Azura insisted they leave their horses behind, though she didn't say why. Morwen assumed she had either bribed guards or found a secret passage that would get them into the city.

She leaned over and whispered into Azura's ear. "How exactly are you planning on getting us over the wall?"

Azura flashed a toothy smile. "We're almost there. I don't want to spoil the surprise."

"I've had my fill of fairy surprises," Lucien muttered under his breath. "Hopefully this one doesn't involve me growing a tail." The remark drew a chuckle from Teelah.

The city's walls loomed ever larger as they approached. Azura led them to a section of wall far from the nearest gate, where no sentries manned the walls.

Lucien frowned. "I don't suppose you mean for us to *fly* over the wall."

Azura was hardly able to contain her glee. "That's exactly what I mean for us to do."

A look of puzzlement replaced his stern expression. "In case you've forgotten, unlike you, we don't have wings."

"I wasn't only looking for information earlier." She reached into her cloak and produced a pouch. "I also wanted to get my hands on *this*." Azura opened the pouch to reveal a powdery substance shimmering in the moonlight.

Morwen recognized it at once. "Fairy dust."

Lucien held up a hand to warn Azura away. "More magic? I'll have no part in it."

Azura narrowed her eyes at him. "Are you too frightened of a little magic to save your kingdom?"

The king glowered at her before relenting. "Very well, but this is the last time I let you use magic on me."

Azura sprinkled fairy dust over Morwen and Lucien, but Teelah—also deeply resistant to the idea of relying on fairy magic—shook her head. "I can scale the wall on my own."

"As you wish." Azura spread her wings and hovered just off the ground. "What are you two waiting for?"

"I don't feel any different," Morwen started to say but stopped short. A strange, tingling sensation spread from her fingers down to her toes. While she was no stranger to magic, this was something else entirely. Lucien stared at her with eyes wide as saucers, and Morwen realized she was floating several inches above the earth.

Her heart soared within her chest. She lifted her arms and rose higher from the ground. Below, Lucien tried desperately to cling to the wall but was lifted feet-first into the air by an unseen force. Azura giggled as he clawed at the air like a drowning man before finally stabilizing in midair.

Although Lucien initially appeared frightened when he glanced down at the ground, a change slowly came over his face as he continued hovering in place. "This isn't so bad." He spread his arms and shot into the sky, climbing higher and higher. "I am Lucien, master of the skies!" For an instant, he appeared every bit the young boy he was. The moment his feet touched the ground on the other side of the wall, he grew serious once more. "Ahem."

Once Teelah finished climbing the wall and dropped

down beside them, Azura again lowered her hood. "Follow me."

They made their way in silence through the night. Patrols were everywhere. Morwen drew on her magic stores to enhance her sight and hearing beyond ordinary levels. They were fortunate Azura knew her way around the city from her years in the Brotherhood. Morwen wondered what it must've been like for her, living in hiding among humans, unable to reveal her true identity or return home.

They took shelter for the night in an abandoned hovel Azura had used as a hideaway more than once in her time as a thief. Azura opened a creaking door to reveal a secret attic room, and Morwen filed in behind her, brushing away cobwebs in her path. A rat scurried away as Morwen lowered herself to sit on the dusty floor. Moonlight entered through boards covering the windows. Although cramped and lacking physical comforts, the hideaway was ideally situated in a deserted neighborhood in the Warrens, far away from prying eyes.

Soon, Lucien was asleep. Teelah joined him not long after, and only Morwen and Azura remained awake. Morwen wrapped herself in her cloak for warmth and watched the fairy with interest. "Where will you go when all this is over?"

"I've lived here these past years, but Dún Aulin is not my home. I've had no home since I was cast out of the Otherworld."

Even in the absence of the bounty on her head, Azura's life would always be in danger, and not just from monster hunters. Only dragon scales and unicorn horns were rarer and more valuable than fairy blood.

"You could come with us. You'd be safe in our company."

Azura chuckled. "I don't imagine your companion would welcome that idea."

"Don't let him fool you. Berengar's not so bad once you get to know him."

"You know him better than I, but I think you might be right." Her eyes lingered on Morwen's amulet. "My path leads elsewhere."

"Do you really think Thane Ramsay is out there?" Everyone in Fál knew the story of Áed's doom. Morwen, a student of magic and its history, was no exception. Although the tale took many forms depending on the telling, every version ended the same—with the death of the king and all his family, Thane Ramsay included. "If Ramsay had survived Connacht's fall, don't you think he would've returned to aid Nora in bringing peace to the realms?"

"Little happens in the kingdoms that is not known in Dún Aulin. I've spent years here searching for answers, and even after all this time, I've found little more than rumors as to his fate."

"What was he like? Was he really as great as the stories say?"

The mere mention of him seemed to bring Azura happiness. "Ramsay's light magic was more powerful than that of the mightiest fairy. He was brave, noble, and kind—everything a proper hero should be. You remind me of him sometimes."

Morwen laughed, struck by the absurdity of the suggestion. "Thane Ramsay was a sorcerer. I'm just a magician, and not a very good one at that."

Azura's eyes twinkled in the moonlight, hinting at her true form. "You are mistaken. True, you are not as powerful as some, or as skilled, but your heart is true. Many powerful old wizards spend their years holed away in some tower, too absorbed in their studies into nature's mysteries to concern themselves with the affairs of others. Lost in their great powers, many sorcerers forget their humanity over the years. You may not be a sorceress, but you have Ramsay's reckless courage, his compassion, and his willingness to aid those in need."

Morwen hesitated, lifted the amulet from around her neck, and offered it to Azura. "You should have this. It belonged to him."

"This is a priceless gift. It is the only thing of him that remains to me." The amulet glowed with golden light when Azura traced it with her finger. "Try to rest now. You'll need your strength for the fight ahead."

Morwen stifled a yawn. "Ravenna was a sorceress, and we handled her well enough. How bad can Valmont be?"

"Völundr is no ordinary fairy. The dark arts have given him power beyond measure. There are few more dangerous creatures in all Fál. Do not let your guard down in his presence, even for a moment."

Morwen yawned again. She *did* feel tired. "Tomorrow, then."

If they could get their forces into the palace unseen, they could depose Valmont and retrieve the cursed blade at the same time. Once Lucien was restored to the throne, the guards and the watch would return their allegiance to the rightful king. Not bad for a day's work.

"This way." Azura's face held none of its characteristic good humor.

Thunder whispered softly above, a promise of storms to come. Bells announced the noon hour from the cathedral. They left the Warrens by way of a dirt path that intersected a paved road in a busy neighborhood. Morwen hurried along, careful to remain close to the others amid the crowds. Muted sunlight provided little reprieve from the frigid breeze. Despite the hour, frost clung to the ground. Morwen looked to the west, where dark clouds gathered over the horizon. *Berengar.* She hoped he was safe.

Her sense of unease had grown from the moment they set out from the hideaway. Some magicians could glimpse events unfolding elsewhere, or even predict the future. Morwen could sense others' intentions and anticipate immediate danger—mostly in proportion to the threat—but other impressions were more limited in scope. Still, she had learned to trust her instincts a long time ago, and she couldn't shake the feeling something wasn't right.

She decided to keep her concerns to herself, at least for the time being. The others had more than enough to worry about, and there was no sense troubling them. Like Azura, Lucien and Teelah were grim, and not without cause. Leinster's fate rested on their shoulders. The companions tried their best to blend into the crowd, but every guard in Dún Aulin was looking for them, and patrols were everywhere. The simmering tension seemed to extend to the city itself. Even with the theft of the cursed blade days in the past, the people remained on edge.

They broke from the multitudes and descended a long stair leading to an older neighborhood in the Grand Square's shadow. While the area was far from deserted, the streets were much quieter than those above. Mercifully, the guards' presence was notably diminished, and most people were preoccupied readying themselves for the coming storm.

They followed a bridge across the river to a grand manor. Trees, bushes, and flowers grew in gardens surrounding a centrally placed well in the manor's secluded courtyard. Banners hanging from the walls waved in the wind. The manor obviously belonged to someone of great wealth, and yet there were no guards in sight.

Lucien glanced around suspiciously. "Is this the place, fairy?"

"Aye." Once Teelah scaled the wall to keep watch in case of treachery, Azura approached a side door and knocked three times in rapid succession. There was a brief pause, the door opened, and a man greeted them on the other side.

Morwen, recognizing him at once, tried and failed to hide her surprise. "You?" It was Jareth, the bard from the Coin and Crown. "What are you doing here?"

"I might ask you the same question, Lady Morwen." Although his manner was as charming as it had been on the stage at the Coin and Crown, up close there was something vaguely predatory about his smile. "Please, come inside." Jareth stepped away from the door to allow them entry.

Morwen followed the others into a well-furnished chamber illuminated by candlelight. "What is this place?"

"This manor and its servants were furnished by my patron, who shall remain anonymous for now. Suffice to say, I am very comfortable here."

"I'd say. Whoever owns this place must live like a king."

Jareth ushered them to a round table beside the fire. "No need for those hoods now."

Morwen hesitated and lowered her hood, and the others did the same. If Jareth recognized Lucien or was surprised to see the king, he hid it well.

Their host poured himself a goblet of wine and settled into a comfortable leather chair. "Tell me, is Warden Berengar here in the city with you?"

Morwen tried her best to keep her face unreadable. "Perhaps. How is it you know me?"

"I am the best bard in Leinster, and quite possibly in Fál. I make it my job to know everything, lass. For every story—every rumor—I am there, listening." Unlike the tailored clothes and elegant cloak he wore for his performance at the Coin and Crown, Jareth dressed in dull brown and gray garments that seemed out of place given the room's finery. "That is why you're here, isn't it? Because of what I know."

"That's right." Azura sounded cheerful again, though Morwen was almost certain it was an act. "Our mutual friend claims you can get us inside the palace."

"There are long-forgotten tunnels that lead to the palace dungeons. The monarchs of old used them to come and go unseen. They inspired those used by the Brotherhood of Thieves in the present, though I suspect you're more familiar with them than I, Azzy—or should I say Azura?" His smile widened. "It's not often one finds oneself in the company of one of the fair folk."

To her credit, Azura didn't flinch. "Can you guide us through these tunnels?"

"I suppose I could—for the right price. The palace isn't as *safe* as it once was, from what I hear. It's said the king has lost his mind. There are rumors that terrible screams come from the towers day and night, and Bishop Valmont has ordered the construction of a great forge in the throne room."

Berengar had warned her not to trust anyone. Something didn't feel quite right, but was her sense of unease coming from Jareth, or was it an extension of the feelings that were bothering her already? Teelah hadn't raised the alarm. That was a good sign, wasn't it?

Lucien remained uncharacteristically quiet, perhaps for fear of giving himself away.

THE CITY OF THIEVES

Azura spoke in the king's stead. "And what is your price?"

"I would have thought it obvious. I want your stories. I'd imagine you and the magician have led quite interesting lives."

Morwen regarded him with skepticism. "You're willing to risk your life just for a story?"

"You'd be surprised just what I'm willing to risk for a story, but I'll also take your weight in gold."

Morwen gestured to the room around them. "You have everything you could ever want. Isn't it enough?"

For a moment, Jareth's expression was deadly serious. "It's never enough." He finished his wine and rose from the chair. "I have another matter to see to. Feel free to discuss my offer among yourselves until my return." With that, he swept from the room.

"Well?" Lucien asked the moment he was gone.

"I don't trust him." Morwen sensed Jareth was being intentionally evasive, even if she couldn't point to a deliberate untruth. She glanced around the room, searching for something out of place. Something was amiss. Of that she was certain.

Azura gestured to the door. "You heard what he said about the forge. Völundr is preparing to reunite the halves of the cursed blade. We're running out of time. If we don't act soon, it will be too late."

Lucien made the decision for them. "Then the choice is no choice at all. We go."

Before Morwen could reply, the sound of footsteps approached from the next room as Jareth returned.

"We accept," Azura said. "You'll get paid, but only after you make good on your word."

Jareth rubbed his hands together. "Agreed. Ordinarily I would insist on payment up front, but given your reputation, I am comfortable with our arrangement. You'll find a trapdoor beneath Labraid's Tower on the other side of a fallen wall. You can't miss it. Meet me there at dusk—and come alone."

Teelah rejoined them outside.

Morwen stole a glance at the manor as they departed. "Did you see anyone, Teelah?"

"No. You were alone."

Morwen bit her lip, unable to shake the feeling she'd missed something.

Azura thought it best to scout the area in advance of their rendezvous with Jareth, so they set out for Labraid's Tower. As Jareth predicted, the trapdoor wasn't difficult to find once they knew where to look.

Teelah glanced at the sky. "I should go. It won't be long before dusk, and I must gather the others before nightfall."

Lucien held up a hand to stop her. "Teelah, wait."

She turned to face him. "Yes?"

"I…" He fell short, as if unable to voice his thought. "We'll wait for you at the tunnel's end. Be safe."

"And you." Teelah lingered for perhaps a moment longer than necessary before hurrying away.

They sought shelter from the inclement weather in the nearest tavern. Lucien and Azura used the opportunity to fill their bellies while they waited for dusk, but Morwen couldn't eat. *Why would Jareth agree to put his life on the line for such a dangerous gamble?* It didn't make sense. Finally, she grabbed her staff and pushed away from her seat. If there was one thing Berengar had taught her, it was to always trust her gut.

"Where are you going?" Azura asked.

"I have to check something. I'll meet you at the tower." She rushed from the tavern and retraced their path to

Jareth's manor. Unlike before, a pair of guards were stationed outside the front, and the courtyard's entrance was shut. Morwen scaled the wall and dropped down to the other side.

Thunder bellowed as she approached the side door. Swirling black clouds gathered over the distant palace like living shadows reaching down to devour the earth. Morwen found the door locked, but although she didn't carry a lockpick like Azura, a simple spell was enough to accomplish her purpose. The door swung open, and she entered quietly and shut the door behind her.

Morwen again looked around the room, seeking what was out of place. She shut her eyes, pressed her thumb against her forehead, and extended her second and third fingers to hone her senses. Darkness seemed to emanate from the fireplace. Morwen opened her eyes and approached. It looked like an ordinary fireplace. *Concentrate.* Again she closed her eyes. *There's something more behind the wall.* Her finger brushed a lever, and the wall opened, revealing a hidden chamber on the other side.

A single chest waited within the chamber, which was otherwise bare. Morwen reached down and lifted the lid. Inside lay a hooded cloak, a set of throwing knives, and a wooden mask. Morwen picked up the mask, which seemed to stare back at her in the quiet room, and her hands began to shake when she remembered where she had seen it before.

It was the mask of the thief king.

Suddenly, everything made sense. Jareth was the thief king. His double life as a famous bard was the perfect cover for a man who spent his time seeking secrets and rumors. He could even enjoy his ill-gotten wealth in plain sight by creating a fictitious wealthy patron. It explained how he'd known everything about them, even from the start. The

Brotherhood of Thieves was the greatest network of spies in Fál.

The hairs on the back of her neck stood on end. *The others must know before it's too late.*

"Is someone there?" The door opened, and a guard entered. Before he could go for his sword, Morwen knocked him out with her staff and fled the manor. Already the sky was darkening. She ran as fast as her legs would carry her, drawing on her magical reserves to boost her stamina. When she reached Labraid's Tower, her heart skipped a beat.

The trapdoor was already open. Morwen equipped her lightstone at the tunnel's entrance and broke into a sprint, hoping she wasn't too late. She followed the tunnel's course for some time before she heard voices beyond the shadows' reach. Ahead, Azura and Lucien trailed Jareth, who carried a torch to light their path. To her relief, her friends were unharmed.

"Stop!"

The trio came to a halt at the sound of Morwen's voice. "What is it?" Azura asked, taking note of her alarm.

Morwen cast the mask on the ground at Jareth's feet, and the torchlight illuminated its shape in the dark. "Jareth is the thief king. He's leading us into a trap."

A sinister smile crept across Jareth's face. When Azura went for her knives, he made no move to defend himself. "I wouldn't do that if I were you."

A shiver ran down Morwen's spine, and she realized they were not alone. Thieves everywhere stepped out of the shadows, their knives gleaming in the dark.

CHAPTER SEVENTEEN

BERENGAR BROUGHT his horse to a stop.

Beside him, Godfrey did likewise. "What do you see?"

He held a finger to his lips to caution against speaking. For a moment, nothing happened. Leaves fell across the trail ahead, and all was calm. Then he spotted a band of goblins marching east. Niall quietly reached for his blade in case the creatures caught their scent, and Berengar did the same. Fortunately, the wind shifted in their favor, and the goblins passed them by.

Niall eased his hand off the blade. "The whole forest is crawling with monsters."

That's not even the half of it. The plan to lead the Acolytes away from the others had worked. Now the monster hunters were on their trail, and the need for caution had slowed their progress. With Prince Tristan's life hanging in the balance, time was something they didn't have, but one false step would bring an army of monsters down on them. Berengar knew their luck couldn't hold forever; the enemy's spies were too many.

Godfrey prodded his horse back onto the path and

beckoned them with his wooden hand. "I don't know about you two, but I don't plan on remaining in these woods come sunset."

Berengar stared ahead. Storm clouds gathered above the Giant's Foot to the east. "We're close."

A change came over the Elderwood as they traveled farther east. Sparsely spaced trees permitted more light into the forest, and the air was no longer quite so stale. Berengar observed forest animals and healthy plants in greater numbers, a sign Cathán's corruption had not yet fully taken hold of the Elderwood.

I hope Morwen's keeping her head down. He still didn't like her pressing on without him, even in the others' company. Dún Aulin was treacherous, especially for a magician, and while Morwen might suggest otherwise, she had a unique talent for finding trouble.

Niall glanced over at him. "What is it?"

"Nothing."

"I know that look. It's not nothing." Niall studied him carefully. "You're worried about the girl, aren't you?" He chuckled. "You know, there was a time when I thought you didn't care for anything other than that hound of yours."

Berengar shot him a dark look.

"I remember seeing her once or twice at Mór's court. We even met once, at some wedding feast or another at Cashel. She was probably too young at the time to remember it. I'm sure you were invited and chose not to go."

"I'm not fond of weddings. Or the south."

"Or any event where people are present, for that matter. She must be quite capable if you've chosen her as a companion."

Berengar resisted the urge to smirk. "When she's not trying to get herself killed."

"How did she come to join you?"

"Before he died, Mór asked me to look after her."

A brief interval passed before Niall spoke again. "I'm sorry I dragged you into this. I know you have an unpleasant history with Dún Aulin." It was an understatement, and they both knew it.

Berengar shrugged. "I did what needed to be done. I always have."

"I haven't forgotten. I was there too."

You're not the one they call monster. Berengar fought back the words. He was a hardened killer long before the riots. His hands were stained with blood, and whatever blood Niall had on his was of a different sort. "I remember. The king sent you to find Prince Tristan before the mobs got him first." Niall's was a rescue mission. He got to play the hero while Berengar got his hands dirty. Like the other wardens, Niall was lauded while Berengar was spat on and despised.

"We've been friends ever since. To tell you the truth, sometimes I suspect I've been a poor influence on the prince. You may find it hard to believe, but I was something of a troublemaker in my youth."

Godfrey, who had pulled up beside them, gave a hearty laugh. "I, for one, don't find that hard to believe at all."

"I hope he's all right." Niall's concern for the prince's safety was evident. Unlike Berengar, he had always been lucky in his friendships. It wasn't surprising. Niall was quick-witted, even-tempered, and always ready with a laugh. The people considered him something of a rogue but loved him all the same. "Do you think Cathán can actually accomplish what he plans?"

"You've seen the pestilence he's wrought," Godfrey answered. "If he's not stopped, the blight will spread."

Niall shook his head, skeptical. "I don't doubt magic is

real, but that doesn't mean it's what it once was. The Fomorians are long gone—if they ever existed at all."

Berengar remained stone-faced. "I never put much stock in the old tales either. That was before Blackthorn, when Laird Margolin attempted to sacrifice Imogen to Balor. Something spoke to me—a giant, wreathed in shadow and flame. I felt its presence again at the henge." He understood Niall's skepticism. Although there were more than enough monsters in Leinster to keep the hunters occupied, Niall spent most of his time dealing with court intrigue and treacherous lords.

Faolán glanced at him, a warning in her eyes. He pulled back on the reins, but it was too late. A goblin scout lurking in a tree spotted them and raised a horn to his mouth. The blast reverberated through the forest, and caws sounded as crows flocked overhead.

Niall swore. "So much for the element of surprise. There's no point hiding ourselves now."

They galloped down the trail, ignoring nearby creatures. Soon the village of Tulach Mhór materialized through the trees. The Giant's Foot was within reach. Berengar spurred his horse forward and raced toward the forest's border. He realized something was wrong just before he broke through the trees.

An army had assembled outside the Elderwood, but not the one he expected. The Acolytes of the True Faith lay in wait. There were at least a hundred in all, maybe more, suggesting Leinster's soldiers were bolstering their numbers at Valmont's command. Archers, infantry, and cavalry gathered in formation, ready for battle.

Winslow was ready for me. If Morwen and the others hadn't taken a separate route to reach Dún Aulin, the Acolytes would have annihilated them.

"Fall back to the woods." Berengar ducked under an

arrow that missed his head by inches and turned his horse around. Niall and Godfrey, already nearer to the forest, closed the distance with ease. An arrow struck Berengar's mount, then another. His horse collapsed just shy of the trees, and Berengar crashed to the ground. When he looked back, he saw the Acolytes' forces advancing.

"Berengar!" Godfrey stared at him with growing horror.

"Go! Save the prince!" Berengar drew his sword, pushed himself to his feet, and scrambled toward the forest as more arrows fell around him.

He didn't get far. Approaching riders followed in pursuit. No matter which direction he turned, another horseman awaited. One charged toward him with a spear. Berengar moved out of the horse's path and met the attack with his sword. Although his strike knocked the rider from the saddle, Berengar hit the ground and lost his blade in the process. Still groggy from his fall, he grasped for the weapon, which lay just out of reach.

"Reach for that sword, and we'll fill you full of holes." Winslow looked down on him from his horse. "Where are the others?"

Berengar met Winslow's gaze without replying.

"Hold him down." Winslow dismounted while two of his underlings restrained Berengar. He smiled at the warden's axe, which he carried in two hands. "Don't worry, I'm not going to kill you. Not yet. But that doesn't mean I can't take some pieces from you first." The monster hunters forced Berengar's hand to the ground.

When Winslow took a step toward Berengar and raised the axe, suddenly the earth began to shake. "What's happening?"

The others peered into the forest. Berengar seized the opportunity to tear himself free, snatch his sword from the ground, and throw himself at Winslow as the army of monsters emerged behind him.

M orwen and the others ascended a winding stair illuminated by torchlight as the thieves led them from the dungeons. The chains binding her manacles rattled when she moved.

"Teelah should have been here by now," Azura whispered. "I should have known better than to trust a goblin."

One of their captors prodded her along before Morwen could respond. "Quiet, you lot."

A door opened at the stair's end, and they emerged into the palace.

"We're escorting the prisoners to the throne room," Jareth—now wearing the thief king mask—said to the guards waiting on the other side.

The guards' captain scowled. His discomfort with the thieves' presence in the palace was obvious. "Entrance to the throne room is barred on Bishop Valmont's orders."

"Rest assured, he will want to see the gift I have brought him."

The captain began to step aside until Lucien tore free from his captors' grip. "Valmont is a liar and a traitor! I am Lucien, your rightful king."

The pronouncement drew murmurs and troubled looks from the guards. "What is the meaning of this?" One guard unsheathed his blade and started forward, but the guards' captain shook his head.

"Stand down. That's an order. These three murdered Bishop Flaherty and plotted to depose the rightful king with a pretender."

Lucien glared at him. "How much is Valmont paying you for your loyalty, treacherous worm?"

The guards' captain ignored him and stared hard at his reluctant underlings to issue an implicit warning against interference. "Make sure they're properly searched before they're allowed inside the throne room."

Morwen frowned. Their captors had taken her staff, and the use of magic without it was too unpredictable to attempt an escape. Besides, with the palace crawling with guards, there was nowhere to run. *There must be something I can do.*

A guard grabbed her satchel and pulled it away. "I'll take that."

Morwen shot a glance at Azura as they resumed the journey to the throne room. Azura hadn't even attempted to resist when the thieves revealed themselves. Despite the discomfort caused by her iron manacles, Azura didn't appear concerned. Instead, she smiled, hinting at an inner confidence.

She wants *them to take us to the throne room. Now that they've caught us, it's the only way we're getting close to Valmont.*

A sudden sensation of dread distracted her from her thoughts. Her skin crawled, and the hair on the back of her neck stood on end. A dark power emanated from the throne room. She'd never felt magic so strong. She hesitated and stretched her hands toward the throne room, and a premonition of destruction flashed through her mind. *Black magic.*

"I sense it too." Azura leaned closer to Morwen and lowered her voice. "Do you remember the spell you used on me the night I stole the cursed blade?"

Morwen didn't bother hiding her confusion. "Why?"

"Do you think you can manage it again?"

Guards stationed outside the throne room parted as the doors opened to permit them entrance. Searing heat greeted them inside, where a great forge cast a shadow across the room. Its fires burned with an eerie blue light. When Morwen's eyes moved from the elite guards and their crossbows to the false king on the throne, she realized what Azura was implying.

"Aye." She intentionally tripped and fell into the guard who had taken her satchel. While the guard was distracted, Morwen deftly slipped her hand into the satchel. *Azura's not the only one who knows sleight of hand.* She *was* a magician, after all.

I'll only have one shot at this. She needed to retrieve the correct rune for Azura's plan to work, and there was only enough time to grab one. She shut her eyes, concentrated on the character of magical energy emitted by each stone, and pulled one from the satchel. The purple stone shimmered in her hand, and she quietly hid the rune in her sleeve before the guard shoved her away.

Only Azura, who met her gaze with a wink, seemed to have noticed. "When I give the signal, you know what to do."

The austere chamber was even more unforgiving than Morwen remembered. It had none of the beauty or splendor found in the throne room at Cashel, which seemed appropriate given the contrast between the kingdoms. It wasn't that long ago she had stood at her father's left hand to advise him about magical threats. The absence of a court magician had left Leinster vulnerable to those very threats, and now the kingdom teetered on the brink of destruction.

Valmont addressed an ornate full-length mirror with his back to them. The mirror hummed softly, and its surface seemed to ebb and flow. As Morwen approached, she saw another figure reflected in the mirror in Valmont's place—a cruel-looking fairy in battle armor. Long black hair framed a scarred face, and atop his head rested a spiked crown.

"The time is nigh." Valmont gripped the shard of the cursed blade by its hilt and held it before the figure in the mirror. "Ready your armies for war."

The crowned figure spoke through the mirror. "I see nothing more than a fragment. Do not forget our pact. You promised me a throne."

The corners of Valmont's mouth curled down in a show of contempt. "And you shall have it. I will uphold my end of our bargain. Take care to uphold yours." When Valmont turned away from the mirror, the crowned figure vanished, replaced by a still glass surface.

"You." Lucien's voice was a hiss. "Treacherous fairy."

Laughter came from the throne, where the imposter-king cackled, spilling wine from his goblet. Although the changeling's appearance copied Lucien nearly perfectly, there were differences if one looked closely enough. Even adorned in the trappings of royal finery, there was some-thing wild and unkempt about the changeling, who had taken Berengar's bearskin cloak and now wore it as a robe while playfully spinning the warden's sword in one hand.

At the sight of Morwen and the others, he broke into song. "A staff, a sword, a throne! A bear, a mage, a fate entwined. A debt, an oath, a life exchanged. One daughter lost, one father lost. At journey's end, one more begins. A home once lost will then be found, and at the end there is a crown!"

Azura regarded the changeling with an icy expression. "You are a fool to aid in his treachery. Once Völundr has what he wants, he will discard you."

The changeling greeted her proclamation with more high-pitched laughter. "Happy fairy, do not fear—the thing you seek is closer than you think! A princess without a crown and a queen of great renown together venture down, into dungeons deep below, where light dies and shadows grow. Beware your wish gone amiss, and joy turned to woe."

"Enough!" Valmont silenced him with a dark stare. Jareth approached the throne and produced the remaining shard of the cursed blade. "You have done well, thief."

"You will honor your word? I will have treasures and riches from the great fairy halls?"

Valmont took the fragment and caressed its surface. "Soon." He returned to the forge with the twin pieces of the cursed blade. He surrendered them to the fire, and blue light from the forge filled the chamber with an ethereal glow. Valmont placed the shards on an anvil and raised a great hammer engraved with charms and enchantments. When he struck the anvil with the hammer, a fierce wind swept through the chamber, and every candle and torch inside the throne room went out at once. Many of the guards looked on in horror, too frightened to act.

Azura quietly opened her fist to reveal a key she'd stolen from one of their captors. Her manacles fell away, and by the time the thieves turned toward her, she was already in motion. Before the others could move to stop her, she opened her mouth and shouted a word of power at Valmont, unleashing a wave of devastation that ripped through the throne room. With the others' attention occupied by Azura, Morwen pitched herself forward, grabbed her staff, and spun it around to knock out the man who had taken it.

"Titim titim amach." The magic flowed through the staff, and her chains fell away. Morwen glanced back at the throne in time to see the smoke clear away from the forge, which remained unharmed.

A crystal wand, longer than those used by human

magicians, vibrated with silent power in Valmont's hand. "You failed."

Azura grinned. "Did I?"

Morwen slid the rune of illusion into a slot at the head of her staff, sprinted forward, and trained her staff on the changeling. "Nocht a nádúr fíor! Let your true nature be revealed!"

The false king's eyes widened, and he tried to shrink away, but it was too late. A tiny, misshapen creature with wrinkled yellow skin sat in the imposter's place.

The real Lucien, freed of his chains by Morwen, stepped forward and pointed at the creature on the throne. "Men of Leinster! I am your true king. The fairy Valmont kidnapped me and replaced me with a changeling to steal my throne and take the cursed blade for himself." Lucien cast his gaze on the guards. "If any among you are loyal to the crown, I call upon you to stand with me now and fight!"

"To the king!" Dozens of guards across the throne room drew their swords and hurried to the king's side.

Valmont bared his teeth. "It matters not." On his command, the Brotherhood of Thieves surrounded Lucien and his allies and forced them to the throne room's heart. "I've filled this palace with those who answer to me. Your defenders are few, child."

Before the enemy could advance, a deafening roar came from behind them, where the doors at the throne room's entrance trembled and shook. A giant crashed through the doors, and goblins and other creatures poured from behind him into the chamber, loosing black arrows and swinging swords.

"Took you long enough," Azura muttered to Teelah with a cheerful smile.

The guards raised their swords and charged the thieves.

"For the king!"

The thieves ran to meet them, and fighting broke out across the throne room. The changeling hopped from the throne and took off running as Morwen and Azura approached. Morwen grabbed Berengar's cloak to restrain the creature, which squirmed out of her grip, leaving the cloak behind.

"Leave him," Azura said. "Our fight is with Völundr."

A guttural cry emanated from Valmont's throat, and claws sprouted from his hands. Two bat-like wings spread behind him as he took on his true monstrous form.

"Get the blade." Azura spread her wings and took flight, and Valmont shot into the air to meet her. Their shouts rippled through the throne room, and each exchange of words sounded like thunder.

Morwen hurried to the anvil where the cursed blade lay. Shadows ran along its surface, whispering to her, and she hesitated. Finally, she managed to tear her gaze away. She unfastened her cloak and wrapped it around the blade to avoid touching it. Before she could spirit the sword away, Azura crashed into the forge and landed on the ground at her feet. Azura had yet to regain her footing when Valmont hit her with a spell that drew a painful shriek from her.

Morwen relinquished her grip on the blade and trained her staff on Valmont. "Leave her be!"

Valmont brushed her aside with a single word and started toward Azura, who struggled to rise. He returned the wand to his pocket, seized Azura, and held her by her throat. "Look at you. Still pretending to be human. Disgusting." Desperate for air, Azura kicked and clawed at his fingers, but he tightened his grip. "You are of the Aos Sídhe. You are more than they could ever be, and you've thrown it all away."

"I'm also a thief," Azura managed to cough out. Before Valmont could stop her, she deftly reached into his robes, and her fingers grasped the wand. "Anwybyddu."

The wand shimmered with an array of multihued light. Not only did Azura's appearance change—revealing her true form—but her clothes did as well. In place of the thieves' garb, she wore an elegant white cloak and silver gown that shone brightly. Valmont was thrown back into the forge, which exploded, leaving a smoke-filled ruin in its place.

Morwen snatched her staff from the floor and scrambled to her feet. She spared a glance back at the unfolding battle, which had turned in favor of Lucien's forces. The giant swept swaths of thieves aside to clear the way for the men and goblins to advance while the smaller broonies and pechs swarmed enemies distracted by pixies flitting about the chamber. When the guards fighting on Lucien's behalf saw the nonhumans were fighting on their side, they put aside their obvious mistrust and joined in a united effort to defeat their common foe.

Azura kept her gaze on the smoking ruin of the forge. Sword in hand, Lucien hurried to their side. The smoke parted to reveal Valmont, wielding the cursed blade with his great, bat-like wings unfurled, perched atop the throne.

"You are too late. The Cliamh Solais is whole once more."

Azura stared him down. "The Bright Sword's power has been perverted by the Lord of Shadows. Nothing good can come from using it. It's too dangerous, even for you."

"You are right to fear its power. This blade can kill immortals. You cannot hope to stand against its might."

"He's right. We can't defeat him in battle." Morwen's eyes darted to the enchanted mirror behind him. If the enchantment worked the way she suspected, there might be a way to use it against Valmont, but that would require Azura's knowledge of fairy magic. "Are you thinking what I'm thinking?"

Azura's face betrayed the hint of a smile. "Distract him and force him back. I'll do the rest."

Morwen thrust her staff forward. "Fórsa tiomáint bhrú!"

Valmont met her spell with a vocal attack that nearly knocked her off her feet. Lucien sprang forward, swinging his sword blindly. Valmont countered each strike with ease and effortlessly shattered Lucien's sword with the cursed blade.

Morwen's eyes widened in fear as Valmont raised his weapon to deliver the killing stroke. *He's going to kill the king.*

Just before Valmont could thrust his sword through Lucien's heart, Teelah pushed the king out of the way. Morwen's mouth opened in shock as the sword protruded from Teelah's abdomen.

"Stupid goblin." Valmont wrenched the sword free, and she dropped to the floor.

With Valmont temporarily distracted, Morwen swung her staff around and tried the same spell again. "Fórsa tiomáint bhrú!" This time, Valmont was pushed back, directly at the enchanted mirror.

Azura, her wand at the ready, darted forward. "Drych yn dod yn fyw!" The mirror hummed, and its surface began to swim. "Gwneud porth i'r byd arall."

"No! You will not cast me out!" Valmont opened his mouth to shout a word of power, but the amulet around Azura's neck glowed with brilliant golden light that filled the chamber.

The sphere of light exploded outward, sending Valmont back through the mirror, and the mirror shattered behind him.

Morwen stared at the thousand glass shards. "He's gone." Valmont, having disappeared into the mirror, was nowhere to be seen. "Where did you send him?"

"Somewhere else."

Morwen turned back to Teelah, who lay in a pool of blood.

Lucien ran to Teelah's side and reached for her hand. "She's dying." He glanced back at Morwen. "There must be something you can do—some potion or spell."

Morwen looked Teelah over and bowed her head. "I'm sorry. She's past my ability to heal. There are limits even to what magic can do."

Lucien trembled, and tears rolled down his face. The fighting had all but stopped, and the throne room had grown quiet.

Teelah's voice was weak. "Who would have thought? Tears from a human, shed for me." She managed a smile. "I spent my life hating you, but it turns out you're not so bad."

"You can't die, Teelah. You can't. You're my friend."

Teelah wiped away his tears. "Don't cry. It's not regal, remember?" She squeezed his hand. "Don't forget your promise. Be a good king. Honor your word."

Lucien nodded solemnly. "I swear it, in the name of the Lord of Hosts."

Content with his answer, Teelah slumped back, and her eyes closed. Morwen fought back tears. Despite her magic, she felt powerless.

Lucien buried his face in Teelah's hair. "I wish we had more time…" He trailed off, unable to finish.

Blinding white light, so powerful she was forced to shield her eyes, enveloped the room. Teelah's eyes fluttered open, and she gasped for breath with new life, her injuries healed.

"I don't understand," Lucien said, still cradling Teelah in his arms.

Morwen began laughing with joy. "Don't you see? It was your wish!"

"A selfless wish, spoken from a pure heart." Azura smiled triumphantly, her wand shining like a star.

B erengar charged. Faolán forged a path to Winslow, whose defenders reacted too late to stop Berengar in time. He brought his sword down with all his might, but Winslow countered the blade with his battleaxe. Even as the sword rattled in Berengar's hand, he brought the blade around in a horizontal slash, and again Winslow parried the strike.

Goblins in the trees unleashed torrents of black arrows, giving cover to the monsters' advance. The Acolytes, seasoned warriors all, held their ground against the first wave of attackers, and the battle began.

Berengar pointed his sword at Winslow. "I'm going to take you apart for hurting Morwen."

"That? I was just getting started." Winslow stared him down, axe at the ready. "I've been waiting for this since the day you cut down my boy."

Berengar kept his gaze trained on his foe. He knew the hate that drove Winslow all too well. It was too dangerous to risk taking his eye off him, even for a moment. "Then what are you waiting for?"

Winslow rushed forward, swinging the battleaxe, and the pair exchanged blows in a fierce clash. Neither gave ground, even with the battle raging around them.

He's good. Berengar knew better than to underestimate his opponent. Winslow was a skilled fighter. A lifetime spent hunting monsters had fashioned him into a lethal killer.

After scoring a strike that bounced off Winslow's breastplate, Berengar rolled away to avoid being struck in turn. Winslow wore mail under his steel plates. Berengar, in contrast, had no armor protecting him. Two spearmen came sprinting toward him, forcing Berengar to divert his attention from his foe. Faolán took care of the first, and Berengar split the other's face in half. Winslow was on him in a flash. When Berengar grabbed at the axe's handle, he caught a flurry of movement out of the corner of his eye. With his free hand, Winslow thrust a dagger toward the warden's heart. When Berengar brought his arm up to ward off the blow, the dagger raked across his forearm, and Winslow stabbed him in the torso.

As Berengar pried the dagger free, Winslow bashed him with the axe's handle and struck him across the face with a steel gauntlet. "Pathetic. I expected better from the High Queen's Monster. You've grown soft."

Berengar growled and drove his forehead into his enemy's face. Winslow's helmet fell away, and he stumbled back. The two circled each other, each waiting for the other to strike. Berengar raised his sword and rushed his foe, who ran to meet him in turn.

Just before they clashed, a rampaging troll stormed between them. Thrown to one side, Berengar found himself staring up at a menacing goblin. Before the creature could impale him with a spear, Faolán dragged the goblin away. Berengar pushed himself to his feet in time to behead another goblin running at him. The troll hurled a stone that crushed a half-dozen soldiers in its path on its way to Berengar, who rolled out of the way, grabbed a spear near a fallen horseman, and cast it at the troll. The spear struck true, and the troll crashed to earth in mid-charge.

More monsters swarmed the area with each passing moment. Berengar scanned the multitudes but could no longer see Winslow amid the fighting. An ogre swung its club at him only to fall prey to an archer's arrow. The archer turned his attention to Berengar, but Faolán leapt on the man before he could take aim. The battle quickly descended into chaos as scattered fighting raged on across the forest, and both sides suffered heavy casualties. Horns blared to sound the retreat as the monster hunters—at a distinct disadvantage, given the terrain—fell back to join the bulk of their forces. Berengar sliced through a spider's leg and joined in the retreat with the monsters closing in behind him. The two armies met on the open field, and the fighting intensified.

Deafening thunder clashed to the east, where lightning flashed above the Giant's Foot. *Cathán.* Berengar knocked an enemy rider from his horse, smashed the man's face in with his boot, and stole the horseman's mount. He used the confusion to make his way to the Giant's Foot.

Crows flocked over the hilltop to greet his arrival. Berengar glanced at the summit. The rubble that once concealed the ruins' entrance had been cleared away. In its place loomed a great stone doorway. Shadows beckoned within. Berengar cut another spider's legs from under it and started up the stone stair. There were fewer enemies waiting above, but enough to cause him trouble none-theless. He fought his way up the hill, using the stone pillars and archways to take cover from goblin archers at the peak. While he occupied the archers' attention, Faolán crept behind them and eliminated them one by one.

They met at the summit. Crows descended, clawing and pecking at them, and they hurried inside. A cavernous chamber reached deep underground. Passages at multiple levels of the ruins emptied into a great atrium, and numerous staircases led to the lower levels. Berengar peered over a precipice and saw Prince Tristan bound to a stone table on a dais. Thick smoke rose from a lid-like seal visible through a hole in the dais. Massive iron chains fixed to the cavern's walls anchored the seal in place. Around the seal there was only darkness—a gaping pit that threatened to swallow all light.

"Eirigh suas!" Cathán chanted at an altar that stretched to the ceiling. A monstrous, wraithlike form moved along the cavern walls in the torchlight, joining its sinister voice to his. Something moved under the earth in response, sending stones falling from above into the dark chasm.

Goblin archers crawled along the cavern walls. Berengar braced himself, anticipating an attack, but instead the creatures scurried toward two figures making their descent to the dais.

Niall and Godfrey. The pair were nearly surrounded by sluagh, which Godfrey did his best to stave off with his crucifix.

Berengar started toward the nearest staircase. When a goblin took note and scurried toward him, Berengar sprinted at the goblin, severed his enemy's bow arm, and kicked the creature from the ledge.

At that moment, Cathán's gaze fell on Berengar. The thunder rune glowed with bright light, and magical lightning illuminated the atrium. Berengar hurled himself out of the way moments before the bolt struck the ledge. His eye moved to the bow the goblin had dropped. He rolled to the bow, nocked a fallen arrow, and emerged from cover to take aim and draw Cathán's attention from Niall and Godfrey. The arrow knocked the ceremonial dagger from Cathán's hands, and it careened into the gaping pit below.

Berengar took cover behind a pillar when Cathán retaliated with another lightning bolt. Cracks spread along the stone floor, part of which threatened to collapse. His sword rested a short space away. As Cathán's voice again filled the chamber, Berengar snatched the weapon from the ground and started for the nearest staircase.

An arrow caught him in the back.

"Where do you think you're going?" Covered in monster blood, Winslow stood at the ruin's entrance. Two archers filed inside behind him. Winslow swung the axe at Berengar, who deflected the attack with his sword. "I'm not finished with you yet."

They clashed at the ruins' entrance as smoke and fire rose from the pit below. The duel took them along the ledge, where a fatal drop awaited any who strayed too far over the side. Their weapons locked, and they struggled inches from the edge. Already weakened from the arrow, it took all the force Berengar could muster to knock Winslow back. Before he could press his advantage, another arrow struck him in the thigh, and the battleaxe knocked the sword from his hands. Winslow delivered blow after blow with his steel gauntlet, and Berengar tasted blood.

"This is where you die, Warden Berengar. You needn't worry. After I'm through with you, I'll find your little friend and take good care of her."

When Winslow raised the axe to deliver the killing blow, a scream came from one of the archers before Faolán silenced him. Using Winslow's distraction to his advantage, Berengar dodged the axe, grabbed his sword, and drove it through his enemy's chest in one fluid motion.

Winslow dropped to his knees, and Berengar pulled the battleaxe free from Winslow's grip. "This belongs to me."

He put his boot against his enemy's back so that Winslow's neck was exposed. "This is for all the lives you've taken. All the people you've hurt."

Winslow stared up at him with pure loathing. "You're a killer, same as me. You always will be. People don't change."

Berengar severed Winslow's head from his body with a single swing. The monster hunter's corpse toppled to the ground, and his head rolled over the edge into the abyss. The remaining archer turned and fled out the entrance in a blind panic.

The floor, already unstable from Cathán's use of the thunder rune, collapsed under Berengar's feet, and he fell into an underground passage full of bones, webs, and dust. He clenched his teeth and pulled the arrow from his thigh. The pain was excruciating. The one in his back would have to wait.

It was all he could do to stand. Berengar limped forward, pressing a bloodied hand against the wall for support. Cathán's voice grew louder as he made his way through the passage. *He's close.* Torchlight flared beyond the shadows. His head was spinning from pain and blood loss, but he forced himself to keep going. *You can't give up now.*

He remembered the last time the city burned. He could still picture the dead in the streets. He couldn't save them. He had put an end to the riots and paid blood for blood, and the people hated him for it. Now another force threatened Dún Aulin, and once more it fell to the High Queen's Monster to fight for those who despised and spat at him. He didn't care about them. Morwen was there. He'd made a promise to keep her safe, and he aimed to keep it, no matter the cost. He'd accepted long ago that he'd be fighting until his dying breath. It was the price he paid for walking the path of vengeance.

He emerged from the passage and made his way to the dais, where Cathán stood at the altar with his back to him. "It's time to end this."

"You dare contend with the will of Balor?" Cathán slowly turned to face him. "Look at you. You can hardly stand."

"I beat you before."

"I was only human then. Now I am something more."

"You were always a monster. You told yourself it was for a greater cause, but power was what you really wanted."

Smoke from the seal below rose between them, momentarily obscuring the druid's figure. "There was a time when the kings of Leinster would lay down their arms at a druid's command. The people have forgotten the old ways. The time has come to remind them."

Berengar pointed his axe at Cathán. "You're wrong. King Lucien pledged to end the persecution of nonhumans in the realm. Now they fight for him."

Cathán stared at him from his place at the altar. "You're lying."

Berengar let out a hard, mocking laugh. "You were wrong about everything, just like you were all those years ago."

"It matters not. The Fomorians will restore magic to its proper place in the world, and mankind will burn."

"Not if I stop you first."

"Come, then, and let us finish what we began in the purges." Cathán's voice reverberated off the cavern's walls, and a powerful gust of wind nearly pulled the axe from Berengar's grasp. Cathán hit him head-on with a jolt of energy from the thunder rune. He nearly screamed from the pain, and the force knocked him to the ground.

Cathán approached, the thunder rune glowing in his

fist. Berengar picked himself up with a growl and lunged at his foe with everything he had. The impact drove the druid back, and they faced each other on the dais.

Cathán swung his scythe at Berengar, who parried the attack with his axe and returned it in kind. The druid moved with impossible speed, blocking each of Berengar's strikes until the scythe grazed the warden's chest.

Cathán raised the bloody scythe, and amid the smoke rose the wraithlike presence, looming hungrily behind the druid. "This is the end, Warden Berengar. You will make a powerful host for Balor until Caorthannach brings about his rebirth in the flesh."

Berengar stumbled backward, clutching the bleeding wound with his free hand and gasping for air. *He hasn't won yet. I have to give it everything I have.* He rushed forward before Cathán could swing his scythe at Prince Tristan, feinting right with his axe. When Cathán countered with his scythe, Berengar slammed into him and struck his foe across the face. The blow shattered half the druid's elk-skull mask to reveal the scarred flesh underneath. "You're no god. Not yet."

Cathán took a step back, his eyes burning with hate, and Berengar saw a hint of doubt for the first time. The cavern shook again, and fire shot from the depths as the two exchanged blows while Prince Tristan looked on. When Cathán unleashed the full power of the thunder rune, Berengar barely brought his axe up in time to shield himself. The silver rune of resistance emitted a high-pitched note, and the axe shook in his hand as it absorbed and deflected excess energy.

Berengar struggled against the force driving him back. It was nearly impossible to keep his grip on the axe, but if his hold faltered, the lightning would incinerate him alive. He roared with fury, relying on his rage to propel him forward. Finally, he drove Cathán back through brute strength and plunged the axe into his chest.

"It's over."

An inhuman rattle emanated from the druid's throat. "There is much you fail to see, Berengar One-Eye. Do you think I am Balor's only servant? His reach is further than you know. The kingdoms of Fál will fall, and your queen with them."

Berengar pulled the axe from Cathán's chest and hurled him over the dais, into the gaping pit below.

CHAPTER EIGHTEEN

HE GAZED across Dún Aulin from the tower bridge. His bearskin cloak swayed in the cold wind. The false king having fled, the warden's belongings were back in his possession. Now that he had recovered his cloak, weapons, and armor, Berengar felt more like himself again. The air was cooler, a sign the seasons were changing. Winter was on its way. He stared at the City of Thieves in solitude, contemplating the past. The purges haunted him, and he supposed they always would.

Faolán's ears perked up, and she eyed the tower door as Morwen emerged and came to stand beside him.

"I thought I might find you here."

"I've been penned inside these walls long enough. It's past time we moved on." A creeping sense of restlessness had set in after his wounds healed, and he was ready to return to the road.

She grinned. "I thought you might say that too. I'm already packed."

"Good." Berengar turned away from the view. He

could save Dún Aulin a thousand times, but he would always be the High Queen's Monster.

"Can we bid farewell to the others first?"

Although he preferred to come and go without fanfare, she asked so earnestly he couldn't bring himself to disappoint her. "The day's still young. There's plenty of time to get on the road."

Bells tolled from the cathedral as the pair made their descent. The king had promised a major proclamation, and the city was abuzz with speculation. Berengar and Morwen moved past the guards and filed inside the throne room, where Lucien had summoned all Leinster's prominent lords and nobles. With church and city officials also in attendance, the room was packed. Teelah stood with the goblins and other nonhumans off to one side.

As Berengar waited for Lucien to appear, he spotted Lady Imogen in attendance. She gave him a curt nod, which Berengar did not return. She too promised peace before she gained her uncle's iron crown. It had not taken long for power to corrupt her. Despite Lucien's bravery, he doubted the boy would be any different.

The bells ceased, and the king's elite guard entered the room. The murmuring crowd fell silent as Lucien took the throne. Despite his small size, the king—clad once more in his silver crown and full regalia—nevertheless cut an impressive figure.

"Welcome, lords and ladies of Leinster, representatives of the church, and"—he smiled briefly when his eyes fell on Teelah—"honored guests. The stories are true. Bishop Valmont attempted to steal my throne. It is only thanks to the help of my new friends and the heroism of my cousin, Prince Tristan—who nearly lost his life to the druid Cathán—that I stand before you now.

"In my exile, I have seen and learned much." He faced

the nobles gathered before the throne. "I always thought Leinster was a righteous kingdom. But I was wrong. You have neglected the needs of your subjects while fighting each other to increase your wealth and power, all in the knowledge the crown would turn a blind eye. No longer. Our church, which should be a source of charity and service to others, has perverted the Lord's will. Thievery and corruption go unpunished while unjust laws target the weakest among us. No more.

"I once believed all nonhumans were monsters. I thought it was our duty to drive them from the land. I was wrong about that too. I have witnessed their capacity for courage, kindness, and selflessness.

"These last few days, I have sought the Lord's guidance on how to heal the realm." Lucien waved a hand toward his scribe. "It is written that 'When a foreigner resides among you in your land, do not mistreat them. The foreigner residing among you must be treated as your native-born. Love them as yourself, for you were foreigners.' To that end, I decree that all peaceful nonhumans within our borders shall be made full citizens of Leinster. Goblins and others wishing to live in peace may come and go freely in our towns and cities. Anyone who harms them will be treated as if they did the same to a human.

"We banned the practice of magic and burned magicians at the stake, but in our hour of need, a magician and a fairy stepped forward to protect this city from certain doom. Therefore, I hereby lift the prohibition on the practice of magic and associated trades and repeal the edicts prohibiting worship of the elder gods. Although the worship of the Lord of Hosts will remain the official state religion, those who wish to worship the elder gods may do so freely."

The decree was met by cries of protest, which Lucien quickly silenced.

"I have not forgotten you, noble lords. Many of the monsters gathered by the druid Cathán remain, scattered to the Elderwood. They are the true enemy. Each of you will contribute forces to protect the inhabitants of the Elderwood from those that would threaten them. Defy me, and your lands and wealth will be seized by the crown. Rebel, and I will show you that I am not as forgiving as my cousin." He turned to the church's representatives, who seemed equally displeased. "To reform the church, we shall need a new bishop—one untainted by politics. Friar Godfrey, are you up to the task?"

No one appeared more surprised by the news than Godfrey, who dropped to his knees, overcome with emotion. "I am not worthy, Your Majesty."

Lucien bade him to rise. "That is why it must be you."

"You honor me, Your Majesty. If it pleases you, I would ask that you outlaw the Acolytes of the True Faith."

"An excellent idea." He turned from Godfrey to the goblins. "A good king heeds wise counsel. I need advisers who care for the good of *all* my subjects. Teelah the Strong-Willed, I would name you my new chief adviser."

A long look passed between the two, and Teelah flashed a proud smile. "I accept."

At this, the goblins in the room gave a great cheer.

Berengar stared at the throne, unable to hide his surprise. *Maybe the insolent whelp's not so bad after all.*

They waited for the king to finish speaking. Niall was also selected for honor. Berengar knew he would receive no such mention. It wasn't his role to play the hero, and that suited him just fine. He didn't like all the fuss anyway.

In the speech's aftermath, Morwen went in search of

Azura, who it seemed had taken her leave. "I would've liked to have seen her one last time before we set out."

"You know fairies. They tend to come and go as they please."

Niall greeted them outside the throne room. "I take it you're leaving."

Berengar nodded. "When you write to the High Queen, tell her it was I who cleaned up your mess."

Niall laughed heartily. "That's not how I remember it. Still, it seems I again find myself in your debt." He reached into his cloak and handed Berengar a message bearing the sigil of a silver fox. "The queen recalls me to Tara. These are uncertain times, old friend. The death of King Mór, the theft of the cursed blade...I expect Nora will want a full report on all the happenings in the realm."

Berengar thought again of Cathán's last words. First Margolin, then Cathán. Just how far did the conspiracy's roots extend? "What of the changeling?" Even with the corrupt guards and the thieves mostly dealt with, there were still a few loose ends remaining. Jareth had managed to escape in the confusion, leaving only the thief king mask behind. Still, with his wealth confiscated and his identity exposed, he would have to get used to a life on the run.

"The changeling was probably glad to be rid of Valmont," Morwen answered for Niall. "I doubt we can expect further trouble from him."

Berengar offered Niall his hand. "I suppose we'll be seeing each other again soon. We'll be wintering at Tara as well."

Morwen, who longed to meet the High Queen, brightened at once. "We will?"

"Aye, but first we must ride north and meet Warden Callahan. He plans to accompany us to the capital."

"Safe travels, my friend." The two clasped hands, and

Niall nodded to Morwen. "Keep an eye on him for me, will you?"

"*She's* the one you should be worried about," Berengar insisted.

Morwen simply laughed.

The pair bade farewell to Niall and set out from the palace. The day was bright and warm—the kind of weather not likely to be seen again for quite some time.

"Do you mind if we stop by the Scholars' District first?" Morwen asked as they made their way through the crowds. "There's something I must do before we leave."

"Suit yourself." Berengar had waited weeks to leave Dún Aulin behind. A few more minutes couldn't hurt.

She glanced over at him from the saddle. "You look rather forlorn, if you don't mind my saying so. We *did* save an entire kingdom recently. I thought you'd be happier."

Berengar kept his gaze on the road, ignoring frightened stares from passersby. "Valmont lives, and with the cursed blade, no less."

Morwen shrugged. "If he finds his way back, we'll fight him and beat him again. Think of all we accomplished—all the people we helped. We rescued the true king and restored him to the throne. After decades of persecution, Leinster's nonhumans are free to live in peace without fear for their lives. Why are you looking at me like that?"

"No reason. You just remind me of Nora sometimes, that's all."

"I understand why you're cynical. Sometimes evil wins. But that also means sometimes—every now and then—good wins too."

Despite himself, Berengar couldn't help but smile at Morwen's unfailing optimism. Finally, they came to a stop outside the Institute. "What are we doing here?"

Morwen reached into her satchel and removed an

acorn. "I took this from the Oakseers' Grotto. It was all that remained of the elder trees." She broke the earth and planted it in the ground. "Maybe others are right to think the time of magic has passed. As for me, I will trust in the hope it will grow again. I still believe times can change. People too." That last part seemed for his benefit more than hers.

"Your father would be proud of you. I know I am." Berengar started toward his horse, but before he could swing himself onto the saddle, Faolán barked loudly in warning. When he turned around, a thief was holding a knife to Morwen's throat. "You."

It was Reyna. Having attempted to kill them more than once already, she was finally in a position to make good on her promise of vengeance. "Did you think I'd let them catch me before I paid you a visit?"

Berengar started to reach for his axe, but Reyna pressed the blade against Morwen's skin.

"Don't move, or I'll cut her throat. And no funny business from you, either, magician."

Berengar eased his hand from his axe. "Let her go. I was the one who took Calum's hand." He shook his head at Faolán, who was waiting to pounce at his command. There was too much distance between them to risk an attack.

Before Reyna could reply, her eyes glazed over, and the knife fell away.

"That's not very nice." Azura, once more in her human form, stepped out of the shadows. "This one's been following you since you left the palace." She held her wand to Reyna's head and whispered in her ear. Suddenly, Reyna dropped to all fours and began to purr before scampering from the area. Azura roared with laughter as Berengar and Morwen exchanged glances. "I don't think she'll be bothering you two any time soon. She only *thinks* she's a cat. It's more fun than actually turning her into one, wouldn't you say?"

Morwen didn't seem to approve but nevertheless greeted Azura with a welcome embrace. "You *were* there for Lucien's speech. I knew you wouldn't miss it."

"It seems our little imp might make a fine king after all. I've seen to it that a list of all my former contacts and associates in the Brotherhood winds up in the city watch's possession. That should delight Tavish to no end." Coupled with the arrests made when Lucien reclaimed the throne, it would help unravel the Brotherhood's empire. "It seems my work here is finally complete."

"Where will you go now?" Morwen asked.

"The Unseelie aren't finished with Fál. Even I do not know where Völundr will end up after his journey through the looking glass. He's still out there somewhere with the cursed blade." Azura traced the edge of Morwen's amulet. "Hopefully, Thane Ramsay is too."

"I hope you find the answers you seek." Morwen wrapped her in a tight hug. "Be careful. Fál is a dangerous place for a fairy." Even without Valmont's bounty on Azura's head, fairy blood was a valuable commodity, and Lucien's proclamation notwithstanding, to many people, the only good fairy was a dead fairy.

"Fortunately, I am quite dangerous myself."

"That you are." Berengar extended his hand to her. "Fál owes you a great debt. Consider yourself under the High Queen's protection. You can always call upon Tara for help if you need it."

Azura lifted the amulet from her neck and returned it to Morwen. "Keep it."

"Are you sure? I can only use it at great cost."

"I think Ramsay would have wanted you to have it.

Farewell, my friends. I am sure we will meet again." Azura gave her wand a slight twirl and disappeared without a trace.

"Fairies. Come on, Morwen. Let's go." Prepared to make their departure from Dún Aulin at last, they returned to the main road by way of Padraig's Gate.

"So, where to now?"

"North. We're to meet Callahan at the Inn of the Wayward Traveler before winter."

"And until then?"

When they passed through the grand square, Berengar's gaze fell on the bounties posted along the wall. He took one notice from the wall and read it before handing it to Morwen. "This looks interesting. Missing villagers in Mucklagh, near the border with Meath. The locals seem to think it's the work of some monster. What do you say?"

Morwen grinned. "As long as it's on the way…" She seized the reins in both hands and spurred her horse forward. "Race you to the gate!"

"You're on." He gave her a head start and took off in pursuit.

THE WILL OF QUEENS

Chapter One

That was the trouble with making promises. Sometimes one actually had to keep them. Berengar had broken more than his share of oaths over the years—either willfully or through no fault of his own—but he never broke a promise to a friend when he could help it. It was probably a good thing that he had few friends for that very reason. He promised to meet Callahan at the Inn of the Wayward Traveler, and even if it meant venturing farther north than he preferred, he planned to keep his word.

Although they were set to reach the inn ahead of schedule, there remained one last job to see to along the way. He and his traveling companions were on their way to the town of Mucklagh at the border Leinster shared with Meath. According to the notice posted in the city square at Dún Aulin, several people in the area had recently gone missing, and others had been found dead. The notice claimed the trouble was a monster's work, but more likely than not it was a band of robbers. In either event the matter needed to be looked into. Berengar fully expected he'd be able to sort out the problem and arrive at the inn to meet Callahan with time to spare.

They'd been on the road almost two weeks. Each day he saw less and less of the sun as the sky took on a gray pallor. The cooling air was yet another sign of fall's retreat under winter's steady advance. The frigid winds rarely bothered him, even without the bearskin cloak he wore. In fact, he felt almost at home in the cool, countryside air. It wasn't the climate that bothered him. He hadn't been north of the Moyry Pass in over fifteen years, and with good reason. Ulster held nothing for him but memories and regrets. There were also plenty who wanted him dead, although that wasn't all that unusual. Truth be told, he wasn't all that fond of Leinster either. Fortunately, if all went according to plan he would soon be back at Tara, just before the worst of the snows hit.

He slowed his horse to a trot and sniffed the air to confirm a growing suspicion. "It's going to snow soon."

His companion, a girl of sixteen with untidy brown curls and a good-natured smile, pulled her mare beside him and shook her head doubtfully. "Are you sure? I don't sense anything."

"Trust me."

Faolán, the enormous wolfhound mix he had raised from a pup, seemed to incline her head in agreement.

Morwen stared into the gray sky. "The last time I checked, only one of us is a magician. Unless you've been a druid all this time and never told me, I think I can predict the weather more readily than you."

Berengar returned his attention to the road. "I know these lands better than you. There will be snow on the ground before we depart with Callahan for Tara."

Morwen trailed closer behind him than before, a

curious expression on her face. "What's he like? Warden Callahan? We've met Niall, and I remember Darragh well from my time at court, but I know almost nothing about Warden Callahan."

Berengar had first encountered Morwen half a year ago during his time in Munster. She was the kingdom's court magician at the time, and together they had investigated the murder of King Mór. As it turned out, Morwen was also the king's illegitimate daughter, and before Mór's death, Berengar pledged to keep her safe. It hadn't taken him long to discover Morwen was more than capable of looking after herself.

She had traveled with him ever since. Although Berengar had always preferred to walk alone, even he was forced to admit it was useful having a magician around. Despite his reservations, he had grown fond enough of Morwen to tolerate her boundless curiosity and tendency to tease him.

"Callahan's probably the greatest monster hunter since the time of Padraig. He's a serious man with little humor. A lifetime of hunting monsters has left him alienated from most others, even when among them. He keeps to himself mostly."

"He's like you, then." Morwen didn't bother concealing a mischievous grin.

"Callahan's the oldest among us. He was a monster hunter long before he was a warden, and he's bloody good at it. The man's a born killer." Perhaps they were more alike than he thought. Still, while Berengar's temper burned hot, Callahan was a cold and ruthless man hardened by his years.

"How did he come to enter the High Queen's service?"

Berengar looked across the forested land on either side of the road, where the trees grew sparse. Eventually the lowlands would give way to mountainous terrain to the north. "Why don't you ask him yourself? You'll meet him soon enough. We're getting close to Mucklagh."

Morwen opened her mouth to respond, but a piercing cry shattered the calm before she could get the words out. Instantly alert, Faolán barked and took off down the road.

There was trouble ahead. Berengar thought again of the notice. His expression hardened, and his grip tightened on the reins. "Come on."

Morwen had little difficulty keeping up with him; men and women from Munster were widely acknowledged as the best riders in Fál, and she was no exception. Faolán ran off the road and into the wild a half-mile down the trail. When she stopped and barked again at a winding stream, Berengar and Morwen dismounted to approach on foot. The dry leaves covering the ground crunched underneath his weight. Faolán waited expectantly, wagging her tail.

She's found something. Sure enough, he noticed a boot sticking out of the brush. Berengar stooped low and uncovered what was hidden underneath. "Look at this. It's a body. Human, from the look of it."

There was blood everywhere. The corpse had been ripped to shreds. Bones and limbs were crushed or mangled. Berengar turned the body over onto its back and discovered a series of gashes across the torso, arm, and upper thigh. *Claw marks.* The innards, torn out and left exposed, attracted no small number of flies. Judging from its closely shorn hair, the corpse was male, though it was a difficult to determine how the deceased might have looked in life given the extent of the damage.

Morwen knelt over the body and lightly touched the man's forehead with the tip of her palm. "He was terrified when he died. Poor man." She withdrew her hand without a hint of the smile she'd worn only a short while ago. "What could've done something like this?"

Berengar shook his head. "There aren't many animals with the strength to cause this much damage." He doubted the man had been able to put up much of a fight. The corpse showed all the signs of a savage attack. "Perhaps there's something to the monster sightings after all."

"I'd say he's been dead since last night, but not much longer than that. The scream we heard can't have come from him. It must've come from someone else."

He probably wasn't out here alone. Berengar glanced around the clearing and observed no signs of a camp where the dead man might've stopped to rest overnight. He took a closer look at the body. *Who were you?* Although shredded, the man's clothes were fine. Likewise, his boots were new and polished. "Merchants often take this road on the way to Meath." He paused. "Interesting."

"What?"

"His coin purse is missing." Berengar rose to his full height. "Come. This body will tell us nothing else."

Morwen shot him a sideways glance. "We can't just leave him here out in the open. He deserves a proper burial."

"If the cry we heard came from someone else, they might still be in danger from whatever did this." When Berengar whistled to Faolán, the wolfhound snapped to alert and began following the scent with her nose low to the ground. He swung himself onto his horse's saddle and started in pursuit.

Faolán led them to a place just off the road where a wagon had crashed into a tree and overturned. There was no one in the vicinity. One of the wagon's wheels was missing—having likely come off and rolled downhill into the brush—and the horse that drew the wagon had also disappeared.

"Something must have spooked the horse. See the damage to the harness? The horse must have torn itself free." He examined the crash scene from the ground. Sacks full of spices and bottled had spilled from the overturned wagon. The discovery indicated his earlier suspicions were well-founded. The passengers were probably merchants from Leinster headed north to peddle their wares across the border.

Morwen inspected a sack's contents. "Saffron. This cargo is worth a considerable amount. It would not have been left behind lightly."

A muddy imprint in the grass suggested someone had been thrown clear of the wagon. With the earth still soft in the absence of winter's bite, the landing would have been a safe one—preferable at least to being crushed underneath the wagon. The rations and supplies had also been left behind. Whoever abandoned the crash did so with great haste, perhaps frightened by whatever unsettled the horse.

"They can't have gone far. We'll have to keep a close eye out for any further signs of trouble." Berengar peered deeper into the woods to make sure nothing was lying in wait. "Let's go. There's nothing more we can do here."

They came across a man wandering along the road not long after resuming their path. When the traveler noticed them, he began waving his hands and frantically shouting for help. Despite his fashionable attire, the man looked untidy and disheveled. Based on the mud staining the man's cloak, Berengar surmised he was the passenger who fled the scene of the crash.

At first, the man seemed relieved at their approach, but as Berengar drew nearer, the man's gaze quickly moved from Berengar's weapons to his face, and he turned and fled in terror. It wasn't the first time Berengar's appearance had elicited such a response, and it wouldn't be the last. The warden was well-aware he looked something like a monster himself. Well-armed, equipped with a short sword at his side, a bow slung over his shoulders, and a cruel-looking battle axe hanging from a harness at his back, he was a sight to behold. Given his size—he was well over six feet tall, with a massive, hulking frame—and the leather armor and bearskin cloak he wore, he probably looked more like a bandit than one of the High Queen's wardens. But it was likely his face that frightened the traveler most. Three uneven scars ran from his forehead to the base of his lip. An eyepatch covered the remains of his right eye, which he lost to the bear whose skin he now wore as a cloak.

Berengar hung back and issued a command to Faolán to remain at his side.

On cue, Morwen caught up to the traveler. "Wait. We mean you no harm."

At the sound of her voice, the man slowed his pace. On the surface, there was nothing about the petite young woman astride the white mare that would indicate she was anything other than an ordinary girl. Unlike Berengar, Morwen traveled with no weapons, and the blue robes she once wore as Munster's court magician had been set aside in favor of less auspicious traveler's garments. Her magician's staff was hidden under a blanket, just within reach. Anyone intending her harm would soon find there was far more to Morwen than appearances suggested.

Apparently deciding she posed no threat, the traveler finally stopped and allowed her to approach.

"I am Morwen of Cashel." She gestured for Berengar to approach. "And this is my companion, Esben Berengar."

Mindful of the traveler's wary gaze, Berengar guided

his horse forward but remained a safe distance away. Morwen's eyes narrowed in his direction, and Berengar managed a forced smile for the traveler's benefit. "We were on the way to Mucklagh when we heard you call for help. We saw the damage to your wagon. Can we offer you our assistance?"

At that, the traveler exhaled deeply and seemed to relax. "Thank heavens. This is the first stroke of luck I've had since the start of this miserable journey."

"You must be thirsty." Morwen passed her drinking horn to the man, who drank a healthy mouthful before handing it back to her.

The traveler was a lean man with sandy brown hair and a well-trimmed mustache matching the color of his cloak. He was younger than Berengar—probably in his early thirties. A coin purse hung at his side, but he had no ring or colors to indicate his clan or house, hinting that despite his means, he was not of noble birth.

"Many thanks." He wiped the sweat from his brow. "Thomas Flanagan's the name. I am a spice merchant on my way to Ulster. Or at least I was."

Morwen returned her drinking horn to her satchl "Then fortune smiles upon you, for we are headed in the same direction. Would you like to accompany us to Mucklagh?"

"Unless I'm mistaken, Mucklagh is less than a half day's ride from here." Berengar's voice was rough and coarse, like a blade scraping against a stone. "This isn't a safe place to travel alone."

The merchant peered past Morwen into the forest, as if half-expecting something to leap out at him, before scrambling forward to accept the invitation. "You're more right than you know. I apologize for my reaction to your sudden appearance, but after what happened to us on the road, I was in a state of terror."

Berengar held out a strong arm and pulled the man onto the saddle behind him.

"Us?" Morwen asked.

"Aye. I set out from Durrow with my associate, William of Clan O'Shea. We hoped to turn a sizable profit selling saffron and tears of the balsam to the northmen. We were beset by ills from the start of our journey. William told me we should have heeded the words of the notice, but I was determined to make up for time we lost due to weather. I should have listened to the warnings..." Thomas trailed off, lost in thought.

"We found a corpse off the road some ways back. Do you think it was your friend?"

"I fear it was." Thomas bowed his head, saddened to learn of his friend's death. "William wandered away from camp last night. I looked for him, to no avail. As I searched, I couldn't help feeling there was something else in the woods with me, watching. It was all I could do to keep the horse from fleeing. Given what happened the night before, I was afraid to remain any longer. I had hoped to assemble a search party once I reached Mucklagh, but now I fear it is too late."

Something about his remarks struck Berengar as odd. "You mentioned that something happened last night. What did you mean by that?"

"I know it sounds strange, but as we neared the end of our travels and made camp near the water, William swore he saw a woman watching from the trees."

"This woman—did you see her?"

"No. When I followed William's gaze, there was no one there."

"What did she look like?" Morwen interrupted. "How did he describe her?"

Thomas absently twirled the corner of his mustache. "William said that she was young and beautiful and wore a red cloak. Naturally, I believed he was mistaken. Why would a woman be on her own in the middle of nowhere?"

"Did anything else unusual happen after that?" Berengar asked.

"Some time after sunset, while we were sitting around the campfire, William imagined he heard singing. When I told him it was the wind, he just stared into the flames with a peculiar look on his face. Later I heard a terrible scream and woke to find William gone."

Berengar and Morwen exchanged glances. Whatever led William away from the camp was probably the same thing that killed him. Already, his mind raced with possibilities, though it was best to avoid discussing them until he and Morwen were alone again.

"I'm sorry about your friend." Morwen's tone was soothing. She didn't need the use of magic to put the merchant at ease. "Were the two of you close?"

"William was like a brother to me. It was he who invested his inheritance to open our business. I'm engaged to marry his sister. This will come as an awful shock to her."

They continued on their way without further interruption. The merchant's spirits improved considerably as Morwen engaged him in conversation. After weeks on the road, she seemed glad of the company—unlike Berengar, who could go an entire day without encountering another soul and remain content. He let them talk, his thoughts on the mystery of the murdered man they found in the woods.

The sun emerged as the morning passed on. Its muted glow lent little warmth. Creeping winds scattered the few remaining leaves from their branches as the companions traveled by underneath. They reached Mucklagh just after midday by crossing a flimsy bridge over a bend in the river. The island of Fál, of which Leinster was but one of five kingdoms, consisted of central lowlands surrounded by outer mountains bridged by lakes and rivers.

It was a modest settlement by any measure. A single dirt road ran the length of town. The homes and buildings —including the church, which seemed to look down over the area from its steeple's lofty heights—were made from wood, not stone. Berengar doubted the town's shoddy split rail fence, with numerous gaps, added a discernable degree of protection.

Chickens squawked and scurried away in a mad panic as the travelers' horses came down the path. Berengar shot Faolán a stern look to warn her against indulging any impulse to give chase. Most of the townspeople, wrapped up in their own chores and tasks, failed to notice their approach or else chose to ignore them, though a few looked up from their work with suspicion or disinterest. The aroma of freshly made bread wafted through the air, thinly masking the scent of the pigs rolling about in their pens.

They dismounted near the town's entrance to continue on foot. Wagon ruts brimming with water, evidence of recent rain, covered the ground. It wasn't long before Berengar's boots were coated in a fresh layer of mud. The trio headed for the tavern, which they had little difficulty finding.

"I am in your debt, friends. Please, take this as a sign of my gratitude." Thomas opened his purse and started to reach for his money, but Berengar shook his head.

"Keep your money. Given your recent losses, I expect you'll need the funds." He didn't work for coin. While one might not guess it judging from his appearance, Berengar was rarely short on gold, one of many benefits to serving the High Queen.

"Very well. I suspect you're right." Thomas closed his purse. "At least let me buy you a round of drinks as a reward for your kindness."

"Maybe later. We have business in town while we still have the light."

The two shook hands. "Then I will see you again tonight. Now I must see about recruiting local help to salvage the wagon's contents and retrieve William's body for a proper burial. Then I'll have to write his family and share this unwelcome news before deciding whether or not to return home or finish the journey."

Berengar and Morwen left the merchant to his task and sought out the tavern's proprietor to make arrangements for their stay while Faolán curled up in a corner of the room and contentedly gnawed on a bone dropped by a diner. Although animals were generally barred from most city establishments, pets were often permitted indoors in more rural settings—not that anyone attempting to show the wolfhound the door would have any success unless she wished it.

The tavern was surprisingly crowded so early in the day. Almost all the tables were occupied, though the atmosphere was anything but lively. Most kept their heads down, muttering under their breath or whispering amongst themselves as Berengar and Morwen made their way toward the proprietor. Even the roaring fire proved not up to the task of dispelling the cold hall's gloom. Only the flames came close to matching the color of Berengar's hair, which was a shade brighter than the somber orange glow emanating from the burning logs.

The tavern's proprietor put on a welcome smile when he noticed them moving in his direction.

Berengar looked over his shoulder at all the patrons gathered in the hall. "Do you have any rooms available?"

"Always room for more guests." The proprietor seemed exceptionally eager.

"In that case, I'd like to pay for a week's stay and lodging for our horses." Berengar laid a stack of copper coins atop the counter. "I'm surprised business is so good, considering the things we've heard on the road. Just today we met a man whose friend died under unusual circumstances."

"Another one?" The proprietor swore then seemed to take note of Morwen. "Begging your pardon, lass."

"Trust me, I've heard worse." She eyed Berengar with barely suppressed laughter, as if to imply he wasn't exactly polite company. Despite her best efforts, she hadn't curbed his tongue any more than she'd tamed his temper.

Berengar chose to let the comment pass. A show of indifference was the surest way to annoy her. "Any truth to the rumors?" In his considerable experience, bartenders and innkeepers were usually the best sources of information around, especially when their palms were plied with coin.

The proprietor shrugged. "I can't rightly say, sir. Most folk around here seem to think there's some sort of monster on the prowl, but of course we get rumors like that all the time in this part of the country. There have been some reported missing lately, mind you."

"Missing?" Morwen raised an eyebrow. "Any suspicious deaths?"

"Those too, though the constable would know more about those affairs than I. Truth be told, all the strange goings-on have driven many indoors. People have taken to keeping together. Strength in numbers and all that, I suppose. The added business has made up for the loss of travelers and the cost of our young king's taxes. Can you believe it, a levy on vices to fill the church's coffers, after the harvest we've had?"

"I have it on good authority the Prince Regent and the new Bishop intend to suspend the vice tax." Berengar doubted the proprietor would believe him if he mentioned that he had heard it directly from the prince's mouth.

The tavern's proprietor brightened at the news. "A right relief, that is. Normally, we get a lot more folks in here this time of year, but you two are the first travelers I've had in some time—apart from those monster hunters, of course."

"Monster hunters?" Morwen shot Berengar a knowing look.

"Aye. Rough looking lot, if you don't mind my saying so. They've caused no shortage of trouble, getting into brawls and frightening my barmaids and all. I've tried talking to the constable about them, but I suppose if they keep the town safe…"

That sounds like a good place to start. "This constable— we'd like to have a word with him, if it's not too much trouble. Any idea where we can find him?"

After squaring things away with the proprietor, the pair returned to where they'd hitched the horses outside.

"So, what kind of monster do you think it is?" Morwen asked as they led their horses to the tavern barn. Faolán lagged behind at the barn's entrance, apparently trying her best to avoid the temptation to snap at the chickens.

Berengar shut the stall door in place. "A beautiful young woman luring a man to his death? A banshee perhaps, or maybe a spirit bride."

"Spirit brides are only found in graveyards. Everybody

knows that. And banshees aren't corporeal—at least not most of the time. The man we found was ripped apart. There's no way a banshee or spirit bride could have done something like that."

After checking to make sure no one else was nearby, Morwen lifted the blanket on the back of her mare's saddle and took out her magician's staff. The staff was made of hazel wood, which according to Morwen was especially useful for 'bringing change,' whatever that meant. Charms and symbols ran the length of its surface, and two runes— one purple and one blue—were fixed at the staff's head. Magicians, who were far less powerful than sorcerers, often used staffs or wands to harness their powers. Morwen, who had not grown into her full strength, was no exception.

She struck the ground with the staff twice. Following a flash of purple light from the rune at its head, the staff took on the appearance of a simple walking stick. It was a useful illusion, though those with a studied eye could see through it. While the peoples of Fál's five kingdoms had varying attitudes in regard to magic, many humans possessed a strong mistrust of magical and nonhuman creatures. Traditionally, Leinster was the least tolerant toward the old ways. Although Berengar and Morwen were at the realm's edge, and many years had passed since the purges, it was still better to avoid drawing unwanted attention.

"Sorry I didn't take the time to consult one of your spellbooks before venturing a guess. If you're so sure of yourself, why don't you tell me what it is?"

Morwen grinned. "I bet you dinner at the Inn of the Wayward Traveler that it's a kelpie or selkie."

"You're on."

Morwen's knowledge of monsters, which vastly exceeded his own, was mostly academic. Berengar's was

THE WILL OF QUEENS

born out of experience. For the most part, he was out of his depth when it came to the subject of magic, even if he had become more comfortable with it due to Morwen's constant presence. Despite his best efforts to train her in the art of combat, she remained something of an avowed pacifist. Between Berengar's skill with his axe and Morwen's use of magic, they complemented each other well.

The pair made their way to yew tree in full bloom despite the season at the heart of town. The great tree towered above all the man-made structures in the area. Its trunk was broad and heavy, and its thick roots ran deep into the ground.

Berengar's attention fell on an ordinance nailed to the tree. "Look at this."

The ordinance declared a regular curfew over Mucklagh after sunset. Along with requesting the townspeople remain in the safety of their homes whenever possible, the noticed warned the town's inhabitants against venturing beyond the town's borders alone. They were also urged to contact the constable if they observed anything out of the ordinary.

As Berengar finished reading the ordinance, he suddenly became aware he was being observed.

"You're not another mercenary, are you? We're not used to having men so heavily armed pass through our town."

Berengar turned and found himself face-to-face with a stout, middle-aged man whose hair held more gray than black. Judging from his clothes and the sword at his side, Berengar guessed this was the constable the tavern's proprietor had spoken of. He reached into his cloak and removed the piece of parchment he had carried with him since departing Dún Aulin. "We're here about the notice."

The constable did not respond. His attention was drawn instead to the image of the silver fox that adorned the booch clasped to Berengar's cloak. He spoke hastily, making a poor effort to mask his surprise. "There's no need for one of the High Queen's Wardens to trouble yourself with our humble affairs. We're more than capable of handling the situation ourselves."

Berengar met the constable's gaze and held it for a long moment. "I can see that. We a dead man on the road." There was a hard edge to his voice. He closed the distance between them and loomed over the constable. "You're not going to make trouble for me, are you?"

The constable took a step back and tugged at his collar. For a moment, it seemed he might reach for his sword, but his eyes darted from Berengar to Faolán, who advanced toward him with a low growl, and he seemed to think better of it. "I was at Hollygrove during the war when the soldiers from Áth Liag came through. I saw what your company did to them at the Ford of the Flagstones. Mucklagh is a respectable place full of decent folk. I don't want anyone getting hurt."

"Then we share the same goal. The High Queen is concerned with the welfare of all her subjects."

He understood the man's angst well enough. Although Berengar enjoyed a high level of infamy across all five kingdoms, he was especially feared in Leinster, and not without cause. His actions during and after the Shadow Wars were not easily forgotten. The farther north he traveled, the stronger the past's grip tightened. None of his deeds in service to the High Queen would ever blot out the stain left by his bloody past or his brutal reputation. There was a reason he had not crossed into Ulster in almost twenty years. Their impending rendezvous with Callahan at the

Inn of the Wayward Traveler was as far north as he was willing to go.

Morwen, ever the diplomat, interrupted in an attempt to defuse the situation. "Please sir, we only want to help. We are experienced in this sort of thing. If it's a monster that's causing you problems, Warden Berengar's one of the best there is at killing them. Why, I personally saw him take on a coatl—a great winged serpent." She held out her hands and increased the space between them to indicate the creature's enormity. "Besides, we've already made arrangements for our stay here, and the people of Leinster are renowned for their hospitality, are they not?"

The constable let out an exasperated sigh and looked as if all the air had been let out of his lungs. "I take it Jerome gave you a room, then. Blast him. He'd turn out his own mother if it meant a paying customer. Very well. I can't deal with those miscreants breathing down my neck while busying myself trying to keep you at bay. Not that I would have any luck against the Bloody Red Bear."

Berengar didn't flinch at the use of one of his less illustrious monikers.

"Excellent." Morwen rubbed her hands together. "Warden Berengar promises not to spill blood unless absolutely necessary."

The constable acquired a resigned expression. "I am Constable Hannelley. What do you want from me?"

Berengar took no offense when he did not offer his hand. He didn't need Hannelley to like him, he just needed his help ridding the area of whatever was killing travelers. "Let's start with the deaths and disappearances. The notice was light on details, but we've heard the rumors that a monster may be involved."

"Oh, there's no question this is the work of a monster."

"What makes you say that?" Morwen asked.

THE WILL OF QUEENS

"It's been spotted by at least a half-dozen people. Folks seem to believe it's a kelpie."

"Aha! I knew it!" Morwen's look of triumph quickly faded when she noticed the constable's expression, and she reddened with embarrassment. "Apologies. Please continue."

"It started over a month ago, before the mercenaries arrived—not just here, but to the north as well. All the attacks seem to take place near large bodies of water, mostly lakes and rivers. Most of the victims were drowned —the ones we found, anyhow."

"How far north?"

"As far as Ulster."

"How did the witnesses describe the monster?"

The constable started to reply but stopped abruptly and stared at Morwen with sudden interest, as if truly noticing her for the first time. "I'm sorry, who are you exactly?'

"My name is Morwen." She kept her tone friendly. I'm a—"

Berengar shot her a withering look. Unlike her native Munster, Leinster was no place to boast about being a magician. There was a reason he told her to keep the satchel containing her spell books and potions closed in sight of others.

"I'm a scholar. The study of monsters is a hobby of mine." When the constable looked away, she aimed a wink at Berengar.

"Those who have seen it say the creature has the appearance of a monstrous black horse with withered, rotting flesh, lifeless pale eyes, and thin limbs resembling flippers. Others have stated its snout is full of razor-sharp teeth used to drag prey into the water. But there are also those who claim to have witnessed a mysterious woman in the same place."

"Kelpies are known to take the form of young, beautiful women to lure their victims into the water." In her matter-of-fact tone, Morwen sounded every bit the scholar.

"Tell me about the victims," Berengar said. "Did they have anything in common?"

"Not that I can think of. Most were either nobles or merchants passing through the area. Does that help?"

Berengar ran a hand through his beard. "Maybe. You mentioned something earlier about miscreants. Did you mean the monster hunters?"

The constable spit on the ground, as if disgusted by the very mention of the mercenaries. "They call themselves the Sons of Leinster. Have you heard of them?"

Berengar shook his head.

"They showed up not long after the attacks started. They said they could protect the town for a price, but they haven't put an end to the killings yet. Most people are downright frightened of the lot of them. Their leader is named Alfric. If you're looking for more information, it might be useful to talk to him first."

"Are there any witnesses we should speak with?" Morwen asked.

The constable considered the question. "You might talk to Brigid, the blacksmith's widow. Her husband was attacked by the beast, but he clung to life for hours before he died. You might also speak with Pollux, the undertaker. I reckon the old foreigner has prepared nearly all the bodies for burial. Now, if there's nothing else, I have other business to attend to."

Berengar stopped him. "One last thing. The bodies you recovered—how many were missing their gold?"

The constable stared at him, slack-jawed. "Nearly all of them. I'd never thought about it before."

"I thought so." Berengar left Hannelley to puzzle over his words. He earned more than a few glances from townspeople who noticed his scars as he walked through Mucklagh with Morwen hurrying to catch up.

"Do you have to try to intimidate everyone we meet?" She sounded like a master correcting a mistaken apprentice. "Oh well. I suppose I should be glad you're not getting answers by hacking off limbs. It sounds like you owe me dinner, by the way. I was right about the kelpie."

"Don't get ahead of yourself," Berengar said, the hint of a smile on his lips. "We haven't caught it yet."

Morwen narrowed her gaze in his direction. "I take it you know something I don't. And what was that business about the missing coins?"

"Just a hunch. Come on, let's talk to that widow."

A calico cat enjoying the shade provided by the yew tree looked up from licking its paw and took note of them. The cat followed them along the road and brushed against Morwen's legs when they stopped to look for the blacksmith.

"Aren't you friendly?" Morwen bent down to pet the cat. Most animals were drawn to her on account of her magic, and Morwen readily returned their affections.

When Faolán barred her fangs, the cat hissed, scurried away, and leapt through an open window to vanish inside a nearby hut.

"Don't worry, Faolán." Morwen scratched the wolfhound behind the ears. "You're still my favorite girl." She straightened suddenly after standing, glancing around as if something peculiar had caught her attention.

"What is it?" Berengar asked.

Morwen bit her lip. "It's probably nothing, but for a moment I was sure I sensed the presence of magic. It's gone now, whatever it was."

Berengar didn't reply.

The clang of a hammer falling against a horseshoe rang out loud and clear, the echo drowned out by each successive strike. Smoke rose from the blacksmith's forge nearby, which was located in close proximity to the other craftsmen and merchants in the area. Whatever its hardships, the town was doing well enough to support such businesses. As they drew closer, Berengar spotted a thuggish-looking individual standing across from the blacksmith's widow, who seemed to be doing her best to ignore him as she pounded the horseshoe into shape.

"Leave me in peace," the woman said in response to a comment Berengar hadn't heard. "I've already told you, I've no money for you. I have mouths to feed, and I'm not about to spend my hard-earned coin on the likes of you."

The imposing figure took another step toward her and lowered his voice. "Are you sure that's wise? After what happened to your husband, I'd think twice about that if I were you. You wouldn't want anything to happen to your children, would you?"

Judging from the sword the man wore, Berengar guessed he was one of the monster hunters. "Is there a problem here?"

The monster hunter turned to face him. He was a large man, though the bulk of his size was girth. His bald head, eggish in shape, shared the same ruddy color as his bulbous face. The patchwork armor he wore had clearly seen better days. "This don't concern you."

"I disagree. The woman asked you to leave. I suggest you heed her words."

At that, the man's face grew even redder. "No one talks to me that way." His hand inched toward the sword at his side.

"Do it." Berengar reached for his axe. "It's been a few weeks since I've had a decent fight."

Each man surveyed the other, the wind sweeping between them. Faolán stepped out from behind Berengar, ready to strike if her master was threatened. As the monster hunter began to slide his blade free from its sheath, Morwen—who had quietly come to stand next to him—reached out her hand and gently touched his forearm.

"Don't you have another appointment elsewhere?"

For a moment, Berengar was concerned for her safety, but Morwen didn't appear intimidated by the man's much larger size in the slightest.

The monster hunter's brow furrowed in confusion. "I don't think so." He sounded uncertain. "I'm to collect protection money from this lot and report back." He seemed not to notice Morwen's hand on his arm.

"Are you sure you're not supposed to gather daisies from the field and contemplate the senselessness of violence?" Morwen seemed to remind him of a task he had forgotten.

"Daisies," the man muttered slowly. "Why, I think you're right."

"Best get to it, then."

The monster hunter removed his hand from the hilt of his blade and marched off toward the outskirts of town with a vacant expression on his face.

Morwen wiped a trickle of blood from her nose. "What were you thinking, picking a fight? You promised the constable not two minutes ago you wouldn't shed blood without just cause."

"I made no such promise. And you would do well to remember not to display your powers so prominently in sight of others."

The blacksmith's widow interrupted their dispute. "My thanks to you, strangers. Although I fear they'll be back tomorrow—meddlesome troublemakers. They call themselves monster hunters, but if you ask me they're just a bunch of cutthroats."

Her words rang true to Berengar. In his experience, monster hunters were usually a pious lot—especially men of Leinster—often driven by a fanatical sense of duty to cleanse the world of evil. They usually wore robes or symbols of their faith. In contrast, the man they'd encountered looked more like a killer for hire. Perhaps more telling, his sword appeared goblin-made. Many monster hunters considered goblins an inferior, unclean species, and would not be caught dead in possession of a weapon made by a goblin forge.

"Why was he bothering you?" Morwen asked.

The woman was probably in her late thirties, though she might have been older. She was thin and hungry looking, and her clothes were plain and dirty. Sweat dripped from her soot stained brow amid the forge's intense heat.

"They say they'll keep us safe from the kelpie—as long as they're given enough coin. Every day they harass business owners and townspeople for more protection money." She set her hammer on the anvil and tucked a strand of frazzled black hair away from her face. "Can I help you with something? I can see that you aren't in need of weaponry. New shoes for your horses, perhaps?"

Berengar shook his head. "I'd like to ask you a few questions about your husband's death. We're here to put a stop to whatever's killing people."

"We're not mercenaries," Morwen added quickly. "We're here on the High Queen's business."

"I see." The woman turned her back for a moment and used a set of tongs to add new iron to the forge before stripping off her gloves and returning her attention to them. "You wouldn't know it from the state of this place, but my husband was more than some simple village black-smith. Quinn worked in the castle armory at Tullamore during the war, but we left to escape the violence that accompanied the purges. He worked hard to make a new life for us out here. Just when I thought our luck was going to change…" She fingered a ring that hung from a chain around her neck. "Quinn received a large order from Athlone. He was so excited that he couldn't stop talking about it. The money would've lasted through the winter and paid for a new forge. He left and traveled west, taking the route along Lough Owel."

"Only he never made it," Berengar remarked.

"That's just it. He reached Athlone safely. Even sent word of how much he'd been paid for the delivery. The next time I saw him, Quinn was not long for this world. To make matters worse, the proceeds from the sale were lost. I've done my best to manage the business in his stead, but I fear what will happen if the winter is long."

More missing money. "Were you able to speak with you husband before he died?"

"Aye." Her voice went quiet. "The things he said…it was as if his last moments were plucked from a nightmare. He spoke of a woman in a red cloak and a horse that came out of Lough Owel and dragged him into the water. I warned him not to go near that lake after the other attacks. If only he'd listened."

"Lough Owel? That's where most of the attacks have happened?"

The blacksmith's widow wiped her eyes and nodded.

"Thank you. You've been very helpful." Morwen laid a reassuring hand on the woman's shoulder. "I'm sorry for your loss."

The widow looked to Berengar, her expression hard as stone. "If you find the thing that did this, I hope you put a sword through its heart and send it back to whatever hell it came from."

Berengar met her gaze and held it. "I give you my word."

That at least, was a promise he could keep.

ACKNOWLEDGMENTS

I started *Warden of Fál* with a very specific approach in mind.

I remember once searching the shelves at a bookstore for a new fantasy book. Every book I found was part of a series. In creating *Warden of Fál*, I decided to make each book stand alone. My hope was that readers could pick up any book in the series and read a complete story, while telling a larger story across the series.

It's been a delicate balancing act at times—nowhere more than in this book, which deals with events and themes from *The Wrath of Lords*. After finishing the story, I ended up rewriting the last act of the book to make the story more self-contained. In a way, *The City of Thieves* is a conclusion of sorts to the arc began in *The Wrath of Lords*. *Wrath* was a dark story. No matter what Berengar did, it didn't seem to make a difference. Then he met Morwen in *The Blood of Kings*, and together they saved Cashel, but only at a great cost. *The City of Thieves* reflects back on past events, including the return of old characters like Friar

Godfrey, while also introducing friends and enemies. It's also the most hopeful book in the series.

The world of the warden will only expand from here. Side characters and familiar faces will continue to come and go as Berengar and Morwen continue their adventures. In *The Will of Queens*, the search for a missing warden will take our protagonists north, where Berengar is forced to face his greatest regret. It's the most brutal and emotional story yet.

The pieces are almost in place. Soon it will be time to bring them all together.

There are a number of people who deserve thanks for their help bringing this project to life. My cover artist, Jeff Brown, continues to knock it out of the park with each cover. Then there's my incredible character illustrator, Matt Forsyth, and my map illustrator, Maxime Plasse. I also want to thank Katie King, my copyeditor, and Margaret Dean, my proofreader, for all their hard work.

My family sees these books before anyone else. I've written almost 1,500 pages of this series in a little over a year, and it's been challenging at times for them to keep up with my writing pace, but I couldn't do this without them. A special thanks to my mother Pamela Romines and my father Robert Romines for all you do to support these books.

I continue to be overwhelmed at all the support I've received from my community, and everyone who has taken the time to leave online reviews or share my work with others.

Finally, I want to thank you—the reader! You make this the best job in the world.

Until next time,

Kyle Alexander Romines

ABOUT THE AUTHOR

Kyle Alexander Romines is a teller of tales from the hills of Kentucky. He enjoys good reads, thunderstorms, and anything edible. His writing interests include fantasy, science fiction, horror, and westerns.

Kyle's lifelong love of books began with childhood bedtime stories and was fostered by his parents and teachers. He grew up reading *Calvin and Hobbes*, R.L. Stine's *Goosebumps* series, and *Harry Potter*. His current list of favorites includes Justin Cronin's *The Passage*, *Red Rising* by Pierce Brown, and *Bone* by Jeff Smith. The library is his friend.

Kyle is a graduate of the University of Louisville School of Medicine, from which he received his M.D.

He plans to continue writing as long as he has stories to tell.

You can contact Kyle at thekylealexander@hotmail.com. You can also subscribe to his author newsletter to receive email updates and a FREE electronic copy of his science fiction novella, The Chrononaut, at http://eepurl.com/bsvhYP.